PRAISE FOR COLLEEN COBLE AND RICK ACKER

WHERE SECRETS LIE

"Clever and full of twists—Colleen Coble and Rick Acker have crafted a page-turner that blends the intellectual intrigue of academia with the high-stakes world of artifact smuggling. With an unpredictable plot, complex characters, and a college campus that holds dark secrets, this mystery will keep you guessing."

—ROBERT DUGONI, *NEW YORK TIMES* BESTSELLING AUTHOR OF THE TRACY CROSSWHITE SERIES

I THINK I WAS MURDERED

"It's a high-octane thriller with the grounding touches of Katrina's Norwegian heritage, the hygge of North Haven, and a very sweet romance between two likable, vulnerable people. Romantic suspense comfort food—just like waffles with cloudberry cream."

—*KIRKUS REVIEWS*

"This fast-paced thriller incorporating today's headline news along with compelling family drama proves that the Coble-Acker partnership (*What We Hide*) will continue to produce hits. Recommend to fans of psychological thrillers such as *Lies We Believe* by Lisa Harris and *Criss Cross* by C. C. Warrens."

—*LIBRARY JOURNAL*

"This is a book that grabs you straight out of the gate. Centered around a bang-up concept with a great techno twist, a rich cast of characters drives you through a twisty plot that is a white-knuckled ride straight to the end. The suspense was killing me as I read! Make sure you're well-rested before you start *I Think I Was Murdered* because it will keep you up at night."

—P.J. TRACY, *NEW YORK TIMES* BESTSELLING AUTHOR

"A timely and intriguing premise played out in a way that keeps readers guessing."

—STEVEN JAMES, NATIONAL BESTSELLING AUTHOR OF *SYNAPSE*

"What a roller-coaster ride! *I Think I Was Murdered* gripped me on page one and didn't let go until the epilogue—after a twist that caught this seasoned reader by complete surprise. If you like thrilling suspense, you won't want to miss this novel by Colleen Coble and Rick Acker."

—ANGELA HUNT, AUTHOR OF *WHAT A WAVE MUST BE*

"Colleen Coble fans will devour her latest offering, which—with the help of thriller writer Rick Acker—cleverly uses AI, family secrets, and a lost treasure to keep readers guessing until the final satisfying page."

—CRESTON MAPES, BESTSELLING AUTHOR

WHAT WE HIDE

"Bestsellers Coble (*Break of Day*) and Acker (*Guilty Blood*) team up for a heart-pounding tale of stolen artifacts and murder . . . The second-chance romance adds dimension to the well-plotted whodunit, which leaves more than a few secrets to be uncovered in the next installment. Readers will be on tenterhooks."

—*Publishers Weekly*

"This is an explosive beginning to a new series and a dynamic author partnership between Coble (Pelican Harbor series) and practicing lawyer Acker. Will appeal to fans of the legal thrillers of Randy Singer and Robert Whitlow."

—*Library Journal*

"Coble and Acker have forged a seamless partnership with a singular voice. I honestly can't tell where one writer starts and the other ends. *What We Hide* is a crisp and hard-charging start to a legal suspense series that tests the boundaries of yesterday's secrets against today's lies, all while trying to escape tomorrow's verdict. From the courtroom to the shadow of a decaying Gothic university, it's a high-stakes ride through love, second chances, and an ending you won't soon forget."

—Charles Martin, *New York Times* bestselling author

"Get ready to be hooked! Brace yourself for a thrill ride as Coble and Acker masterfully weave a web of suspense in *What We Hide*, where secrets simmer and unexpected twists leave you guessing until the shocking finale."

—Kate Angelo, *Publishers Weekly* bestselling author

"This book has it all. Intrigue, suspense, and the mysteries of the heart, woven together masterfully by the great new pairing of Coble and Acker. Fans of their individual books will not be disappointed. New readers will be delighted."

—James Scott Bell, International Thriller Writers Award winner

"Much is hidden in Tupelo Grove and Pelican Harbor. In *What We Hide*, expert storytellers Colleen Coble and Rick Acker will take you on a riveting ride through a picturesque Southern town inhabited by characters who will pull you in and make you care. Hidden truths find their way into the light—sometimes quickly, often slowly in the face of great obstacles and danger. Once you start reading, you won't put this book down."

—Robert Whitlow, bestselling author

"When you combine two brilliant storytellers such as Coble and Acker, the result is a beautiful, well-crafted legal thriller that keeps the reader utterly riveted. If you're looking for a novel that's edge-of-the-seat compelling, emotionally engaging, and nail-bitingly (I know that's not a word, but it fits) suspenseful, look no further than *What We Hide*. With its compelling narrative, well-rounded characters, and intricate plot, this is a must-read, goes-on-the-keeper-shelf, that will stay with you long after the final page is turned."

—Lynette Eason, bestselling, award-winning author of the Extreme Measures series

"*What We Hide* grabbed me with the first chapter and had me reading until two in the morning with its twisty plot and engaging characters."

—Patricia Bradley, author of the Pearl River series

WHEN JUSTICE COMES

ALSO BY COLLEEN COBLE AND RICK ACKER

THE TUPELO GROVE NOVELS

What We Hide
Where Secrets Lie
When Justice Comes

STAND-ALONE

I Think I Was Murdered

ALSO BY COLLEEN COBLE

THE SANCTUARY NOVELS

Ambush
Prowl
Conspiracy (available July 2026)

THE ANNIE PEDERSON NOVELS

Edge of Dusk
Dark of Night
Break of Day

THE PELICAN HARBOR NOVELS

One Little Lie
Two Reasons to Run
Three Missing Days

STAND-ALONE

Fragile Designs
A Stranger's Game

WHEN JUSTICE COMES

A TUPELO GROVE NOVEL

COLLEEN COBLE

RICK ACKER

THOMAS NELSON

Since 1798

When Justice Comes

Copyright © 2025 by Colleen Coble and Rick Acker

All rights reserved. No portion of this book may be reproduced, stored in a retrieval system, or transmitted in any form or by any means—electronic, mechanical, photocopy, recording, scanning, or other—except for brief quotations in critical reviews or articles, without the prior written permission of the publisher.

Published in Nashville, Tennessee, by Thomas Nelson. Thomas Nelson is a registered trademark of HarperCollins Christian Publishing, Inc.

Thomas Nelson titles may be purchased in bulk for educational, business, fundraising, or sales promotional use. For information, please email SpecialMarkets@ThomasNelson.com.

Scripture quotations are taken from The Holy Bible, New International Version®, NIV®. Copyright © 1973, 1978, 1984, 2011 by Biblica, Inc.® Used by permission of Zondervan. All rights reserved worldwide. www.Zondervan.com. The "NIV" and "New International Version" are trademarks registered in the United States Patent and Trademark Office by Biblica, Inc.®

Publisher's Note: This novel is a work of fiction. Names, characters, places, and incidents are either products of the author's imagination or used fictitiously. All characters are fictional, and any similarity to people living or dead is purely coincidental.

Any internet addresses (websites, blogs, etc.) in this book are offered as a resource. They are not intended in any way to be or imply an endorsement by Thomas Nelson, nor does Thomas Nelson vouch for the content of these sites for the life of this book.

Without limiting the exclusive rights of any author, contributor or the publisher of this publication, any unauthorized use of this publication to train generative artificial intelligence (AI) technologies is expressly prohibited. HarperCollins also exercise their rights under Article 4(3) of the Digital Single Market Directive 2019/790 and expressly reserve this publication from the text and data mining exception.

HarperCollins Publishers, Macken House, 39/40 Mayor Street Upper, Dublin 1, D01 C9W8, Ireland (https://www.harpercollins.com)

Library of Congress Cataloging-in-Publication Data

Names: Coble, Colleen author | Acker, Rick, 1966- author
Title: When justice comes / Colleen Coble and Rick Acker.
Description: Nashville, Tennessee : Thomas Nelson, 2025. | Series: A Tupelo Grove novel ; 2 | Summary: "USA TODAY bestselling romantic suspense author Colleen Coble and Rick Acker deliver the final book in their beloved Tupelo Grove series: Hez and Savannah Webster have survived storms that would bury others without a love as strong as theirs—but can they withstand the final battle that threatens to sweep away everything they've fought for?"—Provided by publisher.
Identifiers: LCCN 2025036713 (print) | LCCN 2025036714 (ebook) | ISBN 9781400345731 paperback | ISBN 9781400345748 library binding | ISBN 9781400345755 epub | ISBN 9781400345762
Subjects: LCGFT: Fiction | Christian fiction | Thrillers (Fiction) | Romance fiction | Novels
Classification: LCC PS3553.O2285 W475 2025 (print) | LCC PS3553.O2285 (ebook)
LC record available at https://lccn.loc.gov/2025036713
LC ebook record available at https://lccn.loc.gov/2025036714

Printed in the United States of America

25 26 27 28 29 LBC 5 4 3 2 1

For Karen Solem

For twenty-five years you guided and
shepherded Colleen and others
through the murky waters of publication.
You were a great friend, mentor, and agent.

Walk those heavenly mountains with joy!

WILLARD FAMILY TREE

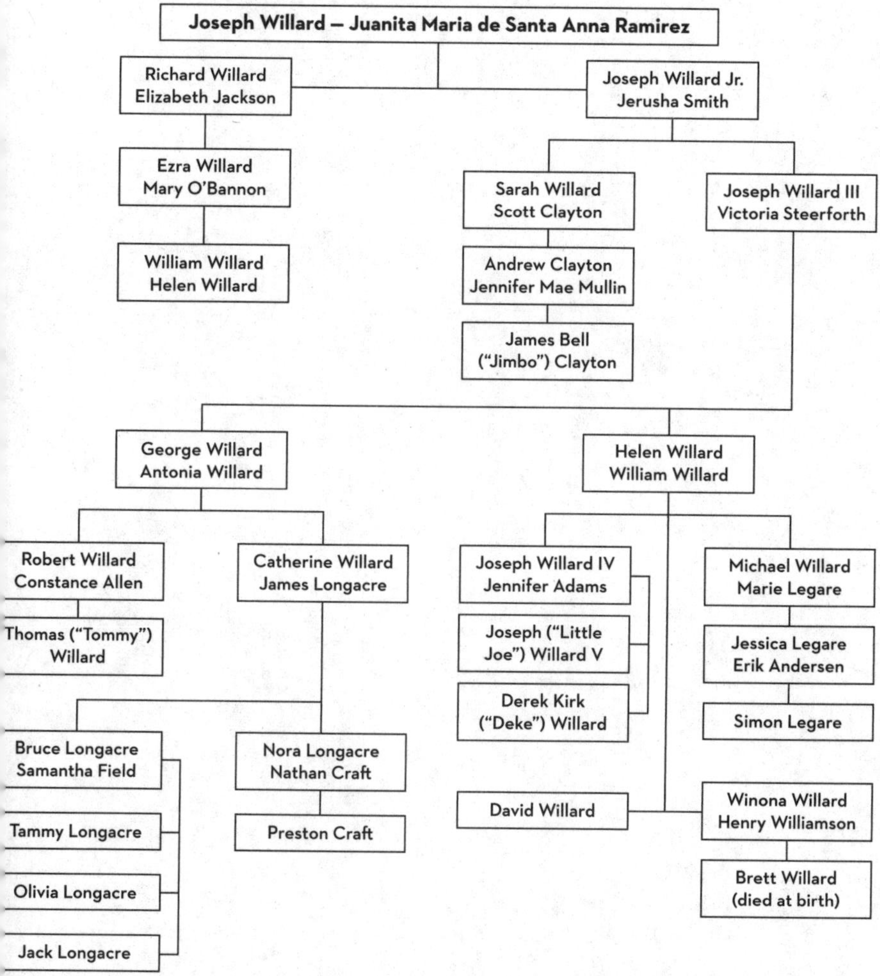

Joseph Willard – Juanita Maria de Santa Anna Ramirez

- Richard Willard / Elizabeth Jackson
  - Ezra Willard / Mary O'Bannon
    - William Willard / Helen Willard
- Joseph Willard Jr. / Jerusha Smith
  - Sarah Willard / Scott Clayton
    - Andrew Clayton / Jennifer Mae Mullin
      - James Bell ("Jimbo") Clayton
  - Joseph Willard III / Victoria Steerforth
    - George Willard / Antonia Willard
      - Robert Willard / Constance Allen
        - Thomas ("Tommy") Willard
      - Catherine Willard / James Longacre
        - Bruce Longacre / Samantha Field
        - Tammy Longacre
        - Olivia Longacre
        - Jack Longacre
        - Nora Longacre / Nathan Craft
          - Preston Craft
    - Helen Willard / William Willard
      - Joseph Willard IV / Jennifer Adams
      - Joseph ("Little Joe") Willard V
      - Derek Kirk ("Deke") Willard
      - Michael Willard / Marie Legare
        - Jessica Legare / Erik Andersen
          - Simon Legare
      - David Willard
      - Winona Willard / Henry Williamson
        - Brett Willard (died at birth)

LEGARE FAMILY TREE
(PARTIAL)

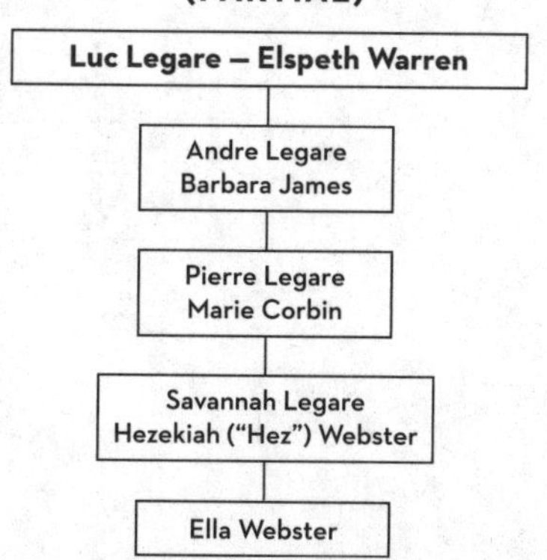

CHAPTER 1

HEZEKIAH WEBSTER DIDN'T NOTICE THE FIRST SCREAM. HE was too focused on the home inspector.

Hez and his former and future wife, Savannah, had a contract on a wonderfully eccentric house outside Nova Cambridge, complete with a little rooftop observatory she had loved since childhood. It was an easy house to love—until you saw the utility and maintenance bills. The windows alone probably added a thousand dollars to the annual electric bill. Though every window was a handcrafted unique work of art, the inspector pointed out that they were all single panes and a number were drafty.

Hez sighed and added another item to his long list of post-closing projects.

Savannah left Hez and the inspector and went to an enormous picture window with a panoramic vista of Mobile Bay from a hillside that sloped down to the water. In the distance the Kate Norris Bridge extended over the inlet to Weeks Bay. Hidden prisms in the window corners cast rainbows when the sun hit them just right.

Hez didn't blame Savannah for preferring to savor the view and hunt rainbows. After the horrors she had endured over the past few months, she deserved it. So did their ten-year-old nephew, Simon. He was out exploring the idiosyncratic landscaping outside. He had promptly discovered the semiartificial sea cave below the house, of course. His laughter and excited yells had been a welcome change from his withdrawn silence in the month since his mother, Savannah's sister Jessica Legare, was murdered.

The second scream finally got Hez's attention. Savannah pointed out the window. "Simon!"

Hez ran to the window. As Savannah rushed to the door, Hez saw Simon's blond head bobbing in the water fifty yards offshore. He was trying to swim back to land, but a rip current pulled him farther into the bay with every second. Simon screamed again, a thin and desperate cry. Hez had heard it a minute ago, but he'd been distracted.

Just like when Ella died.

Hez sprinted out of the house, past Savannah and the inspector, an arthritic retired carpenter. This couldn't happen. Not again. He had to save Simon. Hez's running strides seemed to take an eternity to propel him down the sloping terrain to the pier.

He kicked off his shoes as he reached the boathouse at the end of the pier and hurled himself into the deadly current. He swam through the cold, cloudy water, trying to spot Simon between strokes. The shore receded rapidly behind him, but the distance between him and Simon barely seemed to shrink.

Simon had stopped screaming, which was a bad sign. He seemed to be struggling to keep his head above water. Exhaustion killed many riptide victims, and Hez feared it might be claiming his nephew. He had to reach the boy, but he could feel his own strength starting to fail. He was still recovering from brain surgery and was nowhere near his normal fitness level.

Hez reached Simon at last. His nephew saw him and frantically grabbed for his arm. Hez pulled back. "Simon, listen to me!" He gasped for breath. "We have to get out of this current. Swim parallel to shore. I'll help you."

But Simon didn't listen. Wide-eyed with terror, he flailed toward Hez. Simon went under for a second and came up coughing.

Hez tried to remember the lifeguard training he got during high school summers working at the local pool. He inhaled a lungful of air and ducked under the surface. He couldn't see Simon in the murk, but he caught hold of one of his thrashing legs, spun him around, grabbed his skinny torso, and put him in a cross-chest carry. Hez surfaced and gulped in a fresh breath.

Simon stopped struggling now that his face was above water and he was in Hez's grip, but the effort left Hez nearly spent. He caught a glimpse of shore, which was now just an emerald line on the horizon. They must be nearly a quarter mile out, and there was no way he had the strength to swim back.

He switched to a sidestroke, battling to get out of the rip current and keep both Simon and himself from slipping below the surface. Hez couldn't keep it up much longer.

Something red and white flashed above the waves ahead of him. A buoy. He might be able to reach it. He forced aching muscles to keep moving, willing himself forward.

Spots clouded his vision and he fought for air.

The buoy was fifty yards away. Twenty. Ten.

His hand touched the buoy's hard, smooth side. A single

eyebolt stuck out of the slick surface. With his last strength, Hez put Simon's hand on it. The boy's fingers instinctively closed into a tight grip.

Hez tried to grab the buoy, but his fingers found no purchase. A thrumming roar built in his ears and his vision narrowed to a tunnel. His hands slipped off the buoy and the water closed over his head.

Not again. Savannah clenched her hands together in front of her and barely breathed as she watched Simon clinging to the buoy bobbing in the whitecaps. She stood on the dock with a warm April breeze blowing over her skin. She'd seen Hez's strained face a moment ago, but now she couldn't spot him with the waves rolling toward the shore.

The home inspector patted her shoulder. "I called the Coast Guard," he said in a wavering, gravelly voice. "They have a boat in the area."

"I don't see him," she whispered. "Hez has to be all right. I can't lose him."

A speedboat plowed through the water toward the buoy and slowed as it approached. The vessel's wake dislodged Simon's grip, and he disappeared beneath the waves.

A rescue diver dove in after him and surfaced almost immediately with her nephew. He towed the boy to the boat and delivered him to other crew members, who hauled him into the boat.

She stepped to the very end of the dock. "Hez! Hez is underwater!" Her shout frightened away two gulls near her feet.

The rescuers were too far out to hear her over the boat's motor, but she caught the sound of Simon's hysterical voice screaming, "Uncle Hez! You have to get Uncle Hez!"

The rescue swimmer nodded and dove under the whitecaps again.

Please God, please God. Savannah couldn't form more of a prayer than the desperate plea for intervention. It seemed an eternity before two heads surfaced, and she managed to drag in a relieved lungful of air.

The swimmer towed Hez to the boat, and two other rescuers dragged him over the side. He was much too limp, and his face was way too white. A man and a woman knelt beside him, bending over his inert body. One of them breathed into his mouth while the other performed chest compressions.

For an instant she relived the sight of paramedics bent over her small daughter after Ella had been pulled from the pool. All their ministrations had failed to save their little girl. Unable to watch such a horrific scene again, she slammed her eyes shut for a moment. "God, no, no. Please no."

She forced her lids open again. She wanted to be there holding Hez's hand, but since she couldn't be beside him, the least she could do was pray with all her might.

Her vision blurred as she watched the rescuers. *Two breaths, thirty compressions.* She counted them out as the man lunged down against Hez's chest. *Breathe, Hez, breathe.*

Wait, was that his hand? She swallowed hard and spotted that movement again. Hez raised his arm feebly. Then his face appeared over the gunwale. He retched several times until only dry heaves remained.

After a few more minutes, he was sitting up and leaning

forward against his bent knees. The engine on the boat roared, and the bow headed for shore and the small dock where Savannah stood. She drank in the sight of Simon and Hez sitting with a blanket around them. Both alive. She could hardly believe it.

The boat bumped the side of the dock, and a crew member leaped onto the weathered boards to tie up. Two of the crew helped Hez off the boat, but Simon rushed ahead and threw himself into Savannah's arms.

"I was skipping rocks and my foot slipped," he said in a choked voice. "I nearly killed Uncle Hez." He turned and faced the boat as Hez stepped onto the dock with a wobbly stance. Simon left Savannah's arms and went to his uncle. "Thanks for saving me, Uncle Hez." Tears streamed down his face, and he put his arms around Hez's waist.

Hez bent over and coughed up a little water. He coughed a few more times, but it was beginning to sound less wet. He straightened. "I'm still alive and kicking, buddy. I'm just glad you're okay. I—I couldn't bear to lose you t-t—"

He broke off, and Savannah heard the word *too* at the end of that sentence. She wasn't the only one who had relived Ella's death in the last half hour.

A crew member touched his arm. "Let's sit you down on the bench until the ambulance gets here."

Hez's blue eyes narrowed and he shook his head. "I don't need an ambulance."

"I'm afraid we have to insist, sir." The man led him to the bench. "You'll need to be under observation for a few hours. The boy too."

As soon as the man was out of the way, Savannah rushed to Hez's side and knelt in front of him. The tight containment of her terror and horror dissolved, and she couldn't hold back the tears any longer. "When you went under that water, I was so afraid I'd l-lost you."

He pulled her up and onto his lap where he wrapped his arms around her. He was still shivering, but his smile warmed her as she gazed down into his face. "I've got a wedding to attend, and it would take more than a riptide to stop me from putting that ring back on your finger."

She buried her face in his neck and breathed in the scent of his sage soap under the salty tang of his skin. *Thank you, God.*

CHAPTER 2

MAMA'S HOUSE ALWAYS MADE MICHAEL WILLARD ANGRY. HE loved her and enjoyed visiting over a glass of sweet tea fortified with old-school moonshine. But her home spiked his blood pressure every time he saw it. She deserved so much better than this.

From the outside Mama's house appeared to be abandoned. She lived in a cracked-window, paint-peeling, ready-to-blow-over-in-a-strong-breeze old bungalow outside Nova Cambridge with a weedy garden in back. From the inside it looked like a hoarder house, but Mama was no hoarder. She was a keeper of memories.

The collapsing boxes stacked four high in every room held a priceless archive of documents chronicling the exploits of Joseph Willard, founder of both the town of Nova Cambridge and Universitates Nova Cambridge Willardius, the original name of Tupelo Grove University.

The magnificent Victorian furniture jammed into every free corner once graced the university president's mansion. The faded pictures stacked in the closets recorded the finding of the fabled Willard Treasure, groundbreakings for the university and town, and dozens of other key events, together with the proud, strong faces of Joseph Willard and the other men who made them possible.

Almost everything in the house was one of a kind. There were no other copies of the letters, pictures, journals, and so on that Mama watched over. The Legares and their cronies had seen to that. They had erased Joseph Willard's legacy and even wiped his name from the university he'd founded. If a fire or hurricane ever hit Mama's house, all proof of the Willard family's deeds would vanish.

Michael made his way through a maze of boxes to find his mother sitting in front of a dinky old TV. "Mama, you really ought to let me move some of this stuff into a storage locker. It'll be safer there and you'll have a lot more space."

She didn't turn away from the grainy screen. "Hush, boy. I'm watching the news."

Michael repressed a smile. He was sixty-four years old, president of a trucking company, and one of the most feared men in Southern Alabama's criminal world. And she still hushed him and called him "boy." "Anything interesting?"

She gasped and pointed at the TV. "My great-grandbaby—your grandson—almost died today!"

"What?" He turned to the screen. It showed pictures of Hezekiah Webster and Simon Legare. Simon's resemblance to his mother was almost uncanny. He looked exactly like a male version of Michael's daughter, Jess Legare, at that age. The anchor briefly described the incident and then handed off to a reporter interviewing a Coast Guard spokesman who warned viewers about the dangers of rip currents and letting children play unattended by the water. Then the anchor started a new story about an accident that blocked two lanes of I-10 earlier in the day.

Mama scowled. "Our little boy isn't safe with those two."

Old regrets and new worry needled Michael. "No, he's not."

Mama switched off the TV and glared at Michael. "We need to get him out of there and bring him home to his real family."

"I'm working on it. I've hired a lawyer, and I have some other irons in the fire."

She gave a firm nod, causing her white curls to shake. "Good. We need to take care of family, especially after the time we've had. So many dead, so many lost." She narrowed her eyes. "You're the only one in your generation who's not in a grave or a cell. The little ones deserve a better future, especially Simon. He could be the leader of that generation."

"I see the same promise in him, Mama. We'll make a Willard out of him. Count on it."

Her faded brown eyes grew vague, and she seemed to wander in the past for a moment. "Tell me, why isn't he a Willard now? Why wasn't Jess a Willard? Why did she keep that name?"

Painful memories tried to surface, but Michael pushed them down. "She was biding her time, making connections. The Legare name was better for that."

"Yes, I suppose so. And Jess loved her sister."

More ripples of agony in the dark waters of his past. "Half sister." He changed the subject. "I talked to David's lawyer today. He thinks he'll be able to plead David down to accessory to trafficking stolen goods and get him out for time served."

Her face wrinkled into a smile. "Good, good. I'll make

shrimp and grits to celebrate when he gets out. Your brother always loses weight on jail food."

"I'm sure he'll appreciate it. Your shrimp and grits is fantastic."

"Deke loves it too." Her brow furrowed. "But he's not getting out soon, is he?"

Michael sighed. "No, he's not. I talked to his lawyer too. The prosecution has a recording of him bragging to a jailhouse snitch about calling the hit on Beckett Harrison. Between that and the other stuff they have on Deke, he's probably getting life without parole."

"Oh." She sagged back in her ratty armchair, looking very small and withered. "Poor boy. Poor, poor boy. That'll be hard for him. He always loved the outdoors so much. He is a talker, though. How's he taking it?"

"Not well. It's only just starting to sink in, I think. He's feeling pretty down. He says he's talking to the prison chaplain, which helps some."

Mama's eyes were suddenly sharp. "Talking to the chaplain? Is that still Tim Kramer?"

"Yes."

Her mouth set in a hard line. "Deke's not thinking of doing anything stupid, is he?"

Kramer's favorite verse was "The truth will set you free," and he was a firm believer in the healing power of confession. Prosecutors and cops loved him. "Don't worry about Deke. He'll never turn on family. He's a Willard."

Savannah smiled at the astounding figures in TGU's bank accounts and pulled up a list of long-overdue maintenance projects on her computer. She'd been working on a plan for her vision of the future, and her goals didn't seem out of reach now. She'd even been able to fully fund the scholarships, including one for Hez's favorite student, Ed Hernandez. It seemed impossible that she'd attained the position of university president at only thirty-five years old.

The azaleas flowering on the other side of her office window were a sweet reminder that beauty and life still existed in the midst of grief and change. It wasn't just the turnaround in money that signaled new life for the university—applications for next year had surged as well, and reporters were clamoring for interviews on what she had planned. With the influx of money, the school's college ranking would get a nice boost, and she intended to be prepared.

The first order of business was to finish Legare Hall, the half-built embarrassment her father had started two decades ago but never had the money to complete. It loomed above Tupelo Pond, a mossy marble mess that every campus visitor drove past. It was like the set for a horror movie—hardly the impression Savannah wanted to make on prospective students and professors.

The plans drafted by her father's architect were impressive—and expensive—but she didn't intend to use them. Her father had wanted a majestic, Gothic-style building with a luxurious office suite for himself and a cavernous, mahogany-floored grand foyer he could use for entertaining. The academic function of the building seemed to have been an afterthought. An early version of the plans identified internal rooms as labs and classrooms, but later versions labeled them as a library or storage space—probably because cost had become an issue and shelves were cheaper to install than lab benches or desks.

The corner of one of Great-Grandfather Luc's leather journals peeked out from under a stack of papers, and she pulled it free. An initial glance through this one over a month ago had revealed notes about a hall he'd intended to build, but she hadn't studied it closely. She flipped through the pages, relishing the feel of the quality paper and the faint scent of fine leather. Her fingers paused in the middle of the pages at the sketched floor plans and facade of a building. While it bore some resemblance to the plans her father had sent over, the more historic lines and design of the grand hall appealed to her. The cost would likely be lower, which would leave money for other upgrades.

The door opened and Hez, dressed in khaki slacks and a blue shirt, appeared in the doorway. "Got a minute?"

She closed the journal and eyed the two University Grounds beverages in his hands. "How'd you know I didn't get my drink this morning?" She stood and stepped to the side of the desk.

He entered and shut the door behind him. "I spotted you sprinting for the office after I dropped Simon off at school this morning in my Uber ride. You had your bag and no coffee." He set the drinks on her desk and pulled her into his arms. "I can't wait until we can wake up together again. I missed you this morning."

Letting go of all other thoughts, she relaxed into his embrace and kissed him, relishing the tenderness encircling her. When he finally released her, she opened her eyes and traced his strong jawline with her finger. "That was a pretty impressive rescue for a thirty-seven-year-old guy." He seemed to have fully recovered from the near-drowning incident, and his brain injury was healing well too. Not being able to drive still chafed at him, though.

"You're forgetting your iced mocha," he said with a smile tugging his lips.

"You're good at making me forget everything."

He snagged a lock of her hair and wound it around his finger. "It's my favorite thing to do." His hand fell back to his side.

She chuckled and reached for her mocha. The bright taste of peppermint lingered on her tongue. "How did our boy seem this morning?" Simon had been so subdued that Hez had taken him to his condo to play video games after church yesterday, and Hez had kept him overnight.

"Still withdrawn. I encouraged him to study last night for his math test today, but he gazed off into space more than he did at his textbook. I doubt he'll pull that B back up to an A this semester."

Worry tried to push out her morning euphoria, but she refused to let it spoil this moment. "Healing will take some time. He misses his mother. So do I." The last sentence lodged behind her lips.

"I know you do, and I'm here for you. We'll both be there for him." A frown settled on his forehead.

Was that worry lurking behind his smile? "What's wrong?"

"I hate to spoil your morning, but we have a problem."

The *we* clued her in on the direction of the issue. "Is there an issue with the adoption proceedings? Jess appointed me as Simon's guardian. The court will surely listen to her wishes."

Though Savannah had told herself that over and over, there had been so many hits in the past eight months that she kept waiting for the next shoe to fall.

He set his cup on the desk. “Brace yourself, babe. We always knew one person had a stronger claim to him than us.”

Her stomach bottomed out. “You found Erik Andersen?”

“Worse. He came out of hiding on his own and is armed with one of the top attorneys in the state. He’s filed a challenge to our adoption petition.”

She set a hand to her neck and stepped back. “We can fight him, can’t we? I mean, he’s a criminal.”

“He hasn’t been convicted of anything yet.” Hez’s jaw hardened, and his frown deepened. “It’s going to be a battle.”

“We have to win,” she whispered. “I just lost Jess, and Simon needs us.” There was no way she’d let a lowlife like Erik Andersen raise Simon. Her nephew needed and deserved parents who would love him and be good role models. He was the last piece of her sister, and in her heart he was already their son. She couldn’t lose him now.

CHAPTER 3

THE MINUTE THEY GOT NEAR BOO RADLEY'S LAIR IN TUPELO Pond, Savannah let go of Hez's hand and wrapped Marley's leash several times around her palm. Twilight had nearly obscured the gator's scaly back. "Don't let Cody get too close to Boo," she told Simon, who had Cody's leash. It was mating season and the bull gator was trying to impress his new love, Pika. Right on cue, Boo slipped into the water and slapped his massive tail.

The streetlights around the path flickered on, and Marley stiffened when he caught sight of his nemesis. "Sit."

Her Aussie obeyed with reluctance in every line of his black fur. Cody hadn't noticed Boo Radley yet since a pigeon had caught his attention. Simon had taken Hez's dog as his own, though Cody still seemed to think Hez was his ultimate authority and rarely listened to the boy's commands. Who was she kidding? The dog rarely even obeyed Hez, who had rescued him three years ago. She still wasn't sure what breed to call Cody with his Chihuahua legs, oversized Great Dane ears, and greyhound body. His crooked Chesapeake Bay retriever tail added to his comical appearance. But he was a lovable little dog with his cowlicks and crazy-tooth grin. And he'd been a lifeline for her nephew to cling to in his grief.

Hez squinted in the dusk. "I think I see Pika on the other side of the pond. She's heading his way."

The appearance of the female gator had caused a stir among the students at TGU during mating season when Boo had caught her eye. Her bullet shape stirred the water as she approached the male gator, and they rubbed snouts.

Simon watched in fascination. "Gators are lit. Maybe I'll be a biologist or something when I grow up."

Savannah exchanged a long glance with Hez. The perfect opening. They'd agreed she would take the lead on the unpleasant topic that had to be addressed. "You'll have to bring your grades up if you want to be a biologist. You just failed a math test."

Simon grimaced. "I don't need math if I want to be a biologist. Just lots of science classes."

"All your grades matter for college, and you'll use math the rest of your life." She kept her tone gentle. "I know things haven't been easy, Simon, but letting your grades slip will just add to your trouble and frustration. I can have Will tutor you if you need help."

His chin came up, and his blue eyes, so like Ella's, narrowed. "I don't need Will—I don't need anyone. Math doesn't matter to me."

Will Dixon, Simon's tutor and the police chief's son, had mentioned Simon had been increasingly withdrawn and uncommunicative lately, just like he'd been with her and Hez. He'd been spending more and more time alone in his room with the door shut, and she needed to fix that.

She reached out to brush his hair off his forehead, and he flinched from her touch. She lowered her hand. "I love you, Simon. We both do, and we want to help." The streetlight's glow illuminated the bruise under his eye. "How'd you get the shiner?"

He knelt and pulled Cody to his chest. The dog's snaggle tooth showed in a doggy grin at the attention. "I just tripped at school. I don't want to talk about it."

She felt the blow of the lie in her chest. "That's not what happened, Simon. The school called me. You want to try the truth this time?"

He stayed bent over the dog. "Fine, I got into a fight with Liam, who made fun of me for using the word *posh* instead of *fancy* during English. I shoved him and he hit me in the eye, so I jumped him."

"But you guys are friends, right? I've heard you talk about Liam Jackson, and you guys have hung out to shoot hoops sometimes."

Simon scowled at her. "He's a jerk, and we haven't hung out in a while."

This was spinning out of control. "So who are you hanging out with now?"

"No one. I just want to be left alone. I wish I could take Cody to school with me." He bent to nuzzle the dog again. "He's the only one who understands me."

She flinched and glanced at Hez. Simon's hostility was on full display, and she should have expected it. His sullen moods and angry outbursts were coming more frequently. The good days came less and less often. His grief over the loss of his mother was getting worse, not better. It seemed to be corroding him from the inside like emotional acid. What was happening with him, and how could she help him heal? She'd prayed and prayed for God to help him through this.

Hez took her hand. "You just lied to us, Simon, and there are consequences for fighting at school and lying. No screen time for a month except for schoolwork." He paused and she could see the sympathy in his blue eyes. "But you're not grounded. In fact, I'd like your help at the Justice Chamber. We're getting ready to take on some new work, and I think you'll have fun."

Simon stood with Cody still in his arms and glared at them with a black expression. "Whatever."

She took a step toward him, but he backed away and wouldn't look at her. A boulder formed in her throat. Maybe they'd handled this all wrong. Should they have punished him when he was still reeling from Jess's death? They couldn't ignore discipline, though, not for such serious offenses. They had to figure out a way to reach him before he went too far down the wrong path.

There had been so many changes in his young life lately, and he'd run away from boarding school in England several times before they brought him here. If they were too hard on him, would he try to run again?

"Look out, Will!" Simon jumped to his feet, spilling Hez's popcorn. "Run!"

Will Dixon couldn't have heard Simon's shout over the crowd's noise in Schwarzburg Stadium, but he somehow sensed the linebacker barreling toward his blind side. Will spun and stepped back as the defender lunged for him. He tucked the ball under his arm and darted forward. The crowd roared as he burst through the line untouched and raced twenty yards downfield before a defensive back managed to snag one of the flags fluttering from Will's belt.

"Wooooo! Chomp! Chomp!" Simon made the traditional TGU Gator Chomp with his arms to celebrate Will's play.

Hez smiled at the excitement in Simon's high, young voice. The annual Flags for Food game pitted TGU's first string offense and defense against each other in a flag football battle that benefited the local food bank. It usually drew a few thousand spectators, but this year the Schwarz was filled to capacity, thanks to the gorgeous spring weather and Will's athleticism.

Familiar faces sprinkled the crowd. There was Hez's cousin Blake Lawson and his girlfriend, Paradise Alden. And almost the entire Pelican Harbor Police Department was in the bleachers. Chief Jane Dixon and her husband, Reid, cheered on their son. Savannah's good friend Nora Craft sat next to them with her boyfriend, Graham Warner, and her niece Tammy Longacre. Other members of the department sat in the row behind them. In fact, the only one missing was Detective Augusta Richards, who must be keeping law and order for the entire town.

Simon sat down and noticed Hez brushing popcorn off his lap. "Oh, did I do that? Sorry, Uncle Hez."

Hez didn't mind. Seeing Simon back to his old self was worth a little mess. How long would it last? Hez pushed the question away, determined to savor the moment. "Don't worry about it, kiddo. Are you having fun?"

"Oh yeah. Will's so good. I bet he'll be in the Super Bowl someday."

"You might be right." Hez glanced at Simon. This could be a good time for an important question. "Hey, buddy, I need a best man, and there's no one I'd rather have beside me when I marry your aunt than you. Would you be my wingman?"

Simon's eyes widened. "Me? Really?" He squared his shoulders. "Do I have to wear a tux?"

"I think your aunt will spare you that if you don't want to."

"I want to look nice."

"I take it that's a yes." Hez high-fived him. "Thanks." His phone buzzed with a text from Savannah: Meeting over. Is the game still going?

Hez glanced up at the game clock. Less than a minute left and Will's team led by three touchdowns. Perfect timing for an early exit. Almost, he tapped out. We'll meet you outside the main entrance.

He turned back to Simon. "He's a terrific QB, but I think he's done for the day—and so are we. Aunt Savannah is picking us up outside. What do you say to beignets on the boardwalk? After that, we can play Frisbee on the beach with the dogs while we watch the sunset."

Simon beamed. "I'd love it! You're the best, Uncle Hez."

They headed for the exit and joined the throng coursing through the stadium's shadowy concrete interior. Savannah's Honda Civic pulled to the curb as they walked out of the Schwarz's cavernous redbrick main entrance. She gave Hez an inquiring look as he got in, and he responded with a discreet thumbs-up. Simon chattered happily in the back seat for the entire drive to Hez's condo, where they'd stashed Cody and Marley.

Savannah parked on the street outside Petit Charms. Hez's condo was right above the café, and the tempting scent of coffee and frying beignets greeted him every time he opened his door. He'd put on five pounds since he moved in last semester, despite daily runs.

Hez pulled out his keys as they walked around the corner of the building, but he halted at the foot of the iron staircase leading to the condo. The door wasn't quite shut. He held out his hand to stop Savannah and Simon. "Wait here."

Savannah followed his gaze, then set a hand on his arm. "Let's call the police."

He shook his head. "Augusta is the only one on duty. I don't want to bother her if we don't have to. That door sticks sometimes—it's possible it didn't latch when we left."

She hesitated, then released his arm. "Be careful, babe."

He nodded and crept up the stairs, making as little noise as possible. Every muscle in his body tensed as he gripped the doorknob and gave a tentative tug. It was indeed stuck—and probably had been ever since they'd left for the game. He relaxed and pulled the door open.

The condo was quiet and peaceful—which was wrong. Where were the dogs? He walked in, scanning the floor and furniture. "Cody? Marley?" He stopped when he reached the kitchen. Two furry lumps lay on the floor. "Cody!"

He knelt by the still dogs, but before he could touch them, a cold male voice spoke behind him. "Don't get up. Take your phone out slowly and slide it across the floor. Then lie down with your hands behind the back of your neck and close your eyes."

Hez froze. The intruder was smart. He'd waited until Hez was distracted and in a vulnerable position before making his move. Hez had no choice but to comply. He pulled the phone out of his pocket and tossed it on the floor.

Steps rang on the metal staircase. "Uncle Hez!"

Hez turned to see Simon in the doorway, with Savannah hurrying up behind him. A man clothed in black crouched to pick up Hez's phone. He wore a ski mask and a small backpack, and he held a gun in his free hand, but he had turned toward the door—and away from Hez.

Hez scrambled to his feet and launched himself at the intruder. The man reacted fast, jumping to the side and deflecting the force of Hez's bull rush. Before the burglar could regain his balance, Hez kicked his feet out from under him.

The intruder crashed to the floor as Savannah raced into the room and grabbed a butcher knife. But before she could use it, the burglar rolled to his knees and leveled his gun at her.

Hez jumped in front of her, bracing himself to feel a bullet tear into his body.

The burglar cursed and got to his feet, keeping the gun on the two of them. "Move a muscle and you're both dead." He shot a glance toward the door, where Simon still stood frozen. "Get out of the way, kid."

Eyes round and face pale, Simon nodded and walked over to the couch.

"Now you freeze too." The intruder backed toward the doorway, alternately training the gun on the Websters and Simon. Then he vanished through the door and slammed it. His steps clattered down the stairs.

CHAPTER 4

THE ICE IN SAVANNAH'S VEINS DISSOLVED WHEN THE MAN in the ski mask yanked the door closed behind him. Hez crouched by the inert forms of the dogs, and she and Simon rushed to join him. Her tongue was too dry to speak, and she was afraid to touch the dogs and find them as cold as the shudders coursing down her spine.

Simon threw himself down beside Hez and Cody. “Cody!” He touched the dog’s cowlick. “He’s still warm and breathing. He’s going to be okay, isn’t he, Uncle Hez?”

“I hope so, buddy. We’d better not move them. Can I use your phone, babe? I saw Blake and Paradise at the game. I’ll ask them to come right away.” Paradise was the vet in Nova Cambridge.

Savannah dug her phone out of her purse and gave it to him with a shaky hand. Marley’s back legs twitched, and she touched his ears. “I’m here, Marley.” She was barely aware of Hez’s terse voice asking Blake for help. Were both dogs going to die? Marley had been her solace through so much. How could someone mistreat their dogs like this?

Simon was crying hysterically, and she moved to embrace him. He buried his face against her, and his chest heaved with his sobs. His tears soaked her neck and blouse, and she pressed her lips against his hair, which smelled of Hez's sage soap and little boy sweat. She shot up a prayer for God to spare them another loss. Simon needed Cody right now.

"They'll be here in five minutes. Both dogs are starting to move. I suspect the guy gave them something to knock them out." He handed back her phone and touched her hair. "You okay? Can you call the police while I see if there's anything missing?"

Savannah smoothed Simon's damp hair and nodded. His touch calmed her erratic heartbeat. "What was he doing here, Hez? Do you think he was just a burglar?"

"He wanted my phone." Hez's voice was grim. "I'll see if anything else is missing."

She dialed 911 as Hez's footsteps went down the hall to his office. The operator said they'd have someone there as soon as possible. She wanted Savannah to stay on the line, so she put the phone on speaker and set it on the counter.

Simon's sobs finally subsided, and the boy pulled away to crouch beside his beloved dog again. Her gaze fell on the butcher knife lying on the floor beside Marley. She must have put it there when she knelt beside her dog. She'd been about to kill a man or die trying—and he'd been about to try to kill her. She shivered. What would have happened if Hez hadn't jumped in front of her?

His expression was hard when he returned to the kitchen. "My laptop is gone too. I'll bet it was in his backpack." He tossed a nod toward the living room.

Simon seemed calm, so she rose and followed Hez so they could talk privately. He took her hand and led her to the bathroom, where he pointed to the trash. "Look there. An empty hamburger package. The burglar must have fed it to the dogs."

She gasped and bent to examine the package. "Poison?"

"I hope he just drugged them with a sedative, but Paradise will probably be able to tell."

A thousand what-ifs rolled through her mind. "The second Simon heard you call out Cody's name like that, he bolted past me up the steps. I told him to stop, but he didn't listen and went charging in. The burglar could have shot him. You too."

"And you." Hez took her in his arms and held her tight. "I can't lose you."

They embraced for a long moment. The trauma of the last few minutes played in her head like a video she couldn't turn off. And she noticed something odd. "Why didn't he shoot you? As soon as you got in front of me, he swore and backed away."

"I've been trying to figure out what he was after, and I think it's the key to the dead man's switch. Killing me would flip the switch, so he couldn't do it."

Savannah relaxed against him. "You came up with the right way to stay alive."

The dead man's switch had kept Hez alive ever since he beat a shady financial firm named Hornbrook Finance. Hornbrook had nearly destroyed TGU, but Hez discovered that they'd been cheating their clients, some of whom were very dangerous people. Hez and a computer whiz named Bruno Rubinelli had set up a mass email to all those defrauded clients and threatened to send it out unless Hornbrook repaired TGU's finances and repaid everyone it had cheated. Hornbrook had caved.

To make sure they didn't try to seek revenge, Bruno had set up what he called a "dead man's switch"—a mechanism that would only be triggered if either Hez or Bruno died. Bruno's switch was a computer program that would automatically send out the mass email to Hornbrook's victims if either he or Hez failed to prove they were alive every twenty-four hours.

If those emails were sent, Hornbrook Finance would implode and its founder, James Hornbrook, would be lucky to live a week. So unless James Hornbrook and his company found a way to disable the switch, they had no choice but to let Hez and Bruno live.

"Aunt Savannah!"

Savannah wheeled around at Simon's urgent call, and she ran to the kitchen. Both dogs were standing on wobbly feet with their tails wagging feebly. "Marley." She fell to her knees and buried her face in her dog's fur.

"Hey, Cody," Hez said in a gentle voice. He sank to the floor to pet the little mutt.

A sharp rap sounded on the door and Blake entered with Paradise behind him. Her mane of light brown hair had exploded around her shoulders from the humidity, and she smiled when her amber eyes glanced from Savannah to the dogs. "They're awake. I'll examine them, but I think they'll be okay. The intruder must have used a sedative."

Savannah and Hez moved out of the way, but Simon refused to budge from Cody's side while Paradise checked them out. They'd all survived this incident, but they had to get James Hornbrook behind bars before he attacked Hez again.

A siren wailed outside, so Savannah ended her call with the 911 operator.

"I'd better call Bruno and warn him," Hez said. "If they're taking my electronics, I'm sure he's targeted as well."

"Good idea." She pulled up Bruno's number, dialed, and switched to speaker mode.

The call went straight to voicemail.

Detective Augusta Richards looked up from her notebook, her brown eyes sharp with interest. "Can Hornbrook turn off this dead man's switch now?"

"I don't think so." Hez wished he could give a more definitive answer. "I think the whole thing is encrypted. I punch in a randomly generated code every day and then call a number, and a robotic voice says a nonsense phrase, which I repeat. If the thief can hack into my phone and computer, he'll have the website and number, but I don't think that's enough to turn off the switch. At least not right away. Bruno would know more, of course. He set it up."

"The San Francisco police have already sent a unit to check on him." Augusta clicked her pen and closed her notebook. "Until they find him, there's not much more for us to do." She turned to Savannah's best friend, Nora Craft, a forensic tech at the Pelican Harbor Police Department. "Let me know when you're done processing the scene."

Nora's brown curls bobbed as she nodded. She had come straight from the game and still wore her red-and-white TGU sweatshirt. "It'll just be a few minutes. The burglar didn't leave much evidence beyond that hamburger package. There are some scratches around the lock that might indicate it was picked. I took pictures, and I'm just about done dusting for prints."

Nora's arrival with Augusta had been a relief. Savannah had hugged her friend before turning her attention back to a groggy Marley while Nora worked. Hez also felt better with Nora and Augusta in his condo. The PHPD had an unknown traitor in their ranks, but Hez knew—and trusted—Augusta and Nora. He'd been comfortable turning his back on them while he said goodbye to Blake and Paradise as Augusta interviewed Savannah.

Savannah's phone buzzed, drawing a growl from Cody, who disliked objects that suddenly came to life. Savannah grabbed her phone. "It's Bruno!" She took the call and put it on speaker. "Bruno! Are you okay?"

"Yeah, though I had an unexpected visitor about half an hour ago." Bruno spoke casually, as though this was a common occurrence for him. Maybe it was. "The guy got past my security system, which was impressive. He grabbed my phone and one of my laptops and then ran. How about you guys? Hez's phone is dead. Did they get to him?"

"They did." Hez walked over to her phone. "They got my phone and laptop at about the same time they hit you. How long will it take them to reach the key to the dead man's switch?"

"So they have phones and computers from both of us. Hmm . . ." Hez hovered over the phone as Bruno hummed tunelessly. "Depending on how good they are, it'll take between forty-eight hours and forever."

Forty-eight hours? Hez's stomach muscles clenched. "How will we catch these guys in forty-eight hours?"

Augusta leaned forward. "We'll call the FBI's Cyber Division, and we'll do what we can to keep you safe while they investigate."

Bruno gave a sharp laugh. "Cyber usually calls me for this kind of case. Don't worry about it. We should be fine—at least for a while."

Hez relaxed a fraction. "Why is that?"

"Because I switched the files as soon as the guy left. They're not gonna find the key when they finally get in."

The tension in Hez's gut eased. "What will they find?"

"A Rick Astley video."

The room was silent for a second, then Savannah burst into laughter. "You—you Rickrolled Hornbrook?"

Hez guffawed at the thought of James Hornbrook falling for a juvenile old internet prank, and even Augusta chuckled. Then the implication of Bruno's words hit Hez. "Let me make sure I have this right: It'll take at least forty-eight hours for Hornbrook and company to hack through your security, but you can switch the files and move the key almost instantly. So we can stay a step ahead of them indefinitely."

"Bingo! And they can't kill us because they need us to check in every twenty-four hours."

Hez tugged his lower lip. "What about that email database? What happens if they find that?"

Bruno scoffed. "There are multiple encrypted mirror copies on the dark web—which any decent hacker will know."

Hez wished he shared Bruno's confidence. "That's great, man. It sounds like the techno side of this is tied up with a bow, but there are other ways to get to people."

"I'm not a meat-space expert," Bruno admitted. "I deal with virtual stuff."

Savannah turned toward Hez. "Did James Hornbrook strike you as the kind of guy who'll just give up after this?"

Hez remembered the hatred in Hornbrook's glacial blue eyes when he realized Hez had beaten him. "No. No, he didn't. I hate to say it, but I'm pretty sure this was just his first move."

She fingered the beads on her bracelet. "What do you think he'll do?"

"I don't know. I'm going to start carrying my gun. I can't let anything happen to you or Simon."

"I have bear spray somewhere. I'll find it and stick it in my purse."

"Good plan," Augusta said. "And I'll have a car drive by as often as possible."

An occasional police car cruising the neighborhood wouldn't be enough to protect his family. Hez went to get his gun from the safe in his bedroom.

CHAPTER 5

HEZ PAUSED AS HE PASSED JESS'S OLD OFFICE. THE BRASS nameplate beside the door still said JESSICA LEGARE, CHIEF FINANCIAL OFFICER, but the office was empty. Or almost empty. Her presence still haunted the room in small ways—the faint indentations on the floor where her stylish office furniture once stood, the little scratches on the walls where her TGU and NYU diplomas hung, and so on. The invisible marks Jess left on Tupelo Grove University went much deeper, of course.

Hez took a deep breath and blew it out. Jess's legacy was complex, to say the least. She had tried to destroy TGU financially, but her plan ended with the university flush with cash and debt-free for the first time in generations. She did her best to undermine Hez's relationship with Savannah, but she wound up strengthening it. She hid Simon's very existence from Savannah and Hez, and now they were about to become the boy's parents. Or at least that's what they hoped.

Erik Andersen's lawyer had called Hez the same day she filed her appearance and objection in the adoption case. She had requested a meeting and volunteered to come to TGU. Hez checked his watch—she'd be here in five minutes.

Hez walked down the hall to his office. He gave the room a quick scan. Nothing confidential on his desk or monitor. The remnants of his to-go breakfast sandwich from the university cafeteria went in the trash. So did the used pod from the little Keurig machine on his credenza.

He adjusted the pictures on his computer stand. Both were unposed snapshots from the engagement party last month. One caught Savannah on the verge of a laugh, her green eyes sparkling in the early evening sun, which brought out the gold highlights in her auburn hair. The other photo showed Savannah, Hez, and Simon walking barefoot along the sand after the party, the reds and oranges of the sunset glowing on the water behind them. An excited grin split Simon's face from ear to ear as he showed them a shell he had just found. That day had felt like a new beginning for all three of them. Had it really been an ending, at least as far as Simon was concerned?

The receptionist called to let him know Andersen's lawyer had arrived, and Hez walked out to get her. He had never practiced family law, but he'd met Nita Hendrix at several bar functions over the years. She'd always been friendly, but he'd heard opponents call her "Nita the Knife"—usually right after she'd slashed them.

She smiled as she rose to greet him. She was around sixty, with warm brown eyes and a round face framed by salt-and-pepper curls. A pink blouse, navy slacks of some stretchy material, and sensible shoes completed her outfit. She appeared more like a beloved kindergarten teacher than a knife fighter, which was one reason she was so effective in court.

"How are you doing, Hez?" she asked as they entered his

office. "I saw that news story about you and Simon almost drowning the other day. Are you both okay?"

"We're both fully recovered, thanks." He walked around the desk. "Can I get you something to drink?"

"Decaf with creamer would be wonderful. You must have been terrified."

"I didn't really have time to be scared." Hez popped a decaf pod into the coffee maker and slid a fresh mug under the spout. "I was too focused on saving Simon."

Her gaze rested on the pictures behind Hez. "You love your nephew, don't you?"

Hez didn't hesitate. "Very much."

"He seems like a special boy. Erik is very much anticipating getting to know his son."

The Keurig hissed as it spat the last drops of coffee into her mug. Hez handed it to her along with the little box of creamers he kept in the drawer under the coffee maker. "They already know each other, or did Erik forget to mention that?"

Nita emptied two creamers into the mug. "He mentioned finding Simon and Savannah in his living room, but that didn't sound like it really qualified as getting to know each other." She smiled. "It sounded more like breaking and entering—but you're the criminal-law expert."

Hez smiled back. "I personally would have charged it as unlawful imprisonment because he wouldn't let them leave."

"Followed by assault with a deadly weapon when you arrived, correct?"

Hez shook his head. "Self-defense and defense of others. I'll be happy to tell the whole story at the adoption hearing if that's what your client really wants."

She chuckled. "There won't be an adoption hearing. If the father doesn't consent, the adoption is automatically denied. You'll need to either terminate his rights—which you won't be able to do—or get his consent."

Hez didn't know enough about adoption law to argue with her—but maybe he wouldn't have to. "Are you implying that we might be able to get his consent?"

"Maybe." She took a slow sip of her decaf. "He's been distracted due to the, ah, employment issues caused by his recent absence."

"You mean his claim for back pay?"

"And the unfounded allegations about misconduct with female students."

Hez could hardly believe his ears. "He was seen taking a young woman into a warehouse with a wine bottle. And then he went AWOL for months. He's lucky he still had a job when he came back. We had already started recruiting for a new European history professor when he waltzed back onto campus."

"He had a mental-health crisis triggered by the stress of working under the cloud of that smuggling ring and then being attacked in his own home. Plus, he's a tenured professor, so you can't just fire him."

Hez wished they could do exactly that, but TGU's tenure rules tied their hands and Andersen still had friends in the school bureaucracy despite his antics. "That's the only reason he's back in his old office and not out on the street. Besides, these are HR issues between him and the university. Savannah and I can't—and won't—excuse personal misconduct or use TGU's money to bribe Erik into doing what's best for Simon."

She took a sip of her coffee and switched gears. "You and Savannah love Simon. Despite your busy lives, you're obviously willing to make great sacrifices for him—even to the point of risking your lives. My client is a financially sophisticated individual who also cares deeply for Simon."

Hez resisted the urge to roll his eyes at her description of Erik Andersen. "Go on."

Nita set down her mug. "He is open to a division of labor. You and Savannah would have plenty on your plate with your careers and raising Simon. Erik would take over management of Simon's trust."

So that was it. Andersen wanted access to the fortune Jess left for her son. Hez's stomach churned. "Savannah is the trustee. Are you suggesting that she would appoint Erik as successor trustee and then resign, making him the trustee?"

"That would be one way to do it. She could also just hire him to manage the trust assets. Oh, and one other thing: In light of the, ah, tension between Erik, Savannah, and you, it would be best for the university to arrange a long-term visiting scholar position somewhere appropriate. He believes several schools in southern France would be excellent fits. He would also be open to the University of Hawaii."

Hez could hardly believe his ears. "And if Savannah refuses?"

Nita shrugged. "Then Erik would take custody of Simon and send the trust periodic bills for expenses related to raising him."

"Parents have a duty to provide for their minor children, don't they?"

"Sure, but the bar is low. As long as a parent isn't guilty of child neglect, they're fine."

Anger flared in Hez's chest at the implied threat, but he kept his voice even. "I appreciate your candor."

"I'm glad we understand each other." She gave him a smile that wasn't at all warm or grandmotherly. "Thank you for the time and the coffee." She drained her mug and rose. "Talk to Savannah and let me know what you decide. I know you'll want to do what's best for Simon." She turned and left.

As her footsteps faded down the hall, Hez swiveled to look at the picture of Savannah, Simon, and him. They were so right together. Hez wasn't going to give up Simon—and there was no way he'd let Andersen use the boy as a hostage to extort money from the trust. But there was no way Savannah would—or should—turn the trust over to Andersen as a ransom. That money was Simon's, and they would fight to protect every penny of it. And the idea of using university money to send Andersen on a long-term vacation was the sort of thing Savannah's father, Pierre, might have done, but she never would.

"So what are we going to do?" he murmured.

Boo Radley roared from across the pond, and Marley strained at his leash and snarled. "Stay," Savannah ordered. She let go of Hez's hand long enough to restrain her dog. Marley's hatred of the old gator only grew with time, and Cody offered a snaggle-toothed grimace of support.

Hez's gaze was far away as he watched the sun setting over the tupelo trees lining the water. He hadn't said much since he arrived for an evening stroll while Will Dixon tutored Simon after dinner. The fact Hez hadn't immediately told her about his meeting wasn't a good sign.

A hard knot formed in her midsection. "What happened with Erik's attorney?"

They reached a bench, and he tugged her down with him onto the stone seat. "It's not great, babe. His attorney is good, very good. I don't know enough about family law to recognize if what she said was true, but based on her reputation, I suspect it is. Brace yourself."

Savannah listened with growing horror as he laid out Erik's proposal and how a judge would likely react to his request for custody and his threat to basically hold Simon hostage to get access to Jess's money. If she didn't pay him out of Jess's estate, he might refuse to provide more than the bare necessities for Simon—so she'd have to hand over whatever he demanded. It was a diabolical move.

Savannah rose with clenched fists and paced back and forth in front of Hez. "So let me get this straight—he wants TGU to pay for a permanent vacation so he can strut the beaches of some tropical paradise and target college girls? That's ridiculous, Hez, and I'm not going to do it!" Both dogs cowered at her tone, and she reached down a soothing hand to rub Marley's ears. "It's okay, boy."

"I agree with you, but it'll be an ugly fight. We'll need to hire a top family law attorney."

She fought nausea and wrapped her arms around herself. "I watched my sister become a pawn between my father and hers, and I can't stand by and watch that happen to Simon. He's already been through too much. We have to fix this, Hez—we just have to!"

He rose and opened his arms for her to step into his embrace. She tried to take comfort from his closeness—but failed. If Hez couldn't see a way out of this morass, what could they do? Her thoughts spun frantically, and no quick solution came to mind. She straightened and pulled away. "How do we protect Simon?"

His arms dropped back to his sides, and concern still lingered on his face. "It will take terminating Erik's parental rights. That's not easy to do."

"He's a criminal! Can't we get him sent to jail?"

"When I brought up his actions, his attorney was quick to point out that you and Simon could be accused of breaking and entering."

This situation looked worse and worse. "What kind of a lawyer would take a case with such a slimeball client? Doesn't she care about a child at all?" She raked her hand through her hair. "Don't answer that. She obviously has no more scruples than Erik."

"I've got a few attorneys in mind, and I'll check with Jimmy. He might have some advice for us."

The worry in his voice sent her spirits even lower. "We have to win, Hez."

"I know."

CHAPTER 6

HEZ POKED HIS HEAD INTO HIS NEW HOUSE'S OBSERVATORY— and was instantly ten years old again. An enormous old-fashioned tarnished brass telescope dominated the stuffy little octagonal space. A cracked leather chair sat beside it, and faded astronomical charts covered the low walls. The floor was dusty plexiglass with some sort of design underneath. The ceiling was peaked and supposed to be retractable. Light from a single dim bulb showed a large hand crank protruding from a gearbox.

Hez tried the crank, but it only moved a fraction of an inch. Of course. He sighed and opened the toolbox he'd lugged up with him. He and Savannah had closed on the house yesterday, so it was finally theirs. He had promised to go over it from top to bottom to get it ready, and he'd decided to start at the very top.

One of his father's rules of home maintenance was "Ninety percent of all repairs require pliers, duct tape, or WD-40," so Hez kept all three handy. The pliers made short work of the rusty gearbox lid, and he applied WD-40 liberally to the interior. He tried the crank again. The gears squealed in protest and started to move. Hez got a good workout, but the eight sides of the roof slowly slid down into the walls, letting in the sunshine and very welcome fresh air.

He leaned against the shoulder-height wall and let the late-April breeze cool his sweaty face. Slate shingles sloped down on each side of the roof, and he had a panoramic view of the horizon. The fake medieval tower stood like a sentinel about ten yards from the house, watching over the blue waters of Mobile Bay, and he took in the expanse of water, treetops, boat docks, and the occasional roof.

The bright spring sun showed the floor clearly: The plexiglass protected a giant mechanical star map that took up almost the entire floor. Little knobs stuck out of the floor beside one wall, allowing the map to be adjusted for date and time. The floor of the observatory would be a perfectly labeled guide to the sky above. "Simon is going to love this."

The thought of his nephew brought a pang. Would Simon even see this? The lawyer Hez talked to hadn't held out much hope. Under Alabama law, if the father objected to an adoption, the court had no choice but to deny it. Their only hope was to terminate Erik's parental rights, and that would not be easy. Their only real chance would be to get him convicted and imprisoned for a felony—and he hadn't even been arrested for anything. Hez hoped to change that, and yesterday he'd put in a call to his old mentee at the DA's office, Deputy District Attorney Hope Norcross, now one of the office's go-to prosecutors for major crimes.

As if on cue, his phone rang and Hope's name appeared. Hez's pulse picked up as he took the call. "Hey, Hope. I didn't expect to hear from you so soon. Did you arrest Andersen?"

"No, but I'll let you know if we do. I'm actually calling

about something else. We've run into a dead end in our investigation of Jess's murder, and I was hoping you might be able to help."

"Of course. What's up?"

"Key evidence seems to be missing. We have what's left of your car, but that's about it. No testable explosive residue and very few bomb fragments. There were a lot more at the crime scene, but they vanished somewhere between there and Pelican Harbor PD's evidence locker."

Hez groaned. "I thought you were using state police because of the problems in the PHPD."

"We are. But this came in as a 911 call, so it went straight to first responders, including PHPD. Plus, there was no mention of the smuggling ring, of course. No one connected the dots and alerted my team for almost two hours. And I don't blame them under the circumstances."

Hez winced at her defensive tone. "Sorry, I wasn't trying to blame them—or you either. It's just . . . frustrating."

"I'm frustrated too. There are a lot of good Pelican Harbor cops, and I hate having to freeze them out of a big investigation in their backyard. Hopefully we'll find the mole soon and be able to go back to business as usual." She sighed. "Anyway, I was wondering whether you remembered anything that might be useful from the immediate aftermath of the explosion. Did you see any forensic techs acting strangely? Do you remember which officers put evidence in their cars? Anything like that?"

Hez gazed out at the hazy horizon but didn't really see it. He remembered sitting at his little plywood desk in the Justice Chamber, chewing over his last conversation with

Jess. A distant boom had rattled the windows and shaken the room. Then he had been running, dodging confused students and professors as he raced from Connor Hall to the faculty parking lot.

He'd seen Savannah kneeling in the grass near the flaming wreck of his Audi. She'd been covered in blood, rocking back and forth, her wails mingling with those of the approaching sirens. Then he'd been on his knees beside her, holding her as the scents of acrid smoke and coppery blood assaulted his nose.

Savannah had clutched Jess's mangled corpse, whose sightless, glassy blue eyes stared at the sky—just like Ella's had as Hez held her three and a half years ago.

He made an effort to steady himself. "Sorry, no. I wasn't really paying attention to anything except Savannah and Jess."

"That's what I guessed. I figured it couldn't hurt to ask, though. I'll give Savannah a call too. And Hez—" Hope hesitated. "Stay safe."

His shoulders tensed. "What do you mean?"

"I have a little news on our old friend James Hornbrook."

"What?"

"He's staying in countries that don't have extradition treaties with us, but we're keeping tabs on him when we can. He's continuing to make comments about you that could be construed as threats."

"Like what?"

"Like that he'd love to dance on your grave."

Hez grimaced. "I'll grab his ankle and pull him down to join me if he tries."

Hope chuckled. "And we'd arrest him before he reached the cemetery dance floor. There's more: He's sent significant amounts of money to offshore accounts connected to organized crime, and he's been communicating with someone in the US. He's being careful about security, so we don't know who it is."

"You think he's coming up with plan B after the attack on Bruno and me failed?"

"That's our best guess, but we don't have any details."

"Okay. Thanks for the warning."

He ended the call and slipped the phone into his pocket. Hope's news wasn't a surprise, but it did make the skin on the back of his neck crawl. He had cost Hornbrook and his company, Hornbrook Finance, tens of millions of dollars. Maybe hundreds of millions. Of course Hornbrook wanted to kill him. Guys like that didn't just walk away from a big loss. The dead man's switch would keep Hez safe—for now. But how long would it be before Hornbrook found a way around it?

Savannah sighed contentedly at the sight of the swath of pale blue paint on their new master bedroom's accent wall. It was perfect against the creamy white paint on the other walls. It blended with the water just outside the window, though she couldn't hear the waves over the leaf blower Hez's cousin Blake Lawson was using in the backyard. "Hez, it's so tranquil. It makes me think of Jamaica. Wait until you see the print I found to put above the headboard." Her smile faltered. "Is it wrong to feel so happy right now? My sister is still dead, we're facing a formidable battle with Erik, and Hornbrook wants to do the twist on your grave."

He put the roller back in the tray and opened his arms to hold her. He didn't have to say anything—the steady beat of his heart was enough reassurance. They were together, and their love was strong. They'd already been through so much, and God had made sure they were still standing. Together they could weather anything—couldn't they?

"I'm happy too," he murmured against her hair. "We've faced tough odds in the past, and we'll get through all of this. And hey, we found the perfect house. It even has an attached nursery."

She pulled back to be able to see his expression. His clear blue eyes held no clouds, only love and confidence. Thankfulness settled in her chest at the wonder of how they'd found each other again. "I want a baby right away."

"Me too. Though I'll admit to a bit of terror at the thought of a newborn. Remember how Ella used to be up all night? We would take turns trying to keep our eyes pried open."

She could almost smell that unmistakable scent of a new baby's head. Her arms ached to hold a little one again, and the longing for Ella grew and spread through her chest with a weight that took the air out of her lungs. "I—I think it will be hard, Hez. We'll miss Ella all the more with a new baby in the house." She touched the best friends bracelet Nora had given her and rolled the beads between her fingers.

"We'll never forget our little girl, but maybe a baby will help heal the wounds that are still bleeding." He palmed her face and leaned in for a kiss.

She wrapped her arms around his neck and the familiar passion sparked between them. It was tempting to forget they weren't married yet. She sighed and pulled away. "Whose idea was it to put off the marriage anyway?"

"That was all you, babe. I was ready to put that ring back on your finger and start trying for that baby right away."

Her cheeks heated at his raised eyebrow. "It was the right thing to do. We've been able to work through any lingering issues. We can start our marriage on fresh footing."

"Maybe so, but I'm regretting that decision about now." He gave a rueful grin and picked up the paint roller. "I guess I'd better get back to work. Simon should be along any minute too."

She turned for the door. "Oh right. I want to meet the school bus so the driver knows we're here. It's Simon's first time being dropped at the new place."

The scent of fresh paint lingered in the living room as she went through the house to the front door. The bright yellow school bus lumbered around the curve and came toward her. It didn't slow, and the woman driver waved as it rolled past to the next driveway. Savannah frowned and jogged over as a little girl descended the steps.

The door started to close, and she rushed to stop it. "Excuse me, but where is Simon Legare? He's supposed to get off here too."

The driver was in her thirties with brown hair up in a bun tight enough to heighten her cheekbones. "His grandfather picked him up in the office."

"What? That was never cleared with me. Who gave him the authority to take Simon?"

"You'll have to take that up with the school." The driver glanced at her watch. "I'm running late. Sorry for the mix-up."

Savannah ran for the house to get her phone. Wait until she got ahold of her dad. How dare he whisk Simon away without permission?

"Hez!" She let the door slam behind her and grabbed her purse off the kitchen counter to dig out her phone.

Hez's brisk steps sounded on the hardwood floors, and he came rushing into the room. "What's wrong?"

"The arrogance of my dad," she muttered as she called up his number. "He took Simon out of school."

"Why would he do that? He hasn't bothered much with him."

"Cold, hard cash is the only thing that motivates him." The call rang four times before going to voicemail. "He's not picking up. He probably knows I'm livid." She called Simon next, but it went straight to voicemail. "Simon's phone is off."

Hez wheeled toward the door. "Blake and I will check the marina for Pierre's car. Maybe he took Simon fishing."

"I'm going to strangle that man. I'll stay here and keep trying to reach him while you search. The cell coverage is awful along the route." Savannah followed him out as he called for his cousin. She tried to call her dad again as Hez and his cousin drove off.

Her pulse throbbed in her neck. What should she do? This wasn't a normal situation, and Simon's lack of response was even more worrisome. What if someone had pretended to be his grandfather? Stories of child predators dominated the news constantly.

She couldn't put this off—she had to call 911. Before she could punch in the numbers, a gleaming black GMC Sierra Denali pickup rolled up the driveway, and Simon climbed out. Savannah's pulse stuttered in her chest when she saw a familiar face behind the wheel.

Michael Willard. *Grandfather.* It all clicked into place.

She clenched her fists and rushed to the driver's side as Michael lowered the window. "I was scared to death and about to call the police. No one said you could take Simon from the school."

The wind ruffled his blond hair. "I don't need permission to see my own grandson."

She curled her fingers into her palms hard enough to make her wince. It was all she could do not to slap the arrogant smirk from his face. "I have custody of Simon. No one can take him from the school or anywhere else without my permission. Who allowed you to take him?"

Michael raised one shoulder in a dramatic shrug. "The school receptionist knows I'm Simon's grandfather, of course. We both knew it was fine and there was nothing to worry about."

"You did this so I would worry, and you know it." She rounded on Simon. "And Simon Legare, you know better than to go off with a stranger."

Simon's wide eyes went from her to Michael. "He's not a stranger—he's Mom's dad, right? You don't have to go ballistic. Sheesh, Aunt Savannah, chill."

His defense of Michael raised her ire even more. "Never go off with anyone without permission. Do you understand?"

Simon's eyes widened, and he gave a slight nod. "And why was your phone off?"

Michael stepped out of the truck and pushed close enough for his overpowering cologne to envelop her in a choking wave. "Don't take your anger with me out on Simon."

She put the heel of her palm on his chest and shoved him out of her personal space. "Back off, Michael! I'm not intimidated by you. You've caused enough problems for today. Get in your fancy truck and get off my property."

Something dangerous flashed in Michael's eyes, but his voice stayed calm and smooth. "He turned off his phone because I told him to. Kids spend too much time on their screens. Don't blame me for your irrational panic. As soon as you heard he was with his grandfather, you could have called me. I'm the only grandfather he has, so it should have been clear." Michael smiled at Simon. "We had a great time, didn't we, son? We had root beer floats at Mac's."

"And Pawpaw told me some cool stories about Mom, Aunt Savannah." Simon's voice shook, and his gaze darted between her and Michael. "Stuff I've never heard."

Michael's low chuckle held only contempt. "You can't object to that, now can you, Savannah? The boy wants to know his true family."

Her fury went from red-hot to cold determination at his haughty tone, and she closed her lips against the things she shouldn't say in front of Simon. "You will not take him again without permission, Michael, or you'll be in jail. That's kidnapping." Michael was enjoying pushing Savannah's buttons way too much, and she was letting him get away with it.

She stepped back. "Simon, go inside. We'll talk about this later."

Michael's lips flattened, and he gave her a pointed glare before climbing into his truck and driving off. The school would hear about this, and Savannah intended they would understand the repercussions if they ever allowed it to happen again.

CHAPTER 7

HEZ STOOD AND STRETCHED. A RIPPLE OF CRACKS WENT UP his spine and along each arm. He took a swig of icy water from his bottle and surveyed the day's work. The rambling wildflower garden behind the patio was now weed-free and had a stone border. He pictured sitting in Adirondack chairs on the cobblestone patio and sipping sweet tea with Savannah as Simon chased lightning bugs across the wide sweep of lawn.

Hez wished they were here now. The patio had a firepit, and it would be fun to roast hot dogs for dinner. But Simon had homework to do, and Savannah needed to get to some paperwork she'd left sitting on the counter in her cottage's little kitchen. Plus, she probably also didn't want Simon to be here if Michael Willard decided to drop by again.

Hez's blood boiled at the thought. He had been furious when he heard what happened, of course. He'd also felt a little guilty that he hadn't been here, though there had been no reason to think he was leaving Savannah to face an ominous confrontation alone. Still, he wouldn't mind an opportunity to have a few harsh words with Michael. In fact, one reason Hez had decided to finish the garden today was that he'd half hoped Simon's grandfather might make another visit.

The setting sun turned Mobile Bay to gold and blood as it touched the watery horizon and then slipped beneath it. The sea breeze brought the mingled scents of wildflowers and salt water and blew away the last of the sweat from Hez's face. He leaned against the rough stone of the firepit and took another drink from his bottle. Venus appeared in the darkening sky, and the first lightning bugs winked from a little copse of trees on one side of the lawn.

Time to go try the new showerhead he'd installed in the master bathroom. After that, he'd stretch out on the air mattress he'd brought. He had tomorrow off and he wanted to spend as much time as possible working on the house. He wanted it to be perfect before he carried Savannah over the threshold.

Hez stripped and turned on the shower. They'd splurged and gotten a fancy showerhead that boosted water pressure and had an excellent massage setting. It was Savannah's idea, and Hez silently thanked her as he stepped toward the shower. He'd sleep well tonight.

He stopped with his hand on the door of the shower stall. Was something out there in the night?

The bathroom window had old-fashioned blinds rather than frosted glass, and Hez hadn't bothered to close them because the nearest neighbor on the bay side of the house was across Mobile Bay. A full moon hung low in the western sky, silhouetting the tower on the hillside—and what appeared to be a figure on it.

I'm an easy target.

Hez immediately turned off the bathroom light and ducked. He crept out of the bathroom, staying out of the line of sight of the tower. The master bedroom also faced west, and he risked a peek through one of its windows. The figure on the tower had vanished. Hez pulled on dark sweats to make himself a little less visible and checked the Glock 22 he'd kept nearby since the attack in his condo.

Heart racing, Hez slipped out the front door and circled around to the back of the house, keeping to the shadows as much as possible. Now that he was outside, the moonlight seemed incredibly bright. He would have little trouble seeing the watcher in the tower—and vice versa.

He reached an old oak ten yards from the tower and pressed against its trunk, listening. The only sounds he heard were his pounding heart and the rhythmic rumble of waves reaching the shore. He risked a quick look. Nothing but silvery grass between him and the tower. No movement in its black windows or arched entrance.

Hez swallowed hard, then dashed across the open ground. He stumbled as he reached the tower's gate and it clanged. Anyone in the tower knew he was there now, so he abandoned stealth and raced up the curving staircase inside. The steel steps rang under his feet, and he kept his gun trained on the trapdoor above.

He paused at the top, crouching under the trapdoor. He held his breath and listened. Nothing. He threw open the door and burst out, sweeping his pistol around the small parapeted stone platform. It was empty.

A quarter mile away, an engine roared to life and headlights came on. Tires squealed as the vehicle sped away. The distance was too great for Hez to make out the make or model, but the engine sounded powerful—maybe a pickup or a large SUV.

Hez lowered his gun and examined the platform. There was no sign that anyone had been there, and the springy turf around the tower's base wouldn't hold footprints. All the neighbors had large lots and houses set back from the road, so it was unlikely that a security camera caught anything useful. The only evidence of an intruder would be Hez's claim that he thought he saw someone on the tower—and he was still recovering from brain surgery, which could cause vision problems.

He sighed and trudged back down the tower steps and into the house. He decided to send Hope a short email describing what happened, but there was little she could do. Then he'd take that shower and lie on the air mattress, but no way would he sleep tonight.

There was no line at University Grounds this morning, which was a pleasant surprise to Savannah. She'd spent the night mentally composing what she wanted to say to the school at her scheduled appointment at three, and she was no closer to being confident she could get across how serious the transgression had been.

She glanced at her watch as she approached the counter. Nora would be here in fifteen minutes. Just enough time to get their order. The familiar aroma of coffee and steamed milk eased Savannah's distress for a moment, and she studied the chalkboard of daily breakfast specials. She wasn't hungry but ordered two acai bowls to go with the coffees anyway.

The woman at the other end of the counter poured cream in her coffee and turned back toward the door. Savannah bit back a gasp when she recognized the school receptionist's dyed red hair and skinny arms. Ruth Wells's faded hazel eyes darted toward Savannah's face and just as quickly veered away. Her already pale skin went a shade lighter. The older woman had been a fixture at the elementary school since Savannah had been in the fourth grade, and she had always seemed so kind and encouraging. Now Savannah saw those traits as much too weak to deal with the likes of Michael Willard.

Ruth wetted her lips. "Savannah, good morning."

Savannah stepped into her path. "I need to speak to you for a minute, Ruth."

"I—I took the day off, so perhaps you should speak to the principal."

Savannah wanted to confront Ruth directly. "This won't take long." She steered Ruth toward a back corner before crossing her arms over her chest and fixing a stern stare at the older woman. "I did not give permission for anyone except me or Hez to pick up Simon from school yesterday. Would you care to explain why you let a stranger take him without permission?"

Ruth gave a weak laugh. "Stranger? His grandfather is hardly a stranger and was surely an exception."

"There are no exceptions. When Simon didn't get off the bus, I panicked. You didn't even call me—the bus driver was the one who told me his grandfather had taken him. I couldn't reach my father and had no idea where to find my nephew."

"You thought your father had him?" Ruth gulped, and the

cup in her hand trembled. "I supposed Mr. Willard had cleared it with you."

"You supposed. That's not how safety issues are supposed to work."

"B-but it was Michael Willard!"

"All the more reason to at least call me first. The man is a sociopath!"

Ruth's gaze widened, and she took a step back. "Mr. Willard has been the school's main benefactor for many years, Savannah, and his mother has been one of my best friends for decades. He's a wonderful man, and Simon is lucky to have him in his life. Mr. Willard often picked up Jess, and she would come back to school the next day just glowing from the love he lavished on her. He adored her."

Savannah opened her mouth to refute such nonsense, then closed it again. What proof did she have that anything her father had told her was true? Who was the real villain in this situation? It was humbling to realize she didn't know.

When she didn't answer right away, Ruth squared her shoulders. "I'll make sure no one takes Simon without your permission again, Savannah, and I apologize for my lapse in judgment. Now if you'll excuse me, I have a busy day." She brushed past Savannah without waiting for an answer.

That hadn't gone in the direction Savannah intended. Her order was called, and she went to pick it up as Nora entered the coffee shop. She'd been a steadfast friend since they bonded in a grief group.

"Good morning." Nora followed Savannah to a corner table. "I'm so glad you called. I wanted to hear how the house reno is going."

"I can't wait to show it to you! Hez and I started painting the interior yesterday."

Nora slung her bag over the side of a chair and got situated. "I've driven by a few times. That tower is amazing."

"Stop next time if you see a car there." Savannah sat in her chair and checked her phone. There were no messages with problems she had to deal with at the office. "How are things going with Graham?" Nora had been dating the TGU bookstore manager for a couple of months, and Savannah was thrilled her friend was moving on with her life.

Nora poked her glasses up on her nose. "Great! I—I think I might be falling for him. Hard. He's so kind and supportive. He's very understanding when I get called into work at odd hours too."

Savannah reached across the table and squeezed Nora's hand. "I'm so happy for you."

"I feel the same about you. I'm thrilled everything is going so well for you and Hez."

"And that brings up an important question. Would you be my maid of honor?"

Nora's smile was wide. "I'd be honored! I wouldn't want anyone else propping you up. How's the wedding planning coming? Have you picked out the flowers yet? How can I help?"

Wedding flowers were way down Savannah's priority list. "Oh, uh, not yet. And I can use all the help I can get."

Nora took a sip of her coffee. "You seem a little distracted this morning. Is something wrong?"

Michael was Nora's uncle. Would she be likely to open up about his true nature? Savannah raised her voice above the hiss of the milk steamer. "Have you spent much time with your uncle Michael?"

Nora lifted a brow and set her cup back on the table. "More when I was growing up than lately. Why are you asking about him?"

"I realized I don't know the Michael Jess knew as a father, and I'm not sure how to take him. Jess always described him as a stern but attentive father who took her on motorcycle rides, taught her to shoot, told great stories, and took her to Mimi Willard's for homemade ice cream and cobbler. Did you ever see Jess there?"

Nora nodded. "And I saw those traits she described often. He really loved Jess."

Had Savannah believed the wrong man all these years? "What's his character like? He seems overbearing and arrogant to me."

"His strong personality can be overwhelming. If he likes you, he's great—especially if you're part of the family. But if you're not a Willard and you cross him, he's apt to show you why his nickname is the Punisher."

And Savannah had just crossed him.

CHAPTER 8

HEZ HUMMED AS HE WALKED DOWN A DIMLY LIT CORRIDOR in Connor Hall. He stopped in front of a battered office door with a gray plastic sign in the nameplate holder that read JUSTICE CHAMBER. He turned the knob and shoved with his shoulder to pop the door loose from its jamb. Then he walked into his favorite spot on campus.

The Justice Chamber had been Hez's dream ever since he got sober over a year ago. It was technically a legal clinic operated by the TGU Law School, but it was Hez's baby. He opened it in February, and he spent as much time there as he could spare.

The Chamber occupied the second-worst office in Connor Hall. It held a much-used table, a tiny desk bearing an old computer, and a scattering of mismatched office chairs. A grandiose trefoil window did little to keep out the weather, which fortunately was pleasant today. A plaque over the desk read: *But let justice roll on like a river, righteousness like a never-failing stream!—Amos 5:24.* Hez flipped the light switch, tapped the plaque, and fired up his Italian coffee maker, which was probably worth more than everything else in the room combined. He worried a little that something might happen to it, but it definitely drew people to the Chamber—including him. With his classes over, he could enjoy a coffee reward.

"Smells good," a familiar bass voice said behind him. "Captain Davy's?"

"You know it." Hez turned to greet his friend, AA sponsor, and former boss, Jimmy Little. Jimmy was an enormous man, but most of his bulk was still muscle, and he carried it with the grace of a dancer. He was dressed for court in a navy suit and a perfectly tailored cream shirt that complemented his dark brown skin. He also wore his 1992 national championship ring, which only came out of its display case for special occasions. "You look like a million dollars."

Jimmy grinned and his eyes twinkled under bushy salt-and-pepper brows. "Five million, actually."

"Congratulations!" Hez extended a hand, which Jimmy enveloped in a meaty paw and shook. "Have a seat and tell me about it. That's a million more than you thought you could get, right?"

Jimmy eased into the sturdiest of the chairs. "It is, but Judge Hopkins really let the other side have it during the pretrial conference today. Their lawyers had been getting under his skin for a while—patronizing him, ignoring his advice to consider settling, and so on. They walked into court this morning with six lawyers surrounding the client like an entourage. The judge looked straight at the client and said, 'How many lawyers would you trade for one good fact?'"

Hez leaned against the rickety desk and laughed. The Honorable Achilles Hopkins was a plainspoken ex-cop, and

Hez had no trouble picturing him saying that. "Ouch! Did they see reason after that?"

Jimmy shook his head. "Nope, they decided to make it worse for themselves first. Their senior lawyer started going on about all the big cases he'd won and how he'd win this one. Blah, blah, blah. The judge let him talk for about ten minutes and then said, 'Let me tell you what's going to happen at trial, Counsel. Mr. Little is going to walk in and sit at the plaintiff's table wearing that ring, and you're going to lose half the jury. They're going to like a former Crimson Tide player a lot better than some fancy lawyer from way out of state. And that's before you open your mouth and lose the other half."

"Ha! What did you say?"

"Nothing. I just smiled and held up my hand so they could get a good view of the ring." He repeated the gesture and the ring glittered like a disco ball in the flickering fluorescent light. "The judge took them back to chambers after that, but I had a pretty good feeling about how negotiations would go."

"I'll bet you did. This calls for the good china." Hez found the only two matching and unchipped mugs in the cabinet under the coffee maker. He filled them and handed one to Jimmy. "Thanks for stopping by. You always have solid advice."

"Which you usually ignore." Jimmy took a long sip. "I was down from Birmingham anyway, so it's no inconvenience at all to stop by TGU. And between you and me, I'm also doing a little recruiting. You've bragged on your students, and I'd like to see them in action a little more."

"Here they come now," Hez said as voices reached them from the hall. The three Justice Chamber student volunteers entered together. Toni Casey, a blonde former accountant of about thirty, came in first, followed by Ed Hernandez and Dominga Steerforth. Ed was a scholarship swimmer who was using a final year of eligibility as a law student. Dominga was a senior history major who had an eye on law school—and Ed. They'd been dating for the past month, and things seemed to be getting serious.

Ed helped himself to a mug of coffee. "Hello, Mr. Little. Are you here to help us brainstorm our next case?"

Jimmy nodded. "Though I'm not sure you need my help. Y'all managed to take down a major smuggling operation."

The students beamed. "Well, we helped some," Toni said. "But that was mostly a law enforcement operation, and the kingpin is still—"

Running steps sounded in the hall. A breathless Simon appeared, followed by a boy and a girl Hez didn't recognize. Both appeared to be around Simon's age of ten. "Sorry I'm late," Simon panted. "One of my teachers wanted to talk to me after class."

Hez had reluctantly allowed Simon to join the Justice Chamber to keep him out of trouble. But he hadn't said anything about Simon bringing classmates. "We're just getting started. Who are your friends?"

"They're my cousins." Simon glanced toward the girl, a brunette with large solemn brown eyes. "That's Olivia." He nodded toward the boy, a stocky youth with shaggy blond hair and hard blue eyes. "And that's Jack."

Hez eyed the children. "Pleased to meet you both." He turned back to Simon. "I didn't know you had cousins."

"Neither did I, but Pawpaw Willard introduced me to them

when he took me to get a root beer float." Simon's blue eyes shone. "We go to the same school too. Isn't that great?"

So these were Willard kids, handpicked by Michael to befriend Simon. Was Michael just helping his grandson get to know family members his own age? Or did he have other motives? "Yes, that's great. Why did you bring them to the Justice Chamber?"

Jack shuffled his feet. "My sister Tammy brought us. We met Simon out front and came up together. Tammy works in the police department with Aunt Nora. They say we're too young for police stuff, but Simon told us about the Justice Chamber, so we thought maybe we could help too." He licked his lips. "If that's okay with you, Mr. Hez."

Hez hesitated. Jack's words rang true, but he was a Willard and several Willards had been involved in the artifact smuggling. On the other hand, Nora was also a Willard and Savannah completely trusted her. It wasn't fair to assume everyone connected with the sprawling Willard clan was a criminal, especially young children like Olivia and Jack. And it was good to see Simon happy and connecting with other kids again. That tipped the scales. "It's okay with me. Just make sure your parents know what you're doing."

Olivia nodded. "We texted them and they said it's fine."

"Okay." Hez turned to Toni as the children settled into chairs. "You were saying something about the smuggling ring?"

Toni shot an uneasy glance at the newcomers, but she apparently decided not to question their presence. "Well, there are some loose ends left from that case."

Hez sipped his coffee. "You mean the New York angle?"

She nodded. "Police raids nailed every link in the supply chain from the illegal digs in Mexico to just outside the Big Apple."

"But the worm in the core escaped," Jimmy said.

Toni leaned forward. "Exactly! The money trail led to James Hornbrook, but he somehow escaped the raid and got out of the country before the DA could indict him."

Hez shifted his weight, drawing a creak from the desk. The police raid in New York had caught Jess—but the police had assumed she was innocent and let her go. Hez didn't want to discuss that in front of Simon, of course. "Isn't that an issue for the DA and the New York authorities? The university already settled with Hornbrook and his company."

Jimmy arched a brow. "But this isn't really settled, is it? Hornbrook sent guys after you and your computer expert, right? And he threatened to kill you."

Hez's heart rate ticked up at the memory. "True."

"Then he's an issue for you too." Jimmy gestured at Hez with his mug.

Ed's jaw muscles flexed. "If he's an issue for you, he's an issue for all of us."

Nods and murmurs of agreement came from around the room.

Warmth glowed in Hez's chest. "I appreciate the loyalty, but this is a police matter."

Jimmy folded his tree-trunk-like arms. "And the local police are compromised, right?"

"Everyone knows there's a mole in the Pelican Harbor department," Hez admitted. "That's why Hope is handling the investigation without them."

Jimmy sighed. "Hope is great, but the DA's office isn't set up to investigate crimes. They rely on the police to do that—and you know it better than me."

Hez set his mug on the desk and stood. "Look, Hornbrook is a dangerous guy. I don't want any of you getting hurt."

Simon stirred. "Did he kill my mom?"

The room went silent. Hez turned toward Simon. The boy leaned forward, every muscle in his little body taut. The icy focus in his eyes was a carbon copy of his mother's stare. Hez held the boy's gaze. "I don't know."

Determination filled Simon's voice. "I'm going to find out."

A chuckle rumbled in Jimmy's chest. "Seems like everyone here is on the same page except you, Hez."

Hez glanced around the room and shrugged. "Okay, I guess the Justice Chamber is going after James Hornbrook." He waggled a finger at Simon and the Willards. "But we're going to be very careful about it, and you kids can't be directly involved. In fact, you can't do any Justice Chamber work at all unless I have your promise to do only what I tell you and nothing more."

"We promise," Simon said without hesitation. Jack and Olivia nodded.

Hez wished he could trust Simon to keep his word.

"I'm sorry." Scott Foster held his hands palms up. "I wish I had better news for you two."

This was not what Hez wanted to hear from the family law expert he and Savannah had hired, but it wasn't a surprise.

Hez had done some legal research on his own and knew things didn't look good. He'd hoped Scott would tell him he was wrong and there was some obscure statute or judicial rule that would let them keep Simon, but he hadn't counted on it. Still, a black fog shrouded his heart when he heard Scott's words, and he reached to take Savannah's hand.

"B-but Erik is a criminal." Savannah's voice shook as she spoke. "And he has affairs with students—we caught him on video. Doesn't any of that matter?"

Lines of compassion creased the weathered skin around Scott's eyes. "It matters outside of the courthouse in the real world. It matters a lot. But it won't be enough in court. Alabama law is very protective of parental rights, and terminating them is hard."

Her eyes flashed and she tilted her chin up. "What about Simon? Isn't the judge supposed to consider what's best for him?"

Scott nodded, his fading reddish-brown hair turning almost yellow in the afternoon light coming through the wooden blinds of his office in Pelican Harbor's French Quarter. "Yes."

She leaned forward. "So the judge should give Simon to us. We're best for him. Erik doesn't care about Simon at all. He didn't even know he had a son until a few months ago. You know what the first thing he did was? He threatened Simon and me. And then he vanished until he smelled money. How can it be in Simon's best interest to live with someone like that?"

Scott's expression grew grim and his thin face looked skeletal. "Did he ever put out a cigarette on Simon's face because the boy talked back to him?"

Savannah gasped. “What? Of course not!”

“Or routinely lock him in a closet whenever Erik needed to go to work?”

“No.”

“Did Simon almost die from an asthma attack because Erik took money that was supposed to buy inhalers for his son and used it to buy fentanyl?”

“No.” Savannah’s face was pale. “D-does that kind of thing happen around here?”

Scott nodded and seemed to age a decade. “All the time. Those are the sort of custody-termination cases judges are used to hearing.”

Savannah went white and bit her lip. “I didn’t know.”

Scott sighed. “We live in a very broken world.”

“That I did know.” Savannah squared her shoulders. “And we’re going to do everything we can to protect Simon from it. We have to at least try to get custody of him.”

Hez cleared his throat. “Let’s game that out, Scott. Before we could get custody of Simon, we’d have to terminate Erik’s rights. We’d need to show that he’s an unfit parent, and we’d need to do it by clear and convincing evidence, right?”

“Right. And we wouldn’t have the type of evidence the judge is used to seeing—serious physical abuse, long-term incarceration, obvious abandonment, and so on.”

Just as Hez had expected. “There would be a trial, correct?”

“Yes. This is a factual question that needs to be determined in court.”

Hez had to ask, but he didn’t want to hear the answer. “Trials are expensive, aren’t they?”

Scott nodded. “Yes, very expensive. I’ll do everything I can to keep my bills down, but set aside fifty thousand dollars. At least."

Savannah's sharp intake of breath revealed that this was news to her. For his part, Hez was surprised at how low Scott's estimate was. "And what would you say our odds of winning are?"

Scott thought for a moment, then lifted one shoulder. "Maybe 10 percent. No more than 20."

Savannah swallowed hard. "It's worth it if we have a chance to save Simon."

"What's the downside if we lose?" Hez asked.

Scott looked him in the eye. "Kids usually pay the highest price in these cases. Simon will see his father portrayed in the worst possible light, and then he'll have to go live with him. Also, Erik is likely to completely cut off your contact with Simon, of course."

Now for the question this had all been leading up to. "What do you recommend?"

"We should insist on a DNA test to prove paternity. But if that confirms that Erik is Simon's father . . ." Scott grimaced. "I hate to say it, but I recommend that you try to find a way to make a deal with Erik."

CHAPTER 9

THIS CANNOT BE HAPPENING.

A dull pain throbbed behind Savannah's eyes that even the salty scent of Mobile Bay and the lull of the waves couldn't ease. Seated on a weathered bench on the pier at their new home, she and Hez ate their beignets in stunned silence as the sunset's gold and orange hues settled over the water. The news had been too overwhelming to wrap her head around.

She tossed the last of her treat to the seagulls, watching their avid black eyes before she turned toward Hez. "We can't lose Simon, Hez, we just can't! Scott has to have missed something. Erik is a criminal."

The worried crease on his forehead deepened. "Babe, Scott Foster is an excellent attorney with an illustrious career here in Alabama. Based on initial research I did, I thought we'd hear exactly what he told us. I'd hoped I was wrong, of course, but I trust Scott's expertise."

She clenched her hands into fists. "I want to tell Erik that he'll take Simon over my dead body. I will fight this with everything in me."

Hez frowned. "We don't want to tip our hand with Erik. Passions run high around custody issues, and the last thing we need is to make him fight harder just to 'win.'" He put air quotes around the last word. "Let's wait for any discussion with him until we have more evidence. If we can dig up some actual proof about his criminal activity, we can terminate his parental rights while he's in prison and proceed with the adoption. And besides, we both know Erik doesn't really want custody of Simon—he wants Jess's money. If we slow-walk the whole process, maybe he'll be more apt to take a reasonable settlement—and maybe we won't need a settlement at all because he'll be behind bars."

"I suppose so. We don't have a real choice." It felt wrong to entertain the idea of giving that man a single cent of Jess's money, but Simon's well-being was more important than ensuring he had a fortune in his bank account. "Jess entrusted Simon to us. We have to save him from Erik."

"Our best hope would be if the DNA test showed they weren't related. Think back to your knowledge of your sister. Are you certain Erik is Simon's father?"

She forced herself to run through the moment she'd discovered Simon's existence. "Jess said something about never wanting Erik to know he had a son. And the timing is right. Jess never dated anyone after she and Erik broke up."

"That you know of."

"Yes." His reminder that she hadn't known her sister as well as she'd thought stung in the worst way.

"What should we say to Simon about all of this?"

She thought for a moment. "Nothing. At least not yet. He would just get upset and worry about something that will hopefully never happen. He finally quit asking when my dad was going to come see him. I had to explain to him that you can't ever trust anything he says."

Simon is used to adults keeping secrets from him and being untrustworthy. Savannah winced at the thought, but it was true. Jess hadn't been any more open with her son than anyone else. She had likely carried plenty of secrets to the grave with her. Had some of them involved the Willards?

A gull hopped closer to try to yank the last bite of Hez's beignet, and he tossed it down. "I can see the wheels turning. What are you thinking?"

"I talked to Nora this morning about Michael Willard. Our discussion made me realize there's probably a lot I don't know about Jess's involvement with that family. She seemed to love them, and they loved her. Maybe everything my dad told me was lies." Nora had warned her about getting on Michael's bad side, so Savannah needed to keep that in mind. The only way to know the truth was to dig it out.

"Is there anyone around who knew about your mom's relationship with Michael? A best friend, a relative?"

She shook her head. "Mom was an only child, and none of her cousins lived around here. Mom never talked about it either, but Dad had plenty to say."

"Maybe she wrote diaries or something."

Savannah gasped. "You're a genius! There is a treasure trove of old family papers in the storeroom where I found my great-grandfather's journals. Maybe Mom left diaries there."

It was worth exploring. She couldn't pinpoint why the truth about her mother mattered after all these years, but maybe it was at the root of the vendetta between their two families.

Hez's phone buzzed and a text appeared. Meet me in five minutes at the Seabreeze.

He frowned. The Seabreeze Saloon had been a favorite local watering hole ever since he discovered it while courting Savannah a decade ago. Not a safe place for a recovering alcoholic like him to visit.

The sender of the text also wasn't reassuring: Martine Dubois. Hez knew her from law school and they'd dated briefly before he met Savannah. Martine was smart, funny, and built like a swimsuit model, with almond-shaped brown eyes from her mother, a French-Vietnamese Parisian model. Hez and Martine stayed on friendly terms even though they'd occasionally crossed swords in court, but Hez had broken up with her for very good reasons. And Savannah turned into a porcupine the minute Martine's name was mentioned. It might be best to keep his contact with Martine to himself and not rile Savannah.

What's up? He texted back.

Tell you in person.

If he was going to meet her in person, he preferred to do it on more comfortable turf. And few places were more comfortable than the café below his condo. How about Petit Charms? It's closer.

Not safe. Her ellipsis appeared, disappeared, then reappeared. Hurry.

His frown deepened and his stomach muscles tensed. Martine was representing an anonymous client who had been feeding Hez crucial clues about Hornbrook. Could she have more news? He didn't trust her—at all—but he needed the nuggets of information she gave him.

He clipped his Glock holster to his belt and changed into a loose-fitting Birmingham Barons jersey that hid the gun. The Seabreeze was two blocks down the street from Hez's condo, where he'd been staying for the past two nights. Ralph Mossberg, the TGU architecture professor who had built the house he and Savannah bought, had apparently done his own electrical and plumbing work—which Hez discovered after a wet spot appeared on the kitchen ceiling and the power went out in half the house. Hez knew better than to try to fix either problem on his own, so he shut off the power and water and called an electrician and plumber he trusted—both of whom were tied up for several days.

The Seabreeze was a two-minute stroll away by street sidewalk, but Hez decided to walk along the beach instead. If Martine was right about Petit Charms not being safe, there was a good chance the street in front of it wasn't either.

He left the condo, painfully aware of the clanging his feet made on the steel steps. But once he reached the beach, only the murmur of waves and the distant strains of jazz from the French Quarter reached his ears. Clouds cloaked the moon and stars, but windows cast long streams of light over sand and seagrass. Hez stayed in the shadows as much as possible, alert for any movement.

He relaxed a little when he reached Pelican Harbor's boardwalk. The busy strip of restaurants, cafés, bars, and shops flanked the old Bayfront Inn and opened onto a wide sweep of sand and beach volleyball courts with few places for an assassin to hide.

The Seabreeze Saloon's exterior was decorated with net floats, shells, and other picturesque detritus that had washed up on local shores during storms. Martine sat alone at a table in a corner of the bar's little outdoor seating area, her gaze flicking between her phone and the door. The patio lights touched her tanned skin and brought out the beauty of her high cheekbones and delicate bone structure. A large hurricane lamp stood in the middle of the table, and a glass of water and a tall mojito sat in front of her. Mojitos used to be his favorite summer drink.

Hez walked up behind her. She was texting with someone, but she put down her phone before he could make out the name.

He stepped into the glow of the bar's lights. "Boo."

Martine jumped and gave a little yelp. "Don't scare me like that! What are you, twelve?" She patted the only other chair at the small table, which was just inches from her seat. "Sit down. I have something to show you."

He moved the chair a quarter of the way around the table and sat. "What's up?"

"What?" She cupped her hand to her mouth and puffed. "Do I have bad breath or something?"

"I'm sure you smell fine, but something about this situation stinks. Are you going to tell me what it is?"

"Sure, but you'll have to get within three feet of me." She took a long sip of her mojito. "Mmm. Okay, now I know I smell minty fresh. Now get over here." She picked up her phone and tapped it while he reluctantly dragged his chair closer. She leaned toward him, her shoulder touching his, and held up the phone. It showed a blurry picture of a bearded man wearing sunglasses. "This is Anton Todorov. He's the brother of Ivan Todorov, who works for Hornbrook Finance's European office, which is based in Sofia, Bulgaria."

What was up with her behavior? She had always been a flirt, but she knew better than to come on to Hez. Did this have something to do with her mystery client? "That's an odd place for an American financial firm to have an office."

"Unless the firm is looking for someplace that's in the EU but doesn't have sophisticated financial regulators. It probably doesn't hurt that Bulgaria is close to the Middle East."

Hez studied the phone. "Okay, but why do I care about Anton, the brother of Ivan, who works for Hornbrook?"

"Because Anton also works for Hornbrook—or at least he did until recently—and this picture was taken last week in Pensacola."

Hez's blood ran cold. "Where is he now?"

"I don't know."

"Does your client know?"

"I don't know that either."

"Can I talk to your client?"

"No, they want to remain anonymous. That's why they're paying me to talk to you."

"Can you at least send me a copy of that picture?"

"If I could, I would have done it already."

He gasped and stared over her shoulder. "Have you ever seen a spider that big?"

She whirled. "Where?"

He snatched the phone from her hand and texted the picture to himself. "Thanks."

She grabbed her phone back and anger flared in her eyes, but then she laughed and shoved him playfully. "Spiders? That wasn't fair!"

"Are you playing fair with me, Martine? What's really going on?"

She grew serious and held his gaze for a long moment. "As fair as I can."

"Anything else you can give me?"

Her breath was indeed minty fresh. "Just this." Quick as a flash, she leaned in and kissed him on the cheek. "Good luck, Hez. Stay safe."

Before he could respond, she got up and walked off into the warm darkness. Unease stirred as she sashayed away. She was trying to play him again, but what was the game? And how could he win it?

CHAPTER 10

THE SATURDAY LUNCH CROWD HAD MOSTLY LEFT BY ONE thirty when the hostess led Savannah and Simon to a table at Mac's Irish Pub. Simon paused to gawk at the dollar bills attached to the wall and pointed out pictures of celebrities. Watching his interest in every new experience was almost enough to push away her worry about the danger from Hornbrook. Would he target Hez with a bomb like he did Jess? Or had Hez been the target that time too?

She rubbed the gooseflesh on her arms as she glanced around the dining room for bearded, dark-haired men, then shook off the notion. The guy could have shaved or dyed his hair. And besides, God had a plan and living in fear wasn't an option. A server carried a tray of food past, and the aroma of shepherd's pie and Reuben sandwiches wafted in her wake.

Simon's gaze followed the tray as he got settled on the bench against the wall. "I want one of those bussin' Reubens. I haven't had one since Fairhurst."

He seldom mentioned his disastrous years at the London boarding school where Jess had kept him hidden. "I think this will be your new favorite place. I'll order one for your uncle

Hez too. He'll be here once he finishes at the Justice Chamber clinic."

"Can I have root beer too?"

"Wouldn't you rather have milk or apple juice? Those would be healthier."

A calculating expression came into Simon's eyes. "If I have apple juice, can I get dessert?"

She opened her mouth, then closed it again when a familiar profile caught her attention. Michael sat at a table by the window. She was tempted to rush out before Simon saw him but gave a slight shake of her head and lifted her menu. Michael might intimidate the school, but she refused to let him do the same to her. "Let's see if you're still hungry after your Reuben."

The server appeared with two root beer floats on her tray. "The gentleman by the window sent these over for you." She set one in front of each of them.

Michael twisted their way and lifted his hand in greeting. There was no way out of acknowledging him, so Savannah nodded stiffly. Simon was eyeing the root beer float in front of him and hadn't noticed his grandfather yet, but it was only a matter of time.

Michael's voice boomed out before he reached them. "Well, if it isn't my favorite grandson."

Simon turned and his eyes widened. "Pawpaw!"

"Mind if I join you for a minute?" Without waiting for an answer, he pulled out the only empty chair and settled in it. "I'll bet you've never had a float as good as Mac makes them."

The adoration on Simon's face turned Savannah's stomach almost as much as the thought of eating the treat his grandfather had paid for. She'd resolved to find out more about his relationship with her mother, but she didn't want to give him the satisfaction of twisting things in his favor. Jess had gotten her blonde hair from him, though his was going gray at the temples now. The man's resemblance to Jess was likely one reason Simon had so quickly fallen under his spell.

Michael leaned back in his chair and smiled at the boy. "Are you excited at the thought of going to live with your father?"

Savannah's pulse stuttered, and she barely managed to bite back a gasp. "He's not going to live with his father." How had Michael heard about it? She hadn't even told Nora.

"What are you talking about?" Simon glanced from his grandfather to Savannah. "What's going on, Aunt Savannah? I thought maybe my dad was dead or in jail. Is he looking for me?"

The hope in his voice broke her heart. She'd assumed his father's behavior had destroyed Simon's yearning to know him. "I don't know where he is, Simon. His attorney has shown up with a custody demand from him. Your uncle Hez and I have retained a family lawyer and don't intend to let you go. Your mother wanted us to take care of you."

Michael raised a brow. "You don't want him? You're just honoring Jess's wishes?"

"Of course not! Hez and I love Simon dearly. He belongs with us and we belong with him." What was she doing answering this obnoxious man? She turned her attention to Simon. "You know we love you, don't you?"

He gave an uncertain nod, but his attention went back to his grandfather.

Savannah bit her lip. Michael's influence on the boy was

already more profound than she'd expected. A couple of hours with Michael and Simon idolized him. How had that happened?

Michael shook his head. "It doesn't sound like love to me when you hide things from the boy, Savannah. You're not telling him the truth. I'm sure that attorney you hired has already told you Erik will get custody. The court won't take into consideration he's good for nothing and only wants the boy for Jess's money."

She winced and her jaw tightened. Simon didn't need to hear this kind of talk about his father. "We're determined to find a way to keep Simon with us." She spotted Hez coming their way, and hope surged through her. He'd know how to refute Michael's description of the custody case.

Hez's eyes widened when he spotted Michael. His long legs ate up the distance between them, and he stopped at Michael's chair. "I think you're in my chair. I want you to leave my family alone."

Michael lazily got up but didn't back away. "I could say the same thing to you, Webster. Simon is my blood. You two are going to let Erik have Simon, but his pawpaw isn't."

Savannah locked gazes with Hez, and dread curled in her belly. What did Michael plan to do?

Michael pulled into Erik Andersen's driveway, parking his truck less than six inches from the rear bumper of Erik's Mercedes. He didn't want Erik trying to leave before they were done.

Michael got out and walked to the door of the single-story

home. Mossy oak trees shaded the house and rustled in the gentle breeze. It was a quiet, peaceful scene.

He rang the doorbell and waited. And waited. Could Erik have tried to flee on foot out the back door? That would be foolish—but then, Erik was a fool. Michael frowned.

Michael rang the bell again, then knocked hard. The door finally opened. Erik stood in the entrance, little lines of annoyance creasing the tan skin around his mouth and blue eyes. He stood a few inches taller than Michael's five-foot-eleven and still had the broad shoulders and thick blond hair that caught Jess's eye when she was a student at TGU, but Erik had started to go to seed in the decade since his engagement to Jess ended.

"Hi, Mike. It's been a long time," Erik said in a voice that indicated it hadn't been long enough.

"Mind if I come in?"

"Well, I'm in the middle of grading student projects, so—"

"This is more important." Michael pushed past the bigger man. Erik tensed for an instant, but he didn't resist.

Michael walked into Erik's living room. It had hardwood floors, an antique desk, dark leather furniture, a glass-and-brass coffee table, and framed photos of Erik in front of European landmarks. A bright pink backpack sat on the love seat. Michael picked it up and read the nametag. "Kaitlyn Wilson! Come on out."

A young woman with mussed hair and round eyes appeared in the hallway on the far side of the living room. She appeared to be in her early twenties—about the same age Jess had been. Disgust roiled in Michael's stomach. He turned to Erik. "You were grading student projects, right? What grade do you give her?"

Erik's face reddened and his muscular arms flexed. "What's that supposed to mean?"

"Figure it out, Professor." Michael's voice made the last word an insult. He turned back to Kaitlyn and held out her backpack. "You need to leave, honey."

Erik reached for the backpack. "I'll drive her back to campus. I'll call you to arrange a more reasonable time and place to discuss whatever brought you here."

Michael took a step toward him. "Call her an Uber. You're not going anywhere."

Erik seemed about to object, but he stopped short when he saw Michael's expression. "Go ahead, Kaitlyn. I'll pay you back."

The girl's gaze darted back and forth between the two men for an instant. Then she hurried forward, grabbed her backpack, and vanished out the door.

Erik crossed his arms. "Okay, Mike. What's so important?"

"My grandson."

Erik raised his brows. "You mean my son?"

"For the moment." Michael walked over to the love seat and sat, forcing Erik to follow. "That's what I'm here to discuss."

Erik sat on the edge of the sofa. "I'm not sure I understand."

"Look, you don't really want Simon. He'd interfere with your 'student projects,' for one thing. I do want him, so I'll adopt him and you'll consent to the adoption."

A crafty smile lifted Erik's face. "You're not the only one who wants him. His aunt and uncle already filed an adoption petition. How do you know I won't consent to theirs?"

Michael had expected—even counted on—Erik's willingness to bargain away his own son, but it still made him want to punch the guy in the face. Simon deserved a better father figure—

and Michael would give him one. “Because that wouldn’t be in Simon’s best interests—or yours.”

“Why is that?”

“I’ll pay you a hundred thousand dollars for your consent.”

Erik scoffed. “It’s worth a lot more than that. The kid has a trust fund worth millions.”

Michael’s opinion of Erik reached a new low. “You’re going to skim off your son’s trust fund? Seriously?”

Erik shrugged beefy shoulders. “I’d make sure it was used to provide a high quality of life for Simon. That would also mean a high quality of life for me, of course.”

Michael gripped the arm of the love seat. “Your quality of life? You should be worried more about your quantity of life.”

Erik turned pale beneath his tan, but he said nothing.

Michael took a pen and a folded sheet of paper out of his jacket pocket and set them on the coffee table in front of Erik. “You know what? I’ll sweeten the deal for you. Sign the consent now and you not only get one hundred thousand dollars. You also get my personal promise not to take you into the swamp, stake you to the ground, and leave you for the gators and rats like you deserve.”

Beads of sweat appeared on Erik’s forehead. Michael could almost read his thoughts. The man was a coward. He’d run away last year because he was afraid of TGU’s late provost, Beckett Harrison. Beckett was dead because he’d crossed the Willard clan. Would Erik stand up to the head of that clan? Of course not. He couldn’t run, so he’d roll over like a scared puppy in front of a junkyard dog.

Erik licked his lips and signed the consent with shaking hands.

CHAPTER 11

EVEN AS A LITTLE GIRL SAVANNAH HAD LOVED POKING through the stacks of old books and boxes in the presidential records room. Her love of history had often driven her to spend time here discovering the stories behind the Willard Treasure and the early days of the university. It felt a little like coming home to step into the space steeped with the scent of old leather and paper. She had a few minutes before meeting Hez and Simon for dinner.

The only way she could end the vendetta with Michael was to find out more about the way it had started. Her father's old journals might hold the answers.

She flipped on the overhead lights, and one of them began to hum loudly. She made a mental note to let maintenance know, even though she was likely the only person to come in here much. Had past presidents spent time in here hoping to glean wisdom?

Her mother had often spent afternoons scribbling in journals when Savannah was growing up, but she wasn't certain those records had been kept. If they were incriminating to her father, he would have destroyed them, but maybe he'd missed one or two. Savannah hadn't found them among her mother's belongings after her death, but maybe a few had made it to the records room because Mom had been the president's wife. It wouldn't hurt to search, and Savannah would even be happy to find some of her mother's poetry. She had all the published works, but it would be wonderful to discover poems that hadn't made it to publication.

Stacks of old books stuffed every inch of the bookshelves lining all four sides of the room. The back ones held her great-grandfather's journals, and those records would be older than the ones she hoped to find, so Savannah turned to the ones on her right. She started with the shelves to the right of the door. When she lifted the top book, dust motes tickled her nose. It was an accounting ledger, so she moved it to one side and delved farther down into the stack.

She gasped at the sight of her parents' wedding album. She hadn't seen it in decades, and she flipped through the pages before stopping at an engagement picture. Her mother's green eyes were so hopeful and joyous. At this captured moment in time, Marie Corbin had no idea of the tragedy her life would become.

Savannah's gaze went to her father, and she couldn't help the old admiration from surging a bit. He'd always been handsome, and charm oozed from him in the photo. They'd had so much going for them at the start of their marriage. How had it all gone so wrong?

She closed the album and moved it atop the accounting book to reveal a fine leather journal. She sneezed and opened the cover to discover her father's distinctive bold script sprawling across the first page. While she'd hoped to discover her mother's words, her father's perspective might reveal things she longed to know. She carried it to the table by the door and pulled out a chair.

The dates at the tops of the pages ranged from 1985 to 1990. She turned to the first entry.

> *My first day as president of TGU. I've dreamed of this day. My father will never raise his fist to me again, and he'll never control me with money either. There will be no more whispers of how Andre Legare ruined Tupelo Grove University. My visions will remake it all. Once I implement all my plans, this university will rival Yale and Harvard. I started raising money for Legare Hall last month, and the architect's plans will ensure it's a monument to my vision for this place.*

Savannah grimaced at the thought of his grandiose plans for the crumbling marble building. She'd been struggling with whether to have it razed or try to finish it. It was more of a lesson in how to mismanage money than any kind of accolade in her father's honor. His extravagant ideas rarely came to fruition.

Her attention caught on the "raise his fist" comment. Had her grandpa Andre beaten Dad? The text seemed to say that. She'd always wondered about her father's unquenchable desire for admiration and power. Maybe he'd been powerless to stop his father's abuse growing up. Grandfather Andre's blight on the university could have trained her father in corruption too. If so, he'd been an apt student.

She scanned through the next pages where he cited distractions and his need for more and more money. It was one thing they could agree on—funding was a constant problem, and she'd found life as TGU's president to be full of meetings where her role was to stroke egos and hold the hands of donors and staff. It wasn't how she'd envisioned making a difference here.

The next page was written in 1987.

> *$10 million in TGU's coffers! A generous gift from the Willards in memory of Helen's daughter and grandson. I can put the money they got from the malpractice suit to much better use than her sons. They must be such a disappointment to her.*

Such callous boasting. Reading her father's journal made her feel dirty and guilty, and she almost shoved it aside but made herself turn to the next page dated a month after her birth.

> *My private burdens make it difficult to accomplish the great works set before me. Marie blows hot and cold between depression and condescension. She insists on thinking the worst of me and locks me out of the bedroom. It's hardly my fault that women can't keep their hands off me.*
>
> *She barely speaks to me since Savannah was born, and I caught her with a bottle of pills yesterday. She saw me watching her and dumped them down the kitchen sink. She had the nerve to say she*

couldn't leave our daughter in my care. Like she's any kind of a decent mother. All she does is cry and watch me with accusing eyes.

Besides, I've heard rumors she's been dallying with Michael Willard, so she has no moral high ground. She denied it when I confronted her, but I'm not so sure. It would be just like Michael to use Marie to get back at me. He's full of hate after the misunderstanding about his sister's settlement. He'd like nothing more than to humiliate me by shaming me with my wife. She's a beautiful, fragile flower, and she could be crushed by—

The door opened behind Savannah, and Hez burst into the room. Her gut clenched at the sight of his agitated expression. She rose to face him. "What's wrong?"

"Michael filed his own adoption petition—and Erik has agreed to it."

She pressed her hand against her heart where it hammered against her chest wall. "We can still fight it."

"We can try, but I don't think we can win, Savannah. I'll talk to Scott, but . . ." He gave a helpless shrug.

The anguish in Hez's face hammered home the truth. They were going to lose Simon.

"What are our odds?" Still warm after a run with Hope, Hez tugged on the collar of his shirt.

Scott frowned and drummed long, bony fingers on his walnut desk. "Of getting your petition granted without Andersen's consent? Probably zero now that he provided a DNA test confirming he's Simon's father. You might be able to defeat the Willard petition, but that will depend on the evidence we can present."

Hez's ears perked up. "What kind of evidence would that take?"

Scott shrugged thin shoulders. "Proof that letting Michael Willard adopt Simon wouldn't be in his best interests. The judge is supposed to consider anything relevant to Simon's best interests, so we can put on basically whatever evidence we want as long as it's arguably tied to Simon's well-being. Also, the court will appoint a guardian ad litem for Simon, so we'll want to persuade both the guardian and the judge."

Hez chewed that over for a moment. "Several drivers for Michael's trucking company got caught smuggling artifacts a few months ago, and law enforcement raided the company. Michael and the company weren't indicted, but maybe they were just more careful than the others. Plus, I've heard rumors that Michael has other criminal ties."

Scott shifted, drawing a creak from his leather chair. "I've heard the same rumors—but rumors won't do us any good in court, of course."

"Of course. If we can get admissible evidence to back up those rumors, would that be enough?"

Scott stared into the middle distance for a moment, rocking his chair as he thought. "Probably. It would depend on how good the evidence is, but it should be easy to persuade the judge that Simon's best interests aren't served by letting a career criminal adopt him."

Hez's spirits lifted. Building a criminal case was his strong suit. Maybe he'd even find enough evidence to get Michael arrested. He got up, eager to get started. "Great, I'll start digging."

Scott rose and walked him to the door. "You know you'll be digging in a minefield, right?"

"Because Michael is a dangerous guy?" Hez shrugged. "I'm used to dealing with those."

Scott's gaze went to the left side of Hez's head, where a craniotomy scar peeked out of his hairline. "And you almost died not too long ago, right?"

Hez's stomach muscles tensed at the memory. "I'll be careful."

Scott gave him a grave final stare. "Good. Let me know how it goes."

Hez walked out into the warm spring sunshine. A gentle sea breeze blew down the street from Bon Secour Bay, carrying the mingled scents of salt and coffee from the French Quarter cafés. Smooth melodies floated down from a second-story apartment where a skilled jazz pianist practiced. It was a nice day.

Hez had been about to go back to campus and put in a few hours of work before spending the evening investigating Michael Willard. But maybe a coffee and a walk on the beach would be better—especially if Savannah could join him. They had a lot to talk about.

A silver Mercedes E 350 pulled to the curb beside him. The passenger window slid down and Pierre Legare smiled at Hez from the driver's seat. His perfect teeth and white polo contrasted with his tan. Aviator sunglasses hid his brown eyes. "Can I give you a ride back to campus?"

Hez didn't really want to talk to anyone except Savannah, least of all her father. "No, thanks. I was about to grab a cup of coffee and head for the beach."

"Great, I'll join you." The window slid up before Hez could respond, and Pierre turned off the engine.

Hez exhaled with resignation as Pierre got out of the car. "Were you waiting for me?"

Pierre nodded as he walked around the Mercedes. "You're sharp. I always liked that about you. The secretary said you had a meeting here, so I thought I'd try to catch you."

"Why did you want to catch me, Pierre?"

He clapped Hez on the back and gave an easy laugh. He smelled of cherry pipe tobacco and lemon drops. "For one thing, it's always good to see my once and future son-in-law. Let's get that coffee you mentioned. My treat."

Pierre made small talk about the university and sports as they walked down the block to the Petit Charms take-out window and placed their orders. He grew serious as they strolled toward the beach with their cups. "We haven't always seen eye to eye, Hez, but we're on the same side when it comes to Simon. I don't want that slimeball to get our boy any more than you do. I can help you stop him. I beat him once and I can do it again."

Hez stared at the older man. "What do you mean?"

"Do you know how I got Marie back after Michael stole her?"

"No."

A triumphant grin split Pierre's face. "I hired a private investigator who dug up the truth about Michael Willard. I showed his dossier to Marie, and she came crawling back to me. And I told Michael that if he ever came near her again, I'd make sure he spent the rest of his life in prison. He left with his tail between his legs." Pierre's smile turned crafty. "And it just so happens that I've been updating that dossier every few years."

Hez clamped down on the hope surging in his chest. He knew Pierre too well. "Great! Can I have a copy of the dossier and talk to your investigator?"

"Of course. I'm happy to help you and Savannah—if you'll help me too."

Here we go. "What kind of help did you have in mind?"

Pierre looked him in the eye. "Put back the money you took out of my trust. Restore the income streams you cut off. Drop the lawsuit you filed against Education Management."

Hez crossed his arms over his chest. "The lawsuit was brought by the university, which Education Management cheated. And that money isn't yours or ours. It belongs to the university. It never should have been in the trust in the first place."

"Nonsense!" Pierre's face darkened. "I'm the former president of TGU, and I deserve an adequate retirement. Savannah has the power to give it to me. And as the university's lawyer, you can write whatever documents are necessary to make it all legal."

"We can't just give you university money. That's not how it works."

Pierre flicked his hand like he was shooing away an annoying insect. "That's how it worked when I was president."

The way things worked during Pierre's presidency had nearly

destroyed the university. And it sickened Hez that Pierre was using Simon's fate as extortion leverage. Hez took a long sip of his coffee to give himself time to think before he responded. "Things are different now. I'll talk to Savannah, but don't get your hopes up."

Pierre smiled. "I have faith in you. Like I said, you're sharp—and I know how much you both care about Simon." He glanced at his watch. "I have a tee time I need to get to. Let me know when you've made a decision."

Pierre turned and walked back toward his car. Hez watched the retreating figure, loathing the man more than ever. At least his sleazy proposal had been a subtle ray of hope: If Pierre could find enough dirt to checkmate Michael Willard, Hez could too. But could he do it before the hearing on the adoption petition?

CHAPTER 12

HAVING THEIR OWN BAY VIEW WAS MORE THAN SHE'D EVER expected. Savannah parked in the driveway of their new home and walked across the fragrant, freshly mown grass to find Hez. Early May showers had greened up the lush vegetation. He'd initially suggested meeting at the Pelican Harbor beach, but she'd had some work to finish and reminded him they had a perfect spot to watch the sunset from their dock. Simon was at a tutoring session with Will, and they had three hours to themselves.

She paused to enjoy the view of Hez against the backdrop of the sunset. He'd changed into shorts and a tee, and his thick dark hair was still damp from a shower. His muscular legs dangled over the edge of the dock where he sat tossing bits of bread to the gulls.

Another month and they'd repeat their wedding vows. She still marveled that they'd found their way back to each other through the trauma. She never wanted to take that blessing for granted. How many couples managed to find the bedrock under their relationship and withstand the storms that battered them like she and Hez had done? Not many.

When she stepped onto the weathered boards, the vibration

alerted Hez to her presence and he stood. When he smiled at her, the sun almost seemed to change its mind about setting. Hez really saw her and always had. He opened his arms and she stepped into his embrace. He kissed her like he'd been as hungry for her as she was for him. With his lips on hers, she forgot the ordeal of the past few weeks and their fears for the future.

She finally pulled away and smiled up at him. "I should have left the work on my desk and come here as soon as you called."

"It gave me time to grab shrimp étouffée and take a shower."

When he settled back on the dock and tugged on her hand, she sat beside him with the water reflecting the colorful sunset beneath her feet. "Wonderful! Neither of us has to cook, and we can actually talk." He slipped his arm around her, and she leaned her cheek against his shoulder. "But no problems are allowed to intrude. I want to focus on the wedding and our honeymoon."

"That's a plan I can get behind."

He kissed her again, and she murmured against his lips, "Or maybe we don't have to talk at all." So they didn't for several delicious minutes until he finally sighed and pulled away.

"June can't come soon enough. Are there any decisions to make for the reception?"

She pulled out her phone to show him some photos. "I was unsure on the cake. We were going to have a traditional cake, but what if we do cupcakes? I saw a display that alternated tiers of cupcakes and macarons. It was so pretty and different." She handed him her phone.

He scrolled through them. "I approve. We could even skip the cake entirely and serve beignets. And I have a surprise I want to do if you'll let me."

"You can do whatever you'd like. What is it?"

He kissed the tip of her nose. "It's a surprise. It will come at the end. Will you trust me?"

"I think you know I do." He had impeccable instincts and great ideas. She couldn't wait to see what he'd planned.

They discussed the guest list and decided to expand it a little. Talking things over made it all seem more real and imminent.

Her tummy rumbled. "I wouldn't mind some of that étouffée you bought. I don't think I had lunch."

"It's in the Crock-Pot keeping warm." He rose and helped her to her feet.

They strolled toward the house to the sound of doves cooing. She tensed to see a truck like Michael's rumble past. "It wouldn't be him."

"I wouldn't put it past him to try to see what you're doing. I talked to—" He clamped his lips shut. "Sorry, no talking about problems tonight."

Dread curled in her chest. "I need to know if it's bad." He reached out his hand to lead her toward the door, and she clung to it. "It's that bad?"

"I had two conversations today—one planned and one not planned."

"You talked to Scott?" She knew he had an appointment coming up but wasn't sure when. Hez held open the door, and she stepped into the fragrant aroma of shrimp étouffée. The scent of Cajun spices and shrimp usually made her mouth water, but her stomach clenched with the blow she sensed was taking aim at her heart. She stopped by the kitchen counter next to the Crock-Pot. "Tell me."

"Scott confirmed our chances were slim without Erik's consent. But it wasn't all bad."

As Hez laid out his plan to dig up evidence on Michael's criminal activity, she reached up and traced the still-healing ridge of flesh from his injury. "Hez, you nearly died. This is risky—too risky."

His jaw flexed, and he narrowed his eyes. "It's our only chance unless you want to cave to your dad's extortion."

"He was your unexpected appointment?"

"He was waiting for me to leave Scott's and ambushed me. I will say this, though—if he hadn't mentioned all the dirt he had on Michael, I might not have come up with the idea to prove him unfit to raise Simon."

Hez went over her father's demands, and she clenched her fists. "He's despicable. Doesn't he care at all about Simon?"

"Probably not. His first love is money, and Simon isn't really his grandson. In spite of the way he seemed to want to get to know him, I'm afraid he only wanted access to Jess's money."

"Like Erik." She flexed her fingers and made herself relax her hands. "I think Dad was always this way, but I wouldn't let myself see it. If I'd had the courage to stand up to him sooner, maybe I could have saved my mom. If I'd defied him, maybe Jess wouldn't have gone down that dark road of hatred and revenge." Her throat thickened. "There are so many things I wish I'd done differently."

He palmed her face and gazed down at her with tenderness in his eyes. "We each make our own choices, babe. You were just a kid. I doubt your mom would have appreciated the stress of constant warfare, and it might have made Jess worse. We can't change what is or the choices any of them made.

Dwelling on the might-have-beens is a sure way to destroy the future. It was only by the grace of God that guilt didn't ruin my life. It's been hard to let go of the burden of guilt and accept forgiveness—both from you and from God." His voice shook. "I have to work on it every day. You need to do that too. This is not your fault."

He was right. She wrapped her arms around him. "We've overcome so much, Hez. Even if Simon goes to Michael, he's still our nephew. We'll get to see him and have a part in his life." The thought stabbed her heart, though.

He stiffened. "I don't intend to let that happen. I'm going to work hard at finding a crack in Michael's armor. There has to be a way of proving he's a criminal."

She inhaled. "Do you think Michael wants Simon's money too?"

"I don't get the sense he cares about that. I think he really believes Simon should be raised as a Willard." Hez rubbed his thumb along the ridge between her eyes. "That's your thinking frown. What are you planning?"

She ran her fingers over her bracelet. "Maybe it wouldn't hurt to find out Michael's motives and offer him an olive branch. We'll need to deal with him no matter who has custody. Open warfare isn't good for Simon no matter who he lives with."

And she knew just who to talk to. Nora might be willing to help her figure this out.

Hez sat alone in the Justice Chamber, staring at his monitor. The quiet space away from the busy administration building always helped him focus and think. The information about Anton Todorov hadn't gone anywhere. Hez had sent the man's name and picture to Bruno to research, but there'd been no trail to follow. Even the metadata on the picture had been scrubbed. Martine's client was being very careful to keep his—her? their?—identity secret. Why?

Then Hez got an email from Bruno that took his mind completely off Martine and her client. Hez gave a soft whistle. "Is this what you used to get Marie back, Pierre?"

Hez had been digging into Michael's background ever since Pierre's comments about a dossier of dirt—and he'd finally caught a gleam of gold. Or rather meth.

The trail began back in the 1980s, when Michael Willard had just started his trucking company, Southern Transport, with a single used truck. By 1989 he'd been arrested twice for receiving stolen property, but each time the charges were dropped because he claimed he didn't know his load was stolen and the police couldn't prove otherwise. Even taking questionable cargo hadn't been enough to keep Michael afloat financially. His original truck got repossessed and Southern Transport filed for bankruptcy.

And then something happened. By the early 1990s Southern Transport was out of bankruptcy and had seven new trucks. Around the same time the outlaw biker gang that had controlled the local meth trade suddenly started avoiding the area. That might have had something to do with what happened to two low-level gang members: Their bodies were found in Gum Swamp, tied to stakes pounded deep into the soft earth. The gators had been working on both, hopefully after they were dead.

Police records and news accounts showed that the meth kept flowing despite the bikers' departure. Did Pierre find evidence that the drugs traveled on Southern Transport trucks? That might have been enough to shock Marie into leaving Michael. It also would have given Pierre leverage to—

"Hi, Uncle Hez."

Hez immediately closed the browser window and turned to face Simon, who stood in the doorway. "Hi, Simon. I didn't hear you come in. I thought you were in the library doing your homework."

"I finished, but Aunt Savannah was in a meeting, so I came over here." He stared at Hez's monitor. "What are you working on?"

"Just researching an old case."

Simon's eyes locked on Hez. "Is it about James Hornbrook?"

"No, it's completely unrelated."

"Oh." Simon deflated. "I hoped maybe we were going to catch him soon."

"We're working hard on it."

"If we catch him, can we make him tell us if he killed my mom?"

"He has a legal right not to say anything if he doesn't want to, but I'm sure Hope will do everything she can to get him to talk."

"Good." Simon was silent for a moment. "I wish I knew who to be mad at. Now I just feel so . . . so mad at everything."

Hez nodded. "I know. That's kind of how I felt after Ella died—except I knew who to be mad at: me. But I was also mad at everything, just like you. I was mad that Ella was dead and there was nothing I could do to bring her back and—" His throat constricted and he fought to hold back tears. The sudden surge of emotion surprised and embarrassed him. Would he ever be able to talk about Ella's death without risking a scene?

Simon walked around the desk and put his hand on Hez's shoulder. "I'm sorry, Uncle Hez."

Hez steadied himself. "Thanks. I'm really sorry about your mom too. You can tell me the things you miss about her and any memories you want to share. Or even just how it makes you feel. I know it hurts to talk about it, but it helps too. I wish I'd figured that out sooner after Ella died. So I want you to tell me when you're feeling angry or you're having other bad feelings, okay? I can take it. I understand."

Simon buried his face in Hez's shoulder and hugged his neck with surprising strength. "Thanks, Uncle Hez."

CHAPTER 13

MARLEY BEHAVED SO MUCH BETTER WHEN CODY WASN'T around. Dressed in black leggings and a green tee, Savannah walked at a fast clip down Tupelo Street in Nova Cambridge. Lacy moss draped on oak trees swayed in the light breeze, sweet with the scent of roses blooming along the sidewalk. The fragrance brought a stab of pain, reminding her of the overwhelming odor from the floral arrangements at Jess's funeral. Would she ever be able to enjoy their smell again?

She hurried past the flowers and sighed with relief when the aroma of freshly mown grass replaced their scent. The *click-clack* of a train's wheels on the rails four blocks south reached them, and Marley paused to stare that way.

"It's a train," she reassured him as she stopped to catch her breath.

She glanced around and realized she was nearly to the intersection with Pecan Street. Erik's house was a block away, and she obeyed an impulse to walk past it. There it was. The single-story home looked bereft even with mossy oak trees shading it. Weeds poked through the mulch in the flower bed under the picture window, and the grass could use a trim. This place was the site where Simon confronted his father for the first time. Had he been back since he discovered Erik was suing for custody?

She'd tried to keep Simon too busy to wander, but the boy had a mind of his own. She approached the house cautiously, but Erik's car wasn't in the driveway, and he didn't seem to be home. She stared at the house from the sidewalk. A glint of red caught her eye, and she stepped into the grass to see what it was. A small red double-decker bus key ring lay in the vegetation, and she scooped it up. Simon had one like it, and she clutched it in her fist.

Her intuition had been correct. She should have thought of it sooner. When he first came to town, Simon had constantly been jetting off in pursuit of his father. Of course he would be spying on him.

She sighed and tucked the key ring in her fanny pack beside her phone. She would need to have a conversation with her nephew. There could be serious trouble if Erik caught him. Taking stock of her surroundings, she decided to walk to University Grounds to grab an iced peppermint mocha and maybe an acai bowl.

Marley willingly fell into step beside her, and Savannah's sneakers slapped the pavement as she got into the rhythm of a jog. The exercise allowed her to push away her worry for now. She had to talk to Michael and see if they could come up with a solution that worked for both of them. Surely he would see reason. A fight wasn't in anyone's best interests—least of all Simon's.

She slowed when she reached the coffee shop and spotted Nora's car in the lot. A smile curved her lips at the thought of seeing Nora. She would have advice on how to approach

Michael. Though he and Nora weren't close, she might have heard what he hoped to gain by taking custody of Simon.

A reedy voice floated her way, and she spotted Helen Willard on the porch with Nora. They stood beside a table that held two cups. This might be Savannah's opportunity to talk to Helen. Though the tiny woman held no love for the Legares, she might be persuaded to help avoid a battle that would only hurt all of them. And her son listened to her.

As Savannah ascended the steps, she caught a phrase from Nora. ". . . get real ugly."

Helen replied, "No one will ever know."

The phrases implied something unpleasant or nefarious, and Savannah struggled to put on a passive expression when Helen's brown eyes widened at the sight of her. "Hello, Helen." She smiled at her friend. "Nora, I was just thinking about calling you."

Color surged up Nora's neck and lodged in her cheeks. "Savannah." Her voice was flustered.

Helen didn't reply to Savannah's greeting but instead brushed past her with a smug expression. She clung to the railing with a frail, liver-spotted hand as she went down the steps. Savannah knew better than to try to stop her.

Savannah climbed the steps with Marley, who went to sniff Nora's sandals. "Everything okay?" She pulled out a chair at the table and settled in it.

"F-fine. Everything is fine." Nora made no eye contact as she bent to rub Marley's ears. "I probably should be going."

Savannah hesitated for an instant. Should she push for more information? Lack of trust had been a sore spot between them recently. Her fingers went to her bracelet—and she had her answer. The bracelet had been a gift from Nora, and it spelled *best friends* in Morse code. There was no need to press for more information. Nora wouldn't keep something important from her. "You have a minute?"

"Just a few. I need to get back to work." Nora perched on the chair opposite Savannah's. "How's the house coming along?"

Was she afraid of what Savannah might ask? "It's progressing. We should have it ready before the wedding." She leaned forward. "You've probably heard this, but Michael is suing for custody of Simon—and Erik has agreed to give up his rights."

Nora's eyes widened, but she didn't appear to be all that shocked. "I'm sorry, Savannah. I know that's very upsetting when Jess wanted you to raise her son."

"Exactly—Jess was his daughter. Wouldn't he want to follow her wishes? Do you think he'd listen if I approached him about shared custody?"

Nora took a quick sip of her coffee. "I don't have much to do with Uncle Michael, but he owns a trucking company and is used to negotiations. I don't know how he'll react when this is family. He's fiercely protective of Mimi. I—I wouldn't get your hopes up."

Savannah sighed and sank against the back of the seat. "I was afraid you'd say that. I have to try, though."

What choice did she have when she was hemmed in by laws that didn't allow for following a mother's wishes?

"Forty-six." Hez frowned at the floor he had just finished polishing. The living room in his new house had forty-six different kinds of wood inlaid in striking geometric patterns. He hadn't even heard of most of them—like bloodwood, ipe, pink ivory, and zebrawood. Movers damaged a couple of pieces, and it took over a week and two visits to the TGU biology department just to figure out what kind of wood to order and where to find it. Then he'd discovered that the exotic woods needed a special polish that had to be ordered from Japan.

But the floor was done now—and it was worth it. The afternoon sun slanting in through the prismed windows gave the room a magical feeling as it brought out the different hues and patterns in the wood, which complemented and enhanced the geometry of the design. He imagined slow dancing here with Savannah as the sun set and the stars came out. He'd put together the perfect old-school playlist for their first Valentine's Day together. It had lots of the Righteous Brothers, some Johnny Mathis, and a few songs by Frank Sinatra. Did he still have that somewhere?

His phone rang. Bruno. All thoughts of romance vanished as Hez took the call. "Hey, Bruno. What's up?"

"Weird stuff. Someone went after a copy of the Hornbrook database."

"Oh." Hez thought for a moment. "Why is that weird?"

"Because it's obviously a copy. I mean, the file name is literally 'Hornbrook.Sucks.Copy.94.' If they're going to go after one copy, they should go after all copies simultaneously. They're not doing that. They're not even trying."

Hez frowned. "That, uh, seems like a pretty easy file to find."

"Yeah, it's supposed to be." Bruno's voice held the patient tone of a teacher explaining something to a slightly slow student. "I put a couple copies basically in plain sight, if you know where to look. We want Hornbrook to know that we really do have a database of all his illegal videos."

"Oh. Isn't there a risk that someone other than Hornbrook will stumble across a copy of that database?"

"Yep, but all the copies are encrypted, and my encryption is very tough to break. So if they find a copy, all they'll get is a big encrypted file, a couple of basically harmless unencrypted videos from our Hornbrook collection to prove the encrypted file is real, and a really good deepfake video of Hornbrook singing Taylor Swift's greatest hits."

Hez laughed. "Remind me never to make you mad."

"Never make me mad."

"Thanks. So when you say someone 'went after' the copy, what exactly did they do?"

"They accessed the unencrypted files, tried to access the encrypted file, and then downloaded everything. And they weren't trying very hard to cover their tracks."

"Huh." Hez tugged at his lower lip. "Why would Hornbrook do that?"

"That's an excellent question. And here's another: Why would he use an American? I'm pretty sure Hornbrook has contacts in Russia, and they have lots of good, cheap hackers. Russia also has totally corrupt cybercops, so a well-connected hacker has nothin' to worry about. But this particular hacker came in through an American portal and downloaded the database to an American URL."

An unnerving thought popped into Hez's brain. "A guy like Hornbrook probably made some enemies in New York. Maybe one of them somehow heard about the database."

Bruno groaned. "That's what I was wondering. I think there's another player in our little game."

CHAPTER 14

WITH ELVIS BELTING OUT "JAILHOUSE ROCK" FROM AN OLDIES playlist on Spotify, Savannah positioned a piece of tile on the cutter and turned on the saw. A perfect cut. She was getting good at this. She handed it to Hez, who was on his knees spreading thinset on the master bathroom floor.

They'd nearly finished the traditional black-and-white checkerboard pattern, and it was perfect for the house's character. "If you decide to give up practicing law, you could be a professional tile layer."

"My back wouldn't take it. Or my knees." He set the final piece into place around the doorjamb, then stood to admire it. "Though I admit there's something to be said for working with my hands and transforming the space so dramatically."

"I had the easy job of cutting."

He smiled her way, and his blue eyes softened. "And you're beautiful doing it." Gray goop speckled his arms and coated his fingers.

Savannah wiped a glob of mortar from his hair. "I think you got as much on you as you did the floor." She swept the mortar onto a damp towel they'd been using to clean the tiles.

He reached for her with messy hands, and she squealed as she danced back. "Don't touch me!"

His grin widened. "I thought you loved me and would do anything for me. What a fair-weather fiancée."

Though he was smiling, she felt a sting in her soul. What was a little mortar? It came off with water. She stepped into the circle of his arms. "Do your worst."

He held his hands out from her green tee. "Oh no, I wasn't born yesterday. I'm not falling for that. If I ruin your shirt, I'll never live it down." He kissed her on the nose before dipping his hands in a bucket of water by his feet. He scrubbed the mortar from his fingers, and the water turned a dirty gray.

While he got cleaned up, she put ice in plastic tumblers and poured in sweet tea from the jug she'd brought from home. She settled on the bedroom floor with her legs tucked under her and sipped her tea until he joined her on the old rug they planned on replacing. The main bedroom smelled of Lysol and paint.

The song on her phone changed to "The Power of Love" by Huey Lewis and the News, and she gasped. "Hez, that song makes me so sad. I ran across it when I was researching the feud between the Willards and the Legares after Dad said something about Michael being full of hate after what happened to his sister."

"What's that have to do with a song? And I don't think I knew he had a sister."

Men were always so literal. "I'm going at it backwards, but stay with me." She reached for her phone and scrolled to the picture she'd taken. "This is Michael's sister, Winona Willard." Savannah had found the picture of the pretty girl with enormous blonde hair in a late-eighties yearbook. "I found an old article from a newspaper that talked about how Winona and her baby died in childbirth a year after that picture was taken. It was heartbreaking. The article didn't mention a grieving husband or anything, so I think she got pregnant out of wedlock."

He rubbed his forehead. "That's why the song makes you sad?"

"No, no. I haven't gotten to the song yet. There was a lawsuit when Winona died, and the Willards sued the doctor, which resulted in a ten-million-dollar judgment, and the doctor lost his medical license. The article said the Willard family was donating most of the proceeds from the lawsuit to build a pregnancy and neonatology center at TGU in Winona's memory so other young women wouldn't suffer her fate."

Hez frowned. "TGU doesn't have a neonatology center."

"I know, right? And even in the eighties it would have cost more than ten million dollars, so that didn't make sense either. I dug through the ledgers to see what happened. The records aren't very clear, but it appears the money was diverted into the school's general fund, which then made a multimillion-dollar deposit into Dad's trust fund."

Hez winced. "If I were Michael, I'd be furious. You think that ramped up the feud?"

"I think it's likely, don't you?"

He took a gulp of his sweet tea and nodded. "That kind of betrayal would be hard to forgive. But what about the song?"

There was a reason Hez was such a good attorney. His mind held on to every detail. "While I was reading Dad's journal, I came across the lyrics to that song and he said it was 'their' song, his and Mom's. The chorus talks about how unimportant money is when compared to love—yet look what happened in their marriage. Dad's obsession with power and money grew and grew. It was his fault Mom became Michael's target. Dad blamed her for everything, but it was his betrayal. What happened to him?"

"Francis Bacon said, 'Money is a great servant but a bad master.' Your dad learned that the hard way. The more he had, the more it controlled him. With the way he pillaged TGU, he should be incredibly wealthy, but he's squandered it all. I'm thankful you're nothing like him."

His gaze roved over her face. "Yeah, I'm a man, and the first thing I noticed when we met was how gorgeous you are. Your auburn hair and green eyes caught my attention immediately." He leaned closer and wrapped one of her locks around his finger. "But it didn't take me long to see you're even more beautiful inside. You love people, not things. You care about what's right and you try to take care of everyone, even me when I didn't deserve it. I thank God you gave us a second chance."

She cupped his face in her palms, relishing the rasp of his evening stubble against her skin. Setting her tea aside, she climbed onto his lap and vowed she would never let their love morph and die. She'd fight with everything in her to keep what they had.

Michael Willard had an ugly meeting in five minutes, but he paused to gaze up at the graceful limestone arch framing the weathered oak doors that led into the TGU administration building. He used to swell with pride when he walked through those doors as a child, holding his grandfather's hand. Grandpa Ezra had been dean of students here. He had guided and supported a generation of TGU students, and everyone had expected him to be named president as the capstone to a long career serving the university he loved. But the university hadn't loved him back. The trustees passed over Grandpa and chose a smooth-talking young Legare named Pierre. As a consolation prize, they gave Grandpa a small pension and a long lease on the big house that used to be the president's mansion. And then they kicked him to the curb.

Grandpa made the mistake of trusting the university and the Legares. Michael was about to meet the woman who embodied both: Savannah Webster. She had requested this meeting "to talk about Simon's best interests," but when had a Legare cared about the best interests of anyone else, especially a Willard? Michael would have rejected the meeting out of hand, but he had his own agenda for it. He glanced down at his battered steel briefcase and smiled. This would be fun.

Michael pushed open the heavy doors and walked down the middle of the wide hall, his leather-soled shoes clicking on the marble floor. The place had a faint smell of must under the janitorial disinfectant—the odor of old money that had started to rot. What must it have been like before Savannah's grandfather Andre started the university down the dark path of corruption and the resulting decay?

The old guard behind the security desk glanced up from his phone long enough to point Michael toward the carved oak doors leading to the presidential conference room. The Websters rose as he entered, and Savannah caught him with those gold-flecked green eyes that were so like her mother's. She had

Marie's auburn hair, too, but the rest of her face had the aristocratic lines of a Legare.

Savannah spoke first. "Thanks for coming in, Michael. Please have a seat."

Hez eyed the door as they sat. "Should we wait for your lawyer?"

Michael sneered. "I won't need a lawyer for this."

Savannah gave a tentative smile. "Good. I hope this can be a friendly conversation. We all want what's best for Simon, of course." She swallowed hard. "We'd be open to some form of joint custody."

Michael glanced down at the briefcase beside his chair, but he decided not to open it just yet. "Why should I agree to joint custody?"

Hez cleared his throat. "Because no matter who wins a custody fight, the child usually loses."

Michael turned to Hez. "So don't fight. You can't win."

"But you can still lose."

Michael stared Hez in the eye. "What's that supposed to mean?"

Hez's gaze didn't waver. "You need two things to adopt Simon: Erik's consent and proof that the adoption would be in Simon's best interests. You've got the consent, but you may have difficulty proving that it's in Simon's best interests for you to adopt him."

Embers of anger glowed in Michael's chest, but he kept his voice calm. "I'm his grandfather. I'll raise him better than you could."

"Jess disagreed."

Michael smacked his palms onto the table. "How dare you use my daughter against me!"

Hez shrugged. "Her words will carry a lot of weight in court."

Michael's fury flared and he reached for the briefcase, but Savannah spoke before he could open it. "Please respect her wishes, Michael. I know how much you loved her—and how much she suffered from the conflict between our families. Let's not make Simon go through the same pain."

"She suffered because the Legares hurt her. Not the Willards. I'm going to keep Simon safe from y'all."

Hez scoffed. "Oh, come on. You know Simon is safe with us. Probably safer than with you. We know about your criminal connections—and those will come out during a custody fight. You really are better off making a deal with us."

So they were going to play the same game Pierre did all those years ago, blackmailing Michael to keep him in line. It wouldn't work this time. "Simon almost drowned when he was with you. Should I wait until he's dead, like your daughter?"

Hez turned a satisfying shade of red, and Savannah gave a little gasp.

Michael picked up his briefcase and put it on the glass-topped table. He opened it, pulled out a thick envelope, and tossed it on the table in Hez's general direction. "My lawyer just filed this. It's an emergency motion for full custody of Simon because he's in danger. See you in court."

Michael got up and walked out of the conference room. His anger cooled as he walked back down the hall and out of the building. Thunder rumbled and a gusty wind tossed the moss-draped tree branches overhead. He first kissed Marie on a day like this, sheltering under a huge old oak as a storm swirled around them. He held her tight that day—and he never should have let her go. He hadn't known how to fight the Legares back then, but he was older and savvier now. Everything was going according to plan. Even Erik Andersen had a role to play, though Michael didn't trust him.

The first fat raindrops splattered Michael's truck as he got in. It had rained on the night Marie died too. Pierre should have paid for her life with his, and maybe it wasn't too late to arrange that.

Would Hez Webster need to die too? Michael wouldn't let anyone get between him and his grandson, and if Hez chose to put himself in harm's way, that was his fault. Besides, James Hornbrook might just do the job for Michael.

Michael smiled and drove off into the storm.

CHAPTER 15

KIDS CARRYING BACKPACKS STREAMED FROM THE SCHOOL doors. Savannah parked in the pickup line and craned her neck through her open window to watch for Simon. Ever since Michael had taken her nephew without permission, she'd made sure to pick him up herself. The man had gone rogue, and there was no reining him in. Rules didn't apply to him, and he made sure everyone knew it. The problem was he was right—everyone fell in line with his demands, and she wasn't sure how she and Hez could win this battle.

She glanced at her watch, then fingered the double-decker bus key chain she'd found. Simon had some explaining to do. She drummed her fingers on the steering wheel. Where was Simon? He should be used to the new routine now. A flash of red caught her eye, and she spotted her nephew step out from the back side of the school on her left. He glanced furtively around before heading west at a brisk pace as if he had somewhere to go.

Why would he walk home when he knew she would be waiting? And even more importantly, why was he being so secretive? If he wanted to go to a friend's house, all he had to do was ask. Had he arranged for Michael to pick him up somewhere else?

For the first time she felt uneasy at how obstinate the boy had been about obeying her and Hez. He was only ten, but he already carried Michael's penchant for doing what he wanted no matter what he was told. How did she and Hez keep a wandering boy safe in today's world?

She pulled out of the line of waiting cars and drove slowly along the street as she tried to keep him in sight. She spotted his red shirt again and called to him through the open window. "Simon, over here!"

He glanced her way and frowned, then vanished through a row of shrubs. She gritted her teeth and parked at the curb, then flung her door open and rushed after him. Branches scratched her bare arms and snagged her hair as she forced herself through the shrubs. A heel broke on one of her pumps as she caught it in a crevice along the stone path. She took off her shoes and tried to keep up the pace. The vegetation opened up and sunlight filtered through the leaves overhead.

A path led off toward an extension of Gum Swamp, but Simon had no reason to wander there when he was supposed to be in her back seat. But he wasn't on the main path either, so he had to have gone that way. She veered toward the swamp, and the scent of pine trees mingled with the salty tang of brackish water. The sweet scent of wildflowers wafted her way.

She hadn't gone more than ten feet from where the path ended and the swamp started when the mosquitoes began to buzz around her face. Cold mud sucked at her bare feet and a snake slithered into the vegetation ahead of her. She shuddered at the black and coral markings and slipped her pumps on again. Her pace slowed with the uneven heels, but at least she had a bit of protection for her feet.

Something large splashed in the water off to her left, and she spotted a gator gliding through the black water. She paused to shout Simon's name. No answer. She checked for footprints and caught an occasional impression, but the boy had gotten good at hiding his tracks since the first time she'd brought him here. The few marks he left led her out the other side of the swamp, and she still didn't know his purpose to be out here. Could he have doubled back into the water to try to lose her again?

But after pausing to catch her bearings, she recognized the neighborhood. Erik lived only a block away. Her lungs tightened at the realization of where her nephew had gone. He'd called his birth father a "git" after their first meeting, but here he was again. The poor boy must be desperate for family. She exhaled an exasperated huff and vainly brushed at the mud on her skirt. Even a dry cleaner wouldn't make it wearable again.

She marched to Erik's door and took in the black Denali in the driveway. It had to be Michael's truck. She pressed the doorbell with a muddy finger. The door opened after what felt like forever. "Where's Simon?" she demanded. "Do you have him?"

Erik's glower turned to a grin. "Did you lose that boy again? I'm sure the judge will be interested in hearing about that." He turned and called for Simon.

Simon's eyes widened when he stepped beside his dad. "Aunt Savannah, you look like you were wrestling Boo Radley. You'll track mud all over Dad's clean floor."

In spite of his joke, Savannah thought his blue eyes held

concern. At least she tried to tell herself he cared that she'd braved gators and coral snakes to find him. "I'm glad you're okay, but you knew I was waiting for you. Now we'll both have to traipse back to where I parked the car."

Erik's smile fell away. "Simon and I have things to discuss—privately. I want what's best for him, and with the way you keep losing him, I don't think his future is safe in your hands. I'll bring him to your cottage when we're finished talking."

The door shut in Savannah's face before she could respond. She reached for her phone, then pulled back her hand. He was Simon's father, and calling 911 would get her nowhere.

Michael stood over Marie's grave, which lay in a well-tended corner of the overgrown Legare cemetery. The first rays of dawn rimmed the horizon, but the moon still glowed overhead. Michael held a book of Marie's poems, but he didn't need it. He knew them all by heart. He recited one:

I lost the Moon
My young eyes knew it well
Silver and magic
But someone slipped a rock in the Moon's place
Airless and dead
My grown eyes know it well
I lost the Moon

Those were the first words he'd heard Marie speak—her musical voice weighed down with the sadness of lost dreams.

Much later she'd confided that the "rock" in the middle of the poem referred to the giant diamond on her finger. That hadn't been a surprise—Michael knew all about her marital problems before he set foot in her poetry reading. They were the reason he went.

After Pierre stole the money from the malpractice settlement for the deaths of Winona and her son, Michael had vowed revenge. And what better way to get it than by stealing Pierre's wife?

The whole town knew Marie was Pierre's greatest conquest and prized possession. She was the gorgeous daughter of an old New Orleans society family, and he set his sights on her the moment she arrived on campus to pursue a master of fine arts in poetry. He wooed her, playing the suave and sensitive scion of the local aristocracy. She fell for his act and he had her on his arm at every party or fundraiser thereafter, showing her off to professors and alumni.

Then Marie got pregnant and no longer fit into her elegant evening gowns. Pierre's eye began to rove. Rumors circulated. A local newspaper ran a story about him billing the university for escorts in New Orleans. Pierre claimed it was a misunderstanding and the bill was for a "concierge service" while he was entertaining a wealthy donor.

After Savannah's birth, Marie had published a volume of poetry—and Michael had decided to attend her first reading. He sat on a folding metal chair in the back of a drafty classroom with a creaky floor. A dozen or so people attended—mostly pale-skinned artistic types who appeared to be fellow students. Pierre wasn't there.

Winning Marie's heart had looked easy that night—but

Michael hadn't counted on losing his own in the process. He still didn't have it back over three decades later.

He knelt beside Marie's grave, feeling the dew-wet grass through the knees of his work jeans. He laid a single red rose against the white marble headstone. "I also lost the Moon." His gaze traveled to Jess's grave, and he recalled Marie's name for her. "And our Morning Star."

He glimpsed the statuary group over Ella Webster's little grave. It depicted Simon as part of the Webster family. "But I won't lose him. That's a promise. I'm going to court tomorrow and I'll get him for us." He caressed the cool stone, tracing Marie's engraved name with a calloused finger. "I'll protect him like I should have protected you. No matter what the cost."

Michael pushed himself to his feet. Savannah came up here frequently, and he didn't want to run into her. He started toward the exit but paused as he passed Jess's grave. "Why did you give him to Savannah? The boy is a Willard—you knew that as well as me. Why put him in the hands of a Legare? Were you still mad about how I raised you? I had to make you strong. You knew that too. Why did you do it, girl?"

The only answer was the cooing of a dove in one of the trees dotting the hilltop graveyard.

Whatever Jess's reasoning, she was wrong. She made a mistake, and it was up to him to fix it. He strode down the hill, determined to claim his grandson.

CHAPTER 16

HEZ TRIED NOT TO FIDGET. HE FIRMLY BELIEVED THE ADAGE that a lawyer who represented himself had a fool for a client—but he still hated sitting in a courtroom without being able to argue his own case. He wanted to be sitting next to Scott Foster at the counsel table, scribbling notes and whispering last-minute advice, but that would be counterproductive.

He turned to Savannah, who sat beside him just behind Scott. She gave a nervous smile, took his hand, and squeezed it. He squeezed back and put on what he hoped was a reassuring expression.

Michael Willard sat on the other side of the courtroom, whispering with his attorney, a middle-aged woman with sharp features whom Hez didn't recognize. The only other people present were the clerk, the court reporter, and the bailiff. The two sides had agreed to hold the hearing while Simon was in school so he wouldn't have to hear his family arguing over him.

The bailiff was unusually muscular and well armed. A veteran police officer once told Hez that family law hearings were more likely to turn violent than any other court proceedings, which would explain why the bailiff had a Taser, gun, and billy club. Most bailiffs were retired cops with extra time on their hands, but this guy could have been a SWAT door kicker. And he had given both Hez and Michael appraising looks as they walked in, as if he were deciding the best way to take down each of them if things got ugly.

The door behind the judge's bench opened, and everyone in the courtroom rose. The clerk cleared her throat. "The probate court for Baldwin County is now in session. Please take your seats and come to order." A broad-shouldered short man of about fifty emerged from the chambers. Aloysius O'Keefe had been a star high school running back thirty-five years ago. Reporters named him "the Bowling Ball," and he looked the part in his black robe.

Judge O'Keefe settled in as everyone sat down. He flipped through the papers in front of him, then peered over the side of the bench and nodded to the clerk.

The clerk looked at her monitor. "Calling M. J. W. versus S. L. W. and H. M. W." Adoption dockets were confidential, so the case name used only the parties' initials.

The attorneys rose and Scott spoke first. "Scott Foster for petitioners Savannah and Hezekiah Webster."

Michael's lawyer spoke in a harsh contralto voice. "Agatha Morgan for counterpetitioner and movant, Michael Willard."

Judge O'Keefe nodded. "Thanks. Have a seat. This is our first hearing, but both sides have already been busy. We have not one but two adoption petitions, both of which are contested. And now we also have an emergency motion for custody." He glanced at his papers again. "Normally, the first order of business in a contested adoption is to appoint a guardian ad litem."

Morgan stood. "In light of the urgency of the situation, Mr. Willard respectfully requests that his motion be heard first, Your Honor."

The judge nodded. "I thought he might. I've read the motion papers and the allegations are quite serious. If the child's life truly is threatened by the current custody arrangement, that needs to be addressed immediately. Since this is your motion, you go first."

"Thank you, Your Honor." Morgan picked up her notes and moved to the lectern. "May it please the court, Simon Legare is in danger every hour he stays with the Websters. The facts in our affidavits are undisputed. In the few months Simon has been in their custody, he was kidnapped, nearly drowned, and was held at gunpoint. Further, their own child drowned while under the supervision of Mr. Webster."

The judge held up a hand to stop Morgan and turned to Scott. "Do you agree that all of this is undisputed?"

Scott stood. "It's undisputed that those things happened, Your Honor."

The judge's gaze moved to Hez and Savannah, and judgment showed in his brown eyes. "And they happened while the children were in the Websters' custody and under their supervision?"

Scott nodded. "Yes, Your Honor. However, Mr. Willard's nephew, Deke Willard, kidnapped Simon, so it's hardly fair to blame the Websters for that."

Judge O'Keefe turned back to Morgan. "Is that true?"

Morgan whispered with Michael, whose face had turned red. "Yes, Your Honor. Deke got manipulated into participating in the kidnapping. He is now serving a life sentence without possibility of parole and is no threat to Simon." She picked up a document and handed it to the clerk, who handed it up to the judge. She handed another copy to Scott. "Moving on. Simon's father, Erik Andersen, consented to Michael Willard's adoption petition. Mr. Andersen also submitted an affidavit supporting an immediate custody change. Mr. Andersen met with Simon and Mr. Willard just yesterday and witnessed their loving interactions. Simon said he wanted to live with Mr. Willard and—"

Hez grimaced and a little gasp escaped Savannah. So that's why Erik and Michael somehow lured Simon to Erik's home. Scott jumped to his feet. "Objection, hearsay and lack of notice. This wasn't part of the materials served on my clients."

The judge nodded. "Sustained. If you want Mr. Andersen's testimony in the record, bring him in to testify and give the other side proper notice. The same for the child. I'll allow his testimony, assuming the guardian ad litem doesn't think it would be harmful to him."

Morgan gathered her papers. "Understood, Your Honor. One final point and my argument is finished—the DNA tests prove Mr. Willard is Simon's grandfather."

"All right." Judge O'Keefe turned to Scott. "Argument, Counsel?"

"Yes, Your Honor." Scott stepped to the lectern as Morgan resumed her seat. "May it please the court, the dying wish of Simon's mother—Ms. Webster's sister—was that Ms. Webster take care of Simon. Her will says the same thing. Ms. Webster is in court and will so testify if necessary. His father—confirmed by DNA—is Erik Andersen, who fled during the investigation into the murder of the university president. Ms. Webster is his closest and most logical guardian."

The judge glanced at Savannah, then turned to Morgan. "Do you want to put her on the stand?"

"One moment please, Your Honor." Morgan turned to Michael, who appeared unsettled. They held another whispered conference. Morgan turned back to the judge. "That won't be necessary at this time, though we do reserve the right to take Ms. Webster's deposition at a later date and cross-examine her in future hearings."

"Of course." The judge looked at Scott. "Anything further, Counsel?"

"Yes, Your Honor." Scott turned over a sheet of paper on the lectern. "Deke Willard isn't the only relative of Michael Willard who is in prison for serious crimes. So is his brother, David, and three of Michael Willard's nephews are awaiting trial. They were all involved in a smuggling ring. Michael Willard hasn't been arrested—yet. But he appears to sit at the center of a criminal conspiracy. It clearly wouldn't be in Simon's best interests to—"

"Objection!" Morgan was on her feet, and Michael glared at Scott's back so hard that he seemed to be trying to drill holes in the lawyer's skin. "There's no foundation for any of that."

Judge O'Keefe shrugged. "I can take judicial notice of other proceedings pending in the circuit court. The rest of Mr. Foster's comments are argument. I wouldn't allow them in front of a jury." He pointed at the empty jury box. "But we don't have one. Overruled."

Scott handed documents to Morgan and the clerk, who passed them up to the judge. "This is the affidavit of Oliver Hampton, a licensed private investigator who interviewed a number of witnesses stating that Michael Willard abused several relatives who—"

Michael jumped from his seat. "That's a lie!"

The bailiff stepped away from the bench and pulled his Taser from its holster. Judge O'Keefe grabbed his gavel and slammed it down. "Take your seat! Another outburst and you'll be expelled from the courtroom and arrested for contempt of court. Is that clear?"

Michael eyed the bailiff, then nodded and sat slowly, his eyes still full of fire.

The judge nodded to Scott. "Proceed, Counsel."

Scott somehow appeared unruffled. "Thank you, Your Honor. As I was saying, the affidavit makes clear that Mr. Willard engaged in repeated acts of discipline that crossed the line into abuse. He would be a danger to Simon."

Morgan stood. "Objection. This affidavit is hearsay and presented without proper notice. I'm seeing it for the first time."

The judge nodded. "I'm going to exclude this for the same reason I excluded the Andersen affidavit." He shot a dark glance at Michael. "But Mr. Willard's behavior today does indicate that he has difficulty controlling his temper."

Michael sat in stone-faced silence.

Scott picked up his papers. "Thank you, Your Honor. That concludes my argument."

Judge O'Keefe turned to Morgan. "Any rebuttal, Counsel?"

"Thank you, Your Honor." Morgan rose. "Just that I'm confident Your Honor will base your decision on the best interests of the child, which seem clear here. The alleged danger to Simon if he lives with Mr. Willard is that he might get too severe of a spanking. The admitted danger if he stays with the Websters is that he'll be killed."

The judge nodded as Morgan resumed her seat. "Succinctly put. To be honest, I'm not thrilled with either alternative." He glanced from Michael to the Websters and back again, then sighed. "I'm going to grant the motion in part. Simon Legare will be delivered to Michael Willard within twenty-four hours." The judge's words were a dagger in Hez's gut. He felt Savannah stiffen beside him like she'd been struck. "Mr. Willard will have custody Monday through Friday hereafter until there's a final custody determination. Savannah Webster will have custody on the weekends. Hezekiah Webster is to have no contact with the child for two reasons. First, Alabama does not permit an unmarried couple to adopt, and it would be inappropriate to give temporary custody of a child to a couple who can't adopt him. Second, Mr. Webster's presence appears to increase the danger to the child. For whatever reason, all the child endangerment incidents have occurred when he was with Simon. He was the only one present when the Websters' daughter drowned, for example. The intruder who pulled a gun on Simon was in Mr. Webster's condo. And so on. Finally, when he is in Ms. Webster's custody, Simon is not to be allowed within one hundred yards of any body of water deep enough to be over his head."

The judge and the lawyers moved on to discuss setting a final custody hearing, appointing a guardian ad litem, and other matters. Hez couldn't focus on what they were saying. He was too stunned. Was the judge right that his presence put Simon in danger? Would he ever see his nephew again?

The scent of flowers in the warm May breeze did nothing to calm Savannah's agitation as she and Simon walked the dogs along the field fronting the swamp. There was only one road along the meadow, and it usually had no traffic. She'd hoped the serenity would ground her, but her insides vibrated with outrage.

It was Sunday afternoon and they should be at their new home. She should be working on the new kitchen with Hez while Simon explored the house grounds. But her nephew would never be allowed to live there. The judge's order specifically said he couldn't be within one hundred yards of water. Their home was closer than that to Mobile Bay, so where did that leave them? Would they have to stay in a hotel on the weekends or with friends? It was all so unfair.

Simon chattered excitedly about getting to be with his grandfather. "And my cousins are going to teach me how to shoot a gun and drive an ATV."

Savannah stopped short to face him, and Marley plowed into her leg. "Simon, those are not safe activities. Do you know how many kids are injured and killed on ATVs every year? I want you to be safe."

He rolled his eyes as only a kid could do. "I can't wait to

be a part of my family. Being with my cousins is almost like having brothers and sisters. And Pawpaw is great! You just don't want me to have any fun."

There was no comeback she could make to that. No matter what she said, she only succeeded in pushing him further away. Were she and Hez being selfish by trying to keep custody of him when he so desperately wanted to be with his grandfather? The Willards were his family too, and Jess had loved them and spent time with them. But in spite of that, she hadn't appointed any of the Willards as Simon's guardian. There had to be a reason for Jess's decision. Savannah believed her sister had known the dark depths in that family and had wanted to protect her son from them.

And Savannah had failed.

Cody squirreled around Simon's legs, and the boy knelt to pet him. "I'm going to miss my dog, though. Pawpaw doesn't want his big dogs to hurt him."

"Marley is big and he's good with Cody. Are Michael's dogs mean?"

"Well, they're guard dogs, I guess. They aren't very friendly."

Not only did she have to worry about guns and ATVs, but she had to fear a mauling. The judge had made the wrong decision, and there was nothing they could do about it.

Simon threw a tennis ball, and Cody sprang after it. Watching the dog run on those short Chihuahua legs with his Great Dane ears flopping made Savannah chuckle in spite of her morose mood. "Get it, Cody!" The dog galloped after the green ball toward the street as a black SUV approached and screeched to a halt.

Three masked men jumped out and came toward them

across the grass. Savannah froze and glanced around for help, but no one else was out here. Her adrenaline surged, and she reached for Simon, but he wasn't paying attention and ran toward the dog. One of the men grabbed Cody by the collar, and the dog yelped and struggled.

Simon sprang at the man and pushed him. "Leave my dog alone."

Savannah rushed forward and yanked him back from the man, then gave him a slight shove in the opposite direction. "Hide in the swamp!" She balled her fists and pummeled the guy in the belly as he started after the boy. He wrestled to try to get her out of the way, but she kneed him in the groin and scratched at his face with her nails.

"Get the kid," he snarled to the other two. He flipped Savannah around and got her in a chokehold.

No matter how she tore at his arm, bulging with muscles, she couldn't budge his grip. As her oxygen ran out, she saw stars, and then his free hand rose with a syringe.

A slight sting pricked her neck before he hauled her across the grass to the SUV and tossed her inside before crawling in beside her. Savannah tried to throw open the door, but it was locked and her brain couldn't figure out how to unlock it.

Another man threw Simon in beside her and went around to the driver's door. Marley growled and snapped at the third man's legs, but strong hands grabbed Marley and dragged him away. Savannah's captor climbed into the passenger seat and shut the vehicle door. Her vision began to fade.

Stay awake, stay awake. But the drug was swirling in her veins, dimming her senses. She closed her eyes and fell into the blackness.

CHAPTER 17

IS THE CUSTODY EXCHANGE OVER? **HEZ SENT THE TEXT TO** Savannah, then waited for the pulsing ellipsis to show she was responding. He drummed his fingers on the steering wheel of his new GMC pickup. His neurologist had finally cleared him to drive two weeks ago, and he'd planned to buy another Audi, but Blake persuaded him that the rural back roads required something a little tougher. Driving it felt a little like walking on stilts, but Hez appreciated the extra power and ground clearance.

He had parked by the side of the road half a mile from Savannah's cottage so he could stop by as soon as Michael left with Simon. Hez hated having to leave Savannah to face such a hard moment alone, but Judge O'Keefe's order had been very clear: Hez had to keep at least five hundred yards from Simon.

A minute passed since his text. Two minutes. Three. He called her, but it went straight to voicemail without ringing.

Could she and Simon still be walking the dogs along the old swamp road? Cell coverage was bad out there. Maybe that was the problem.

He checked his watch: 6:40 p.m.—ten minutes after Michael was supposed to pick up Simon at Savannah's cottage. She wouldn't be late for that if she could help it. Missing a custody exchange would just give Michael an excuse to go back in front of Judge O'Keefe and ask for even more.

Hez frowned. Had Michael tried something? That made no sense—he was getting what he wanted: Simon. Still, the man was a violent thug, and Hez wouldn't put anything past him.

He called again—and again it went directly to voicemail. Dread coiled in his gut. Something had happened.

He put the truck in gear and drove toward Savannah's home. He turned the corner onto her street and saw Michael's black Denali in her driveway. Michael stood beside it with his phone to his ear. He scowled and gesticulated with his free hand before spotting Hez. He gestured for him to pull over.

Hez parked on the street in front of the cottage, mind whirring. Where were Savannah and Simon? Why was Michael still here?

Michael shoved his phone in his pocket and stomped over. "Where's my grandson?" he demanded as Hez stepped down from the truck.

Hez shut the door. "What are you talking about?"

Michael's face darkened and his eyes flashed. He jabbed a finger toward Hez's face. "Do not play games with me! I was supposed to pick up Simon at six thirty. Where is he? And where's your Legare wife?"

Before Hez could respond, his phone rang. A picture of a cream-colored golden retriever appeared on the screen. The number was blocked.

Michael stared at the phone. The fury vanished from his face and voice. He turned pale. "Put it on speaker."

Hez complied. "This is Hez Webster."

"If you want to see Savannah, Simon, or your dogs again, you will do exactly as I say." The flat robotic voice indicated electronic masking. "You have thirty-six hours to do two things. First, find and eliminate all copies of the database of materials you stole from Hornbrook Finance. All copies—whether created by you or not. Second, find and eliminate whoever is blackmailing Hornbrook."

Hez's pulse thundered in his ears. "If you hurt them, I'll—"

"Thirty-six hours."

The call ended.

CHAPTER 18

A SWEET AROMA ENVELOPED SAVANNAH'S SENSES AND EN- ticed her out of slumber. She stirred with her eyes still closed. An exotic sound penetrated her stupor—it sounded like a parrot or some other tropical bird. *What a lovely dream.*

She opened her eyes, blinked, then saw a pitched ceiling overhead with white-painted boards and a fan in the shape of palm leaves. Ignoring her stiff spine, she bolted upright and swung her gaze around her surroundings.

She was on a twin bed with pale blue sheets. The walls were creamy white with tasteful tropical prints. Simon snored softly in the bed next to hers, and Cody curled on the end of his bed. A tropical breeze stirred gauzy curtains at an open window that peeked out at palm trees swaying next to a white-sand beach. The glimpse of turquoise water enticed her to come closer. A parrot squawked from its perch somewhere, and her eyes widened.

This is not Alabama.

She eased her legs over the side of the bed to check on Simon, and Marley, tail wagging, trotted to her to get his ears rubbed. The touch of his soft fur under her fingers anchored her to the present, and her memory flooded back to the men who'd leaped from the SUV. She probed her neck where she'd felt the prick of a needle but couldn't feel a mark.

She stood and took a step toward the other bed and discovered the weight of a monitor on her left ankle. She frowned and moved to Simon's side to press her fingers against his carotid artery. His pulse was nice and steady, and so was his breathing. He was just asleep, but he wore an ankle monitor too. Cody turned his snaggletooth her way before tucking his muzzle into his tail again.

The scent of fresh coffee turned her attention to a carafe with mugs, tropical fruits, and pastries on a table in the corner. She poured herself a mug of coffee and took a gulp that tasted like Guatemalan, her favorite. Whoever the men were, they didn't stint on quality coffee. Carrying her mug, she went to the door and tried the knob. Unlocked. "Stay with Simon," she told Marley before stepping outside into a beautiful tropical day. Where was this place?

Two fit and muscular men holding scary-looking guns rose from chairs under a palm tree. They both wore sunglasses that masked their expressions. "Do you need anything, ma'am?" the taller one asked.

She tried to place his accent. Serbian, Bulgarian, somewhere in southeast Europe maybe? "Where are we?"

His grin showed very white teeth. "In paradise, ma'am."

She didn't care for his flippant answer. "I need to leave. Right now."

The two men glanced at each other, and the other one laughed. "Good luck, lady. We're on an island ten miles from any other land mass. The strong currents will yank you farther out to sea, and the sharks are very hungry around here."

The guy with the accent gestured with his gun. “The boss wants to have a chat.”

“I don’t want to leave my nephew alone. He might be afraid when he wakes up.”

The other man chuckled. “That little man ain’t afraid of nothing. And he’ll be sleeping off his meds for at least another hour. This way.” His tone left no doubt he intended her to go if he had to drag her.

She stiffened and took another swallow of coffee for courage before she set it down on the porch railing. Was “the boss” Hornbrook? If so, they were in a lot of trouble.

The men led her along a path of crushed shells toward a low-slung building with a large porch that overlooked the water and the pier behind it. Colorful tropical flowers filled the planter beds and spilled their scent into the air. The large house stretched out into three wings and appeared welcoming, but she knew better than to think she would find any help inside.

Shoulders squared, she mounted the wide steps and entered the house. The guards followed her inside, where Mozart’s Serenade No. 13 played from speakers around the room. The rousing melody elevated her pulse even more.

A silver-haired sixtyish man rose from a chair with a cautious smile and extended his hand. “Ms. Webster, it’s a pleasure to meet you. Welcome to my island. I’m James Hornbrook.”

Hornbrook. She masked her dismay and ignored his hand. “It’s hardly appropriate to welcome me when your goons kidnapped me and my nephew. I demand you let us go immediately.”

"Hey." The guy with the accent shoved her. "We're no goons."

"Keep your hands to yourself, Anton," Hornbrook barked. His attention returned to Savannah. "You're in no position to make demands, Ms. Webster. Not if you value your life and your nephew's. If you don't do as I request immediately, I'll see that young Simon is taken out to sea and fed to the sharks." His blue eyes grew colder with every word. He picked up a newspaper and a phone. "I'd like you to read the article here about the PGA tournament. When you're done with the first paragraph, say the words *twenty-four hours.*"

She wanted to tear the newspaper to shreds and scatter it on the beautiful mahogany floor, but she had Simon and the dogs to consider. Anton. Hadn't Hez mentioned someone named Anton Todorov who worked for Hornbrook? And he was dangerous.

When Hornbrook held out the paper, she took it. He lifted his phone and she began to read in a clear voice. Though her legs trembled, she wasn't about to let him know how terrified she was. She finished with the phrase "twenty-four hours."

None of them were hiding their faces, which told her they didn't plan to let her and Simon describe them to law enforcement. They didn't intend to let them leave this tropical paradise. And Hez had only twenty-four hours to find them.

"Twenty-four hours."

The recorded message ended and the Justice Chamber fell silent. Hez clicked off his phone and dropped it in his pocket. "I got that via text at seven. Thank you all for getting here so fast." How was his voice so calm when he was dying inside? Every nerve in his body hummed with tension. What was Savannah going through? And Simon? He'd already experienced so much trauma in his young life. Hez cleared his throat and looked around the room at the group gathered there.

The cold, unnatural light from the fluorescent bulbs overhead gave everyone a sickly color that matched their expressions after hearing the message from Hornbrook. Dominga gripped Ed's hand as they hunched over the little table, which was dominated by an old speakerphone Hez had found in a closet. Arms folded and face grim, Toni sat beside them. Hope, who was there at Hez's invitation, occupied the final seat at the table and seemed deep in thought.

Michael, who had basically invited himself, paced the small room, muttering. He knew about the Justice Chamber from his grandchildren and had demanded to be involved in any efforts to rescue Simon. Hez hadn't objected. Maybe Michael could help.

Hope's phone chimed and she glanced at it. "That was the FBI. They're already analyzing the audio and the text Hez received. They also gave me an update on the black SUV the police found on the beach last night. It was reported stolen two days ago, and they discovered a fingerprint from Simon and three strands of auburn hair in the back seat."

Michael scoffed. "That's all you've got after thirteen hours? We'll never find Simon in time. Do better!"

Hope grimaced. "We're doing everything we can, Mr. Willard."

Hez released the edge of his desk. He'd been unconsciously

holding it in a death grip and his fingers ached. "What about Hornbrook's claim that someone was blackmailing him?"

Hope nodded. "That appears to be true. The Cyber Division has confirmed that an extortion demand was delivered to Hornbrook Finance."

Michael stopped pacing. "So Hornbrook was telling the truth? Who's the blackmailer? What do they want?"

Hope drummed her fingers, her nails clicking on the weathered wood tabletop. "All I know is that someone contacted his company and demanded five million dollars. If they don't get it, they'll release a database of damaging videos." She glanced at Hez. "I assume it's the same one."

Michael glared at her for a moment, then turned to Hez. "What's this database? Everyone seems to know about it except me."

Hez wouldn't trust Michael with more information than necessary. "All you need to know is that we're aware of what he wants and we're working on finding it."

Michael's eyes flashed and he took a step toward Hez. "What I need to know is whether we can give Hornbrook what he wants. Can we?"

Hez tensed further at Michael's demanding tone. "If we give him what he wants, he has no reason to keep them alive any longer."

Michael nodded. "Yeah, but if we can offer him what he wants, that gives us leverage."

Hez gave a grim half smile. "Exactly what I was thinking." He leaned over the speakerphone. "Bruno, how are you doing?"

"Better 'n the bureau." Static from the speaker distorted

Bruno's voice. "I took down all copies of the database we put online and did some hunting to make sure I didn't miss any. I still have a copy of the database on a hard drive in a secure location, of course. Unfortunately, someone else does too."

Hez's phone buzzed. His heart rate jumped as he pulled it from his pocket—but the screen only showed an incoming call from someone named Tim Kramer. Probably a wrong number. Hez sent it to voicemail and turned back to the speakerphone. "The blackmailer?"

"Excellent guess. They're close to y'all—that's what you say down there, right? Maybe a mile from where you are right now. Two miles tops. And they're running Google Chrome on a 2023 MacBook."

"This is a university," Michael growled. "Lotta people have MacBooks."

"I'm sure." Bruno seemed unruffled. "This particular MacBook has two external monitors and an external five-terabyte Seagate hard drive. And that hard drive has a copy of the Hornbrook database. Oh, and your blackmailer is an amateur. They may know computers, but they don't know hacking or cybersecurity. They didn't even use a VPN."

"Uh, thanks. Can you get us a name or street address or phone number—something specific like that?"

A burst of static came from the speaker as Bruno blew out a long breath. "Maybe. I'd need to get into the blackmailer's machine, which could take time. Right now I don't have much more than the device fingerprint."

Hez looked at his watch. "We've got twenty-two hours and forty-three minutes. Can you find the blackmailer before then?"

The line was silent for a long moment. "I dunno, man."

CHAPTER 19

THIS ISLAND WAS A PRISON, NOT A PARADISE. UNDER other circumstances Savannah would have loved the chance to sit on the white-sand beach and let the sea breeze deposit the scent of salt in her hair. She watched Simon throw sticks for the dogs and laugh at their antics. At least he didn't realize the gravity of their situation, and she planned to keep it from him if she could.

The guards laughed and played poker on a little bamboo table in the shadow of three palm trees. They mostly ignored her and Simon, but Savannah left Simon building a sandcastle and approached the men. If she could engage them in conversation, maybe she'd learn more about the location. Five beautiful golden retrievers left their side and approached Savannah, tails wagging.

She ran her hands over their silky cream-colored coats. "You guys are a whole herd. I've never seen such gorgeous dogs," she said to the men.

The bearded guy, Anton, whooped and scooped the pot of coins into his hands. "Count yourself lucky the boss is a big dog lover. It would have been easier to shoot your mutts rather than bring them here." He grinned, but his dark eyes were cold.

Savannah held back a shudder at his tone. A black Lab appeared from the side of a gazebo and came over to say hello. Its tail hung between its legs, and it licked her hand before settling at her feet and staring up at her with sad eyes. "Is this Lab okay? Maybe it needs a vet." *Please mention the nearest vet.*

The other guy shuffled the cards. "Nah, he's just a little sad. A previous guest, um, left him behind last week, and he hasn't quite recovered. He will, though. The boss is giving him special attention, and there isn't a dog alive who doesn't love Mr. Hornbrook."

Her gaze surveyed the horizon of endless blue water. Did that guest disappear out there? "Where is this island anyway?"

"That's a need-to-know question, and it's above your pay grade," Anton said. "Look around if you like, though." His tone encouraged her to wander off and leave them alone.

She backed away, and the Lab watched her go with soulful eyes. Simon jumped to his feet at her approach and brushed sand from his hands. "Can we take a walk? I want to see the rest of the island."

"Sure." Their dogs followed them, and the goldens trailed them too. The guards ambled along about ten yards back, talking and laughing.

Behind the main house she spotted the dock she'd seen when talking to Hornbrook. A yacht bobbed in the waves. She kept walking. To the left of the main house, the beach curved around to reveal a perfect little cove. Several small boats were tied to a small pier. A spit of land curled protectively around the harbor on the other side.

Simon's gaze darted toward the boats. "Could we take one of those and get out of here?" he whispered.

The boats were small with low-power engines that wouldn't putt along more than a few miles an hour. "I don't think so. For one thing, the engines likely don't have much gas, and there's no way to get our bearings on which direction to head. And even if we tried, that yacht behind the big house would catch up to us in no time."

The bright hope on his face ebbed. "So we're stuck here?"

"I'm sure your uncle Hez will find us." He had to be frantic after that message from her.

"Pawpaw too. He knows lots of people, and he won't let anyone get away with this."

When they got out of this mess, she needed to figure out a gentle way of making sure Simon knew his grandfather was no angel. If she didn't do something about her nephew's misplaced admiration, Michael would lure him into the Willard crime web. She couldn't let that happen.

The waves tossed a soggy wrapper of some kind onto the pristine beach, and she stepped over to grab it. She shook the salt water from it and smoothed it out to examine the writing. It was a food take-out bag for a restaurant in Caracas. Her gaze traveled down the beach to the dogs frolicking in the turquoise water. This had to be a small island off the coast of Venezuela, and an idea began to germinate on how to reveal their location to Hez.

Who was blackmailing James Hornbrook?

Hez tugged his lower lip as he stared out the Justice Chamber's lone window. Rain pelted the glass and dribbled in through the poorly fitted lead frame, staining the cement sill. The window wasn't the only thing that leaked—someone had told a tech-savvy extortionist about the Hornbrook database, but who?

Hez had assumed the answer lay in New York City. That's where Hornbrook did business and where most of his victims—and probably his enemies—lived. But why would the hacker who found and downloaded the database be so close to TGU? It made no sense—unless the leak happened here. Not many people in Southern Alabama knew about the database, but there were a few: Hez, Savannah, Hope, the TGU trustees.

Of that group, the trustees were the most likely culprits. They were mostly semiretired, prominent businessmen, and none of them struck Hez as potential hackers, but they were talkers. Could one of them have told about Hez and Bruno's exploits at a tailgate party or similar event? Hez had sworn them to secrecy before briefing them, but it was a good story and they might have "forgotten" their promise. If a greedy computer science professor or student overheard the tale, that could explain both the blackmail and why Hornbrook immediately tried to force Hez and Bruno to solve his problem.

Could they do it in time? Hez's gut told him catching the blackmailer was the key to rescuing Savannah and Simon, but they had less than thirteen hours to do it.

What would happen to Savannah and Simon if they failed?

He closed his eyes and tried to push away the dark images crowding his mind. "Dear God, please keep them safe."

His phone buzzed with a text from Martine: Meet me at the Campbell Motel. Room 26.

He frowned. The Campbell Motel was a cheap old motel on Highway 98 that catered to truckers and migrant laborers. Why did Martine want to meet him there? Was she deliberately trying to sabotage his relationship with Savannah? Something had seemed off in all his meetings with her, but she had provided him with valuable information about Hornbrook. Maybe she would do it again, but he had to be on his guard around her. He texted: Pick another place.

I'll wait here for fifteen minutes, then I'm gone and so is my information.

He sighed, grabbed an umbrella from the desk, and headed out to his truck. The rain increased as he drove to the Campbell Motel, and so did his fear. The tantalizing clues Martine had given him in the past wouldn't be enough this time. He needed clear and complete answers to his questions. Where were Simon and Savannah? Who was blackmailing Hornbrook? If they didn't get solid information fast, Savannah and Simon would die.

Hez pulled into the Campbell Motel. The weedy, cracked asphalt parking lot was mostly empty. Green-painted doors faced the lot under an overhanging eave. The lot held a few older pickups, a black Ford Taurus with primer spots and blue doors, and a little red Jaguar coup outside room 26. He parked next to the Jaguar and got out, not bothering with the umbrella.

He jogged a few steps until he was under the motel's eaves, then slowed to a walk. He glanced up and down the row of rooms. Was someone hiding in the overgrown hedge at the edge of the lot? Before he could be sure, room 26's door flew open and Martine took his hand and pulled him inside.

She shut the door and stood with her back to it. She wore spike heels and a black cocktail dress that left little to the imagination. Her thick blonde hair tumbled down her shoulders onto her chest, and her full lips wore bright red lipstick. Her enticing perfume wafted to him. She stared at him, panting.

He backed away and glanced around the room. The sheets on the double bed were pulled back and rumpled. An empty wine bottle and two used glasses stood on the bedside table. An open box of condoms lay beside them.

Hez's pulse thundered in his ears. This was a setup of some kind, but he couldn't worry about that now. "What is this?" He took a step back. "Whatever your game is, forget it. I need answers and fast. Someone has kidnapped Savannah and Simon. Who's your client, Martine? I need that name."

Her eyes filled with tears. "I'm sorry." She jerked open the door and ran out.

Hez followed, determined to get information that would help him find his family, but she jumped into the Jaguar, started the engine, and roared out of the parking lot.

Hez scrambled into his truck and gunned the engine to life. He started to back out but then stopped. He could never catch her Jag, but he would waste precious time trying. Every minute counted, and he needed to get back to the Justice Chamber. He looked toward the hedge. The shape he had seen there was gone.

He put the truck in Drive and headed back to TGU, his mind whirling.

CHAPTER 20

A WOMAN ABOUT SAVANNAH'S AGE CARRIED A STAINLESS-steel tray of food toward the porch of the small house where Savannah sat playing Uno with Simon. Colored beads snaked through the woman's hair, and a red-and-white ruffled skirt fluttered around her ankles. She was beautiful with dark eyes, but she didn't smile or even glance their way.

She set the metal pan on the table and walked back the way she'd come. Savannah stood and caught a whiff of chorizo and cheese. A basket held small rounds of some type of bread on one side of the tray, and small containers of chorizo, black beans, mozzarella cheese, avocado chunks, pickled onions, and jalapeños were on the other side.

"That smells good." Simon reached for a bread round. "They have slits at the top like pita bread. Maybe we're supposed to stuff them."

"I think they're arepas. They're a traditional Venezuelan food I've heard of." She picked up a piece of bread. "I think these are made with corn flour. I'll prep one for you."

"I want to do my own." Simon slid small spoonfuls of each of the ingredients into the pocket of his bread and took a bite. His eyes widened. "Bussin'," he mumbled past his full mouth.

She prepped one for herself and the explosion of flavors had her reaching for another one right away. The morning's coffee was the last thing she'd put in her stomach, and she'd saved the breakfast pastries for Simon. At least Hornbrook wasn't starving them. She wouldn't mind a shower and a change of clothing, though. The lack of normal supplies wasn't a good indication of their expected longevity.

Anton approached with his usual grim expression. He jerked his thumb toward the main house. "The boss wants to see you." He eyed Simon and the dogs begging for a bite of food at his feet. "Alone."

Her gut clenched, and she wiped the juice from her fingers with a napkin before following him across the oyster-shell path dappled with late-afternoon sunlight. Had Hez replied to Hornbrook's demands yet? She slowed her steps, but Anton grabbed her arm and propelled her faster toward their destination.

She jerked her arm out of his grasp. "I can walk by myself."

"Step up the pace or I'll drag you."

She clenched her hands and quickened her steps. The theme music from *Jaws* greeted her when she opened the door to the house. A shudder went down her back at the grin Anton directed her way, and she remembered Hornbrook's threat about feeding Simon to the sharks. She crossed the mahogany floors to the living room.

Hornbrook rose from the leather sofa. His cold, appraising gaze swept over her. "Your fiancé hasn't complied with my demands yet, and I think he needs a reminder of what he stands to lose."

"Why are you doing this?" she burst out. "Hez planned to leave you alone. It was over as far as he was concerned. He didn't want a war with you."

"I didn't start this war—you have Hez to blame for your situation. His ransom demand set it in motion."

Ransom demand? "It couldn't have been Hez. We just wanted to get on with life and forget all about you."

"Did you really think you could hold me hostage for twenty million dollars and demand debt relief for TGU without repercussions? I'm sure Hez thought I'd roll over at the next demand of five million, but he was wrong. It's time to eliminate the threat altogether."

Savannah took a step back as the obnoxious music continued to play. "It wasn't Hez. Maybe someone in your own organization thought he'd implicate Hez and fleece you for money."

"My staff wouldn't dare cross me like that. They've seen what I do to my enemies." He shrugged. "At any rate it doesn't matter now. At some point I would have had to ensure there weren't copies of that database floating around, waiting to blindside me. You and the boy are perfect leverage to make sure Hez and Bruno destroy all the copies. His time is running out—and so is yours."

Savannah considered her options. As soon as Hornbrook was assured the copies of the database were gone, he'd have to remove the risk that she and Simon presented. He couldn't trust they wouldn't testify against him, and he'd make sure their bodies were never found.

She laced her hands together and smiled when two of his goldens approached. "These guys are gorgeous. The fact you take care of dogs that are left behind makes me think you might be a man of your word."

Hornbrook's eyebrows rose, and he smiled for the first time. "My grandfather raised award-winning golden retrievers, and I learned to appreciate dogs from him. They're loyal, love their people, and never lie—except about whether they've been fed. Every dog that sets foot on this island is well treated and safe. Including your two."

Savannah forced a chuckle. "I appreciate hearing that. My dogs are important to me too. I recently picked up a rescue named Cass that's afraid of Cody and Marley, so she wasn't with us when we went on our walk. I hope she's okay."

Hornbrook shuffled papers and glanced at his Rolex before turning a computer monitor to face her. "Enough chitchat. Read the headline and say the words *twelve hours* when you're done."

She'd prepped all afternoon for this moment. She read the headline. "Yankees Beat Mets 6–3." She paused and cleared her throat. "Hez, take care of our new puppy, 'kay? Take care of Cass, 'kay?" She slurred the words slightly as though she was nervous. "I'll see you soon, 'kay? Twelve hours."

Now that she'd delivered her lines, it felt impossible that Hez would get what she was trying to tell him. The ominous music from *Jaws* swelled to a crescendo. If Hez didn't figure it out, she and Simon would be food for the sharks.

"Focus!" Hez leaned back in the Justice Chamber's lone decent chair and shook his head so hard that he got a warning twinge from the still-healing surgical site on the left side of his skull. But he couldn't shake the memory of Martine out of his brain. He needed to devote every neuron to saving Savannah and Simon—not analyzing the incident at the Campbell Motel. That would have to wait. And yet his mind wouldn't let it.

What had happened at the motel? It had the trappings of a secret tryst—the cheap motel, Martine's dress and makeup, the wine—but Martine hadn't even tried to seduce him. She apologized and ran as soon as he was in the room demanding answers. Why? The only explanation that made sense was that the whole thing was a setup. But what exactly had been set up? Presumably, the room had been staged to make it appear they'd been having an affair—but was that all? Did Martine flee the room so it would look like Hez attacked her? And was that shape in the hedges a photographer? Had there been a camera hidden in the room too?

Hez shook his head again, more carefully this time. He inhaled—and got a whiff of Martine's perfume from his TGU sweatshirt. He tore it off and hurled it across the room. It hit the opposite wall and slid down, landing in a heap on the floor. None of this was important now when he needed to find Savannah and Simon.

His phone buzzed—and all thoughts of Martine vanished when he saw the name on the screen: Hornbrook. Hez tapped the recording app Hope had asked him to put on the phone, then took the call. "Hez Webster."

"You're down to twelve hours." Hornbrook's cold tone came

through despite the voice-altering software. “Did you finish the jobs I gave you?”

Hez licked his lips. “We’re making progress. We’ve destroyed all copies of the database, just like you asked. We’re closing in on the blackmailer, too, but we need more time.”

“You don’t have it.”

“Let me talk to Savannah. How do I know she and Simon are still alive?”

“They’re still alive—for the moment.” Another recording of Savannah reading a current headline, followed by the ominous words “twelve hours.”

The line went dead.

Hez played the recorded conversation twice to make sure he caught every nuance. Savannah’s voice was a dagger in his heart, but it was more than that. She was telling him something more than Hornbrook intended—but what?

Hez forwarded the recording to everyone who’d been at the last meeting, including a Zoom link in the email. Then he opened the Zoom meeting and waited, his mind racing.

Bruno’s bald head appeared first, followed a few seconds later by Hope and Michael. Ed, Dominga, and Toni were probably in class. There was no time to wait for them.

Hez jumped right in. “Savannah left clues for us in that last message. She doesn’t have a dog named Cass, and something was off about how she was talking.”

Hope’s brow furrowed. “Off? How exactly?”

“She kept saying ‘’kay’ and she slurred her words. She worked hard on her diction when she started teaching, and it’s instinctive for her now. She doesn’t normally talk like that.”

Michael grunted. "Think she's drunk or drugged?"

Hez thought for a moment. "It's possible, I guess, but that doesn't explain why she's asking me to take care of a fictional dog."

Hope leaned her cheek against her hand. "I also have some clues to add to the mix. The FBI did an acoustic analysis on the first message and picked up what sounded like seagulls and possibly waves in the background."

"So they might be near a beach." Michael rolled his eyes. "That doesn't mean much around here."

Hez snapped his fingers. "Yes, it does! I'll bet she's on a cay. There are lots of private islands and cays in the Caribbean. We stayed on Fowl Cay during our honeymoon. She wasn't saying 'okay.' She was saying 'cay.'"

"Maybe." Michael scratched his jaw. "What about the dog thing?"

"Oh." Hope tapped her keyboard. "There's a group of islands called the Dog Islands. Maybe she's there."

Michael nodded slowly. "Could be."

Bruno cocked his head and frowned. "Dunno. She said to take care of a dog named Cass, which seems weirdly specific if she's just trying to get us to think of dogs. Is one of the Dog Islands named Cass or something?"

Hope typed some more, then sat back. "No, and there's no town called Cass on any of them."

"Wait—let's listen to exactly what she said." Hez played the message again. "She's really only slurring her words when she says 'care of Cass.' Maybe she's running them together on purpose. She's actually saying 'care-a-Cass.'"

Michael frowned. "So what does that mean?"

No one responded.

Bruno chuckled. "I had an uncle in Chicago who thought Care-a-cass was the capital of Venezuela." His eyes widened. "Hold on a sec!" His hands flew over his keyboard so fast that his typing sounded like static. "Ha! Bet I found 'em!"

"Where?" Hez and Michael asked simultaneously.

Bruno's face split into a wide grin. "Private island about ten miles off the coast of Venezuela, near Caracas. It's owned by a shell company controlled by Hornbrook."

Hez punched the air. "Yes! We can contact the Venezuelan authorities and— What's wrong?"

Hope was shaking her head and grimacing. She sighed. "The Venezuelans don't cooperate with us at all. They hate American law enforcement—partially because we've arrested some of their government officials for drug smuggling and other crimes. If we ask for their help, we'll be lucky if they just ignore us. More likely, they'd send forces out to the island to protect it against Yankee intervention."

Michael reddened. "So we don't ask! We send in the Marines, take out Hornbrook, and get my grandson!"

Hez felt a migraine forming behind his eyes. "The Marines won't do that, Michael. They'd be invading another country. It would be an act of war."

"He's right." Hope seemed to deflate. "Hornbrook is in Venezuelan territorial waters. The American government can't do anything. You're on your own. I'm sorry."

Hez exchanged a long look with Michael.

"I have someone who can help us," Michael said. "He used to work for the CIA, and he owes me a favor. Flight time is six hours, plus an hour or two to get to the island. Grab your passport and Savannah's and Simon's as well. I'll call my friend on the way and have him get his team together. It's a tight timeline, but we have to make it work."

Whatever his faults, Michael's love for Simon just might save Savannah and Simon this time.

CHAPTER 21

"SAVANNAH."

Hez's voice was a sure sign Savannah was dreaming, and she buried her face in the pillow. She didn't want to be pulled from a pleasant dream and face the fact that she and Simon were likely to be herded aboard a boat to be tossed off for a shark snack.

A hand shook her. "Babe, we have to get out of here."

Hez's harsh whisper jolted her awake, and she opened her eyes to blink the sleep away. A form moved in the faint glimmer of moonlight through the gauzy curtains of the cottage. Was she still dreaming?

But no, Hez's strong hand grabbed her arm and tugged. She sat up and glanced around. Simon still slept in the other bed, and both dogs came toward her with tails wagging.

She licked her lips. "Hez, it's really you?"

He tore off the black mask so she could see his face, grim with determination. "I'm getting Simon, and you corral the dogs. The guards will be coming any minute. Hurry."

She swung her feet to the floor and patted her thigh for the dogs to come to her, while Hez moved to Simon's side and roused him. The boy woke up instantly and didn't ask questions. He and Hez followed her to the door, and they stepped out onto the porch. Armed figures in dark clothing and black masks stood guard watching the area, and for a moment she thought they were Hornbrook's men. But one of them put his finger to his lips and gestured for her to go with him.

She raced after him with Hez and Simon on her heels. Three other men brought up the rear. The shell path to the beach bit into her bare feet, but she barely noticed as she raced for the inflatable Zodiac boat that bobbed in the surf ahead of them.

Hez caught up with her and pushed her nephew toward her. "Get Simon to the Zodiac."

She paused to grab Simon's hand as Hez dropped behind her and raised his gun. Her feet left the shell pathway and sank into soft sand. When the salty breeze hit her face, she felt the first surge of hope that they might escape. Before she could relish the burst of optimism, four men, two on each side, leapt from the shadows.

Cody barked ferociously, then snarled and ran at the closest of the two men, who kicked Cody away. Cody yelped but leaped back into the battle.

"Leave my dog alone!" Simon tore his hand free from hers and ran at Hornbrook's men. Marley snarled and followed the boy.

Hornbrook's top goon grabbed Simon and yanked him away. Simon's kicks and punches did nothing to deter Anton as he and the other guard hauled Simon toward the main house.

"Get to the Zodiac!" Hez shouted to her. "I'll get Simon." He ran after the men with his gun up.

The three other rescuers ran after him, and Savannah pivoted to see Anton and two other guards disappear into the mansion with Simon. The dogs barked helplessly outside the heavy oak door.

Gunfire rang out, and Hez and the other men hit the manicured turf as bullets zinged over their heads. Hez would be hampered by being unable to return fire with Simon in the fray. They scrambled into the shadows and got to their feet. Hez tucked his gun away before he and the other men disappeared around the corner of the house.

She waded into the waves, and warm water lapped at her legs. She clambered aboard the rubber boat and grabbed the oars instead of starting the engine, which would alert Hornbrook's men to her approach. The tide was going out, so it was an easy maneuver to navigate it to the end of the pier on the far side of the house. She grabbed hold of the bottom rung on the pier's ladder, pulled herself up, and threw a rope around a piling so the Zodiac wouldn't float off. Heart pounding, she ran toward the house.

Gunfire still echoed above the sound of the surf, but it came from the other side of the building and didn't seem to be aimed at her. Still, the dock was well lit, and if anyone saw her she'd be an easy target.

She reached the house. Back flat against the stucco exterior, she gulped and listened. Voices came from inside, but no more gunshots. Crouching low, she tried the door. It opened into a small room with life vests and other boating equipment. An unlit hallway stretched away into shadows. She had to find Simon and Hez, but she couldn't call out without alerting Hornbrook and his men.

She crept along the darkened passage, listening for any hint of movement. Her skin crawled every time she passed a door.

They were fighting on Hornbrook's turf and she hated it. It seemed to take forever to creep along the passage and search the nooks and crannies as she went. Where were they?

"Aunt Savannah." Simon's whisper was just ahead.

She spotted him crouched down behind a chair with his arms around the dogs. She didn't see Hez and the other rescuers. Her heart squeezed at the thought that Hez might already be shot. The gun battle had raged for several minutes. Was everyone else dead?

Please, God, no.

She reached her nephew and buried her face in his hair, smelling of little boy as she embraced him. "Have you seen your uncle Hez?"

He nodded toward a side passage. "He's somewhere down there. I got away from the guards and hid here. The dogs found me when Uncle Hez and the other guys were able to get into the house. He shot one of the guards, but I don't know where he is now. The guys with him will keep him safe. I think they're CIA or something."

Her mind filled with a horrific image of Hez lying dead in a pool of blood. She shook it away. The thought could paralyze her, and she had to find him. "Stay here. I'll be back soon."

She edged along the hallway and passed through a large open room. Marley followed her despite her whispered order to stay with Simon. She spotted several motionless figures face down on the rich carpet. The acrid smell of gunsmoke hung in the air. It was too dark to determine if they were Hornbrook's men or the rescuers. She squinted in the dark. Where were Hez and Hornbrook?

The hall turned a corner and she heard shouted curses from

that direction. Hornbrook's voice. Bright light poured from an open door. Blinking and crouching low, she moved that way and spotted two figures struggling on the floor of a small room lined with racks of wine bottles.

Hornbrook, his face distorted in a fierce snarl, was on top of Hez with both hands around Hez's neck.

Hez clawed at Hornbrook's fingers with his right hand. A red puddle spread out from under Hez's left shoulder.

She had to help him, but how? She needed a weapon! She ran into the room and yanked a bottle from one of the shelves. Hez's face was nearly purple now, and she slammed the bottle down with all her strength on top of Hornbrook's head. It shattered, then he toppled over onto his side and his hands fell off Hez's throat.

Hez choked in a gasp of air, and Savannah started to go to his side, but Marley let out a snarl. A volley of frantic barking followed, and she turned to see Hornbrook, his face a grimace of hate and rage, getting to his hands and knees.

She swung the shattered bottle, hitting him in the neck. Blood fountained from a severed artery.

Hornbrook grabbed his neck and tried to stagger to his feet, but he collapsed and lay motionless.

She rushed to kneel by Hez and helped him sit up and lean against her. The solid feel of him against her brought tears of relief rushing to her eyes, and she hugged him.

He gasped in oxygen. "Simon?" he whispered.

"He's safe." She glanced at the blood pooling under Hornbrook's head. "I think Hornbrook is dead."

He noticed her weapon and gave a faint grin. "Never thought a wine bottle would save my life." He pulled away and tried to stand. His face was pale, and the bullet had torn through the outside of his shoulder. "Let's get out of here. There might be more guards on the way."

She helped him up. "This way."

They reached Simon's hiding place. "Uncle Hez, you're okay!" He ran to hug Hez around the waist. "You saved us."

Hez winced as he put one arm around Simon. "Thank your aunt Savannah. She let us know where you were." He shot a tender and proud glance her way.

Two men in black burst into view. "Let's get out of here. I think we eliminated all four of them. This way."

They left the house and hurried down the pier. The Special Ops guys steadied the Zodiac for them to climb aboard. Hez pointed out a fishing boat's lights ahead. "We're joining up with that fishing boat."

The little craft's powerful engine rapidly closed the distance to the fishing vessel. Savannah squinted in the dark and gaped at the figure standing at the rail. Michael? She couldn't wait to hear about the chain of events that had led to this moment. God had to have orchestrated it.

Michael leaned over the rail and waved. "Thank you for saving my grandson." His voice was choked. "Now let's get out of here and back on solid ground."

Hez leaned against the gunwale in the fishing boat's darkened bow with Savannah snuggled against his right side. The little ship chugged along at what he guessed was top speed, sending a gentle sea breeze over them. The fresh salty scent was a welcome change from the smell of rancid fish in the muggy cabin.

The captain had switched off the lights as soon as they returned from Hornbrook's island to make the small ship less visible to Venezuelan authorities. The night was moonless but clear, and the Caribbean stars hung so low that Hez thought he could almost reach up and grab one.

"You were amazing back there," she said, her voice barely audible above the rush of water against the hull. They were alone, but the boat was small.

He stroked her cheek. "You too." All he could manage was a hoarse whisper through his damaged vocal cords. "Hornbrook tackled me after I got this." He touched his now-bandaged left shoulder. "If you hadn't taken him out, I'd be dead on the floor of his walk-in wine fridge." He gave her a squeeze. "I'm glad you didn't stay in the Zodiac like I asked."

She shivered despite the blood-warm air. "I don't want to think about what could have happened—or what did happen. I-I'm glad I stopped him, but the blood . . ." She stopped and swallowed. "I keep seeing it in my head."

"He chose his path, babe. If you hadn't been there, I'd be dead instead."

She looked up at him, her face ethereal and silver in the starlight. Her eyes glimmered with tears. "God brought us through safely. And I'm so thankful. I'm never going to let you go."

He bent and pressed his lips against hers. He wasn't aware of anything except her—the taste of her lips, the feel of her against him.

At last their lips separated and she rested her cheek on his shoulder with a contented sigh. She lifted her head a moment later. "How did you do it? How did you arrange this boat, the rescue team, all of it?"

"To be honest, I didn't. I brought my own gun, but that's about it. This is almost all Michael. As soon as we figured out your clues, he got on the phone. He seems to have many, uh, business connections, including a former CIA guy who pulled in more help. Michael called in a lot of favors to make this happen."

"He really cares for Simon."

He held her tighter and kissed the top of her hair. "So do we."

Hez stared up into the Milky Way, unnerved by the words they had just spoken. Michael cared enough about Simon to launch a deadly raid on Hornbrook's island. Five men lay dead back there because of how much Michael cared. And Hez and Savannah cared at least as much as Michael. How far would they go to do what was best for Simon? How far would Michael go?

Hez fingered his throbbing shoulder. He'd already taken one bullet in this fight. Would he take another? And would Michael fire it?

CHAPTER 22

THE SERENITY OF THEIR NEW HOME USUALLY SOOTHED SA-vannah, but she couldn't sit on the sofa and relax. She stood at the picture window looking out at Mobile Bay. The waves were huge today, battering their bit of land and foaming over the weathered boards of the pier. Simon should be here with them. He'd be chattering away and talking to Cody like he was a person. He'd want to go out after the waves subsided and search for shells. He'd be calling for her to make him fish and chips or one of his other favorite meals.

The house wasn't home without him. She started pacing again.

Hez set aside his yellow pad of paper and patted the sofa beside him. "Sit down, babe." Even after three days his voice was still hoarse. "You're going to wear the finish off our floors."

She sighed and dropped onto the cushion beside him. His throat was a swollen mass of black and purple. She'd never forget the sight of his face as Hornbrook choked the life out of him. He put his arm around her, and she leaned against him. "You don't think they're coming back, do you?"

He pressed his lips against her temple. "I hope they are.

Simon is due back to us tomorrow. Michael knows we get him on the weekends."

"Like he cares what the laws says." She reached for her phone on the coffee table. "I'm going to call Simon."

Her nephew picked up immediately. "Hi, Aunt Savannah. How's Cody? I'm amped to see him."

She'd never been so glad to hear her nephew's voice, and he seemed happy. "He's eager to see you, buddy. What time are you coming home?"

"Pawpaw is dropping me off at eight. Can you fix pancakes?"

They were back in the country. She closed her eyes and exhaled with relief. "You bet."

"Bussin'." A man's voice spoke in the background. "We're leaving for dinner, um, and Pawpaw said to remind you that Uncle Hez can't be there . . ." Simon's voice trailed off. "That's crazy. The judge shouldn't have done that."

Savannah bit her lip. "Have fun at dinner, and I'll see you in the morning." She tossed the phone onto the table, but she wanted to hit something. "They're in town and Michael said to remind us you can't be here."

Hez's smile fell away. "That's not something I'm likely to forget."

"This can't go on, Hez. Simon wants to see you. We need to figure out a way to make peace between us all. It's what's best for Simon."

"I've been thinking about that too. Michael cashed in a lot of chips on the rescue, and there's emotion in that grizzled heart of his. He really loves Simon. I thought he only wanted him because he hates us, but he showed me I was wrong. Yeah, he's a bayou crime boss, but we owe him." Hez pulled her close against his side and nuzzled her neck. "I owe him. If not for his connections and determination, you and Simon would be fish food."

She kissed him, soaking in his scent. "Don't remind me of that. I'll never see the ocean the same again." She started to kiss him again, then bolted upright. "Wait a minute. What about that money meant for the neonatal unit, the funds my dad diverted into his trust fund?"

He gave her a quizzical look. "What does that have to do with Simon?"

"If we're going to make peace with Michael and his family, maybe we can start by righting an old wrong. The Willards donated millions to build that center in memory of Winona, and Dad basically stole it. Can we get it back?"

"Nice try, but the statute of limitations has run. He got away with the theft. Besides, Pierre's trust doesn't have much in it after the Justice Chamber and Jess finished cutting off his illicit income streams."

Hearing her sister's name was sweet torment. No one mentioned her much, and Savannah wished she could talk over the current dilemma with Jess. But her heart knew what Jess would say. "We have the funds to build it anyway. We'll finish Legare Hall and do some maintenance, and there will still be money left over to do the right thing. It's right for TGU and right for Simon and the Willards. And it just might rebuild some bridges that were burned down a long time ago."

"Are you sure, babe? That's a lot of money. And you wanted to be married in the chapel on campus. You'll have to focus your efforts on the new unit."

"We can get married on the beach. I'll get to work on making arrangements. I have a lot to make up for. I'm going to call Helen." Savannah reached for her phone again, and her hand trembled as she placed the call.

"Savannah?" Helen's voice was cautious. "What do you want?"

At least the Willard matriarch hadn't hung up on her. "Helen, I was going through some old journals and discovered what my dad did to you, how he stole money meant for a neonatal unit in memory of your daughter. I'm so sorry, and I want to make amends. I'm going to build it."

"Y-you're going to build the unit? Is this some kind of joke?"

"I wouldn't joke about something like that. I'm ashamed of what my dad did, and I want to do the right thing. We'll name it after your daughter and pray we save women in the same circumstances."

Silence answered her. Savannah pulled the phone back and looked at the screen. They were still connected. "Helen?"

"I don't believe you," the older woman spat out. "This is some kind of trick to get access to Simon, isn't it? I know the games you Legares play, but I'm not stupid."

This time when the phone went dead, no one was on the other end.

Hez switched off the power washer and stood back to survey the results. The cobblestone patio and firepit seemed fresh and new after he'd blasted away the years of grime. Once the sea breeze blew away the dampness, he would put out the new Adirondack chairs and matching table. It would be the perfect spot for a romantic dinner as they watched the sun set over Mobile Bay. He'd spent the weekend working so he didn't miss Savannah and Simon so much. He hadn't seen his nephew in over a week, not since the rescue.

Savannah had to spend the afternoon at the university, but she'd promised to be back by seven. It would be their last evening together for a few days because Michael was dropping off Simon at Savannah's cottage in the morning, so Hez wanted to make it a little special. He had shrimp bisque and crab cakes ready to go on the stove and in the oven, plus Savannah's favorite garden salad in the fridge.

He smiled at the thought of her coming home and seeing dinner—or no, she'd smell it first. She'd walk in the door, catch the scent of cooking seafood, and light up with a smile that would make those gorgeous green eyes dance. It would be a perfect evening.

A vehicle turned into the driveway. Hez frowned. Savannah wouldn't be back for over an hour and the deep-throated engine didn't sound like her Civic. He walked around the side of the house and saw a black Denali.

The cab opened and Michael stepped out. He spotted Hez and walked over, carrying a thick envelope in one hand. "How's the shoulder healing?"

"Fine. I'll have an interesting scar, but that's all. What can I do for you?"

Michael looked him in the eye. "It's time to end this fight over Simon. It's not good for anyone."

Hez's brows went up. Maybe Savannah's olive branch had worked. "I agree. What did you have in mind?"

"After what happened with Hornbrook, you should withdraw your adoption petition."

Hez shook his head. "No way."

Michael pressed his mouth into a thin line and blew out through his nose. "Simon could have died, Hez. And this isn't the first near miss. Or the second. He's in danger whenever he's around you or Savannah."

"Hornbrook was the danger, not us."

Michael nodded toward the water. "Did Hornbrook let Simon almost drown out there?"

Hez winced internally at the memory. "We're keeping him away from water, just like the judge ordered. If you want to discuss some sort of shared custody, we'll be flexible. But we won't give up Simon. We love him and we won't let him go. His mother—your own daughter—wanted Savannah to raise him. Why won't you respect Jess's wishes?"

"Keep her name out of your mouth!" A vein stood out on Michael's neck. He tapped the envelope against his jeans. "You've got more at stake here than custody of Simon. A lot more."

Hez was glad he'd started carrying his Glock whenever he was out here. "What exactly do you mean?"

Michael held out the envelope. "I know you've worked very hard to repair your relationship with Savannah. It would be a shame to throw away all that."

Hez opened the envelope. It contained a stack of pictures of Martine and him. The first showed them at the beach—she carried her shoes in one hand and had her other arm around him. His arm curled around her waist. In the second they sat very close to each other at the Seabreeze Saloon, and he had a half-empty mojito in front of him. The third picture was also from the Seabreeze and showed her kissing his cheek. The next photos showed him pulling into the Campbell Motel, Martine holding his hand and taking him into the room, and—

Hez gasped. "These are fake!"

Michael grinned. "There's security camera video from the bar and motel corroborating those pictures."

"Not those last ones!" The pieces clicked into place. "You're Martine's mysterious client. You've been using her to set me up."

Michael sighed. "Face the facts, Hez. If you and Savannah keep trying to take away my grandson, these are going to come out in court. It can't be in Simon's best interests to have parents whose marriage is on the rocks before it even begins."

Hez threw the pictures on the ground and thrust a finger in Michael's face. "You're not going to blackmail me!"

Michael's right hand went to his hip, pulling back his jacket. A pearl-handled pistol hung at his belt. "Careful."

Every muscle in Hez's body trembled with rage. He wanted to smash in Michael's face or even pull his own gun and see just how fast Michael could draw—but the rational part of his brain kept his hands at his sides. He glared at Michael. "Get off my property, pond scum."

Michael chuckled and stepped back slowly toward his truck. He opened the door and got in, then turned back to Hez. "Do the smart thing, Counsel." He shut the door and drove away.

CHAPTER 23

SAVANNAH PULLED INTO THE DRIVEWAY OF THEIR SOON-TO-be-together home and smiled. The sight was just what she needed after a day of interviewing applicants to replace Jess, followed by a meeting of the board of trustees. Lights sparkled through the prisms of the big front window in a welcoming burst of color. Lights glowed from the folly as well, which drew her gaze out toward the dock stretching into the waves with the sunset glimmering on them.

Hez had thought of everything, and she wished Simon could be with her to see it—though the thought of a romantic evening alone with Hez made up for it. She hated the armed-camp atmosphere that strained their relationship with her nephew. She feared he'd be awkward with her tomorrow morning when she got him after Michael had appeared as a rescuing hero.

She bounded up the steps with an anticipatory smile and opened the door to the mouthwatering aromas of garlic, butter, and seafood. "I smell shrimp bisque and crab cakes." Her voice faltered when she saw Hez's ashen face. "What's wrong? Is it Simon?"

He stepped nearer to take her hand. "I have something I need to tell you. I think we'd better sit down."

She eyed the envelope in his hand. Was it about the adoption? Had they lost?

He led her to the sofa and tugged her down with him onto the cushions. "Michael showed up an hour ago." Hez raked his hand through his hair. "I knew something was up, but I couldn't figure it out. I never expected anything like this."

"You're scaring me. What is it?"

"There are pictures." He swallowed hard and tried again. "Michael was so determined to stop our adoption petition that he hired Martine to help him blackmail us. He brought pictures of me with Martine and demanded we drop our suit or he'll use them in court."

Pictures? Hez's extreme reaction told her more than his words, and all thoughts of a romantic dinner vanished. He would never betray her, never. She clung to that belief. "I need to see them."

"I'd rather you didn't, babe. Some of them are fake and th-they look bad."

She held out her hand. "Now."

The first picture showed Martine, shoes in one hand against a beach background, gazing up at him with an adoring expression. Savannah focused on Martine's proprietary arm around Hez—like she had a perfect right to embrace him. Even worse, his arm curled around her trim waist. Savannah forced herself to the next picture and recognized the setting of it too—the Seabreeze Saloon. She winced at the half-empty mojito in front of him.

She shot an accusing glare his way. "Is this fake?"

He shook his head. "No, but I haven't touched a drop of liquor since I started AA."

She held on to the thin shred of hope that he hadn't and went to the next picture, also at the bar. Martine, eyes closed, kissed his cheek. He didn't seem to be objecting. Savannah flipped to the next picture, one at the door of a motel room. A seductive smile on her face, Martine led him through into the darkness inside. Pressure squeezed Savannah's heart, and she struggled to pull in oxygen. She didn't want to see the next pictures, but she forced herself.

The lurid photos of Hez and Martine in bed slammed into her brain. The last thing she saw before she shut her eyes against the onslaught of pain and disbelief was the birthmark on his bare hip. There was no mistaking the irregular star shape. Bile churned in her chest, but she managed not to vomit.

Hez's voice pushed past the roaring in her ears. "Those last pictures never happened, Savannah. I promise you. Look at me." His voice held pain.

She forced her lids open. "If those are the only faked photos, were the other ones real? You let her kiss you, you had your arm around her? You met her at a bar?"

"I didn't touch a drop of alcohol, I swear." His blue eyes begged her to believe him. "She was providing information about the case, and in every instance, she instigated inappropriate behavior, but I thought it was worth the risk if I could find Hornbrook. Then you and Simon were kidnapped, and I thought if I could talk to her client, I could find you."

He massaged the bridge of his nose. "I thought she was just flirting like she always does. It's never meant anything—she acts that way with all men. I had no idea she was on Michael's payroll and was providing blackmail pictures."

"You went to a motel with her, Hez. How was that ever okay? Didn't you see for one second how she manipulated you? Didn't the alarm bells ring even once?"

"Your lives were in danger! I realized it was a peculiar meeting place but went anyway, hoping it would lead to finding you. I swear to you those last pictures are fabricated. They're completely fake."

She wanted to believe him when his voice vibrated with passion and outrage, but how could she when the last pictures . . . She gulped and couldn't bring herself to see them again, so she shoved them at him. "Explain how Michael faked your birthmark! How would he know you had one?"

"I don't know how he faked that, but I know he did because this never happened." Desperation tinged his words. "I—I hadn't noticed the birthmark, but I would never do this, Savannah. In your deepest heart, you know I love you more than my own life. From the first moment I met you, I've never been interested in another woman. Not once."

Anger and hurt raged for control of her emotions, and she didn't know what to believe. "I can't talk to you right now. I'm going for a walk to decide if I've been wrong all this time about the man I love." Her voice wobbled, and she lurched to her feet and rushed for the door.

She didn't want to admit to herself she'd used the word *love* in present tense. If his betrayal ended up being true, it would rip the heart right out of her.

Michael took a long pull at his beer and put his feet up on the porch rail. He smiled as he watched Simon, Jack, and Olivia chasing lightning bugs in the late-evening shadows. They darted among the loblolly pines at the back of Michael's wide lawn, their high voices ringing in the cool air as they called out each new catch. They didn't seem at all tired, even though they'd spent the day fishing in the pond that glimmered through the trees and riding ATVs in the four-hundred-acre pine forest that stretched out around Michael's house.

Tammy, her curly dark brown hair blowing around her face, sat on a swing down by the pond with her boyfriend Austin. They were sipping sweet tea and keeping an eye on the younger children. Mama rocked on a well-cushioned chair on the porch, keeping an eye on Austin and Tammy.

Michael turned to his mother. "They remind me of Jess, Deke, and Little Joe when they were the same age."

She chuckled. "They put me in mind of you and David. I remember many a night watching you two chase lightning bugs."

"Some things never change, I guess."

Mama rocked in silence for a moment. "Didn't Marie write a poem about that?"

"About what?"

"Boys playing." Mama nodded toward the lawn. "I remember her sitting on this porch and watching my grandsons playing out there. She scribbled something in that little notebook she always carried. I thought it was a poem."

"It was." Michael reached for a well-thumbed volume on a little table. "It was published in her last book." He held the book in the light from a window, found the poem, and read it aloud:

Boys
Yelling, jumping, throwing, catching, fighting, laughing,
wrestling, fishing, swimming
Runningrunningrunningrunningrunning
Flop!
Lying on backs, green-smudged and gasping
Turning clouds to dinosaurs and rockets

Mama smiled and nodded. "I like her happy ones. I wish she wrote more of them."

"Me too, but she said a poet had to tell the truth." His mind went back to when she'd first told him that. It was a week after the poetry reading. He had "accidentally" run into her in the park where she regularly walked baby Savannah. He quoted one of her poems to her, charming her. They walked together and talked about poetry and TGU. She seemed to know nothing about how her husband's family had treated the Willards, and Michael didn't enlighten her. If she knew the truth, she might be more cautious around him, and he didn't want that.

He'd told her he was writing a poem for his mother's fiftieth birthday and asked for her help. It was a lie, of course, but he needed an excuse to meet her again. She agreed and they met several times to talk about Mama's life and go over drafts of the poem. When Michael told her about Winona's death, Marie was moved to tears—and wrote a verse on the spot that did the same to Michael. She had taken his hand as he wept over the new lines and old grief.

He should have known then that he was laying a trap for his heart as well as hers, but he had been young and stupid.

Mama shifted in her seat. "Savannah Webster called

yesterday. Says she's going to build that pregnancy center her daddy promised."

Michael stilled for several long moments. Building the neonatal center was the sort of thing Marie would have done if she were university president. Could Savannah have inherited her mother's heart? He batted the question away before taking another swig from his beer can. "Do you believe her?"

"Actions speak louder than words." The porch boards squeaked under Mama's rocker. "And we both know what Legare words are worth."

"That we do."

"It's probably just a trick to soften us up about Simon." She sighed. "Such a sweet boy. Too bad you have to take him back tomorrow."

Michael drained the can. "I may not have to."

She stopped rocking. "Why not?"

"Because staying here is best for him—and because I just made a persuasive argument to Hez Webster." He told her about the photos of Hez and Martine.

Mama was silent for a minute. "I don't like it."

"Why not?"

"It's underhanded, it's cruel. It's the kind of thing a Legare would do."

"So?" He crushed the can in his fist. "We're fighting Legares."

"But that doesn't mean we have to fight like Legares. We're better than that, better than them." She smacked him on the arm. "This isn't how Willards fight, boy."

"And look what happened to us. Every. Single. Time." He stood. "This is how Willards win, Mama."

He turned on his heel and stormed off the porch.

Blake savored the last spoonful of bisque and turned to Hez. "Ahh. You should patent this, man."

Hez forced a smile. "I'm glad someone is getting to enjoy it. I wasn't hungry after seeing those pictures, and I don't think Savannah was either."

Sympathy in his blue eyes, Blake set down his bowl and leaned against the newly installed black quartz kitchen counter. "She must've taken it pretty hard."

Hez's gut clenched as he remembered the shock and hurt in her face—and the anger. Her reaction was multiplied a hundredfold by betrayal—but he'd never cheat on her, never. "Yeah, she did. Thanks for coming over. I know things have been hectic at the Sanctuary."

"True, but Mom and Paradise have things under control for the evening. Besides, you know I'm always here for you—especially when you're making bisque."

Hez nodded toward the stack of photos on the kitchen table. "This feels like the wine bottle thing again. The only difference is this time I've got a shot at nipping it in the bud. Bruno is going to run some powerful AI-detection software on the fake pictures."

Hesitation clouded Blake's eyes. "Umm . . ."

"Um what?"

Blake cleared his throat. "Well, you never went to the Seabreeze Saloon to meet a wine bottle."

"If only that were true."

Blake laughed. "You know what I mean, Hez. I know you had

good intentions, but Martine obviously didn't. She's been raising red flags since she showed up. Not just the Seabreeze, but the thing on the beach and pretty much everything else she's done. And the Campbell Motel? As my aunt used to say, 'That place is for trucks and tramps, and I don't see eighteen wheels on her.'"

Hez winced. "I hadn't heard that one." He held his hands up in exasperation. "I didn't trust her, but what was I supposed to do? Savannah and Simon were in danger, and I was desperate to get some kind of handle on where to find them. She said I had fifteen minutes to get there or she was gone. I had no leads to follow and needed one."

Blake shrugged his muscular shoulders. "I don't know, man. I'm just saying that this isn't exactly like the wine bottle thing. There was nothing you could have done to prevent that."

Hez stared through the kitchen window into the gathering darkness outside. "Savannah said the same thing. I tried to apologize, but she stalked out."

"Keep trying. She deserves major groveling." Blake ladled another helping of bisque into his bowl. "Any idea how Michael's AI knows about your birthmark?"

Hez paced, his stocking feet silent on the hardwood floor. "No, and that's been bugging me."

"Maybe they got a picture while you were unconscious at the hospital."

"True. I had pants when I blacked out and none when I woke up." He pinched his lower lip as he evaluated the idea. "But I was in surgery or the ICU basically the whole time I was out. How could Michael or his minions get access to me?"

"Good question—and I don't have an answer. Just tossing out ideas."

"I appreciate it." Hez paused and wiped a tiny spot off the sparkling countertop. "I guess it doesn't matter. Once Bruno has results, we'll hopefully be able to prove those are fakes and put this whole thing in the rearview mirror."

Blake rubbed his forehead. "Don't count on it."

"Why not?"

"Because the non-AI pictures aren't great. Because Nova Cambridge is a small town. Because you're the husband of TGU's president. Because a lot of people like to gossip. Because they'd rather believe a sexy lie than a boring truth." Blake put a hand on Hez's shoulder. "Even if you can prove those last pictures are fake, I'm afraid this will get messy."

CHAPTER 24

THE COFFEE MACHINE HISSING IN THE DISTANCE AND THE hum of conversation in University Grounds tried to penetrate Savannah's thoughts, but nothing made it past the lurid pictures still residing there. She swallowed down the lump that kept trying to form in her throat. She hadn't slept much last night.

Nora reached across the table and squeezed her hand. "Try not to jump to conclusions, Savannah. Hez brought the pictures to you as soon as he got them. He didn't try to hide them and hope you wouldn't find out. That speaks to his integrity. And I'm sure he wasn't thinking straight when you were kidnapped. He's a smart guy. Under any other circumstances, he wouldn't have gone to the motel."

Savannah bobbed her head and picked up her cup, inhaling the aroma of her peppermint mocha. It did nothing for her agitation. She and her counselor had decided she'd progressed enough to stop appointments for now, but Nora had always been her best confidant. "That's one thing I'm clinging to. But Nora, that birthmark! If the picture was faked, how did they know about his birthmark?" Nausea churned in her stomach, and she set her coffee down without taking a sip. She wished she'd never seen that particular set of pictures.

She raised her gaze to Nora's. "Michael is ruthless about pushing us out of Simon's life, but I won't let him keep us away. He's my nephew, and Jess wanted me to raise him. Michael doesn't even have kids—what does he know about raising a child?" She rubbed her forehead. "I'm sorry—I know he's your uncle, but you're the only one I can talk to."

Now that Jess is gone.

The unspoken thought made her tear up. Jess wouldn't be as kind toward Hez as Nora was, but she had always been there for Savannah. Jess would let her rant and would get angry at Hez with her. Nora's calm presence was probably better for Savannah's peace of mind even if she'd rather pace and rage about it.

"Uncle Michael is no angel. But he loves Simon."

"His kind of love is one that gobbles up the recipient. Kids can't have too many people who love them. It's Michael's desire for revenge that's made him so determined to push us out."

"You have to find a way to resolve this with Hez."

Nora clearly didn't want to talk about her uncle, and Savannah decided to let it go. She'd already put her in an awkward position. "I'm trying not to jump to conclusions like I did with the wine bottle, but even if the pictures were staged, how could he be so stupid about Martine? It makes me so mad he walked right into her trap! I knew immediately what kind of person she is."

"His obsession with finding Hornbrook probably blinded him to the danger she posed."

Savannah rubbed the bridge of her nose. "Maybe. While

Hornbrook was out there, Hez knew we were all in danger. He was determined to get Hornbrook behind bars."

Nora stared down into her cup. "And sometimes it can be hard to do a complete one-eighty in how you deal with someone you've known for a long time, even if you know you should."

Savannah realized what she needed to do. "Then it's high time I dealt with her on my own since he can't."

Nora looked up. "What do you mean?"

"I'm going to confront her right now." Savannah pulled out her phone and searched for Martine. "I thought so. Her law office is down the street. Will you come with me?"

"You go, girl! I wouldn't miss the fireworks." Nora rose and grabbed her coffee. "Lead the way."

Savannah shoved back from the table and dropped her coffee cup in the trash on the way out. She didn't need to be more jittery. Her ire rose as they walked down the street toward a block of old Victorian buildings that housed several professional offices. They passed a diner wafting out the aroma of bacon before they reached Martine's block.

Martine's office was the last one, and Savannah marched toward the cute Victorian building painted creamy white with navy shutters. She'd make the woman admit what she'd done to Hez. But what if Martine offered up further proof? Savannah's nausea intensified. How had her bright hope for the future turned so dark?

Nora put her hand on Savannah's arm. "Wait up. Something's wrong." She pointed at the front of the building.

Savannah gasped at the police tape across the broken door hanging open several inches. The wood casing around the entry was splintered where someone had forced their way in. Had Martine been injured?

Savannah took a few steps closer and found red spray paint on the big front window. DEAD MAN WALKING. Was that a warning for Hez? Maybe Martine would know.

She fumbled for her phone from her purse and pulled up Martine's number, but the call wouldn't go through. "Her phone isn't working. Can you find out anything from the office?"

"I'm on it." Nora pulled out her phone and turned away to talk to her office.

Savannah hesitated to call Hez. Police might think she assumed he'd tried to hurt Martine.

Savannah's phone rang with *Unknown Caller.* She hit the silence button, then reconsidered. What if it was about Simon? She sighed and answered it. "Savannah Webster."

"Ms. Webster, my name is Tim Kramer, and I work with inmates here at Baldwin County Correctional Facility. I've been counseling Deke Willard, and he has become a Christian. He's quite insistent he needs to ask forgiveness from you and Mr. Webster. Would it be possible for you to come see him today? He's distraught and wants to get it off his chest before he's transferred."

Savannah glanced at the gaping front door to Martine's office. She might not be able to track Martine down today. "I think we can do that. I'll call Hez. What time?"

"Would later today work? Like maybe noon?"

It was only eight, so they had time to get there. "We can do that. If Hez can't make it, I'll have him text you."

"Thank you so much. See you then."

Nora dropped her phone back in her purse. "Martine has disappeared. Someone broke into her office, and it's trashed. Her computer is missing as well as her files."

Savannah's gut clenched tighter. "Was she kidnapped?"

"I don't think so. A security camera at her apartment building showed her leaving with a suitcase this morning. She seemed to be in a hurry."

"She fled?"

"That's the suspicion." Nora gestured to the phone still in Savannah's hand. "The call upset you. Anything I can help with?"

Savannah told her about the Kramer call. "I'd better call Hez and see if he's free, but we're not driving up together. I'm not ready to hear more lame excuses yet."

Hez walked into the Bay Minette jail visiting room. Savannah was already there, perched on the edge of a vinyl chair, eyes focused on the glass partition in front of her. She turned as he entered and gave him a perfunctory nod but no smile. He'd forwarded her a message from Bruno stating the X-rated pictures with Martine were faked, but she hadn't answered. He hadn't expected her to, not yet.

He sat beside her and shot her an apologetic glance, but she didn't seem to notice. She was watching the door at the back of the room on the other side of the partition. It opened and a few prisoners filed in under the watchful eyes of a pair of guards.

Deke Willard appeared younger and less threatening than Hez remembered. The last time Hez had seen him had been at

Deke's sentencing hearing. Deke had stood next to his attorney while the judge read the plea bargain with the DA's office and asked Deke if he agreed with it. Deke had fumed, flexing massive muscles as the judge spoke and spitting out curt responses. As one of Deke's victims, Hez had been only too happy to see him sentenced to life without possibility of parole.

Deke still had gorilla arms, and his shaggy brown hair touched the collar of his orange prison uniform, but he was clean-shaven and his eyes were clear and focused. He sat and reached for the phone on his side.

Hez nodded to Savannah as he brought the handset to his ear. She did the same, holding it in both hands.

"Hi, um, thanks for coming." Deke's voice was rough and nervous. "I think Pastor Tim told you I—I decided to become a Christian."

"He did, yes. We're glad for you," Savannah said.

Deke's gaze flicked between them. "Are you Christians too?"

Hez nodded. "We are."

Deke relaxed a fraction. "So you know what Jesus says about the truth settin' you free. Pastor Tim—he's the preacher I been talkin' to—he says that a lot. He asked me to pray on it, so I done that and, uh—" He cleared his throat. "Uh, the Spirit put on my heart that I should talk to you two."

Hez leaned forward. "What do you want to say to us?"

Deke licked his lips and stared at the scarred Formica counter in front of him. "Um, I did those things. I was there both times. That first night, I hit you in the head, Mr. Hez. And I'm the one that put the bag over your head, Ms. Savannah. And . . . well, you know it was me on the boat. You saw the cops pull off my mask. I feel really bad about it. I-I'm sorry, and I hope you can forgive me someday." The last sentence came out in a rush, as if he couldn't wait to get it over and done with.

The memories reached out from the shadows of Hez's mind and grabbed him. He relived the blow crashing into the left side of his skull as he had sat outside Beckett Harrison's house listening to Savannah's conversation with the former TGU provost. He, Savannah, and Simon woke up in the cemetery the next morning—an unsubtle warning about what would happen if they didn't stay away from Harrison and his artifact-smuggling ring. They hadn't, so Harrison and Deke kidnapped them again and took them out to the Gulf to kill them—and make it look like a murder-suicide where Hez killed Savannah and Simon. Hez could still feel the rough nonslip surface of the boat's deck under his cheek as he lay zip-tied, waiting for the killing shots. He could still see the helpless terror in Savannah's eyes.

Deke licked his lips again and jiggled his right knee as he watched their faces. His muscles twitched and his eyes held a mixture of fear and hope.

The career criminal sitting on the other side of that glass pane didn't deserve forgiveness. He'd attacked the love of Hez's life. He'd twice kidnapped a child. He'd been prepared to murder Simon, Savannah, and Hez in cold blood. And he didn't confess his crimes or ask forgiveness until he had nothing left to lose.

But Deke *had* asked for forgiveness—and who was Hez to refuse it? Ella's glassy, dead eyes stared up at him out of the deep waters of memory. He hadn't deserved forgiveness for her death. The boulder of guilt crushed him for years and nearly destroyed him. Would he even be here today without God's forgiveness—and Savannah's?

Hez's hand found Savannah's, and he held her fingers in a tight grip. "I forgive you, Deke. I've done some bad things in my life too."

Savannah's eyes filled and she gave a jerky nod. "I forgive you too, Deke."

Deke leaned back and ran his fingers through his shaggy mop of hair. "Thank you."

A detail from the first kidnapping popped into Hez's memory. "What about the Justin's peanut butter cups?"

Deke froze. "What do you mean?"

Hez's brain switched into lawyer mode. The peanut butter cups had been mentioned in the police file on Ella's death. That detail must have come from a police department insider: the PHPD mole. Deke must know who that was.

"I think you know exactly what I mean, Deke. You left Justin's peanut butter cups on Simon's chest at the cemetery during that first kidnapping. Why?"

The color drained from his face, leaving him a pasty white. "I—I don't remember." His gaze shifted away and revealed his lie.

Hez shook his head. "I can tell you're lying. God can tell too."

Deke's knuckles were white on the receiver. "I was just trying to scare you. I didn't mean nothin' by it." His voice shook and he still didn't look at them.

Hez raised his brows. "How did you know the candy would frighten us?"

A sob burst from Deke, and he covered his eyes with his free hand. "Because of her, the little girl."

Savannah clutched Hez's hand tighter. The trembling in her stomach moved up her back, and her vision dimmed. Ella? How did Deke know about their baby girl? Maybe he'd tell them the name of the mole inside the PHPD.

"Who told you about Ella and the peanut butter cups?" Hez's voice took on his stern prosecutor tone.

Deke's sobs grew louder. "I'm sorry, I'm sorry. We didn't want to kill her. We were just gonna keep her till we got the money. All the money the Legares stole. We thought we could get it back, doubled. We didn't mean to hurt your little girl."

Ice ran through Savannah's veins as his words penetrated. She forgot to breathe, forgot where she was in the horror that encased her. Her baby had died because of revenge? It had never been Hez's fault. Her father's corruption had begun the cascade of events that led to the loss of the most precious person in her life.

Hez didn't speak either, but his fingers tightened around hers in a death grip. His blue eyes stared out of his shocked white face.

"It wasn't supposed to happen that way!" Deke wailed. "I watched the family awhile and knew she didn't eat candy often, and when she did, you guys gave her that Justin kind. So I lured her out with it. We only planned to keep her long enough to get you guys to pay up. It all happened so fast—she slipped and fell in the pool. When she started screaming, the dog went crazy with barking. I—I panicked." He raked his hand through his hair. "I just ran. I'm sorry."

Savannah started to rise, but Hez's hand anchored her in place. "Y-you left her struggling in the water?"

Tears rolled down Deke's face. "I—I thought Mr. Hez would hear and come running, that she would be fine."

"Whose idea was it?" Hez asked in a wooden voice.

"Th-the man called my phone. He used somethin' to make his voice sound like a robot, so I don't know—"

Hez waved the answer away. "Never mind. Michael's fingerprints are all over this."

Deke stood and turned for the door. "Guard!" His shoulders shook with his sobs, and he glanced back one more time before the guard took him away. "I didn't mean for her to drown."

Though she hadn't been there, Savannah had imagined the scenario in graphic detail ever since her baby drowned. Over and over she saw Ella falling into that pool, heard Marley's barking, saw Hez's panicked rescue that failed to revive her.

Numbness traveled down her face to her arms, and her vision darkened again. She heard Hez shout her name before the merciful blackness moved in to claim her.

CHAPTER 25

HEZ STARED DOWN AT ELLA'S GRAVE. SAVANNAH STOOD beside him. Her sobs had subsided to sniffles, but her breathing was still shaky and ragged. He put his arm around her, and she leaned her head on his shoulder.

He had no idea how they'd gotten there. He vaguely recalled gathering her in his arms when she collapsed in the visiting room. Then they'd been in the parking lot, holding each other tight. And then he was driving through the countryside, not consciously aware of where he was going. He'd had one hand on the wheel, while the other grasped Savannah's. They must have left her car in the jail parking lot.

It was a beautiful day, which felt wrong and surreal. The sun hung high in a cloudless sky. A gentle breeze rustled the leaves of the ancient oak and tupelo trees, carrying the scent of wildflowers and newly mown grass. A bird sang somewhere. A single fresh red rose lay on Marie's grave.

Savannah hugged herself and rocked back and forth. "I don't know how to forgive him. I'm not sure I can."

"I know, babe." Hez crouched down and brushed a leaf from the little statuary grouping that marked Ella's resting place. Ella sat on his lap while Simon knelt beside her and smiled adoringly at her. Savannah sat on the sculpted grass on the other side looking toward the children, a peaceful smile on her stone face. “I could forgive Deke for trying to kill us. But Ella—” His voice broke and his vision blurred.

A kaleidoscope of images ran through his thoughts. Savannah holding newborn Ella in the hospital, Ella taking her first wobbly steps on chubby legs, Ella laughing and playing with Marley, Ella looking up at Hez with her blue eyes full of confusion as he tried to explain that “dog” and “God” were very different words.

Those same eyes staring at him, glassy and dead, as he desperately performed CPR on her by that swimming pool.

Savannah knelt beside him and put her arms around him. “Oh, Hez. You carried all that guilt around, but it wasn’t your fault. And you holding me tight by the hand during that ordeal with Deke made everything clear about those pictures. I believe in you. I know you would never cheat on me, never. You might be guilty of being too obsessed with justice, but most of the time it’s endearing. I love you.”

“I’m sorry.” He clutched her to his chest. “I don’t deserve you. I’ll try not to be so stupid ever again.” He wasn’t ready to let himself off the hook about Ella. He rested his hand on top of the headstone. “If I’d been paying attention to her like I should have, she’d still be with us.”

Savannah gave him a squeeze. “She’s with God.”

A new fear gripped Hez’s chest. He touched the statue of Simon. “But Simon is with Michael. We can’t let him hurt another child we love.”

Savannah froze for a heartbeat. “Do you really think Michael would hurt Simon?”

Hez swept his arm around the graveyard. “This cemetery

is full of people Michael hurt. He broke your mom's heart and drove her deeper into booze and pills. He fed Jess's hunger for vengeance until it led her into a very dangerous plot that wound up killing her. And now we know that Michael's scheming caused Ella's death too. He hurts everyone he touches, even the ones he claims to love."

Savannah pointed down the hill to the weedier Willard plot with its smaller monuments. "There are fresh graves down there too. How many deaths has Michael caused in his own family?" She bit her lip. "I wonder what Deke would have been like if he'd grown up without Michael's influence."

Resolve hardened in Hez's heart. "I won't let him destroy Simon too. I'm going to protect our boy like I should have protected Ella. And I'm going to get justice for our little girl, no matter what it takes."

Savannah tore her gaze away from the picture on her office desk at TGU. Ella's dimpled smile was imprinted on her mind forever. If she let herself dwell on what she'd learned from Deke, she'd be paralyzed today, and she needed to work. There was solace in doing what she loved so much, and she found it a place to forget her pain for a little while before it came swooping back. The grumble of the mower outside her window made for a soothing backdrop to the day, and the scent of grass wafted through her open window.

She moved her mouse and pulled up the progress reports on Legare Hall. Construction on the exterior and grand hall was on schedule for completion in three weeks, though the remainder of the building would be unfinished. HVAC, electrical, and plumbing would be completed next week, and construction on the other areas would start next month. She couldn't wait to walk across the mahogany floors and gaze into the dome overhead. It had been an eyesore for so many years, and the completion of the building would show the world the university wasn't only surviving—TGU was thriving.

Ella's picture caught her eye again, and she allowed herself to smile back into her daughter's blue eyes before reaching for her great-grandfather's drawings. She intended to fulfill his vision for details and decor in the hall. She studied the classical moldings in the main hall and snapped a picture of them for the carpenter she'd hired. When she set aside her phone, scrawled words in her great-grandfather's ornate script drew her attention. She'd never noticed his note tucked in the bottom right corner, and she situated the paper in the light to see it better.

Willard Hall, in honor of Joseph Willard and the longtime dean of students, Ezra Willard.

Her great-grandfather had never intended to name it Legare Hall. Her father had corrupted one more way to honor the Willards. Did the man have no shame whatsoever?

She picked up the framed picture of her baby girl, and rage gathered in her chest. "I have to stop him," she whispered. Pierre's ruthless drive to elevate his own position in life had left as much carnage in his wake as Michael's.

Her father's voice boomed through the screen window behind her, and she turned to see him berating the gardener for leaving clippings on the sidewalk. The poor man didn't speak English well and kept trying to explain he hadn't gotten out the blower for cleanup yet, but her father brushed off any explanation. His imperious voice and reddened face transported her to the cowering little girl she'd been. Her lip curled. The only emotion she had left for him was contempt.

Pierre left off haranguing the gardener and walked toward the entrance to the building. She set the picture back in its place, then rose and waited for him to appear with another demand for her to fund his trust. The blood roared in her ears, and she clenched her jaw so tightly a jab of pain shot through her head.

The door opened and her father, dressed in golfing clothes, stepped into her office. He'd always been bigger than life, forcing his way through every circumstance with his entitlement, and his presence soaked up the air in the room. His arrogant stare her direction raised her ire to the boiling point.

She lifted her chin and came around the side of her desk. "You are despicable. The price for your arrogance and greed was Ella's life! My baby girl was murdered because of you. It was no accident." What she'd learned from Deke flowed off her tongue like lava.

Her father's face went white as she laid out the plot. "W-what? How can you blame me for the Willards' treachery? They're a tribe of psychopaths."

She advanced toward him. "If you knew how dangerous they were, why did you cheat them out of millions of dollars? Don't bother trying to tell me you didn't do anything—I've seen the proof. You stole the money for the neonatal unit. Time after time you defrauded them. How did you think they'd react?"

"They never understood how university funding works, and clearly you don't either. Funds dry up and plans change. It happens everywhere."

"The money ended up in your *trust fund*! You planned to seize it all along."

"And you still haven't fixed my trust fund."

She'd had all she could take of his whining, self-serving behavior. "Thanks to your behavior, my nephew is in Michael's clutches too. You might not care about that, but I love him and he's likely to be the next casualty. You've milked this university for the last time. Now get out of my office, or I'll have security remove you. I'm ashamed to be your daughter."

His eyes narrowed, but as she came toward him, he backed quickly toward the door and opened it. "You'll be sorry you crossed me, Savannah. Very sorry."

"I'm only sorry it took me this long!" She slammed the door behind him and stalked back to her desk. If only she'd stood up to him years ago.

CHAPTER 26

HEZ PICKED UP HIS NOTES FROM THE CLASSROOM LECTERN and went straight for the door. Most evenings he hung around for a few minutes in case any students had questions—but not today. He had two hours before his next class, and he intended to make every minute count.

The smell of fresh paint greeted him as he walked down the hall, and the sound of power tools floated through an open window. Savannah's increases to the maintenance budget were paying off. Hopefully she'd find some money for new computers for the law school too, but Hez wasn't holding his breath.

"Professor Webster!"

Hez turned to see Ed Hernandez hurrying after him. "Hi, Ed. What's up?"

Ed caught up to him. "Thanks for putting in a good word with Jimmy Little. He offered me a summer associateship with his firm."

"That's great news!" Hez stuck out his hand, which Ed shook vigorously. "Jimmy was impressed with your work at the Justice Chamber."

"Do we have any new cases coming in? Now that swimming

season is over, I have more time. I'd love to get as much experience as possible before starting my summer job."

Hez paused. Ed and the rest of the Justice Chamber crew would be a big help in the fight to bring Michael to justice, but this wasn't a pro bono case. The Justice Chamber was supposed to promote the public interest—it wasn't Hez's personal law firm. Besides, Ella's death was a personal matter in more ways than one. "Nope, nothing new for the Justice Chamber. I'll let you know if that changes."

Hez walked into his office, shut the door, and tossed his notes on the desk. He pulled out his cell and dialed Hope's number.

She picked up on the second ring. "Hey, Hez. What's up?"

He told her about Deke's confession. He stayed in lawyer mode, describing events from a clinical, legal perspective. It kept him from breaking down—barely. "I'm not objective, of course, but it seems like there are grounds to open an investigation."

"Yes, of course. I . . ." Her voice trailed off. "This is such a shock. I'm so sorry, Hez. H-how are you doing?"

He gritted his teeth. "I'll be doing a lot better once Michael is behind bars."

"I'll contact the Birmingham DA's office as soon as I'm off the line with you. I'll get a copy of the file and make a pitch that our office should handle the prosecution. The murder took place up there, but the perps and witnesses are all here."

Hez thanked her and ended the call. Then he dropped the phone on his desk and buried his face in his hands. Rage and grief swirled through him, but also a thread of relief. Savannah was right: It hadn't been all his fault. Guilt and self-loathing stepped hard on the relief—how dare he feel relieved that his daughter had been murdered! He should have been with Ella, watching her like he'd promised Savannah. His practical side reminded him of Michael's tenacity and determination. If that attempt had failed, he would have kept on trying.

Hez closed his eyes and groaned as he wrestled with the injustice. "Oh, God. Help me get through this. Help Savannah. And give Ella justice. Please." He pictured Ella with God, like Savannah had said in the cemetery. He saw her holding the nail-scarred hand of a young man with kind brown eyes. It helped. A little.

His phone vibrated on the plywood desktop. Hope was already calling back. He took the call. "That was quick."

"I just got off the phone with the Birmingham PD." Her voice was tight and tense. "The file on Ella's death is gone."

The bottom dropped out of Hez's stomach. "What?"

"But the good news is that the thief didn't spot one of the security cameras. We know who Pelican Harbor's mole is. I've told Jane, and they'll make an arrest any minute."

Savannah sat hugging herself as the rest of the grieving parents filed out of the classroom at TGU where the group session was held every week. Spilling the news that her daughter had been targeted had gutted her, but she needed to get it out. She withheld the perpetrator's name, but Michael's insolent smile still hovered in her brain.

Seated beside her in the back row of blue folding chairs, Nora touched her hand. "I'm so sorry, Savannah. Th-this is beyond horrible and tragic. I wish I could take the pain." She leaned down and snagged her purse and Savannah's as well. "Let's get some air. It's stuffy in here with the AC already off."

Savannah nodded and rose to go with her. "I'll take my purse." She retrieved it and slung it over her shoulder. She lifted her face to welcome the cooling night breeze fragrant with the scent of magnolia.

Nora stopped in the lot by Savannah's car. "I know you couldn't say who was behind the plot, but do you want to tell me?"

Accusations against Michael hovered on her lips, but she pressed them together. Did Nora already know he'd been involved? She pushed away the disloyal thought. Nora would never conceal something like that from her. "Deke talked about all the Legares had done to his family. He didn't specifically say who was behind it, but Hez and I have our suspicions."

The illumination from the overhead parking lot light revealed Nora's expression shifting from concerned to uneasy. "I—I don't know what to say." Tears glimmered on her lashes. "I'm so sorry." She moved her purse to her other shoulder. "I put out some inquiries about Martine. She's gone to ground, but I'll find her."

The determination in Nora's voice bolstered Savannah's confidence. While Nora might not be comfortable tearing down her uncle's character, she would help in any way she could. "I appreciate that. I believe Hez was set up, and she didn't come up with that idea on her own. I want to get her to admit who was behind it."

"You think it was Uncle Michael." Nora's flat tone said it all. This was no surprise to her.

"Michael is bent on revenge."

"How did you handle Deke's request for forgiveness?"

"Hez and I both forgave him for trying to kill us." Savannah touched her car door handle and it unlocked. She opened the door and tossed her purse onto the passenger seat, then leaned against the car. She absently fingered the bracelet Nora had given her. "We're still processing what happened to Ella. I'm not sure I can let go of that yet."

"Don't become Uncle Michael." The words burst out of Nora in a rush. "He's eaten up with the need to get even."

In her mind's eye Savannah saw the determination on Hez's face to enact justice. Was that the need for revenge? She swirled the tiny beads on the bracelet. The bracelet couldn't help her with this problem, though. Only God could.

Her phone sounded from inside the car with a text message. She leaned inside and retrieved it to see a message from Hez. Call me. We need to talk ASAP. She wanted to finish with Nora before she answered him, so she tossed her phone on top of her purse.

Two police cars, sirens blaring and lights flashing, pulled into the parking lot and parked behind them. The vehicles' doors flew open, and Jane, still in uniform, got out of the first car. Jane Dixon could have been a younger brunette Reese Witherspoon but was more competent than her youthful appearance implied. Detective Augusta Richards stepped out of the second one, and they both approached where Savannah stood with Nora.

Savannah's gut tightened at Jane's grim expression. Augusta's was equally serious. Had they come to give her bad news? Her fingers curled into her palms, and she held herself erect for the coming blow.

She took a step toward them. "Is it Simon? Is he okay? Or Hez?"

Jane's hazel eyes softened. "Everyone is fine." Her attention moved from Savannah to Nora. "Nora Craft, you're under arrest." She nodded at Augusta, who moved to Nora and turned her around.

Augusta pulled Nora's arms behind her and slapped on the cuffs. "You have the right to remain silent. Anything you say can be used against you in a court of law. You have a right to counsel, and if you can't afford an attorney, one will be provided for you. Do you understand your rights?"

"What are the charges?" Nora asked in a quiet voice.

"Do you understand your rights?" Augusta asked again.

"Yes, but I don't understand. What am I charged with?"

"Evidence tampering, obstructing government operations, and hindering felony prosecutions."

Savannah gasped and took a step back. "I don't believe it, Jane. Nora wouldn't do that."

Jane remained expressionless. "Hez will explain it to you."

CHAPTER 27

HEZ SAT AT THE TABLE IN THE JUSTICE CHAMBER, TRYING to grade papers. That would be easier if he sat at his desk or stopped watching the open door in front of him. But if he did either of those things, he wouldn't know when Erik Andersen walked by. Andersen's office was at the end of the hall, and Hez had urgent business with him.

Last night's phone conversation with Savannah didn't help his focus. He had been so excited to tell her that the PHPD mole was about to be arrested that he hadn't immediately realized she was saying something about Nora—or that she was crying. He'd talked over her tears for nearly a minute before her sobs broke through the torrent of words pouring from his mouth.

He winced at the memory. He had apologized, of course, but he needed to do something to make it up to her. Soon.

Still, he couldn't help being excited. Hope hadn't just caught the mole. She'd caught a Willard—and that meant they were one step closer to catching Michael. Nora seemed like a sweet woman, but she'd clearly betrayed her best friend—even if Savannah didn't want to believe it. Nora must have been taking orders from Michael. And if anyone could find the proof, Hope could. She would draw the net tight around Michael and haul him in—but netting a shark was tricky, and Hez planned to give her all the help he could. That was one reason he had staked out Andersen's office this morning.

There he was! Hez caught a quick glimpse of khaki slacks, black polo, and perfectly coiffed blond hair as his target passed.

Hez dropped the student paper he was reading and hurried after Andersen. He caught up just as the man was turning into his office. Hez rapped on the door as Andersen reached to shut it.

The professor's blue eyes went wide with surprise and he jerked back. "Hez! I'm surprised to see you."

"Likewise."

Andersen cocked his head. "What do you mean?"

Hez glanced around to make sure they were alone. "Well, you offered to consent to our adoption petition in return for control of Jess's trust plus a permanent vacation in France or Hawaii, but then you consented to Michael's petition before we could respond. His offer must have been so good that you didn't even bother to negotiate with us. So I'm surprised you're still here and not off on a private island or something."

A spasm of anger crossed Andersen's face. "I don't want to talk about it."

"Then just listen. Give me five minutes. I don't think you'll regret it."

Andersen eyed him with wary indecision for a moment, then nodded. "Five minutes."

Hez stepped into Andersen's office, which felt a little like a walk-in trophy case. Polished walnut bookcases and a matching table were mostly decorated with awards and honorary degrees Andersen had received as well as pictures of him with famous people. He seated himself behind an ornate walnut desk as Hez settled in one of the leather guest chairs.

Andersen glanced at his watch, then steepled his fingers. "I'm listening."

"Michael Willard is a thug and he'd make a terrible father for your son. I think you know that. So why did you consent to his adoption petition? It wasn't money, at least not the kind of money you were demanding from Savannah and me. If he'd handed you a mountain of cash, you wouldn't be here. So I'm guessing Michael took your consent by force. He threatened you, and the threat was serious enough that you gave him what he wanted."

Andersen's eyes narrowed and little lines formed around the corners of his mouth. "Get to the point."

"The point is that neither of us likes Michael—and we're not the only ones. I still have connections in the law enforcement community, and I have reason to believe someone is investigating him. If he committed extortion or made threats of violence, he could be in serious trouble—especially if he did it to corrupt a judicial proceeding."

Andersen leaned forward. "Like an adoption proceeding?"

"Yep."

"How much trouble would he be in if he did that?"

Hez resisted the urge to smile. "That would be a felony, and probably not the only one. If Michael could also be tied to the artifact smuggling that went on last year, he could spend the rest of his life in prison."

"Hmm. Could he adopt Simon if he's in prison?"

"No."

Andersen's eyes held a crafty gleam. "So my consent to the adoption would disappear and I could consent to someone else adopting my son?"

Hez's stomach churned at Andersen's willingness to sell Simon to the highest bidder. The boy deserved so much better. "Yes."

"I see." Andersen tapped his fingertips against each other. "Tell your law enforcement connections that there's a person who can prove Michael engaged in extortion, artifact smuggling, and other serious crimes. This person will need protection, of course. Immunity too."

"I'll deliver that message."

Andersen gave an oily smile, showing too-perfect teeth. "Good. You were right. I don't regret sacrificing five minutes of my day for this."

Hez ended the conversation and got out of Andersen's office as quickly as possible. Andersen made Hez's skin crawl, and he felt like he needed a shower. He and Hope were going for a run in a few minutes, and he could tell her what he found out. She'd be very interested.

He didn't like the idea of Andersen getting immunity for his crimes. And he really didn't like the idea of haggling over Simon's future with Andersen's lawyer, Nita the Knife. But it would be worth it if Michael was permanently behind bars.

It was no wonder Simon loved spending time at Michael's property. It was a kid paradise with the lush green yard and a tree house at the edge of the woods. Savannah spotted a glimpse of a small lake or pond through the canopy of trees as she drove along the property to pull into the driveway. The wide porch on the two-story home held several chairs and a swing. Helen sat on an Adirondack chair, and Michael rose from the one beside her as Savannah parked.

It took all her strength not to leap at him and claw his face. Hez had warned her to say nothing about what they'd learned from Deke, so she swallowed down the accusations burning the back of her tongue.

She got out, and Helen's hard, suspicious expression dimmed Savannah's spirits even more. If only Hez could have come with her, but the court order forbade any contact with Simon.

Shading her eyes with her hand from the morning sun, she approached Michael as he descended the steps. "I don't see Simon. Is he getting his things inside?" A smoker on a trailer parked by the house puffed out the aroma of brisket, but she was too tense to find it appealing.

Michael folded his arms over his chest, and his biceps bulged in his blue tee. "He's out back playing with his cousins in the woods. I think they're catching crawdads in the creek. I'll get him."

"He is supposed to be ready for custody transfer."

Michael's glowering stare let her know he cared nothing

about a court order. "Stay here." He stalked to the side of the house and went around toward the back. His two German shepherds approached, and one gave a low growl. Savannah froze and eyed the dogs.

"Lie down," Helen commanded.

The dogs backed away and settled on the ground. Savannah's fingers touched the bracelet at her wrist, and she fondled the words *Best Friends*. She'd been doing the same thing when she overheard Nora talking to Helen. Nora needed help, and her great-aunt might have some information to help free her. Savannah was certain Helen knew something.

Savannah mounted the steps and approached Helen. "Mrs. Willard, I need your help. I love Nora like a sister. She gave me this bracelet when I was going through a hard time a few months ago." She extended her arm and showed Helen her bracelet. "I know you love her too. I think you might know who framed her. Please, help me get her out of jail."

"I don't know what you're talking about," Helen said in a dismissive tone.

"I overheard you and Nora talking at University Grounds. Nora said, 'It could get real ugly,' and you responded, 'No one will ever know.' I'm not trying to get anyone in trouble—I just want Nora cleared. What were you talking about?"

Savannah thought she caught a bit of surprise in the woman's brown eyes. Helen's expression went blank, and her lips flattened. She glanced away and then back at Savannah. Her mouth opened, but she shut it when the sound of children laughing floated their way.

Simon came into view first, and he rushed up the steps to throw his arms around Savannah. She relished his tight hug.

"You smell like the creek." She smoothed his sweaty hair. "Did you catch any crawdads?"

"We sure did. Pawpaw is going to clean them and freeze them so we can have them when I come back."

His cousins rounded the corner of the house and ran for the tree house. Simon took a step after them, and she put her hand on his shoulder. "We need to go. Grab your backpack."

"Aw, man." He scowled and trudged to the door. "I wish we could all be together here. Why does it have to be so hard?" The screen door banged behind him to punctuate his displeasure.

The dogs rose and raced toward the side of the house, and Savannah tensed, knowing they'd alerted to Michael's presence. His mood appeared to have worsened, and if looks could kill, she'd be six feet under.

His gaze flickered from her to his mother, then back again. "I told you to stay put. What are you doing bothering my mom?"

"Just chatting." Savannah kept her tone casual and walked down the steps. "Next time have him ready and your family won't have to put up with my presence." He reached toward her as if to grab her arm, and she fixed him with a hard stare of warning. "I wouldn't if I were you."

His hand fell back to his side, but his face twisted into a harder expression.

Simon tore out of the house with his backpack slung over his shoulder. "I'm ready, Aunt Savannah."

Michael's hands curled into fists. "I wasn't going to let him go at all, but my mother talked me into it. Get off my property before I change my mind."

Savannah steered Simon toward her car. He flung his pack

into the back seat, then climbed in on the passenger side. She went around to the driver's side and got in, then shot a final backward glance toward Helen, who stared after the car with a thoughtful, remote expression.

Nothing seemed to get through to the Willard family. Did Helen care nothing about Nora?

CHAPTER 28

MICHAEL WAITED IN THE DARK. HE SAT ON ERIK ANDERSEN'S leather sofa, facing the front door. It was the same sofa where Michael saw a girl's backpack on an earlier visit. He thought he smelled perfume, but that was probably just his imagination. Had Jess ever sat on this sofa while Andersen eyed her with a predatory smile?

Michael grimaced. Jess should have talked to him before she ever got involved with Andersen. He would have warned her off—and beaten some sense into her if necessary. What could she possibly have been thinking?

Andersen's thoughts, on the other hand, were obvious. He had been an ambitious young professor. Jess was a beautiful and brilliant young woman with connections to both the Legares and the Willards. Andersen figured he could milk those connections for all they were worth. He planned to use Jess as a stepping stone and abandon her whenever she ceased to be useful. But she'd abandoned him first, after catching him with another female student.

Fresh anger swept over Michael, heightening his blood pressure—and his anticipation of what would happen tonight.

The door opened. Andersen walked in and clicked on the

light. He spotted Michael and froze. Before he could react, a masked man stepped from behind the door, put a gun to Andersen's back, and shut and locked the door with his free hand. He shoved Andersen in the small of the back, pushing him away from the door and creating some open space in case Andersen tried anything.

Michael smiled. The masked man was his second cousin, Jimbo Clayton. This was Jimbo's first muscle job, and he was handling it like a pro so far. Little Joe and Tommy used to do this sort of work, but they both died in a police raid a few months ago.

Andersen licked his lips. "Mike, what's going on?"

Michael stood. "Evening, Professor. Glad you're alone tonight. That'll make things easier."

"What do you mean? Make what easier?" Andersen's gaze slid to Michael's hands. "Why are you wearing gloves?"

Michael reached behind the sofa and pulled out a suitcase he'd found in Andersen's closet. "You're going to disappear again."

Andersen relaxed slightly. "Okay. Do you mind telling me why?"

"You talk too much and to the wrong people."

"I—I don't know what you mean."

Michael frowned. "You also lie too much. I know about your conversation with Hez Webster. And I know you're scheduled to meet with the DA tomorrow."

Andersen gulped and turned pale.

"So you're going to disappear again," Michael continued. "At least until the adoption hearing is over. And you're not going to talk to the DA. Ever."

Andersen nodded. "Okay, sure. I'll leave now."

Michael walked toward the garage door, pulling the suitcase. "We're going to escort you out of town."

Jimbo took the phone from Andersen's hand and tossed it to the floor. "You won't need that tonight." He nudged Andersen toward the door with the barrel of his gun. "Get in the back seat."

Andersen climbed into the back of his own car, followed by Jimbo. Michael put the suitcase in the trunk, opened the garage door, and got behind the wheel. He glanced in the rearview mirror. "Keep your hands in your lap. If you touch the door handle, you'll die. Understand?"

Andersen moved away from the door and clasped his hands in his lap. "Got it."

The Mercedes purred as Michael pulled out of the garage. He drove through the countryside, avoiding towns and making sure to stay under the speed limit and follow all traffic rules.

They entered Gum Swamp. The night was chilly, and patchy fog filled low spots and sent streamers of mist across the road. Michael broke the silence in the car. "Do you like poetry, Professor?"

Andersen stirred. "What?"

"Poetry. Do you like it?"

"Uh, sure."

Michael cleared his throat and recited:

Because I could not stop for Death–
He kindly stopped for me–
The Carriage held but just Ourselves–
And Immortality.

We slowly drove–He knew no haste
And I had put away
My labor and my leisure too,
For His Civility–

We passed the School, where Children strove
At Recess–in the Ring–
We passed the Fields of Gazing Grain–
We passed the Setting Sun–

Or rather–He passed Us–
The Dews drew quivering and Chill–
For only Gossamer, my Gown–
My Tippet–only Tulle–

We paused before a House that seemed
A Swelling of the Ground–
The Roof was scarcely visible–
The Cornice–in the Ground–

He broke off as a black pickup truck loomed out of the darkness on the side of the road. Michael pulled up behind it and parked. Jimbo opened his door and got out, keeping his gun trained on Andersen.

Michael turned to Andersen, who was pale and sweating. "Get out."

"W-what are you going to do to me?"

"It will be worse if you don't get out now."

Andersen opened his door with a shaking hand. He launched

himself out of the car and ran into the swamp, splashing and stumbling.

Jimbo was ready. He fired two quick shots. Andersen stumbled and fell face down in the shallow water. He didn't move.

Michael watched with satisfaction as Jimbo picked up the shell casings without needing to be told. "Strip the body and stake it someplace the gators will find it. Burn the clothes and the suitcase. Leave the car near the Greyhound terminal. I'll pick you up there in an hour."

Jimbo nodded and got to work. Michael climbed into his pickup and started the engine. He smiled as he drove off and finished the Emily Dickinson poem:

Since then–'tis Centuries–and yet
Feels shorter than the Day
I first surmised the Horses' Heads
Were toward Eternity–

"Look at the bream I caught in the pond, Uncle Hez!" Simon turned his phone around to face the Zoom screen on the laptop in Savannah's office. He flipped through pictures of fish. "Pawpaw let me fillet my fish all by myself." He extended his left index finger. "I only cut myself in one tiny place, and it only bled a minute."

This was news to Savannah, who sat beside him, but she resisted the temptation to peel back the sticky bandage and examine the wound. With Michael giving Simon adult chores, her nephew wouldn't appreciate being made to feel like a little boy. Why did the man have to make things so hard?

Her face ached from the fake smile she kept pinned in place. Simon's constant praise for everything Willard hurt her heart. How did she coax him back into the fold of this family? Michael had an insidious way of pulling the unwary into his orbit, and she would do anything to keep Simon from ending up like Little Joe.

Hez shot her a glance of commiseration but maintained his smile. "Nice catch. Did you fry it up too?" He appeared relaxed in shorts and a blue tee that brought out the color of his eyes. Mobile Bay was in the background from his spot on the back patio of their house.

"Mimi and Tammy did the cooking." Simon puffed out his chest. "But Pawpaw said they were the best fish he'd ever eaten. I ate two plates full. Mimi's homemade lemonade was even better than LuLu's."

That was saying a lot since Simon loved everything at LuLu's. The restaurant was owned by Jimmy Buffett's sister and was an icon in the Gulf Shores area.

Simon swiped his phone again. "And look at this, Uncle Hez—we found an old still behind one of the shacks me and my cousins have been using as a hideout." He turned the phone around again proudly. "We're going to build a raft and take it out on the pond."

Savannah tensed. "How deep is the water?"

"I don't know. I'm not going to swim in the pond, Aunt Savannah. I'll just push a raft across it with a pole. I'll be fine."

He hadn't been in the ocean since the near drowning. She pressed her lips together. "Did you get your homework done while you were there?"

The excitement left Simon's expression "Uh, no. I didn't have time."

"Better get to it then. You've got three hours before bedtime. I know it's very exciting to be with your cousins, but school is important." A confrontation with Michael might be in her future.

"Fine." He got up in a huff and stomped down the hall to his bedroom.

Savannah exhaled. "How do we combat Michael's influence, Hez? I don't know what to do. He needs *your* influence, not that of the Willards. I hate that you can't be with us. I miss you."

"I miss you even more. I've been trying to keep myself busy by working on the house, but the minutes go by way too slowly." His expression on the screen went somber. "I can't go into details, babe, but the pressure on Michael is about to go way up. He's already unpredictable, so be prepared for him to react poorly."

React poorly? "What does that mean?"

"I can't say more, but he could lash out. I want you to be careful."

Unease rippled down her spine. She already felt like her neck was a swivel. Anytime a strange car drove past her cottage or she heard the squeal of tires, she tensed. "I wish you'd tell me what you know. Did you do something to him?"

The doorbell rang before Hez could answer. She started to get up, but Simon came out of his room and ran past the office door on his way to the entry. "I'll get it," he called.

"Wait, Simon!" She leaped up to try to intercept him, but he threw open the door and stepped onto the porch. She raced after him and found him holding a manila envelope.

No one else was on the porch and no cars were in the cottage's driveway or parked on the street. She smelled freshly cut grass, not the odor of gasoline. Was someone hiding alongside the house in the bushes? She grabbed Simon's shoulder and pushed him back inside.

"It's addressed to you." Simon handed it to her.

She took it gingerly. "Thanks, Simon. You can get back to your schoolwork now."

He eyed the envelope with curiosity but retreated to his room.

Savannah locked the door and carried the envelope to her office. She held it up for Hez to see. "No one was out there. No cars, no pedestrians. Someone dropped it and ran."

"I don't like the sound of that," he said. "I should come get it."

"I don't like it either." She studied her name in block letters. "I'm going to open it."

The envelope wasn't sealed, just closed with the metal clasp. She straightened the flattened clasp and lifted the flap to draw out the contents. "There are two pages." She studied the top one. "The first is a prisoner record for an inmate in Louisiana. Francois Dubois." She turned the paper around to face the camera on her computer so Hez could see. "Could he be related to Martine?"

He frowned and leaned closer, then shrugged. "It's possible. What's the other document?"

"It's a handwritten note in a foreign language—French, I think. I can't pronounce it." She held it up to the camera.

He squinted and leaned close to the screen. "*'Papa, je te protégerai. Je ferai ce qu'ils veulent.'* My French isn't great, but I think it means 'Papa, I'll protect you. I'll do whatever they want.' "

"Papa! I'll bet Francois is Martine's dad. Can you find out? Maybe Hope could tell you."

"It would make sense. Maybe Martine set me up to save her father. Snap a picture of the documents and email them to me. I'll send them to Hope. The big question is, who dropped them at your door?"

She took in the block letters on the manila envelope. "I—I think maybe it was Nora. She promised to help me find Martine."

"But Nora's in jail."

"She still has friends in the police department." Savannah leaned forward and stared into the camera, willing Hez to see how much this meant to her. If they were together in person, she knew she could convince him. "She should get bail on Monday, right?"

"Probably. She's charged with a felony, so it won't be low."

"She hardly has any money. It's not fair that she'll be stuck in jail just because she's poor."

The furrow on his brow deepened. "Babe, I see where your thoughts are going. Bailing her out won't be cheap. We've dropped most of our savings on the down payment for the house and even more on renovations. I'm estimating bail might be as much as fifteen grand."

She winced, but the cost didn't sway her. "We've got that much in our wedding fund. We'll get it back at trial, right?"

"If she shows up."

"She will." Her fingers touched the bracelet on her wrist. "I'm sure she sent this information. I can't stand by and let her rot in jail for something I don't think she would do."

He sighed. "I won't fight you on this. We can get a home-equity loan for the wedding if we have to."

She made a kissing sound in the air. "I wish you were here so I could thank you properly."

The tension left his face when he smiled and touched the screen as if he were touching her lips. "Me too, babe, me too. It's going to be a long weekend without you."

CHAPTER 29

HEZ LEANED BACK AND GROANED. BIRDS SANG OUTSIDE THE Justice Chamber's open trefoil window, and late-May sunshine cast warm golden bars across the floor and touched the edge of the much-used plywood desk. The scent of sun-warmed grass wafted in on a gentle breeze. It was a beautiful day, but the bad news on the monitor in front of him cast a pall over it all.

Hez reread Scott Foster's email. As expected, the probate judge had appointed a guardian ad litem for Simon in advance of the upcoming custody hearing. The guardian was a veteran social worker and attorney named Janet Henderson. She had already visited Michael Willard's home to meet Simon and observe his interactions with the family—without notifying Scott in advance. When Scott complained, Henderson explained that it was "just an informal visit" because she was stopping by anyway to see Helen Willard, a friend from church.

Scott planned to ask the judge to appoint a new guardian, but he didn't have high hopes. Henderson was qualified, and the judge wasn't likely to replace her just because she had an undisclosed preliminary interaction with Simon and was friends with a relative of someone connected to the adoption. Nova Cambridge and Pelican Harbor weren't big places—the odds of finding a qualified guardian candidate who had no contacts at all with a large local family weren't great.

Hez stood and paced the small room, drawing creaks from the old floorboards under the thin carpet. The guardian issue was aggravating, but it wouldn't matter. Not once Michael was behind bars for extortion, smuggling, and possibly more. Henderson couldn't recommend that Michael get custody under those circumstances. Hez and Savannah just needed to make sure she felt comfortable recommending them. So they needed to be nice and cooperative—despite her actions so far. Just like they needed to be nice and cooperative with Erik Andersen and find a way to cajole him into consenting to the adoption without giving him Simon's trust fund. Hez grimaced at the thought, but he'd find a way to do it for Simon.

His phone buzzed and he pulled it out of his pocket. Hope. His heart rate ticked up. Was she about to tell him Michael had just been arrested?

He accepted the call. "Hey. What's up?"

"When was the last time you had any contact with Erik Andersen?"

Hez thought for a moment. "Right before I told you about him."

"Have you seen him since then?"

He didn't like the direction of her questions. "No. Why?"

She exhaled. "He didn't answer the door when we went to interview him, even though we'd scheduled it in advance. He also didn't answer his phone, so an officer entered the house and did a welfare check. Mr. Andersen wasn't there. His car was missing and indentations in the carpet in a closet indicated that a suitcase was also missing. Several drawers in his dresser were open, and there were no toiletries on his bathroom sink. His car was found parked on the street near a bus terminal." She paused. "I think he ran, though if he did, he left his phone behind. We found it on the floor."

The bottom fell out of Hez's gut. This couldn't be happening. "Are you sure? He seemed more than willing to talk. Maybe something happened to him. Why would he leave his phone behind if he was leaving of his own free will?"

"This is the second time he's disappeared, and the first time seems to have been voluntary. He could have forgotten his phone. Or he was afraid it would be used to track him."

"Hold on a minute. I'll go check his office." Hez walked down the hall to Andersen's office. It was empty and the only light came in through the window. Nothing seemed out of the ordinary. Hez scanned the desk—and spotted something odd. "TGU is switching insurance plans, and there's a half-filled-out form on his desk. If he doesn't submit it by tomorrow, his premiums will double. I don't think he was planning to take a trip."

"Hmm. Maybe not."

"Hold on a sec. I'm putting you on speaker." Hez got on his hands and knees, turned on his phone's flashlight, and shone it on the underside of Andersen's desk and shelves. His heart jittered when he saw a small round object. He got to his feet, hurried into the hall, and took the phone off speaker. "There's a bug under his desk."

The line was silent for a heartbeat. "I'll submit a missing person report and get an investigator assigned. Have you checked your office?"

Hez walked back to the Justice Chamber. Thirty seconds

later, he found an identical bug on the underside of the room's table. No wonder Michael always seemed one step ahead of them.

Savannah parked in the lot by Pelican Harbor Beach and got out into the salty breeze. Whitecaps foamed on the sand and retreated to repeat their hypnotic movement. A tern did a slow roll and dive-bombed to snatch a hapless crab before it could scuttle to safety in the waves. She hadn't been sleeping well while Nora was in jail, and she needed this walk along the water. Everything felt off-kilter.

She spotted Nora tossing pieces of food to a brown pelican and waved, then picked up the pace to reach her. "Looks like Pete knows a soft touch when he sees one." Jane had rescued Pelican Harbor's unofficial mascot when he was a baby, and he loved people.

Nora wiped her hands on a napkin before she rose from the bench. "I couldn't eat all my shrimp, but Pete was happy to take my leftovers." She enveloped Savannah in a fierce hug. "Thanks for coming to meet me. I still can't believe you paid for my bail. I—I didn't expect you to do that. It was fifteen thousand dollars!"

Savannah squeezed her tightly. "You kept me sane when I was drowning in grief. I know you arranged for me to get that prisoner file too. Even in jail you tried to help me like you always do. I couldn't let you rot in a cell. We'll get it back."

Nora frowned. "What prisoner file?"

"Martine's father's file."

"That wasn't me." Nora released her and stepped back. "Hez was okay with the bail money?"

"We took it out of our wedding fund." When Nora's eyes filled with tears, Savannah took her hand. "The wedding's not in jeopardy, so don't assume you wrecked our plans. I realized I trusted Hez enough to believe him. Michael orchestrated the pictures somehow." She took off her shoes, dangling them in one hand, and nodded toward the beach. "Let's walk while we talk. I need to feel the sea breeze in my hair. Now that you're out, we have to figure out who used your credentials to steal Ella's report at the Birmingham PD. Any ideas?"

Nora walked beside her but said nothing for a long moment. Savannah stopped and studied her downcast gaze. "Nora? You must have possible suspects in mind."

Nora pushed her glasses up on her nose and gripped Savannah's hand. "You don't know how much I appreciate your loyalty, Savannah, but I can't let you get in the middle of this. I—I don't want you to get hurt."

"Who would hurt me? Your uncle Michael? I'm used to dealing with him now. There's something you aren't telling me."

"There's nothing you can do about this, Savannah. Let it go."

"Not until you tell me what's going on."

"I can't talk about it!" Nora walked ahead with a jerky gait and didn't look back.

Savannah started after her and slipped in the thick sand. She went down on one knee as she lost the fight to keep her balance. "Nora, wait!"

Nora turned and saw her struggling to get up but didn't approach. "Please trust me, Savannah. Stay out of it."

Savannah struggled to her feet and brushed the sand from

her hands before walking toward Nora, who had gone pale. "You can't ask me to trust you with no information. This is about Ella. You, of all people, know what I've gone through. You understand. I have to know. You can't cover for her killers, Nora—you just can't!"

"I'm sorry, I'm sorry." A sob tore from Nora, and she turned to run off down the beach.

Savannah clutched the bracelet circling her wrist, and the beads bit into her skin. Nora couldn't have been involved in the theft of Ella's file—Savannah refused to believe it. There had to be another answer. But no matter which way she examined the known facts, she couldn't come up with any other reason Nora's credentials had been used. No one could have "borrowed" them without her knowledge.

Hez knew there was a problem the instant Savannah opened her cottage door. Her puffy red eyes told him the meeting with Nora hadn't gone well. He stepped in without saying a word and held her tight.

She buried her face in his chest. "I can't believe Nora would do this."

He reached back and closed the door behind him to block prying eyes. "I'm sorry, babe."

"I—I cried my eyes out over Ella again and again during grief group, and Nora held my hand and put her arm around me each time. She understands. She must understand."

Hez guided her to a sofa, sat, and pulled her onto his lap. "Did she confess to stealing the file?"

"No, but she asked me not to investigate. She said I might get hurt." Savannah inhaled. "She said I needed to trust her."

Trust me—the motto of every untrustworthy person in the world. Including him. He'd asked her to trust him over the pictures, and she'd done it. He wished he was wrong about Nora, but he didn't think so. "Her betrayal must be really hard, especially after Jess."

Savannah stiffened and went silent for a moment. "No, Hez, you're wrong. Hearing you say the word *betrayal* brought it all into focus, and the one thing I know is that she's never let me down. Besides, this is about Ella." She fidgeted with her bracelet. "I don't believe she would cover for Ella's killers. She's hiding something, but I'm sure she would be the first to accuse the murderer. I—I trust her."

Just like Savannah trusted Jess—right up until the moment she stuck a knife in her back. Savannah didn't have a great track record when it came to trusting Willard women, but now wasn't the time to bring that up.

Hez sighed and mentally said goodbye to the fifteen thousand Savannah blew on Nora's bail—and bit his tongue about that too. The last thing he wanted was to start a fight, especially when he had his own bad news to deliver.

"Ella's killers may have struck again." He told her about his conversation with Hope and the bugs he discovered in Andersen's office and the Justice Chamber.

She gasped. "You think Michael was listening when you persuaded Erik to talk to Hope? And then murdered him before he could testify?"

Hez nodded. "I can't believe I never thought to search for bugs earlier. I knew Michael and the Willard kids had been in Connor Hall and in the Justice Chamber itself, but it somehow never occurred to me that they might have left something behind." He tapped his left temple. "Some people never completely recover after a craniotomy. Maybe I've permanently lost a step."

She gave him a tender kiss and stroked his hair. "I didn't fall in love with you because you're the smartest man I know—even though you are."

"I'm not smarter than Michael Willard. Without Andersen's testimony, Hope doesn't have a basis for an arrest warrant. And if Andersen doesn't revoke his consent to Michael's adoption of Simon, we'll have a hard time stopping it. A really hard time."

Her fingers stilled in his hair. "What are our chances?"

"Close to zero," he admitted. "I let you down. Worse, I let Simon down."

"I'm scared for our boy. What will Michael do to him?"

Fear gripped Hez's heart with iron talons. "He's a cold-blooded killer, and I think he murdered Simon's birth father. And that PI we hired for the first hearing reported that Michael was physically abusive to family members. If he hurts Simon . . ."

Savannah shivered. "I'm not just worried about him physically harming Simon. Michael corrupts everyone around him. Look at Jess, his brother David, his nephews Deke and Tommy and Little Joe, the other Willards who are dead or behind bars after those smuggling raids. And those are only the ones we know about. I'll bet there are more."

"And he's hard at work on the next generation. Simon gushes about how much fun he has with his cousins at 'Pawpaw's place.' He idolizes that sociopath. I so much want to go over there and get Simon and take him someplace safe—to protect him. But I know I'd be doing the opposite. Michael's court case would get even stronger, and there could even be bloodshed." Hez closed his eyes. "This is like those nightmares I have about Ella. I know she's drowning, but there's nothing I can do to save her."

Savannah took his hand in both of hers. "You're wrong."

"What do you mean?"

"There is something we can do: Pray for Simon. We don't have the power to protect Simon, but God does, and he works through our prayers. Especially when we pray together." She squeezed his hand. "Let's pray for our boy right now." She bowed her head.

Hez blinked. She was right. God could protect Simon despite Hez's repeated failings. This wasn't all on him. A weight lifted from his heart as he inclined his head. He cleared his throat and began, "Lord, we thank you that you love Simon and hold him in the palm of your hand. He faces great danger, but not too great for you. Keep him safe, Lord, please."

CHAPTER 30

THE FOYER OF LEGARE HALL WOULD SOON BE FINISHED. SAvannah stood in the grand entrance with its rounded dome ceiling soaring overhead. She had cut out some of the needlessly ostentatious—and expensive—flourishes in her father's plans, and the classic grace of the space shone through. The beautiful room with its refurbished mahogany floors and exquisite moldings was everything she'd dreamed it would be. She had big plans for the hall and smiled as she envisioned rolling out its name and purpose once the entire building was completed.

The contractor called out to her, and she went to join him outside by the southern magnolia tree on the lawn. The tree's white blooms filled the air with fragrance. "It's beautiful, Sergie. Well done. Where is the issue on the facade you called about?" With Sergie's attention to detail, there couldn't be much of a problem.

He pointed to the roof. "We haven't discussed guttering. With the style of the building, I'd suggest copper, but it's very expensive. There are a few options that look like copper but don't cost as much. See what you think." He pulled samples from a bag. "We have copper-coated, which still has the same appearance. And here's zinc. Copper penny aluminum would be the least expensive option, and from down here it would look like the real thing. All of these would be suitable."

She studied her choices and turned to stare at the building. The hall had sat here for twenty years falling into ruin. Did she want to skimp now on this magnificent facade? No. No, she did not. "Let's do the real thing."

His faded blue eyes smiled with relief. "I was hoping you'd say that. I'll get it ordered."

"Thank you." Over his shoulder she spotted Hez coming her way, and she lifted her hand in greeting and walked a few steps to meet him.

He kissed her before taking her hand and beginning the walk back to her office in the May sunshine. "I talked to the prison this morning and asked to see Francois Dubois. 'Franky' turned down a meeting. I wasn't surprised. I did a little digging before I called, and there are several Willards in prison with him. If it got out that he met with me, he'd likely have a fatal 'accident.'" Hez made air quotes with his fingers. "But I had to try. The Willard clan being on-site likely explains Martine's note and Michael's hold over her. If she doesn't cooperate, her father really is a 'dead man walking.' It would be just a matter of time before one of the Willards took him out."

"How important is her testimony?"

"If she tells the truth—the whole truth about how she and Michael set me up—that could tip the scales in our favor. The judge would really have to wonder whether it's in Simon's best interests to be raised by Michael, no matter what the guardian says. Michael could even wind up in prison." Hez sucked in a breath through his teeth. "But without Martine's testimony, we'll probably lose Simon."

Savannah paused the walk and clung to his hand. "What are our options? Can we force Martine to testify? He's her dad, not a spouse. Though it might be a challenge to find her."

"Finding her is the easy part. I have a strong suspicion she's in France, staying in or near her mother's village in the Burgundy region. She spent summers there after her parents divorced and her mom moved back across the pond."

"Out in plain sight? What if Michael sends one of his goons to silence her?"

"He's unlikely to do that. She's proven she's afraid of him and will do whatever he says. As long as he doesn't get a whiff of any disobedience, he'll leave her alone."

Savannah started toward her office again. Her afternoon would be full of meetings with faculty about changes for next year. It was nearly lunchtime, and students sat on the soft carpet of grass with their snacks and meals. "Can we subpoena her to testify?"

"No." Hez paused at the pond until Boo Radley crossed the path to slide into the water. "It's virtually impossible for an American court to force someone in France to testify. As long as she stays there and doesn't agree to testify, she and her father are perfectly safe. I can hire a PI to verify she's at her mother's, then try to talk her into coming back willingly."

Savannah shook her head. "You have too much to handle here. I'll go. Maybe I can appeal to her softer side." She leveled a stern glance at him. "And your track record with her stinks. You still see the girl you used to know instead of the calculating woman she is now."

His cheeks flushed. "I don't like it, babe. Michael could get wind of it and send one of his goons after you."

"I'll say I'm going to London about some funding or business of some kind. It will seem normal to the university. But I'll fly to Paris instead and take the train. Do you remember the name of the town?"

"No, but I can find out." He sounded resigned.

A three-day trip when she had so much on her plate wasn't ideal, but Savannah felt a surge of energy at the thought of facing Martine at last.

Hez wished he could be a fly on the wall during Savannah's meeting with Martine. Then he started to picture the conversation and changed his mind. His name would come up a lot, and the context might not always be positive. Still, he wished he could be there. If anything happened to Savannah in his absence, he'd never forgive himself.

He did his best to focus on the paperwork and emails in front of him. He was keeping an eye on Savannah's inbox as well as his, and he was amazed at how much she had to do. There were emails about the renovations of Legare Hall and the campus chapel, draft graduation schedules, and dozens of other items to sift through. There was even a lengthy complaint about Boo Radley, who had allegedly eaten a professor's cat. Hez very much doubted that Boo could even catch a cat, but the professor was adamant and verbose. The cat hadn't been home for two days and Boo seemed fatter than usual. Therefore, Boo must have eaten the cat. Hez looked up the professor and was relieved that he wasn't on the law faculty.

Hez's email pinged with a message from Scott. The title

was "Guardian's Report" and the first line was "Sorry to be the bearer of bad news."

Hez groaned as he opened the email and groaned again as he read the report. The guardian recommended that Michael's adoption petition be granted and that he get full custody of Simon, with Savannah and Hez getting visitation rights on holidays and birthdays. The guardian came across as thorough and unbiased, which made things worse. She had met Simon multiple times, observed him when he was with Michael and when he was with Savannah, and interviewed all three of the potential adopters.

She didn't criticize Savannah or Hez, but she pointed out that they both had full-time jobs and couldn't always be home for Simon. The report also mentioned Hez's work with the Justice Chamber, which had already put Simon in danger. By contrast, Michael had a flexible schedule and could be home whenever Simon was. Michael also had an assortment of young relatives with whom Simon was already bonding. And no one had ever pulled a gun on Michael in Simon's presence.

The guardian noted that Hez and Savannah had raised concerns about Michael's purported criminal connections, but she observed that those hadn't been proven. Simon's opinion was no help—he loved his grandfather and his aunt and uncle.

Hez tried to think of a way the report could have been worse for him and Savannah. He failed.

A sharp rap at his door jolted him out of his funk. "Come in."

The door opened and Ed, Dominga, and Toni entered, all smiling. Ed spoke first. "You know how you said you didn't have any work for us? I told Jimmy, and he said you must be getting sloppy because there was an obvious loose end from the Hornbrook thing."

"Oh, really." Hez swiveled in his chair. "Did he say what it was?"

Dominga nodded. "We never figured out who was blackmailing James Hornbrook."

Hez frowned. "He's right. We should give that a shot."

Toni's smile broadened. "We already did. Jimmy hired us as externs for the job and paid our expenses. He said not to tell you because you'd want TGU to pay for it."

"He's right about that too—but tell me what you found. You've all got grins as big as a gator's."

Ed pulled a binder out of his backpack. "It took some digging by Bruno, but we managed to pinpoint the location of the MacBook used by the extortionist." He pulled out a sheet of paper and laid it on Hez's desk. "That's where it is—or at least was."

Hez looked down at a map with a circle drawn around a house. His ears roared and he felt lightheaded. "This . . . this is Michael Willard's home."

Ed's expression sobered. "It is. He was behind this all along. I don't understand it, though. Why would he blackmail Hornbrook and then stage a commando raid to kill him?"

"Because of Simon," Hez said without hesitation. "But that also doesn't make sense. Would Michael really put his grandson in danger like that just to gouge a few bucks out of Hornbrook?"

Ed tapped his fingers on his binder. "Did he know Hornbrook was going to kidnap Simon and President Webster?"

Hez snapped his fingers. "That's it! I'm sure Michael wants me gone, and he must have wanted Hornbrook gone, too, because Hornbrook could implicate Michael in the artifact smuggling. So he set up this blackmail scheme to pit us against each other. If he was lucky, one or both of us would wind up dead and he'd make some easy money without ever getting his hands dirty. But then Hornbrook surprised him by kidnapping Simon and Savannah."

Ed nodded slowly. "Yeah, that could be it."

Hez reached for his phone. "We need to get this to Hope ASAP."

The custody hearing was only three days away. Would Hope be able to secure a warrant and execute it in time?

CHAPTER 31

SAVANNAH EYED HERSELF IN THE ANTIQUE MIRROR IN THE corner of the charming room she'd rented in Semur-en-Auxois. Power suit or something she could wear with sneakers for the walk along the cobblestone streets? *Power suit, definitely.* She needed all the backbone and persuasion she could muster to convince Martine to return to Alabama to testify.

She slipped out of her jeans into a muted navy pencil skirt and blazer with a cream top under it. She added a gold paperclip necklace Hez had gotten her and matching earrings. Tasteful and in control. Head high, she exited the hotel past a smiling blonde Frenchwoman and stepped out into the sunshine of the quaint town. According to the map on her phone, Martine's mother lived two blocks east and three blocks south. Savannah should be there in less than ten minutes.

She set off to the east, taking care to watch where she planted her shoes. The sunshine felt good on her face, and she paused to take in the pink bluffs and the ruins of an old castle with a keep and ramparts. If only Hez were here so they could explore. The scent of chocolate wafted from a small shop, and she passed several vendors selling flowers.

She consulted her phone and reached a fence protecting

a red-roofed manor set into the side of the cliff. She pressed a hand to her stomach to still the butterflies and squared her shoulders to approach the gate. It opened easily, and she started for the entry, but before she reached the door, she spotted Martine lounging at the side of the house beside a pool. An older woman was with her. Martine's bikini showed off a perfect figure, and Savannah gulped back her envy.

Neither of the women had spotted her, and she took a moment to gather her thoughts. The estate was beautiful with gorgeous flowers and shrubs. Mosaic tile surrounded the sparkling pool, and Martine's confident laughter rang out as Savannah stepped forward to make her presence known.

As Savannah drew closer, the smile vanished from Martine's face. She pushed her silky blonde hair out of her face, then lowered her sunglasses and peered over the top of them to stare in Savannah's direction. She gaped, then swung her legs to the side of the lounge chair to sit more upright.

"What are you doing here?" She squinted and her gaze traveled past Savannah. "Is Hez with you?"

Savannah stopped two feet away from her. "No. I thought the two of us could speak more openly without him." She smiled at the older woman. "You must be Martine's mother, because she clearly inherited your beauty. I'm Savannah Webster."

"Mama, you remember meeting Hez in America when I was in law school. This is his ex-wife. She's president of a university back in Alabama."

"Fiancée," Savannah corrected.

"Pleased to make your acquaintance, mademoiselle." The former model rose in a fluid movement from her chaise lounge. "I shall leave you two to speak privately." Her reserved smile held a trace of admiration before she walked toward the house.

Sit or stand? There was more power in towering over Martine, but it would be friendlier to sit for the discussion. Savannah perched on a chair beside Martine.

Martine draped a towel around her shoulders. "Let's not beat around the bush. What do you want?"

"You're an attorney, Martine—a respected one. I'm here to ask you to do the right thing. Michael has my nephew, and I fear for Simon's future. You know what that Willard gang is like. Several of Michael's nephews are behind bars or dead after being involved in his schemes. I've already lost my sister, and I don't want to see Simon pulled into a life of crime. If you come back to Alabama and tell how you framed Hez with those fake pictures, we might be able to save a little boy. Michael will be behind bars and won't be able to hurt your father."

Martine blanched and put her hand to her neck. "You know about my father?"

"Hez tried to speak with him, but Francois refused."

Martine narrowed her eyes at Savannah. "Is this conversation being recorded?"

"Of course not."

Martine was silent for a heartbeat. "I wish I could trust you." She grimaced. "I can't help you. Find an expert to testify on your behalf about the pictures."

"We have an expert who testified they are fake, but Michael has one who says they're real. You know the truth. With your testimony we can save Simon."

Martine caught her full lower lip in her teeth, and her dark, almond-shaped eyes held sadness. "I know what happens to those who cross Michael Willard. He took my files and computer to make sure I had no proof he'd hired me to get what he demanded. And he'll go scorched earth if I help you. It won't be enough to kill my father. He'll move on to my mother and to me. None of my family would be safe."

"He'd be in jail."

"Not soon enough. And his reach is long, even if he were behind bars. You don't know what you're asking." She shook her head. "No, I can't do it."

Savannah clenched her fists and stood. "You're destroying the finest man I've ever met, and now you're helping to ruin a child's life. How would you feel if it were your nephew or your own blood? You could change Simon's future, but you're letting fear rule you."

Martine gulped and dashed a tear from her cheek. "I'm sorry, Savannah, truly. I had no choice. I love my father. I had no choice."

"The right choice isn't easy and takes courage. I guess you have no backbone, Martine. I thought better of you. You're making the weaker choice again." She stormed toward the gate to get away before she lost her composure completely.

"Savannah!"

She paused at Martine's call and turned back toward her with a tiny ray of hope. "You'll come?"

Martine was standing with her hands clasped in front of her. She took a step toward her, then stopped. "I—I wanted to tell you I've never seen Hez as happy as he is with you. I wish you both the best, but I can't come back. I just can't." She ran toward the house.

Savannah fought the sting of tears. How would she tell Hez she'd failed?

Hez rubbed his forehead and leaned back in his chair, staring at the tiles on his office ceiling through tired eyes. Savannah had been apologetic when she called to tell him about her meeting with Martine, but Hez didn't blame her at all. He was very familiar with Martine's look-out-for-number-one approach to life. She was witty and fun but hardly altruistic. Her refusal to testify was disappointing but not surprising.

Hez had thought of Martine as a sort of outer-orbit friend—the kind of person you want at your parties but not in your life. That had been a mistake. If you can't trust someone, they shouldn't be around you at all. That should have been obvious to him, especially as a former prosecutor. If anyone was to blame here, it was him.

His phone buzzed—and his spirits rose when he saw who it was. He sat up and took the call. "Hey, Hope. What's up?"

"Hi, Hez. Thanks for that tip on the location of the computer used to blackmail James Hornbrook. I've forwarded it to the FBI and they're verifying Bruno's work. They don't doubt that it's accurate, but they have to check, of course."

Hez stood and started to pace. "Of course. But what about Michael Willard? Were you able to get a warrant to search his house? Did you find the computer?"

Her tone cooled. "You know I can't comment on that, Hez. I can't reveal specifics about an ongoing criminal investigation, especially to someone who's litigating against the subject of the investigation."

Hez ran his fingers through his hair. "Sorry. I know that

when there's news you can share, you'll share it. It's just that . . . well, the adoption hearing is only two days away. If Michael is arrested, that's going to make a big difference."

The line was silent for a moment. "Don't count on him getting arrested."

Hez closed his eyes. "Thanks for letting me know."

"I'm sorry."

He ended the call and shoved his phone in his pocket.

His thoughts traveled back to the call when Bruno had first told them about his efforts to trace the extortionist's computer. Bruno had been on speakerphone in the Justice Chamber and the static had been terrible. Was that the same Justice Chamber meeting that Michael attended? Yes. In fact, he had questioned Bruno about the computer.

Hez winced and flopped down into his chair. The computer and all the hardware Bruno mentioned must have vanished from Michael's house that very night.

Would Bruno's analysis alone be enough to trigger an arrest warrant for Michael? Probably not. He had relatives over all the time, and it would be impossible to prove that one of them didn't own the computer. So investigators would need to find proof that Michael bought the MacBook and other stuff Bruno mentioned. But if Michael was smart—and he certainly was—he wouldn't have bought it himself. He would have purchased it through a dummy company or, better yet, used stolen electronics. So that would likely be another dead end.

Hez tried to force himself to examine the facts like a prosecutor. What would he do in Hope's shoes? He'd be suspicious of Michael, of course. Very suspicious. He was too close to too many crimes—the artifact smuggling, the Hornbrook extortion, Ella's murder.

A surge of anger flooded Hez at the memory of Deke's confession. It was no use. He couldn't put himself in Hope's shoes because he was too personally involved. Besides, she'd already told him he shouldn't count on Michael being arrested. Maybe she suspected him of just as many crimes as Hez did but didn't have hard evidence against him. As the old law enforcement saying went, "We never catch the smart ones."

He put his face in his hands and tried to pray for protection for Simon and justice for Ella. But hopelessness overwhelmed him and the words stuck on his tongue like ashes.

Savannah knelt by Ella's grave, and she pulled a few stray weeds from the lush carpet of grass. The scent of wildflowers and freshly mown hay eased the stress of the past few days. What time was it? Her body had no idea if she was in France or Alabama.

Tomorrow a judge would decide their fate, and she held little hope for that decision. Nothing had gone their way in these proceedings. Michael was too corrupt, too crafty. She wished Hez were here with her, but he was huddling with Scott on any last-minute strategy they might pull out of the hat.

She traced the letters on the gravestone and closed her eyes, calling to mind the dimpled smile she loved so much. This life wasn't all there was. No matter what happened tomorrow, God was in control.

Footsteps crunched on oyster shells, and she opened her eyes with the hope Hez had come after all. She gulped when she spotted the tiny figure climbing the steep path. Helen clutched flowers in both hands, and she paused at the sight of Savannah. Their gazes locked and clung, and Savannah struggled for something to say.

The wind lifted Helen's white hair into a soft halo around her face when she paused and glanced at Ella's headstone. Her stony expression softened. "Is it true TGU is actually starting the neonatal clinic? I saw it on TV, but I never know what to believe from that lying reporter."

"It's true. When I learned the truth about what my father did, I wanted to do the right thing."

"Is that why you paid Nora's bail? That wasn't cheap."

Savannah stood and brushed the dirt from her hands. "That was for love, and I don't believe she's guilty."

Helen snorted. "That's very out of character for a Legare to help a Willard. You are your mother's daughter. Marie was a very sweet soul."

"Is that why you're here—to visit Mom's grave?"

"Hers and Jess's. Jess was my granddaughter, and there was no part of her with the Legare temperament. She was a Willard through and through."

That was debatable. Jess had learned the art of deception from Pierre all too well. There was much to be said for nurture over nature. Savannah trailed her fingers over Ella's polished gravestone. "Are you here to visit Ella too? I know you've been here before. I've seen the flowers."

Helen glanced away and bit her lip before nodding.

"Why? You never met her."

Helen's back straightened, and she raised her chin. "I know Deke told you what he'd done. I heard about it straight from him a few months earlier, and it about ripped the heart out of my chest. She was Marie's granddaughter, and for that reason alone, she held a piece of my heart. Marie should have been my daughter-in-law. If Pierre had let her go, Michael would have—" She pressed her lips together. "Never mind."

Savannah's mouth went dry. Were they really talking like this? Helen's faded brown eyes held real regret, and Savannah wished she'd finished her sentence. Did Mom's death change him? Maybe he'd really loved her. "I found some of Mom's poetry. It's remarkable."

"She was very gifted." Helen pointed at the stone's inscription. "'For where your treasure is, there your heart will be also.' Claptrap. If God cared about us, why would he let an incompetent idiot take my beautiful daughter? I never forgave God for that. Then I found out my beloved Deke, a sweet boy who loved the outdoors, did the same thing to your beautiful Ella. It makes no sense. What a cruel divine joke for God to throw my anger back in my face by showing me I wasn't the only one with a heavy burden. If you want to know, I came here to give God a piece of my mind. He has a lot to answer for as far as I'm concerned."

Savannah felt an unexpected kinship with Helen. They'd both lost a daughter. "Did he answer you?"

"That's between me and him." Helen peered at Savannah. "Does it bother you that I'm here in the Legare part of the cemetery? Does it feel like the enemy is snooping, searching for another way to hurt you?"

"No, of course not. You're welcome here anytime. I-I'm

touched you care about Ella, about Mom. I knew you loved Jess, but I'm thankful you think of Ella kindly and that you loved my mother. I miss her."

"So do I, child, so do I." Helen laid a bouquet of daisies on Ella's grave, then walked with determined steps toward the other two graves sheltered under the sweeping boughs of an oak tree laced with Spanish moss.

Savannah watched Helen lay a bouquet of roses beside the tulips Savannah had placed there earlier. Helen had known Jess well enough to remember her favorite flower. She stood for several long moments with her head bowed, and Savannah tore her gaze away to let the older woman grieve in peace.

The Willard matriarch had a heart under that stern exterior after all.

Michael had better things to do than sit in a jail visiting room, but Deke had said it was important—though he wouldn't say why. That made Michael uneasy, and his unease grew as Deke walked into the room on the other side of the glass. His nephew sat and hunkered over the counter with the handset gripped in his big paw. He eyed Michael apprehensively, like a dog afraid of getting whipped.

Michael picked up his handset. "Well? Why'd you drag me out here?"

Deke cringed. "Sorry. I, uh, I talked to the Websters. I asked them to forgive me, and I thought I should tell you."

"Why?" Michael pinned Deke with his gaze. "What did you ask them to forgive you for?"

"For kidnapping them and hitting him in the head—you know, the stuff I pled guilty to." Deke licked his lips. "It also slipped out about their little girl."

Michael's gut clenched. How could Deke have been so stupid—especially when guards could listen to everything he said? Michael fought to keep his voice even. "So? What does that have to do with me? I told you I had nothing to do with that."

Deke nodded vigorously. "Yes, sir. You absolutely told me that—and that's what I tried to say. But Mr. Hez wouldn't listen. He thought you was the man who called me. So I figured I should tell you, especially with that big court hearing coming up."

Michael's blood pressure spiked. He wanted to lunge through the window and shake Deke by the neck. Mama had worried that he would run his mouth ever since he confessed to her a few months ago. And she'd been right—the boy couldn't help himself. Now he was going to ruin everything.

A new idea occurred to Michael. He leaned back and studied his worn fingernails. If he played his cards exactly right, he might be able to turn this to his advantage. Everything was going to come to a head at once, but maybe that wasn't a bad thing.

Michael refocused his attention on Deke, who perched on the edge of his chair and held the handset in a white-knuckled grip. "You did right to tell me, Deke. I wouldn't have taken kindly to getting surprised by a murder accusation. As for Hez Webster, the man is confused. And it never hurts to have a confused opponent."

CHAPTER 32

HEZ HELD SAVANNAH'S HAND AS THEY SAT ON THE FIRST-row bench in the probate courtroom, just behind Scott Foster, who was seated at the counsel table with his paralegal. Michael sat behind his lawyer on the other side of the room. Janet Henderson, the guardian ad litem, occupied a chair in the jury box, which was otherwise empty. A scattering of witnesses dotted the gallery, waiting their turns to testify. Simon was in the jury room, totally absorbed in *The Dangerous Book for Boys*, a gift from Savannah.

The door behind the judge's bench opened. "All rise," the clerk said.

Judge O'Keefe came through the door, looking like a black-draped cube. Once he was seated and the case called, he swept his gaze over the room. "Good morning, everyone. We have dueling adoption petitions today rather than a single petition, which makes things a little more complicated. To keep the proceedings as simple as possible, I'll consider the petitions simultaneously and take all evidence for both petitions in one hearing. So, for example, witnesses will only testify once and their testimony will go to both petitions. Do both sides agree?"

Scott rose. "Petitioners Savannah and Hezekiah Webster agree, Your Honor."

Michael's attorney, Agatha Morgan, stood. "Counter-petitioner Michael Willard also agrees, Your Honor."

"All right," the judge said as the lawyers resumed their seats. "Let's get started." He patted a tall stack of paper on the bench. "I have before me objections to various prehearing evidentiary submissions. I've gone through all of them. If we had a jury, I'd rule on each objection individually and carefully filter out anything that might be inadmissible. But since I'm the only fact finder here, I'm going to take a more relaxed approach and let in everything—with one exception. Petitioners' objection to the pictures of Mr. Webster is sustained."

Morgan stood. "If I might be heard briefly, Your Honor. We have the photographer here in court. We also have an expert in manipulated imagery. They are prepared to testify that—"

The judge held up his hand. "I don't care whether the pictures are real. I'm excluding them because they're scandalous and only marginally relevant to the best interests of the child. If you want the technical legal standard, the prejudicial impact of those pictures outweighs their probative value." Morgan opened her mouth to argue further, but Judge O'Keefe kept going. "A lot of dirt gets thrown around in these proceedings—but I keep it to a minimum in this courtroom. Some dirt is regrettably necessary. This is not. Objection sustained."

Morgan closed her mouth and resumed her seat.

Savannah squeezed Hez's hand, her green eyes bright with hope. Hez squeezed back and gave a little smile and nod. Their surprise victory on the pictures was a nice way to start the hearing, but it sent a little ripple of worry through Hez. The judge easily could have ruled the other way—and probably should have. Prejudicial impact really only mattered when a jury was present. Maybe the judge excluded the pictures as a matter of principle—but he could also be preparing to rule against the Websters. If he denied their adoption petition, Hez and Savannah wouldn't later be able to argue that he relied on improper evidence.

Judge O'Keefe turned to Scott. "Your clients filed their petition first, so you can put on your case first. Call your first witness."

Scott stood and moved to the lectern. "We call Savannah Webster."

She rose from her seat and walked up to the witness stand. The bailiff swore her in, and she perched on the chair in the witness box. Scott walked her through the testimony they'd practiced, and she did a great job. She talked about how happy Simon was with her and Hez, the opportunities their connections to TGU would offer the boy, and even the room they were preparing for him in their new home. She ended with Jess's dying insistence that Savannah care for Simon. Her voice was halting and soft, but the entire courtroom was utterly silent as she spoke. Morgan didn't even bother cross-examining Savannah.

Scott then called the guardian ad litem, Janet Henderson. She admitted being friends with Helen Willard, but she said that the relationship didn't affect her report or recommendation. Scott did his best to undermine her judgment, but she was an experienced witness. Also, the judge had appointed Henderson, so Scott had to use kid gloves to avoid offending him. When Morgan stepped up to the lectern, she only asked whether Henderson stood by her recommendation. Henderson said yes, and Morgan sat down.

Hez's turn came next. He spent a lot less time on the stand than he'd expected. His main goal had been to discredit the Martine pictures, leaving him little to do on direct examination except echo Savannah's testimony about Simon.

Morgan's cross-examination of Hez held a few fireworks. She set her notes on the lectern and went straight for the jugular. "Mr. Webster, your daughter drowned while in your care, correct?"

Hez speared Michael with a glare. He sat perfectly still and held Hez's gaze. "My daughter was murdered."

Morgan's thin eyebrows went up. "Oh. The police report at the time indicated an accidental death while the child was in your care, correct?"

"Yes, but that was before Michael Willard's nephew Deke confessed." Hez spared a glance at Michael. A murderous glint sparked in his eyes.

Morgan's mouth hung open for a second. "Objection, hearsay. Move to strike."

Scott rose. "It's an admission against interest and therefore exempt from the hearsay rule."

Judge O'Keefe nodded. "It is indeed. Objection overruled and motion denied."

Morgan turned to Michael, who gave a slight shrug. She studied her notes for a long moment. "Is this Deke in prison?"

"Yes. He was just sentenced to life in prison for other crimes, including another murder," Hez said.

"So he's not a threat to Simon, right?"

"Not anymore, though several of the crimes he was already convicted of involved attacks on Simon." Hez looked at Michael again. "And Deke didn't act alone."

Morgan glanced at her notes. "Simon also almost drowned in your care, correct?"

Hez grimaced. "Correct."

She turned over a page. "You founded a legal clinic called the Justice Chamber, correct?"

"Yes."

"Does the Justice Chamber sometimes take on cases against dangerous opponents?"

"Yes."

"Opponents such as James Hornbrook?"

Hez cut a look at Michael. Amusement flickered in the older man's blue eyes. "James Hornbrook is no longer a dangerous opponent."

"But he did kidnap Simon, correct?"

"Yes."

"And the Justice Chamber may in the future accept cases against other dangerous opponents, correct?"

Hez lifted a brow. "You're implying that the head of a legal clinic is a greater danger to Simon than the head of a crime family? That's really your argument?"

Michael tensed and muttered something. The muscular bailiff stirred, and Morgan reached back to put a hand on Michael's shoulder. "I'll ask you again. The Justice Chamber may in the future accept cases against other dangerous opponents, correct?"

Hez shrugged. "I can't speculate on what cases the Chamber may or may not take in the future—but I can assure you that I'll do everything in my power to keep Simon safe."

Morgan flipped through her notes and apparently decided she didn't want to give Hez an excuse to keep talking. "No further questions."

Hez resumed his seat with the pleasant weight of Michael's glare on his back. Scott's plan was working. They needed to persuade Judge O'Keefe that Simon wouldn't be safe with Michael Willard, despite what Henderson said in her report. If Michael lost his temper and lashed out in the middle of the hearing, that just might be enough. So Hez had pushed his enemy's buttons at every opportunity from the witness stand. It hadn't been hard—all Hez had to do was tell the truth to Michael's face.

Scott stepped up to the lectern. "Petitioners call Erik Andersen."

A few people in the courtroom glanced toward the gallery, looking for Andersen. The rest didn't react at all—except Michael. His eyes widened and he turned pale. He stared at Scott for a moment, then recovered his composure and focused his gaze on the wall in front of him.

Scott glanced over his shoulder. "It appears that Mr. Andersen is not available at the moment. Petitioners call Michael Willard."

Michael walked to the witness box, was sworn in by the bailiff, and sat. His back didn't touch the chair and he eyed Scott warily.

Scott gave Michael a genial smile. "Good morning, Mr. Willard. When I called Mr. Andersen a moment ago, you seemed surprised and looked at me. You were the only one in the courtroom who reacted like that. Why?"

Michael shrugged. "I don't know."

"Could it be because you know Mr. Andersen is dead?"

Michael licked his lips. "I don't know what you're talking about."

"I think you do. This wouldn't be the first time a member of the Willard crime family murdered an inconvenient witness, would it?"

Michael flushed and opened his mouth, but before he could speak, Morgan popped to her feet. "Objection! Counsel is harassing the witness."

Scott held his hands palms up. "Whether Mr. Willard is a murderer and a member of a criminal organization is clearly relevant."

Michael glowered from the stand. "I'm neither!"

The judge gave Michael a warning look. "Wait for a question, Mr. Willard." He turned to Scott. "It's relevant, but you need to prove it with evidence. Don't just throw around terms like 'crime family.' You know better than that, Mr. Foster."

"Yes, Your Honor." Scott looked at Michael. "Let's start with Willards murdering witnesses. Your nephew Deke pled guilty to the murder of Beckett Harrison, who was going to testify against Deke, correct?"

"You'd have to ask Deke about that."

"I'm asking you."

"I don't remember the specifics."

Scott turned to his paralegal, who handed him a document. "I believe you were present at the sentencing hearing. I have a transcript in my hand. Would that help refresh your memory of the specifics?"

A vein stood out on Michael's neck, but he kept his voice level. "I remember in general terms that Deke pled guilty to the Harrison murder."

"And that Harrison was going to testify against Deke in another murder case?"

"Yes."

"Thank you." Scott handed the document back to his paralegal, who gave him another stack of paper. "Deke has an extensive criminal history. Would it be helpful for you to have a copy for reference?"

Michael's nostrils flared. "No."

Morgan stood. "Objection, relevance. Your Honor, we've already established that Deke Willard will be in prison for the rest of his life. He's obviously no threat to Simon."

Judge O'Keefe nodded. "You've made your point, Mr. Foster. I'll accept as proven that Deke Willard is a career criminal. Move on."

Michael leaned forward. "Deke is a troubled boy."

Scott tapped the lectern for a moment. "There are a lot of those in the Willard family, aren't there? Let's talk about Deke's brother, Joseph Willard V."

Michael's face darkened. "Don't speak ill of the dead."

"He died in a shootout with police, didn't he?"

"They murdered him."

Scott reached for another document from his paralegal. "The police report says otherwise. Would you like to see it?"

A muscle twitched in Michael's neck. "No."

"Deke's and Joseph's cousin Thomas also died in the same incident. He fired shots at the police and died in the return gunfire, correct?"

"I'm sure you've got a police report that says so."

"I do. And your own brother, David, is currently awaiting trial for—"

Michael stood. "That's enough!"

The bailiff stepped into the well of the court and put his

hand on the butt of his Taser. Judge O'Keefe stabbed Michael with a cold glare. "Sit down!"

Michael slowly resumed his seat, every eye in the courtroom fixed on him. "I'm sorry."

"You'll be more than sorry if you do that again." There was granite in the judge's face and voice. "You'll be in jail for contempt." He nodded to Scott. "Proceed, Counsel."

"Mr. Willard, you are the only Willard male in your generation or the next younger generation who's not either behind bars or dead from violence, correct?"

Michael clenched his jaw and nodded.

"The court reporter needs an audible response."

"I have cousins and second cousins, but that's true enough of my immediate family."

"So would you agree that it's also true enough to refer to the Willards as a crime family?"

Michael's face mottled and his knuckles went white on the rail of the witness stand. For an instant Hez thought Michael was going to launch himself at Scott. The bailiff tensed and half drew the Taser.

Michael's jaw muscles worked for a moment, clenching and unclenching. "We're not a crime family, Mr. Foster. I'm proud of my family. Very proud. But . . . to tell the truth, the last few years have been hard." His voice roughened. "I-I'm all my mama has left, except the great-grandkids."

Scott gathered his papers. "No further questions."

Morgan stepped up to the lectern as Scott sat at the counsel table. "Do you intend to let Simon follow in the footsteps of Deke or other Willard men who have had trouble with the law?"

Michael scoffed. "Of course not."

"Will Simon have any contact with them?"

"No." Michael shot an icy glare at Scott. "Not unless he visits the cemetery or the prison."

"Do you love Simon?"

"With all my heart. That boy means the world to me."

"No further questions."

The tension in the courtroom eased as Michael left the witness stand and went back to his seat.

Judge O'Keefe glanced around. "Do the petitioners have additional witnesses?"

Scott stood. "No, Your Honor. Petitioners rest."

The judge looked at Morgan. "Does the counterpetitioner have any witnesses?"

Morgan rose. "Counterpetitioner also rests, Your Honor."

The judge nodded. "I believe quick resolutions are critical in adoption cases. And that's what I'm going to give all of you and Simon." He nodded to the bailiff. "Go get the boy so he can be here when I give my ruling."

CHAPTER 33

SAVANNAH LEANED AGAINST HEZ'S SOLID BULK AND TRIED to calm her racing pulse. The bailiff would bring Simon in any minute, and they'd know their future. Hez released her hand and slipped his arm around her. The familiar scent of his sage soap was a reminder of how seldom he lost a case. They would win this too.

She leaned closer to whisper in his ear. "I thought it went really well." Would Simon be allowed to sit with them, or would he sit with Michael? She wanted to take Simon and go home to a new normal life.

"Scott did a good job."

Hez's lackluster response sent a shudder of warning prickles down her back. "You can't think we'll lose—not when it's clear Michael runs a crime family. The judge has to see the danger in letting the Willards be Simon's main influence."

A worry line between his blue eyes deepened. "It could go either way, babe. Morgan made some good points too. Let's see what happens."

She bit her lip but didn't argue as the bailiff entered with Simon in tow. The boy shot her a worried glance, then sidled toward Michael. The bailiff redirected him and had him sit in the jury box with the guardian.

Judge O'Keefe steepled his fingers. "This has been a challenging case. Let me get right to the decision. I accept the guardian's recommendations and am granting Michael Willard's petition to adopt Simon. Simon, you still have a loving aunt and uncle, but you have a new father. You are now Simon Willard."

Simon whooped and leaped up to race to the front row. He flung his arms around his grandfather, who lifted him off his feet in a bear hug. "I'm a real Willard now!"

"It's the best day ever," Michael crowed.

His triumphant grin slammed straight into Savannah's chest, and her heart began to batter against her ribs. The sounds around her grew muffled from the blood roaring in her ears. She couldn't feel her body other than the vague sensation of Hez's arm holding her and the hot course of tears down her cheeks. This couldn't be happening. How could they withstand one more devastating blow? Michael had snatched away the last piece of her sister. He'd throw up a fatal obstacle to any influence they might have on Simon's life. It wouldn't be long before his sweet spirit was perverted and he went down the path of the others in the Willard family.

Her eyes filled. Would he be dead or in jail in ten years? She had to try to keep that from happening, but how?

Her nephew turned and smiled her way. He left Michael and came toward her with that same joyous expression. She couldn't muster up a smile to match his. She couldn't cough up a single syllable past the pain lodged in her midsection.

Simon's smile faltered. "You'll always be part of my family, Aunt Savannah. I love you and I can still come visit, right?"

She nodded and finally swallowed the boulder in her throat. "Your room at the house will always be there, and you can visit anytime."

Shoulders back and a triumphant smile on his face, Michael came toward them like a conqueror. His arrogance and pride had laid waste to the plans Jess had for her little boy, and hatred surged in Savannah's chest. She tried to shove it away, but it would take time to forgive him for the havoc he'd inflicted on their lives.

Michael's smile widened, and he drew Simon against his side in a proprietary hold. "Now you know exactly how I felt, Savannah. The pain of having someone you love ripped away forever is now yours. You shouldn't have underestimated me."

Simon's eyes widened, and his mouth dropped open as he stared up at his grandpa. His appalled gaze darted back to Savannah, and she saw the realization hit him that his grandpa was using him for revenge. He edged out of Michael's embrace and stared at the floor.

Hope stirred in Savannah's heart. If Simon saw Michael for who he really was, maybe he'd guard his heart against Michael's manipulation.

Simon reached for Hez's hand. "Do you still want me to be your best man, Uncle Hez?"

Hez pulled him into a man hug. "Of course I do. We'll always be best buds."

The glee in Michael's face ebbed, and he grabbed Simon's arm and drew him away from Hez. "Say goodbye, Simon. It's time to go *home*."

Simon pulled his arm away. "Bye, Aunt Savannah. I'll call you." He hugged her, and she clung to him until Michael pulled him back with an impatient huff.

Hez clapped Simon on the shoulder. "I'll call you about the wedding."

Michael took Simon's hand and led him toward the exit. Simon glanced back at Savannah with a forlorn expression before the courtroom door swung shut with a finality that broke her heart.

Michael kissed the soft petals, then bent and placed a single perfect red rose on Marie's grave. "We won. Our grandson is a Willard. I promised our love would never die, and it hasn't. The burned and hacked stump has grown a fresh shoot. He'll be a great man, maybe the greatest of us all. You'll be proud of him."

A gust of wind tossed the old branches high overhead and thunder boomed in the distance. A storm had been brewing on that day, but he and Marie hadn't cared. After she finished the poem for Mama's fiftieth birthday, Michael and Marie had kept meeting. They discovered that they both liked bluesy jazz, good coffee, beachcombing after a storm, and walking in the woods.

Tongues started to wag, of course, so they had stayed out of the public eye to avoid any "misunderstandings." It had all been innocent, at least from Marie's perspective. She was lonely and appreciated having a friend and sounding board for new poems. Michael enjoyed her company and—to his surprise—poetry. And he could feel her defenses slowly coming down, like a stone wall undermined by the gentle stream flowing at its base—until it came down with a sudden crash.

The crash had come on a blustery spring day. They had met for a walk at a nature preserve east of Foley. Marie had left Savannah with the nanny, saying she would spend the afternoon composing in the woods, which had been true enough. She and Michael walked under the tupelos and live oaks as wind gusted in the trees, carrying the scent of coming rain. She made up verse, remade it, and asked his opinion. He had loved it all, which alternately pleased and frustrated her.

She'd looked up at him, green eyes even more vibrant than usual thanks to the fresh emerald backdrop of the forest. "How can I get better if you never tell me when I'm bad?"

He smiled. "If you're ever bad, I'll tell you."

She quirked a smile. "You have no standards—which I both love and hate. Here, let me read you something really good." She reached into her purse and pulled out a book—she always had a book of poetry with her—and read to him. It had been E. E. Cummings, mostly poems about spring. Michael still remembered some of them: "i thank You God for most this amazing," "in Just-," "And this day it was Spring . . . us." She started to read "'I carry your heart with me (I carry it in my heart),'" but her voice caught in her throat.

The storm hit then, sudden and fierce. Wind whipped through the trees, followed by a wall of falling water. Michael pulled her against the gnarled bole of an ancient oak, out of the pelting rain. She looked up from the circle of his arms, hair dripping and eyes wide. Her breath had been shallow and uneven. She had been the most beautiful thing he had ever seen.

He bent and pressed his lips against hers as the storm raged around them. She froze for an instant—and then responded with electric intensity. She threw her arms around his neck and kissed him with a passion that stunned him.

Then the moment ended. She broke away from him and staggered back. She gasped and touched her lips as the rain streamed down her face.

He held out his arms toward her. "I love you, Marie! Come away with me! Come away with me forever!"

She turned and ran.

He called her name, but she didn't slow down. He ran after her. He reached the parking lot just as she roared away in the fancy SUV Pierre had bought her. Michael climbed into his pickup and drove home through the downpour, convinced that his plan had failed. Worse, he realized that he'd told the truth in the forest: He really did love Marie. And now he'd lost her forever.

But late that night, his phone had rung. "Did you mean it?" Marie asked without preamble.

"Mean what?"

"What you said today. Do you love me? Do you want me to come away with you forever?"

"Yes!"

She'd gone silent a moment before answering. "Then come get me now."

He had run to his truck and raced across town, eager to reach her mansion before she changed her mind. She walked out unsteadily, dragging a suitcase with one hand and carrying

Savannah in the other. She smelled of alcohol, but he hadn't thought much of it. She must have needed some liquid courage to make a decision that big.

The next six months had been the happiest of his life. Marie moved into his house with Savannah. Pierre had been gloriously furious and humiliated. He first claimed that Michael kidnapped Marie and Savannah. When she denied it and filed for divorce, he switched his story and said Michael had drugged Marie and was controlling her. Marie responded by giving obviously undrugged solo interviews to local and national media. Michael had sat back and enjoyed the show.

Meanwhile, Michael and Marie's love had deepened. They strolled his private forest, had long talks on his porch, and raced around Mobile Bay in his boat. Her poems from this time were happier than any of her other works. She gave him one that she never published:

I live in my lover's love
It is a wide country, beautiful and secret
His laugh like sunlight dancing on water
His eyes the blue of skies where eagles roam
His heart strong as a mountain and gentle as a summer breeze
Our love rushing like a river at flood
Our love quiet as a winter sunrise
Our love delicate as the first flower of spring
My heart at home in its homeland
At last and forever

Michael traced the letters on her gravestone. "At last and forever." If only that had been true.

An old black anger burned in his heart as he remembered what had come next. He comforted himself with the thought that his revenge against Pierre was unfolding beautifully. And the final act was about to begin.

"Justice is coming." A cold smile lifted his lips.

CHAPTER 34

HOLDING HEZ'S HAND, SAVANNAH WANDERED THROUGH their new home. The refinished floors gleamed, and the scents of paint, stain, and polyurethane permeated the air. The kitchen cabinets held her supplies and utensils except for the single skillet still at her house and a handful of old silverware and plates. She and Hez had picked out new dishes, Polish pottery she couldn't wait to use.

She followed Hez down the hall. The open door to Simon's room invited her to enter, but she pulled it shut with a decisive snap. "I can't look at it right now. We have no guarantee Michael will ever let him stay overnight."

Hez squeezed her fingers. "I'll get to work on a visitation agreement."

She caught his forced tone and knew he had his doubts as well. Michael would relish causing them as much pain as possible. The torment he planned to inflict was far from over, and she needed to be prepared for anything he might dish out. All that mattered was getting Simon through the damage his years spent with a psychopath like his grandfather were likely to cause.

Hez tugged at her hand. "Come to our room. Wait until you see it all done." He led her to the massive main bedroom and took her straight to the room's view of the sunset settling its red and gold rays over the water.

She caught her breath at the display of God's handiwork. "I can't believe we get to see that every evening."

Turning toward the room, she took in the furnishings. A gorgeous comforter and pillows in shades of blue and white covered the king bed she'd soon share with Hez, and she'd found a complementing blue rug that stretched under the bed. Bedside tables held matching lamps, and a stack of books waited on her side of the bed.

She stepped closer to examine the titles. The newest Lisa Gardner book was on top. "I didn't realize this was out yet." Under it were other favorite authors, including a new one by Robert Dugoni. "You know me so well."

He folded her in his arms. "You are my favorite area of study."

"I love our home so much. It would be perfect if only . . ."

"If only Simon could be with us." He pressed his lips on the top of her hair.

"It's so wrong, Hez. Justice is supposed to win, and yet it so often doesn't. I don't know how you continue to fight when bad decisions like this one come down."

His arms tightened around her, and he stiffened. "This isn't over, babe. I promise you Michael will pay for his crimes. I'll never give up no matter how long it takes. I know he is responsible for Ella's death, and I won't be able to rest until the truth is out and he's behind bars." His arms dropped away from her, and he turned toward the door. "I started an email to Hope with suggestions for how to tie Michael to Erik's disappearance. I think I'll go finish it and get it sent."

She caught his arm. The last thing she needed now was to lose him to his obsession with work. "Leave things to Hope, Hez, at least until after our honeymoon. I'm weary, and I know you have to be as well. You've worked long and hard on all the problems facing us. Let's rest so we can be ready to fight again later. I don't want to focus on anything but our upcoming wedding for a while. Michael is so unpredictable, so let's not provoke a battle until we're ready to deal with him." She cupped his face in her palms. "And speaking of honeymoons, where are we going? You've been very cagey about it."

They'd stayed in the Caribbean on their first honeymoon, but she wanted something completely fresh and different.

"It's a surprise."

"But how will I know what to pack?"

His blue eyes crinkled, and he waggled his eyebrows. "I have an accomplice for the packing dilemma."

"Nora?"

"Let's just say you don't have to worry about packing. I have it all under control." He took her in his arms again. "And you're right. The wedding is in two weeks, so let's savor these last few days. We can finish the yard and buy any other furnishings you want here before I finally get to carry you over the threshold." His lips claimed hers.

All her worry fled, and she wrapped her arms around his neck and sank into his embrace. She clung to him as the passion flared between them. When she opened her eyes, they were sitting on the edge of the bed. Hez's intense gaze smoldered its way into her heart, and she was so very tempted to shut the door and stay right here with him.

He sighed and stood, tugging her to her feet. "Let's go watch the sunset from the pier before I forget you don't have that ring on your finger yet."

Hez understood her better than she understood herself sometimes. She clasped his hand and went with him.

Hez paced the empty Justice Chamber as he waited for Hope to call. He touched the plaque on the wall and murmured the words like a prayer: " 'But let justice roll on like a river, righteousness like a never-failing stream!' "

It certainly looked like the river of justice had been dammed and the stream of righteousness had failed, but appearances could be deceiving. Michael had beaten them time after time, but Hez only needed to beat him once. If he could just catch Michael in one of his many serious crimes, that would be enough. Michael would be behind bars and away from Simon—and unable to interfere with Hez's investigation of the crime that mattered most.

Hez picked up a framed picture of Ella from the corner of his little desk. She smiled up at the camera, on the verge of a giggle. "Justice is coming, baby girl. Justice is coming."

His phone buzzed and he accepted the call. "Hi, Hope. What's up?"

"Thanks for that email about Michael Willard and Erik Andersen. Your instincts are as good as ever."

He fought back rising elation. "Did you arrest Michael?"

She chuckled. "If we did, the DA would hold a press conference—and he'd kill me if I told anyone before he announced it. I'm actually calling with a question."

He leaned against the side of the trefoil window and watched the workers attaching gutters to what Pierre had planned to call Legare Hall. Savannah had done a remarkable job with it, turning it from a half-finished ruin into a Gothic Revival masterpiece. It would be a campus jewel for generations. "Fire away."

"What do you know about Jimbo Clayton?"

Hez searched his memory. "He's part of the Willard clan, right? The name is vaguely familiar."

"Do you have any information about him? Anything that might give us a clue to his location?"

"Maybe. I think his name came up once or twice in the report from the PI we hired. Why?"

She sighed. "We have a warrant for his arrest, but he got wind of it and ran."

The dots connected. "The warrant is for the murder of Erik Andersen, isn't it?"

She was silent for a heartbeat. "Confidentially, yes. Very confidentially."

Hez punched the air. "I knew it! He forgot to turn off his phone, didn't he?"

"Close. He turned off his phone—but he forgot to turn off his smartwatch. We were able to track him to Andersen's house, through Gum Swamp, and then to the spot where we found Andersen's car. He stopped for a while in the swamp, so we took a cadaver dog out there and found a femur belonging to Andersen. The DNA just came back."

Hez pinched his lower lip as he absorbed the information. "Michael's phone was off at the same time, wasn't it?"

"Nope. On its charger at his home."

Hez rubbed the bridge of his nose. "We never catch the smart ones, do we?"

"No. No, we don't."

A realization hit Hez. "Nora Craft is smart."

"Uh, I guess so. Why? Where is your brain going?"

His brain was going back to Jess's funeral, trying to picture everyone who had been there. "You worked with the PHPD on the warrant for Clayton's arrest, didn't you?"

"Yes. It was in their jurisdiction and we'd caught the mole."

"I don't think so. Nora wouldn't have used her own credentials to steal files from the Birmingham PD. That would have been stupid, and Nora's not stupid."

"So who did it? And what about the security camera picture? The angle wasn't great, but I think that's Nora."

Hez's brain whirred. Who could he trust? "You, Jane Dixon, and I should meet. Now."

CHAPTER 35

SAVANNAH FROWNED WHEN HEZ DIDN'T PICK UP HER CALL. Again. She'd already left two messages, and the unusual silence alarmed her after everything they'd been through. She needed to know he was all right and Michael hadn't come after him. She shot off a quick text: Call me—I'm worried.

The last of her packing tasks at the cottage beckoned, and she finished loading a box of things from Simon's room. Grief pinched hard. Would he ever use the baseball mitt or the basketball in his closet again?

She taped shut the top of the box and carried it to join the others by the front door. Hez would load them in the back of his truck when he came. Movement through the front window caught her attention, and she spotted Nora jumping out of her car to rush to the door.

Savannah didn't wait for Nora to ring the bell and went to join her on the porch. Her smile faded when she saw Nora's tearstained face and red eyes. "What's happened?"

Savannah embraced Nora and hugged her tight as she sobbed against Savannah's shoulder. "I-it's Tammy. The police arrested her. I saw Hez heading into the station with Chief Dixon and Hope, but they wouldn't tell me anything."

No wonder Savannah hadn't been able to get ahold of him. "What were the charges?"

"I don't know exactly, but I have my suspicions." Nora pulled away and moved past Savannah into the living room where she fell into a chair. "You and I've been close a long time, but there's a lot about me you don't know. I hate talking about it, but it's important for you to understand. I did time in juvie myself."

Savannah's eyes widened. She perched on the edge of the sofa with the dogs curled at her feet. "You did?"

Nora nodded. "Uncle Michael can be charismatic, and I wasn't immune to the lure of being with my 'cool' cousins." She made air quotes. "I admired Little Joe, Tommy, and Deke and wanted to be just like them. Until it wasn't so cool and I got caught driving a stolen car. Looking back, it was the best thing that ever happened to me. I got sent to a great facility, and for the first time, I clearly saw the dark side of what Uncle Michael and the others were doing. I turned my life around, kept Uncle Michael and the rest at arm's length, and only saw them at family reunions. I saw Tammy going down the same path, and I wanted to help her. I even got her a job at PHPD so I could keep an eye on her, and she seemed to be on the right track."

Savannah tensed at the word "seemed." "But?"

Nora swiped at her wet eyes and sighed. "But I caught her in the evidence locker without authorization. She didn't have a good explanation for being in there, and I didn't like how evasive she was. I talked to my grandmother, hoping she would help, but she told me not to say anything. That it wasn't anything to worry about, and if I kept my mouth shut, no one would find out. That should have been my first clue that something was very wrong."

"Tammy used your credentials, didn't she? I knew you didn't steal Ella's file."

Nora gave a jerky nod. "We resemble each other, and she could easily pass for me when she borrowed my credentials. I didn't want to turn her in and begged her to do the right thing on her own, but she refused. Now she's ruined her life." Nora buried her face in her hands. "I don't know what to do."

"We can pray for her." Savannah patted the sofa cushion beside her. "Sit by me, and we'll pray right now."

When Nora moved to sit beside her, Savannah took her hand and they prayed for mercy and wisdom, but most of all for Tammy to realize her spiritual condition. They were both weeping when Nora echoed Savannah's "Amen."

"I have to go." Nora rose. "I knew you'd help me. Thank you." She gave her a fierce hug before Savannah walked her to the door.

Sunset was falling, and the streetlights came on. A breeze lifted Savannah's hair as she waved goodbye. Nora's car backed out of the driveway, and Savannah started to enter the house again. An envelope lay partially hidden by the floor mat, and she picked it up. The flap resisted her fingers, and she ripped it open. Inside was a phone bill with Deke Willard's name at the top, and she glanced at the date, which was four years ago. What on earth? An entry halfway down the page was highlighted in yellow.

Hez needed to see this right away. She rushed inside to grab her phone.

Michael's heart rate went up as he turned into the Oyster Hill Country Club in Nova Cambridge. He'd been anticipating this for a long time.

The clubhouse was an imposing old white building with a pillared porch. It had started life as an antebellum mansion, according to the bronze plaque Michael had read when he toured the place last week before buying his membership. Huge old oaks shaded the clubhouse and grass as green and perfect as an emerald carpet.

Michael spotted Pierre's silver Mercedes E 350 in the lot, even though his tee time wasn't for another hour. Pierre must be in the clubhouse or on the driving range. Good.

The sun stood high in a hot, cloudless sky, so Michael parked in a shady spot. He turned to Simon, who was staring at the old mansion. "Have you ever been golfing before?"

Simon's eyes went wide. "This will be my first time."

"Then we'd better start you off with some lessons and maybe a bite to eat."

They walked up the oyster-shell path to the clubhouse entrance and stepped through the double doors into the cool interior. The foyer had a high ceiling and dark wood floors decorated with expensive-looking old rugs. A scattering of antique chairs and tables stood against the walls. Michael inhaled deeply, drawing in the scents of old wood, fresh flowers, and a hint of perfume from a well-dressed woman who walked by. The smell of money.

A glance through the window facing the driving range told Michael that Pierre must be in the clubhouse. Probably in the restaurant. He turned to Simon. "I could use a burger and some sweet tea. How about you?"

Simon grinned. "Sounds great! Can I have a root beer float?"

Michael tousled his grandson's blond hair. "Of course."

They went to the dining room and stood in the entrance as Michael scanned the tables. It was nearly noon, and the place was almost full. Perfect.

Simon spotted Pierre first. "Grandpa Legare!"

Pierre stared at them, his mouth hanging open. He sat with an attractive blonde of about forty whom Michael didn't recognize. She seemed a little surprised at Pierre's reaction but regained her composure and smiled at them.

Michael smiled back and waved to Pierre as a host walked up with menus. Michael took the menus from the young man and gestured toward Pierre. "I see my friend is already here."

Michael walked to Pierre's table with Simon trailing him. He pulled out a chair and sat. "What a pleasant surprise." He turned to the woman. "I'm Michael Willard, and this is my grandson, Simon Willard."

She gave a polite nod. "Pleased to meet you. I'm Susan Beaufort."

"What are you doing here?" Pierre asked, his voice tight.

"Having lunch with you, of course. I'm a member now, so we'll be seeing a lot of each other—or at least we will for as long as you can pay membership dues." Michael spoke loud enough for nearby tables to overhear. "I know money has been tight since you can't embezzle from the university anymore."

The buzz of conversation around them subsided. Pierre turned white. "That's a lie!"

Michael laughed. "As the kids say, I have receipts—and these are actual receipts." He took out his phone and opened a document. "Here's a TGU credit card statement from your time as university president. You charged the university for remodeling at your Pensacola condo." He swiped on his phone. "And oh, look! Here's a charge from Elegant Encounters. That's an escort service, isn't it?"

Pierre glared daggers at him. "I wouldn't know."

"Sure you would." Michael swiped again and held up his phone. It showed a picture of Pierre with a heavily made-up young woman wearing a tight cocktail dress. "This is you and Desiree from Elegant Encounters."

Pierre slapped the phone from Michael's hand, and it clattered to the floor. Cracks spidered across the screen. The dining room was completely silent.

Michael leaned forward and spoke softly. "Touch me again and I'll break your arm."

"Get out of here!" Pierre hissed.

"Or what?" Michael leaned back and smiled. "Say you'll make me, Pierre. Ask me to step outside. *Please* ask me to step outside."

Pierre stood, quivering with rage. He turned to Susan. "Come on. We're leaving." He stormed off without waiting for her.

"See you at First Baptist on Sunday morning," Michael called after him.

Pierre flinched, but he kept walking.

Michael chuckled at his retreating back. He turned to Susan, who still sat frozen at the table. "You're welcome to stay, honey. I've got lots of Pierre stories I can tell you."

She stared at Michael for a second, then rose and hurried after Pierre.

Michael bent and picked up his phone. He turned to Simon, who had watched the whole scene with wide eyes. "That's your first lesson in what the Legares are really like. They may look nice, act nice, and go to nice places—but they're not at all nice on the inside. Poke a hole in that pretty surface and you'll see that they're all fakes and cowards." He patted Simon on the shoulder. "Now, let's get you that root beer float."

"Aunt Savannah is nice all the way through. I don't think I want a root beer float anymore. Can we go now? People are staring at us."

"I'm not ready yet." Conversations restarted around them, this time in whispers. Michael savored it. He imagined similar conversations in the parking lot outside First Baptist on Sunday, around the boathouse in front of the building where Pierre had a condo in Pensacola, and every other place Pierre went. It would be magnificent.

Pierre had taught Michael this tactic thirty years ago, and his brain played back that brutal lesson.

Michael closed his file folder and went to find Marie on the front porch swing of the old house. She sat scribbling in her poetry notebook with her legs tucked under her, and he'd never seen a more beautiful sight than her auburn hair tumbling down her shoulders. And she was all his now that the big influx of cash was in his account. He could give her the house and the life she deserved.

She noticed him, and her smile squeezed his chest. "You seem happy."

"I am. Let's go house hunting."

"What's wrong with this house?"

"Everything. You deserve a mansion like the one you left for me."

"I don't care about houses as long as I have you." She moved her legs and patted the spot beside her on the swing.

Michael started toward her, but a familiar Mercedes pulled into his weedy driveway. Marie murmured, "Oh no," and Michael fisted his hands at his sides and strode to intercept Pierre.

Marie's husband unwound long legs from behind the wheel of the convertible. He wore an expression of satisfaction and held up a sheaf of papers in one hand and a gun in the other.

Michael had left his gun in the house and had no time to retrieve it.

Pierre didn't look at Marie. The bore of the gun pointed at Michael's chest. "I've come for my wife. Marie, get your things."

"She's not going anywhere with you."

Pierre smiled and held up the papers. "No? If she's not in the car immediately, I'll turn these over to the FBI and the DEA. You'll spend the rest of your life peering through bars and wishing you'd listened."

Marie came to Michael's side when he took the papers and flipped through them. Meth sales and extortion statements from businesses in town were neatly chronicled. Pierre had it all.

Marie took a step back. "I'm not going anywhere with you. I'll tell everyone the truth about you when I divorce you. You'll never hold your head up in this county again. I'll leave you without a penny."

Pierre laughed coldly. "My money is in a 'spendthrift trust.'

You'll be bagging groceries and living on food stamps. I own the judges in Baldwin County, and you'll never get custody of Savannah. I'll have your beloved daughter *and* all my money. You'll have . . . nothing." He jerked his head toward the car. "Not another word. Get in."

Marie was so pale that Michael thought she'd faint. He put his hand on her forearm. "Don't listen to him, Marie. He's bluffing."

She pulled out of his grip. "He never bluffs." She rose slowly, as if every movement hurt, and walked into the house. She returned with Savannah in her arms, then walked down the rickety steps. "I despise you," she told Pierre, who only shrugged as she got in the car.

Michael had to watch Pierre drive her out of his life.

Michael blinked and pushed away the worst memory of his life. Since that moment he'd spent three decades doing the same thing to Pierre. He'd had him followed, had surreptitiously gone through his trash, and had bided his time until this moment. Jess had uncovered a treasure trove of sleaze, using her position as TGU's CFO to dig through the university's financial records. Michael was still working on a few details, but he had plenty of acid to dribble over Pierre and his reputation in the meantime.

Would Pierre run away every time Michael confronted him? Or would he eventually take a swing at Michael? Both would be fun.

CHAPTER 36

SAVANNAH SLID THE LAST OF HER BOOKS INTO HER SECTION of the home office bookcases. Hez's legal tomes occupied the ones on the other side of the window looking out onto their driveway. "It's beginning to feel like home."

His dark hair askew and still on his knees, Hez backed out from under the desk where he'd been monkeying with the computer cords. "I think we're all set with the computer." The built-in oak desk wrapped around two sides of the room with plenty of space for them both to have computers or laptops.

She reached out and brushed cobwebs from his hair, then wiped them off on her jeans. "There's nothing sexier than a man chasing away spiders."

He grinned and sat on the floor, then tugged her down onto his lap. "I should get some compensation for braving the cobwebs."

She nestled against him and palmed his face. "I could see my way clear to thanking you for squashing those nasty beasts." She pulled his head down, and his lips captured hers. She'd wrapped her arms around his neck to kiss him back properly when the popping of tires on gravel brought her attention around to the window.

A car had stopped by the brick path to their front door, and she winced at her father's stormy expression when he exited the vehicle. "Uh-oh, he's probably gotten this month's bank statement."

"Let's not answer. He won't see us sitting here on the floor."

"Both of our vehicles are outside." She brushed his lips with hers again before getting up. "Later."

"I'll hold you to that promise."

"You could come with me."

"I think I'll stay right here. Out of sight, out of mind."

"Coward." She didn't blame him. If she could hide out in the office, she would too. It would be her father's first glimpse of what they'd done to the house. Would he notice or comment?

She met her dad at the door. "What a surprise, Dad." Up close his expression wasn't so much stormy as incensed with more rage than she'd ever seen him display. She wasn't sure she wanted to ask him what was wrong, but he'd tell her whether she asked or not. "Coffee or sweet tea?"

He pushed past her. "Is Hez here?" The aroma of his pipe tobacco and lemon gumdrops wafted in his wake.

Uh-oh. "This way." She led him to the office, and Hez rose from the floor. "Dad needed to talk to you too."

Her dad hadn't even noticed the refinishing of the floors or the new paint on the walls. He'd made no comment about the furniture or anything, which shouldn't have been a surprise. Only greenbacks mattered to him.

Her father strode toward Hez. "I've got a present for you—for both of you—but Hez will best know what to do with it." He set a fat file folder on the desk and topped it with a thumb drive.

Hez picked up the items. "What's this all about?"

"It's everything you need to stop Michael Willard from corrupting your nephew. Private investigator reports, surveillance pictures of his activities, and other documents that will show his criminal behavior. No judge will let him have influence over Simon when the truth comes out."

Hez leafed through the documents and whistled when he reached a raft of pictures. He turned it around for Savannah to see, and she winced at what appeared to be a dead man on the ground. "Is this what you offered to sell Hez?" she asked her father.

"It is. My money is running out and I'd hoped to shore up my finances with the sale, but I can't stand by and let Michael get by with his arrogance. The information goes back thirty years to when I used it to beat him when he tried to steal your mother. He's still the same. I've got evidence from a month ago that will prove a leopard doesn't change his spots. With the new proof, you can get Simon back." He took Savannah's hand. "It's my gift to you. You and Hez have proven you're an effective team. I thought about using it on my own, but in Hez's hands, you'll get more done."

"Why now, Dad? What happened today? You were livid when you got out of the car."

His lips flattened. "Michael brought Simon to my country club. He had the gall to say I embezzled money from the university—in front of my date, no less. He spewed all kinds of lies and showed doctored pictures."

Savannah had her doubts about that when his gaze cut away from hers. She should have known only something personal would drive him to give up this information. "I suppose you want money."

He narrowed his eyes. "That's not why I'm here. You have to take that man down permanently, Savannah. He can't ever treat another Legare like he did me today."

Hez's blue eyes gleamed and he smiled. "I'll study what you've given us. It seems promising, though I'm not seeing as much detail in the newer stuff."

Dad nodded. "He's been more careful in recent years. No direct involvement with crimes when he can avoid it. He used burner phones and voice-altering software for all his business. Even when contacting his family, his voice never sounded like himself. He kept everyone guessing. But I got everything I could."

Hez put the file down. "Thank you. We love Simon and want him out of Michael's influence."

Her father's chest puffed out beneath his navy jacket. "When I saw the boy drinking in every word Michael said, I knew I had to do something. There was no love lost between me and Jess, but it's not Simon's fault. He's a good kid, and I'd hate to see him turn out like Little Joe."

Savannah wished she could believe it was concern for Simon that had driven him here today, but she knew better. It was the slur to his own reputation and the fact Michael had dared to confront him on his own turf. No one could ever say Michael cared what people thought, though, and her father couldn't stand that kind of impudence when he cared so deeply about his role in the community. But she'd take whatever help she could get to save her nephew.

Hez had been trying. He really had. Savannah had asked him to leave the investigation of Michael's crimes alone, at least until after their wedding. But the investigation wouldn't leave him alone. First came Tammy's arrest, then the mystery phone bill on Savannah's doorstep, and now Pierre's file. It wasn't completely Hez's fault that he and Savannah were sitting in Hope's office less than a week before their wedding, but he still felt guilty.

As the Websters seated themselves in Hope's guest chairs, she smiled at them and kicked off her three-inch heels. She'd just come back from court and hung her jacket on a hanger on her coat tree. "Thanks for coming in." Her chin-length brown hair swung forward, and she tucked a lock behind her ear, then patted a thick stack of documents. "The new materials you provided include a lot of helpful context. Do you have anything else that could help us fill in some gaps?"

Hez leaned forward. "We're happy to help. Did you have any specific gaps in mind?

Hope picked up the top document. "Mr. Legare's file contains strong evidence of drug trafficking—mostly meth—but a lot of it is over thirty years old."

Hez wrinkled his brow. "I thought there was no statute of limitations for drug trafficking."

"There isn't, but the DA won't invest resources in a drug case from the 1990s, especially when the defendant is a prominent local businessman from an old family."

Savannah scoffed. "Are you sure you're describing Michael Willard?"

Hope gave her a sympathetic look. "I know he isn't what he

seems, but the rest of the county doesn't know that. They see a successful businessman who donates to local schools and"—she cleared her throat—"supports local leaders."

Hez rubbed his temples. "He donated to the DA's campaign, didn't he?"

Hope's tone and brown eyes were blank. "I can't comment on that, but all campaigns must disclose itemized contribution records. That includes district attorney campaigns, of course."

Hez swallowed an unhelpful remark. "Okay, so you're not likely to prosecute the older stuff. What about the more recent evidence in the file?"

Hope picked up some documents and flipped through them. "It's more tenuous, unfortunately—anonymous and somewhat vague reports of Michael trafficking in Mexican explosives and American guns and engaging in artifact smuggling, pictures of him with known mobsters, and so on. If you or Mr. Legare have any additional evidence, we'd really appreciate it."

Savannah slumped, but Hez wasn't surprised. He'd had the same reaction when he read the newer materials in Pierre's file. Michael learned his lesson from his confrontation with Pierre over Marie, and he'd been more careful in recent years. "We'll ask, but I'm not aware of anything. What about that highlighted phone bill someone left for Savannah?"

Hope plucked a copy from her stack. "The number belongs to a burner phone purchased with cash in Mobile four years ago. Any surveillance video is long gone, of course."

"Another dead end." Hez rubbed the bridge of his nose. "That's why you asked for a meeting, isn't it? You're stuck and you hoped we might have more leads."

Hope gave a wan smile. "Guilty as charged."

Hez tugged at his lower lip. "Michael used burner phones for his criminal business."

Hope leaned back in her chair. "So do lots of criminals, including several other members of his organization. That's one reason we weren't able to nail him or his company as part of that artifact-smuggling case."

Hez fought back his frustration. Michael was about to slip through their fingers. Again. "Sorry, I can't think of anything else."

Savannah sat up straight. "Michael doesn't know that."

A little line appeared between Hope's brows. "What do you mean?"

"Michael doesn't know we're stuck." Savannah leaned forward. "Maybe we can trick him."

Hez turned toward her. "Do you have anything specific in mind?"

Savannah nodded. "We know he's been using Tammy to steal evidence from the Pelican Harbor police. What if we make him think we have really damning evidence against him? He can't use Tammy anymore, so he might try to steal it on his own."

Hez snapped his fingers. "The burner phone! If we had that, we could mine it for all sorts of information. If Michael thinks we've somehow found it, that would worry him." He turned to Hope. "What do you think of leaking to the press that Ella's death has been reclassified as a homicide and law enforcement has the burner phone used to arrange the crime?"

Hope looked into the distance for a moment. "I think I can do that."

Hez drummed his fingers on his chair's armrest. "I'll see if

I can talk Bruno Rubinelli into visiting. He said he wanted to try real beignets and shrimp bisque. We could set him up in an office at the PHPD and give him a dirty old burner phone to pretend to work on. It's a small town and people will ask him who he is and what he's doing."

Savannah chuckled. "They will indeed, and then they'll talk about him. All he needs to do is drop a couple hints and word will get back to Michael in no time."

Hope jotted down a note on a pad on her desk. "If you can get Bruno out here, I'm pretty sure I can arrange a workspace for him that's easy to break into—but will have excellent sensors and security cameras."

Hez leaned back in his chair and smiled. "Perfect."

CHAPTER 37

NERVES AND OVER-THE-TOP BRIDAL DRAMA OOZED FROM the walls of the Tropical Weddings shop in downtown Pelican Harbor. Butterflies fluttered in Savannah's stomach as she waited for her wedding dress to be brought out for the final fitting. How many brides over the years had browsed through these dresses to find the perfect one for their special day?

Nora twirled in her knee-length blue dress. The color complemented her complexion and was a beautiful contrast with her brown hair and eyes. The ruffles shimmered down her slim form to end just above her knees. "I love it, Savannah."

Savannah rose and walked around Nora to check out the dress from all angles. "It fits perfectly now that it was hemmed a bit. You look beautiful." She turned to see the owner, Fiona Hamilton, carrying a champagne dress draped over both arms. Her blonde hair was up in a bun, and she wore a skirt and blouse reminiscent of Lucille Ball.

Savannah's pulse kicked. She hadn't seen the dress in several weeks. Was it as perfect as she remembered? "Let's check the fit now. It was a little big last time, but unless your weight has changed, it should be fine now."

She wanted more than fine. She didn't want to be a bridezilla insisting everything had to be perfect, but she wanted to knock Hez's socks off when she walked out. The consultant led her to the huge dressing room, where Savannah disrobed. The lightweight silken folds drifted down over her figure to settle at her ankles. The whisper of the zipper and the scent of the silk took her back to the first time she'd said "I do" to Hez. She was older and wiser now but no less in love with him. Maybe even more so.

Only a few more days until she was Mrs. Hezekiah Webster again for real.

Fiona pushed back the curtain. "Let's take a peek in the big mirrors."

Savannah followed her out into the promenade area with its massive mirrors and stared at herself. The color made her auburn hair gleam in the lights, and the folds of the dress skimmed her waist and hips perfectly. The silk underskirt hugged her skin, and the tiny details of the flowers on the chiffon overlay shimmered in the light. The modest bodice and full skirt flattered her figure in a way she thought Hez would like. It was even more perfect than she remembered.

"Hez might pass out." Nora adjusted the hem of the silk cap sleeve. "The champagne color is perfect." She stepped back and glanced toward the door when a bell attached to it jingled. She stilled and pressed her lips together.

Savannah turned to see what had caught her attention. Nora's niece Tammy had entered. Her dark brown hair was mussed, and she smoothed it as she walked toward them over the beige carpet. She wore jeans and a blue tee. Had she just gotten out of jail?

Tammy's gaze slid from Savannah to Nora and back again, and then she squared her shoulders at Nora's encouraging nod.

Savannah sent a questioning glance in Nora's direction, but her friend kept a soft smile directed at her niece while Tammy's full attention was on Savannah. Why was she here?

Tears dampened Tammy's cheeks, and red rimmed her brown eyes, so like Nora's. The two looked enough alike to be sisters. "I—I owe you an apology, Savannah." Tammy sent an appealing glance toward Fiona.

The store owner backed away. "I'll check on you later, Savannah." She gave Tammy's arm an encouraging pat, then walked toward the back of the store.

Tammy sniffled and hiked her purse strap back into place on her shoulder. "I should have known better than to listen to Uncle Michael. I stole evidence from the PHPD, and I'm in so much trouble." She choked back a sob. "It was so stupid. At first he just wanted me to spy on the police department and tell him what they were investigating, but it got to be more than that. More and more and more. The orders never stopped, but I was a frog in water that was getting hotter and didn't realize I needed to hop out. Now it's too late." She shuffled her sneakered feet.

Savannah's chest stirred with pity. The girl was so young, not even twenty-five. And she'd had a rough life without a lot of role models. Only Nora would have stood in the gap and tried to point the girl in the right direction. "I'm sorry for your trouble, Tammy. Are the charges serious?"

Tammy gave a jerky nod and dug a crumpled paper napkin from her purse to use on her damp face. "I destroyed evidence. Uncle Michael had me burn stuff and throw it off the Kate

Norris Bridge. And I handed some things over to him." She began to shred the napkin into pieces. "Like your little girl's file."

"What did he want with Ella's file?"

Tammy's fingers stilled their shredding. "I—I think maybe he wanted to use it to hurt you and Hez somehow. I wasn't sure how exactly, but he insisted I steal it. Maybe it was something about Simon. I'm so sorry. I hope you can forgive me." Her voice trembled and faded to a whisper. "I'm so ashamed."

"Does he still have the file?" Savannah asked.

"I think so."

"Could you get it back? We now know Ella was murdered, and there are details in that file that could be important."

Tammy's morose expression brightened, and she nodded. "I can try. I might get in trouble if he catches me, but I don't care. If I get it back for you, can you forgive me?"

"I forgive you even if you don't get it back, but it would be helpful if we could study the evidence now that we know the truth."

And maybe there was a clue that had been missed originally.

Hez suppressed a chuckle when Bruno Rubinelli walked into the Pelican Harbor Police Department headquarters. A frown line creased the space between Detective Augusta Richards's brows, and a deputy's hand twitched toward the cuffs on his belt, as if he wanted to arrest Bruno on general principle.

Bruno didn't seem to notice. He carried a skateboard under one bony, tattoo-covered arm and a ratty backpack over the opposite shoulder. He wore ripped jeans and an ancient Skynet T-shirt that had once been black. The fluorescent lights gleamed off his hairless skull as it swiveled on his long neck, scanning the PHPD lobby.

He spotted Hez and broke into a toothy grin. "There he is. You got those beignets you promised me?"

Hez held up a bag from Petit Charms. "Still warm. Let's get you situated."

Hez introduced Bruno to Augusta as they walked down the hall to the office she had prepared for him. Augusta had picked one at the back of the building near an exit and without obvious security to make it enticing to Michael. She tucked a lock of short brown hair behind her ear as she pointed out the sensors and cameras the department had installed. "We've got two hidden cameras watching the window, one inside and one outside. Pressure pads are under the carpet by the window and all around the desk."

She picked up a dirty phone with a cracked screen from the utilitarian desk in the middle of the room. "This is a four-year-old prepaid phone of the make and model sold in the store where our target bought the phone used to call Deke Willard. Do you need anything else at the moment?"

Bruno opened the Petit Charms bag and inhaled. "Ahh. Is your coffee any good?"

A smile cracked Augusta's no-nonsense demeanor. "The chief's is. She just set up a coffee bar in her office. I'll see if I can get you a cup. How do you like it?"

"Black, thanks." Bruno unzipped his backpack as Augusta left. He pulled out a heavily stickered laptop and a couple of metal boxes that sprouted numerous wires, one of which he connected to the phone on the desk. "Might as well make it look realistic."

Augusta returned with the coffee. Bruno accepted the mug gratefully and took a bite of beignet. "Awesome. Good as advertised."

Hez got up. "Glad you like them. I've got a meeting, but let me know if you need anything."

Bruno gave a thumbs-up and swallowed. "Will do. Gonna hang here for a few, then find a skate park or somethin'. Chat up the locals a little like you asked."

Hez thanked him and left with Augusta, who cast a doubtful glance back over her shoulder as they walked to their meeting. "If the FBI didn't vouch for him, I'd be a little worried he'd hack into our computers."

Hez laughed. "He could do that from back in California. Trust me—we're lucky he's on our side."

They walked into Chief Jane Dixon's office, and she rose to greet them. Hope was seated in one of Jane's guest chairs with a laptop on her knees. "Hey, Hez. Did you get my email just now?"

"No. We were getting Bruno set up. What's going on?"

Hope closed her laptop. "Well, the good news is that we've got the area around the Norris Bridge secured—for now."

Hez braced himself. "And the bad news?"

Hope sighed. "It'll take two weeks to get a diver out here. We usually work with the Coast Guard, but they don't have anyone available until the end of the month."

Jane looked grim. "And I can't keep an officer out there guarding the site for that long."

Hez couldn't believe his ears. "The Norris Bridge is right at the entrance to Weeks Bay. It would only take a minute to reach from Mobile Bay. Michael Willard can just wait for your officer to leave and then send in his own diver or dredge the area under the bridge."

Augusta shrugged. "He'd have to be ready with a diver or dredger, of course."

Hez arched an eyebrow. "Have you met this guy?"

Jane drummed her fingers. "Do you have any suggestions, Hez?"

He tugged at his lower lip for a moment. "The diver doesn't have to be a government employee, right? They just must be under police supervision?"

Hope nodded slowly. "Yes. We'll need to show chain of custody and that proper evidence-gathering protocols were followed, but we don't technically need a government diver."

Hez relaxed a fraction. "Then I might have a guy for you. His name is Ed Hernandez and he's a varsity swimmer. I think he's scuba certified too."

"Excellent." Jane pulled up a calendar on her monitor. "I'd love to get my deputy back tomorrow. Can you get him out there that soon?"

"I'll talk to him as soon as we're done." Unease crept into Hez's gut. He might have just put a target on Ed's back.

CHAPTER 38

WEEKS BAY REFLECTED A MIRROR IMAGE OF THE BLUE SKY. Savannah stood with Hez watching Augusta offshore twenty feet in an anchored boat. The breeze left a salty tang on her lips and lifted her hair. The sun glaring off the water made it hard to see what was happening out in the boat.

Curious drivers slowed their vehicles to try to figure out what the police were doing. Ed clung to the side of the boat, and the detective received a dripping-wet dive bag of evidence from him. He adjusted his mask and plunged into the water under the Norris Bridge again.

Hez shaded his eyes. "Ed's exhausted. It's hard work fighting the current between Mobile Bay and Weeks Bay with those tanks. The silt makes visibility bad."

Savannah moved restlessly. "It's been two days, and they've found some good stuff. Shouldn't that be enough to arrest Michael? The gun and who knows what else in those muddy bags should be plenty. There's even a part from your old Audi."

"The police are closing in." He shaded his eyes with his hand and observed the activity on the boat. "I wish they'd let me on the boat to examine the evidence. Michael has to be worried—especially with that 'leaked' article about Ella's murder and the cell phone."

A picture of Bruno entering the rear door of the police station showed how unsecured the office was, and she'd expected a break-in attempt by now. She closed her fingers around Hez's forearm. "You need to stay out of it. There's already a target on your back." She slid her hand down his arm to take his hand and steer him toward their vehicles. "You have a class to teach in an hour."

He resisted her tug. "I'd hoped to see some sudden activity that might indicate they're heading out to arrest him. I'd love to be there and see his shock when they snap the cuffs on him. He needs to pay for what he did to our daughter."

She released him and brushed a strand of hair out of her eyes. "I want to bring him to justice too, but his arrest won't bring back Ella. She'll always be part of us and I will miss her every day of my life, but I keep reminding myself that God's justice is better than anything we can do." She reached up and smoothed the lines between his blue eyes with her fingertip. "I want to see that worry disappear and your smile come back. You've been so focused on getting Michael behind bars that I haven't heard you laugh in weeks."

"It's not just justice for Ella—it's Simon's future I'm worried about too."

"So am I, but I keep reminding myself God loves Simon even more than we do, and he will take care of him. Trust is hard for me—especially after losing Ella—but I'm working on it. I want us both to try to put aside our worry and the need to fix something that's out of our hands. At least for now."

He pulled her close and kissed the top of her head. "I'll try, but I'd sure like to go on our honeymoon with Michael behind bars."

"So would I."

"If by some miracle we get Simon back before the wedding, what do we do with him on our trip?"

"Nora has already offered to stay at our house with him. Being in his own room will give him stability, and he can settle in even if we're not there."

Hez pulled back and studied her face. "You think it's going to happen, don't you? That Michael will go to jail and we'll have Simon back?"

Was that what this sense of peace was all about? "I don't know if he'll be in our custody again before our wedding, but I know God has a plan. I'm clinging to that even though I have to remind myself of it a thousand times a day." She poked her fingers in his ribs. "You might try remembering that too. And Michael's arrest is Augusta's job, not yours. Your job is to think about where you're taking me on our honeymoon. Let's take things one day at a time and not try to micromanage everyone else."

Even though he nodded and walked with her to the car, this battle wasn't over for either of them. All she could hope for was a respite for the wedding and their honeymoon.

Michael watched through binoculars as Savannah led Hez toward their vehicles. He kept glancing back over his shoulder, like a kid forced to leave the toy section at Walmart. The guy spent all his time at the dive site, hanging around the police station, or huddling with that lady prosecutor, Hope Norcross. Put another way, Hez spent every free minute hunting Michael.

It had to stop.

Michael lowered his binoculars. He'd hoped that Hez would give up after the judge granted the adoption petition. But then, he'd had the same hope when he handed Hez those pictures of Martine and him. And when he fired shots into Hez's condo the night before a key hearing. And when his men put Hez in the hospital with a near-fatal brain bleed.

The guy wouldn't give up. He couldn't be bullied. He refused to stay down despite repeated beatings in and out of the courtroom. He just kept coming. Michael admired that, but he couldn't tolerate it.

Besides, Jess's death needed to be avenged.

Michael shoved the binoculars in his truck's glove compartment and put the vehicle in gear. He drove to the back of the woods behind his house and turned onto an old logging road. Two hundred yards in, he stopped and tapped his horn three times in quick succession.

A few seconds later, Jimbo appeared among the thin-trunked pines holding a pistol and eyeing the truck warily. He'd been hiding in the woods while Michael arranged for him to be smuggled out of the country. "I thought the truck takin' me to Mexico didn't leave 'til tomorrow night."

"Change of plans." Michael pointed to the passenger door. "Get in."

Jimbo shrugged and climbed into the truck. "Where we goin'?"

"We're feeding the gators again. Slouch back so no one sees your face."

Jimbo slumped in his seat and turned away from the window as Michael pulled back onto the county road and drove toward campus. If someone glanced in through the windshield, Jimbo would be impossible to identify.

Michael pulled into the TGU parking lot and drove slowly along the rows of vehicles, scanning for Hez's. There it was, parked in a shady spot near the back and away from any security cameras—and Hez was still in it, doing something on his phone. Perfect.

Michael nudged Jimbo. "Our guy is in the silver GMC. We need to get him in my truck and take him out to the swamp, just like last time."

They parked behind Hez's truck, jumped out, and ran to the driver's door, guns drawn. Michael yanked open the door. "Get out! Leave your phone and watch in your truck. And give me your gun, butt first."

Hez's eyes went wide with shock, then narrowed as he focused on Michael. His gaze flicked to Jimbo and recognition dawned on his face. He looked back at Michael. "What do you want?"

"We're going for a drive. Get out now!"

Hez sighed. "Okay." He took off his watch and tossed it and his phone onto the seat of his truck. Then he pulled out his gun and held it out butt-first. As Michael reached for it, Hez flipped it around with a flick of his wrist.

Michael hadn't expected Hez to go without a fight. He jumped to the side and slapped at the gun, throwing off Hez's aim. A shot erupted from Hez's pistol, but the bullet buried itself in the asphalt rather than Michael's chest.

Jimbo grabbed Hez's wrist and yanked him out of the car.

Michael sucker punched the lawyer, stunning him long enough for them to take his pistol and shove him into the back seat of Michael's truck. Michael scanned the area as he got into the cab. No one in sight.

Hez came to as Michael pulled out of the parking lot. Michael glanced in the rearview mirror to make sure Jimbo had everything under control. Hez struggled for a moment, but Jimbo held his arm in an iron grip and jammed his gun into Hez's ribs. Hez winced and stopped fighting. He met Michael's gaze in the mirror. "Okay, we're going for a drive. What do you want?"

"You killed my daughter."

Hez's brows furrowed in confusion. "You think I blew up my own car?"

"You knew the bomb was in it and you gave Jess the keys."

Hez shook his head. "I had no idea there was a bomb in the car. If I did, I would've called the police."

"Then why did you leave it sitting in the lot for weeks?"

"I couldn't drive." Hez tapped the left side of his skull. "Your guys put me in the hospital, remember? No driving for three months."

Michael's knuckles whitened on the wheel. "You knew it was there! You've figured out everything—you must've figured out that too. You knew Jess set you up and tried to keep you and Savannah apart. You knew she put TGU in bankruptcy. So you killed her in a way that kept your hands completely clean. You're a smart guy, Counsel. Stop playing dumb!"

"I'm not like you, Michael." Disgust and controlled rage filled Hez's voice. "I didn't kill your daughter—but you did kill mine."

"I didn't kill Ella."

"Liar!"

Michael looked in the mirror. Hez's eyes glared back at him, full of blue fire. The man had a gun in his ribs and must know where they were taking him, but he wasn't sweating or begging for his life. He was furious and spitting insults.

Michael gave a low laugh. "I should have killed you a long time ago. I would've saved a lot of trouble. Couldn't bring myself to do it, though. I liked you too much. Ah, well. Too bad you weren't born a Willard."

Surprise registered on Hez's face, but he said nothing.

Michael slowed as they reached the edge of Gum Swamp. "Do you like poetry, Counsel?"

CHAPTER 39

A LAWN MOWER GROWLED OUTSIDE SAVANNAH'S OFFICE window. She leaned back in her chair and checked the message she'd sent Hez half an hour ago. It showed Delivered, so he still hadn't seen it, which was very unlike him. She had promised to give the tent supply place an answer by now about the location they wanted for the beach tent. It was a major detail, and while she could run out there by herself to make a decision, Hez always had good input.

She frowned at the phone as if her displeasure would switch the message to Read. Maybe he hadn't heard his phone. He could be talking with students or asking Hope again about the status of an arrest. She called his number, but the connection went to voicemail, which was odd. She tried the office number, but it rang several times before she got his voicemail message there too. The sound of his deep voice released more fear than she'd realized she was suppressing. Where was he?

The Justice Chamber might know. She hated to bother them if they were in the middle of a discussion, but by now she couldn't control her panic. She shouldn't be worried, but fear shuddered down her back. There'd been too many attacks against Hez in recent months, and she kept waiting for something else to happen. Losing custody of Simon hadn't improved her sense of equilibrium.

The line picked up on the second ring. "Justice Chamber, Dominga speaking."

Savannah's fingers tightened on her phone, and she paced the office. "I hope I'm not interrupting anything, Dominga, but I'm looking for Hez. Is he there?" *Please be there, please be there.*

"I was just about to call you." Dominga's voice was heavy with tension. "He's not here, but even more worrisome is that Toni arrived a few minutes ago looking for him too. He didn't show up to teach her legal writing class, which started fifteen minutes ago. As soon as she heard about his no-show, she started searching for him, but he's not answering his phone. Something is very wrong. He is the most dependable person I know. And there was a report of a gunshot this afternoon. Security went to the parking lot but didn't find anything."

Savannah gulped back a gasp. "I'll see what I can find out. Let me know if you find him." She raced out of her office and across the lobby to the exit. Her secretary called out after her, but she didn't pause.

A blast of heat and humidity hit her face when she stepped through the door and headed for where he usually parked. The passing mower threw grass clippings over her bare legs and skirt. She didn't pause to brush away the debris but darted across the yard toward the parking lot.

She paused and scanned the area for Hez's truck. There it was. The door was ajar. She ran over and checked inside. No Hez, but something shiny on the ground caught her eye. A bullet casing.

Her heart seized in her chest. Hands shaking, she called 911. "This is Savannah Webster out at TGU. My fiancé, Hez Webster, is missing, and I think Michael Willard might have d-done something—" Her tongue dried and she wet her lips to try again. "I think he's hurt him or—or—"

She couldn't get out what she feared, but her brain kept inserting graphic pictures of Hez tossed to the gators like Erik. Michael was a monster.

"Hang on and I'll transfer you to Detective Richards."

A few seconds of silence followed before she heard a click and Augusta's voice was in her ear. "Savannah, I'm tailing Michael right now. We see two other men in his truck. Maybe one of them is Hez, but we can't tell. We're about to arrest Michael."

Please, God, let him be alive. "Where are you? I'll be right there."

"It's not safe. I'll call you as soon as we have Michael in custody. There's nothing you can do, Savannah. Pray for a smooth arrest with no bullets flying. I'll be in touch."

The call went dead. "Augusta?" Savannah glanced at the phone screen. Augusta had either hung up or hit a spot with connection issues. Savannah had no idea where the chase was taking place either. She sank onto a bench and prayed with all her strength.

Hez could hardly believe his ears when Michael started reciting poetry. "Because I could not stop for Death—"

A siren blared behind them.

Michael cursed and gunned the engine. His head swiveled back and forth as if he were searching for something in the marshy landscape. He glanced back at Jimbo. "Hold on."

Michael yanked the wheel to the left, turning into the tall grass. He switched the truck into four-wheel drive and followed an almost invisible track. The truck bounced and shook, knocking them around the cab like pinballs. Hez's skull whacked the roof, but somehow Michael maintained control of the vehicle.

Michael looked in the rearview mirror, then slapped the wheel. "Ha! They're stuck!"

Hez's heart sank. For a moment he'd thought he was about to be rescued. He'd have to escape on his own. But how?

The vehicle slowed slightly. The bone-jarring shocks became less intense and frequent. Still, they had to brace themselves continually. Hez glanced down. Jimbo wasn't holding him. The big man held his gun in one hand and gripped his armrest with the other. The gun pointed more or less in Hez's direction, but Jimbo couldn't help waving it around.

Hez stared through the windshield, watching for an upcoming dip or rock. There! A glint in the grass showed where a trickle of water crossed their path, carving a nasty rut in the "road."

The truck jolted as they hit the little gulley. At the same instant Hez opened the door and hurled himself out.

Jimbo shouted and fired through the swinging door. Hez landed in the muddy grass and tumbled along for several feet before crashing into a thornbush.

The truck stopped. Michael opened his door and pointed a gun at Hez.

Hez flattened himself into the mud just as Michael fired. The bullet whizzed through the spot where Hez's head had been a second earlier.

Faint voices shouted from behind Hez. Shots popped like firecrackers.

Michael jumped back into his truck and drove off.

As the sound of the truck's engine faded, Hez disentangled himself from the bush's painful clutches. Augusta Richards and a male officer ran toward him along the barely there road Michael had taken.

Hez got to his feet as the police approached. His right shoulder and left knee throbbed and he had dozens of scratches, but he seemed otherwise uninjured. "Thanks," he said to Augusta and her partner. "I'm pretty sure he planned to kill me and dump me in the swamp like he did Erik. Did someone see him kidnap me?"

Augusta watched the retreating truck for a moment, then sighed and holstered her pistol. "Savannah realized you were missing and called 911, but we were already following him by that point."

"Why?"

"There's a warrant for his arrest. It just issued an hour ago." Augusta turned to her partner. "Update Dispatch and ask for backup."

Augusta looked grim as they hurried through the swamp. As her partner told the dispatcher what had happened, Augusta pulled out her phone and called Savannah on speaker to let her know Hez was safe. "We've got Hez."

He leaned closer to Augusta's phone. "Hi, babe, I'm fine."

"Thank God, thank God." Her voice hiccupped in a small sob. "I need to see that you're all in one piece before I believe it."

"I'll get there as soon as I can." Hez's mind went back to the warrant. "What are the charges against Michael?"

Augusta pressed her lips together in a hard line. "The main one is the murder of Jessica Legare."

Savannah gasped. "Michael killed his own daughter. He seemed to love her."

"He planted the bomb." Augusta frowned at Hez. "He probably meant to kill you."

Hez absorbed the information in silence, barely hearing the conversation around him. So that was why Michael had been so insistent that Hez was really responsible for Jess's death. Hez knew all too well how hard it was for a father to bear the thought that he had killed his own daughter. And then he knew what Michael would do next. He turned to Augusta. "He's going to run, but he'll go home first. You can catch him there."

Savannah's voice was a cry. "Simon!"

Augusta grimaced as they reached her car. She pointed at her mud-caked vehicle, which had sunk up to its wheel wells in the swamp. "That's the only police car in a ten-mile radius."

"I'll get Simon!" Savannah's voice quivered with determination. "I'm less than two miles from Michael's house."

Hez leaned over Augusta's phone. "Savannah, wait!"

But the line was dead.

CHAPTER 40

WHERE HAD THE TRAFFIC COME FROM? SAVANNAH PASSED a slow-driving truck and pulled quickly back into her lane to avoid a head-on with a green sedan coming from the other direction. The oncoming car blared its horn indignantly and she waved apologetically.

Her pulse throbbed in her throat. Michael would know his only weapon now was taking Simon from them, and she couldn't let that happen. The police car was farther away and would never get there in time.

It was up to her to save her nephew.

Jess. Pain radiated from her chest, and she gripped the steering wheel with tight fingers. She'd lost her sister because of a feud that had gone on way too long. If only Savannah had known of all these undercurrents and deep plots a year ago, even six months ago, Jess might still be with her. Michael had used his daughter as a pawn and never really loved her. At least Jess was spared that knowledge. She'd searched for a father's love all her life and had found only deceit and a dark desire for revenge.

Savannah accelerated the final mile along the county road

to Michael's house. The driveway was empty, and no one moved on the porch of the two-story home or in the yard. Maybe she'd made it in time. Michael's dogs barked and lunged as she approached, but they were chained in the yard. She braked and threw the car into Park, then flung open her door and raced up the steps to the house.

She pressed the doorbell, then pounded on it with her fist. "Simon!" She darted to the window and peered past an opening in the curtains and saw movement. She stepped back to the door and slammed her fist on it again. "Simon!"

The door opened, and Simon's startled face came into view. "Aunt Savannah, what's wrong?"

"We have to go. Right now!" She grabbed his hand and pulled him onto the porch.

He hung back and resisted the forward momentum. "I can't leave. Pawpaw texted me to be ready for a trip, and I'm not done packing. What's going on?"

"There's no time to explain. We have to go right now, before Michael gets here." He didn't resist as she pulled him across the porch and down the steps toward her car.

Too late. Michael's big truck pulled into the drive behind her vehicle, trapping her car in its place. She glanced around for a way of escape. They could try to run through the woods, but Michael knew this property and she didn't.

He jumped out of the truck and charged at her with his fists clenched. Jimbo got out on the other side and fingered the gun in his belt holster as he ran toward her too.

Michael reached for Simon, but Savannah stepped between them. "Don't touch him! Isn't it bad enough that you killed

Jess?" She stepped forward and shoved him with both hands. "You are a monster!"

He reeled back at her unexpected attack but caught his balance and came back at her. "I didn't want to hurt you out of respect for Jess, Savannah, but you've caused enough trouble." His fist looped up and grazed her chin.

She avoided the worst of the blow and went at him again. "Respect? You killed her! You don't have an ounce of love in your soul for anyone, not even your own daughter." He wasn't going to hurt Simon—she would give her life to save him. She leaped at Michael and began battering him with her fists. "Simon, run!"

Michael's hands came up in a defensive movement, and she intensified her attack. She spared a glance at Simon, but he stayed frozen in place with his eyes wide. She redoubled her attack to keep Michael's attention off Simon long enough for him to flee. Her hands hurt, but she landed blow after blow on Michael's torso and arms as he shielded his face.

Strong hands grabbed her from behind and forced her arms to her sides. She smelled cigar smoke and bourbon on her captor and whipped around in place. She caught a glimpse of Jimbo's enraged face. She fought to free her arms, but he was too strong.

Face red and lips twisted in a snarl, Michael straightened and marched toward her. "You're a menace, Savannah. I should have gotten rid of you long ago."

She quit her futile fight. "You killed her," she whispered. "How could you, Michael? How could you? She adored you."

His eyes narrowed and she didn't see his fist come up until pain exploded on the left side of her face and the world went dark.

Michael ignored his stinging knuckles. Jimbo continued to hold the unconscious Savannah like a rag doll, an uncertain expression on his broad face. Michael picked up Savannah's phone and key fob and hurled them into a patch of tall grass at the edge of his lawn. "Leave her. And get out of here. You've got a better chance of escaping on your own. Go through the woods, stay away from towns, and head for the border. If you make it to Reynosa, you'll find help. Now go!"

Jimbo hesitated for a moment, then dropped Savannah's limp form and loped off into the woods.

Simon still stood frozen, staring at his aunt. Michael stepped in front of Savannah. "Are you packed?"

Simon didn't meet his gaze. "I-I'm not done."

A siren wailed in the distance. Michael cursed under his breath. "There's no time now. Get in the truck."

Simon crouched by Savannah and touched her hand. "Aunt Savannah, wake up." He sniffled when she didn't answer.

Michael grabbed him by the collar and shoved him toward the Denali. "Get in the truck!"

Simon stumbled, caught his balance, and climbed into the passenger side of the cab as Michael jumped into the driver's seat. As soon as they were in, Michael threw the truck into Reverse and gunned the engine. The tires squealed as he backed out of the driveway, then put the truck in Drive and roared down the road in the opposite direction of the sirens he'd heard.

He looked in the rearview mirror just before he turned a corner that would take him out of sight of the house. No cops in view. They wouldn't know which direction he'd gone or how far he'd gotten. That was a good start, but only a start. He'd need to ditch the Denali as soon as possible. He'd only had the truck for six months and he loved it, but he had no choice. Maybe he could steal something, or they might be able to hitch a ride with—

"Why did you hit Aunt Savannah?"

Michael glanced at Simon, who huddled against the door at the far edge of his seat. He watched Michael with alert, fearful eyes. "I'm sorry you had to see that. She was trying to take you away, and there was no time to argue."

"Will she be okay?"

"Yes, she'll wake up in a minute. She'll be right as rain."

"Where are we going?"

Michael forced a smile. "Oh, it's a surprise! We're going on a big adventure." No need to give the boy details he might blurt out at a truck stop.

"Are we running from the police?"

"You're a sharp kid, Simon. Yes, we are. It's a big misunderstanding, though. We'll sort it out when we reach someplace safe."

Simon hugged the door tighter, his face pale. "D-did you kill my mom?"

Michael grimaced. "I did not. I loved that girl with all my heart."

"Aunt Savannah said you killed her."

"She lied!"

Simon was silent for a moment. Then he seemed to reach a decision. He sat up straight. "Aunt Savannah doesn't lie."

"Well, she did this time."

"Stop the truck. I want to get out."

Michael ground his teeth. "No. And no more back talk. I need to think."

Simon's face flushed. "Let me out!"

Michael backhanded him. "Shut up!"

Simon grabbed for the wheel. "Stop the truck now!"

Michael shoved Simon away, then punched him in the face. The pain in his hand flared. "Get control of yourself, boy! Act like a man! A Willard man!"

Simon retreated to the far side of the cab again, his lower lip bleeding. "I hate you! And I'm never going to be a Willard man!" He opened the door.

Michael swore and slammed on the brakes. Fortunately, the road was deserted. He glared at Simon and the boy glared back, his blue eyes filled with defiant hate. He'd lost the boy, maybe forever.

"Fine!" Michael reached over and shoved Simon out the open door, sending the boy sprawling on the roadside gravel.

Michael slammed the door and drove off. He resisted the urge to look in the mirror. Simon had rejected Michael, his name, and his family. The boy was dead to him now.

Who was left alive?

Michael brooded on the question as he drove. Marie and Jess were both gone. There were lots of other Willards, but his line would die out with him. Simon had been his last hope for the future, the final green shoot.

He hadn't felt like this since Marie died. He'd been a young man then, with his life ahead of him. Now he had nothing. He was just an old man who'd spend the rest of his days alone, running from the law.

His thoughts wandered back to the day of her death, as they often did in black moments. He hadn't spoken to her after she drove away with Pierre and his henchman, but Michael saw her from time to time. She looked broken—slumped shoulders, unfocused eyes, never a real smile unless it was for her girls. People said she was day-drinking and popping pills, and Michael didn't doubt it.

Then one stormy morning came the news he'd feared and expected: Marie was dead. The night before, she had driven off a sharp curve near Magnolia Springs. Her car had plunged into Eslava Branch and she drowned. Toxicology reports found alcohol and antidepressants in her blood, and the crash was ruled an accident.

The day after she died, he got an envelope from her. It contained a final handwritten poem:

I wander
    Hemmed in and hopeless
    In a gray and sunless land
The wind mutters
    Among sharp, cold rocks
    Whispering rumors of shame and judgment

The ferryman waits
By the river's edge, silent and shrouded
His coin heavy in my pocket
Our oak tree beckons
From the far side of the river
Limbs swaying in an Elysian breeze

He had cried when he read it. He did more than cry—he came completely unstrung. He shouted and cursed and punched the wall so hard he broke three bones in his hand. Then he drank until he passed out. Mama worried that he might "do something desperate," so she came over and took charge of him for a week.

Maybe he should have done something desperate. Maybe he should do it now.

He discovered that he had been driving toward Eslava Branch for the last several minutes. He gunned the engine and headed for the curve that claimed Marie's life. He accelerated into it and let the truck drift off the road between two houses. He crashed through underbrush, startled several ducks into flight, and hit the water with an enormous spray and splash.

Water gushed through the vents, cool and relentless. It soaked his feet, his calves, his thighs, his belly, his chest. Dim green-brown replaced the bright sunlight outside. He closed his eyes and pictured Marie waiting for him under the huge oak where they'd first kissed, her hair blown by a heavenly breeze.

Something smashed through the door window. The last air bubbled out of the truck as strong hands reached in. They grabbed Michael and dragged him through the window frame and to the surface.

Michael choked and gasped as his rescuers pulled him to shore. He finally got a look at them as they dropped him on the muddy bank: Hez Webster and Augusta Richards.

Richards went to retrieve handcuffs from a utility belt she'd left lying by the water. Hez leaned over Michael, face dripping. "You're not getting off that easy."

CHAPTER 41

SAVANNAH TRIED TO MOVE HER HEAD AND COULDN'T. THERE was something on her neck. Her senses began to return with the scent of mud and grass and the sounds around her. Was that a siren? Pain filtered in and her memories with it.

Simon.

She opened her eyes and winced at the lights flashing on top of an ambulance. Hez's worried face swam into view, and she reached for his hand. "Michael has Simon!" She tried to sit.

"Whoa, whoa." He pressed her back. "The paramedics are going to take you to the hospital. And we've got Simon." He gestured to her other side.

She cast her glance that way since she couldn't move her neck. Simon hovered on his haunches beside her on her right side. "I'm okay, Aunt Savannah. You're not supposed to move." His blue eyes studied her face. "You're going to have a shiner for the wedding." He rose. "I'm going to go pack the rest of my stuff. I'll be right back. Don't leave without me."

She touched her puffy face. A shiner? At least they were all alive. "We won't go anywhere without you." When Simon walked toward the house, she reached for Hez's hand. "Where's Michael?"

His hand touched her hair gently. "In custody for Jess's murder. They caught Jimbo too."

She closed her eyes a moment as her chest contracted with pain. Jess would still be here, ready to be her maid of honor at the wedding. Instead, Simon was an orphan, and Savannah would never see her again. No, that wasn't true. Jess was safe with Jesus, and the knowledge they'd be together again someday meant everything.

Hez's lips touched hers. "I'm sorry, babe. I know it hurts to realize her own father killed her."

She opened her eyes. "How do they know it was him?"

"I was with Augusta on her way to make the arrest. Your dad's file had a picture of Michael standing next to a truck. Augusta had it examined to see what was in the back of the vehicle, and it contained boxes of industrial explosives—a very powerful and rare type. When they went through the evidence baggies Ed retrieved, they found residue from the same type of explosive on fragments of my car. That's enough for an arrest warrant. They should find more evidence once they search his home and business."

"He was after you."

"Yes. We think he was determined to stop me from interfering with his elaborate plans to destroy TGU and your family."

"Jess was part of it, all of it. His desire for revenge had infected her too. She believed he loved her, but she never stopped to think about how a father's love didn't include putting her in danger and sending her on a path of deceit and destruction. My father is no better. He modeled selfishness and a drive for control and wealth that made it easy for Michael."

His hand cupped her unharmed cheek. "I think Michael really loved your mother. Losing her warped him, and he never recovered from it. He tried to kill himself at the same spot Marie died, but Augusta and I stopped him. To tell you the truth, I feel sorry for him. I'm thankful I didn't have to watch you live with another man."

Her heart swelled with love and gratitude. "You are the strongest man I've ever met. You saw how you needed to change, and you did it. You came here determined to restore our relationship, and I'm thankful you're the kind of man who wasn't puffed up with pride like my dad and Michael. You were willing to do whatever it took to restore our marriage." She reached up and cupped his face with her palms. "I'm so blessed you're mine."

His smile turned even more tender. "This is all you, babe. The thought of that fierce heart of yours never really let go of me. I hit bottom and knew I had to have it back—have you back. You forgave me, and not many women would have been so generous. Who would have thought we could slog through all this to get to where we are now? And we'll have a son soon."

"We'll be able to adopt Simon?"

Hez nodded. "There shouldn't be any hiccup to adopting him. And after today I think he won't mind having his name changed to Webster. He saw Michael for who he really is." Hez's blue eyes hardened. "Michael threw Simon out of the truck, Savannah. Like an unwanted dog."

Her eyes burned, and she planned to hug Simon and tell him how much she loved him. No ten-year-old should have to go through what he'd endured. She put her hand to her forehead, which had begun to throb in earnest. "Can I just get something for the pain? I don't need to go to the hospital. There's so much to do before the wedding."

"Sorry, babe, you have to get checked out. We need to take some pictures of that beautiful head of yours and make sure you don't collapse on me before you can say 'I do.' They're coming to load you now, and I'll wait at the hospital with Simon. The three of us can go back to the house when you're released. Simon will get to sleep in his new room for the first time."

Hez rose and his smile widened as the paramedics shouldered him out of the way. "It's over, finally over, and the future is waiting."

Tears filled her eyes and she nodded, unable to speak. God was good to have brought them through so much. She couldn't wait to see what he would do next.

Hez raised his glass. "To stolen hours."

Candlelight danced in Savannah's eyes, bringing out the gold flecks. The purple-and-yellow bruise under her left eye drew a few curious stares, but she wore it like what it was: a badge of honor. She raised her glass and tapped it against his with a soft chime. "The sweetest kind."

They'd slipped away to Billy's Seafood Restaurant for a quiet date—and made a point of not telling anyone where they were. The craziness of the last few days had been overwhelming, and they craved a little quiet time just to connect. Will was staying at the house with Simon.

Hez sipped his citrus-infused sparkling water. Billy's made

it themselves with fresh fruit and local spring water, and it was delicious. He could almost forget that it wasn't champagne. "Every hour alone with you is sweet, babe."

She rewarded him with a luminous smile. "We haven't had many of those recently, have we?"

"Nope, but I intend to fix that as soon as possible. I can't wait to carry you across the threshold of our new home and have you all to myself for a loooong time."

"It's very mutual." She winked. "Poor Simon. If everything goes right, he's going to get adopted and abandoned on the same day." She took a sip from her glass. "I can't believe the wedding is only two days away. I wonder how many messages will be waiting for us by the end of the evening."

"I don't want to think about it. Or about the legal loose ends I have to tie up before then."

She dipped a morsel of bread in a little dish of spiced olive oil. "Is there any news?"

The server delivered their oyster appetizers before Hez could respond. He slid one into his mouth, savoring the salty meat. "Mmm. I always think these can't be as good as I remember, and I'm always wrong." He pulled out his phone and put it on the table. "I hate to do this—but now that you mention it, I'm waiting for a text from Scott confirming that the judge signed the adoption order. The guardian supported our new petition, so I don't think the outcome is in doubt—but the timing might be. The judge is going on vacation tomorrow, and Scott is pulling in every favor he can to get this signed before His Honor leaves."

"If it were anything else, I'd make you put that phone right back in your pocket." She popped an oyster in her mouth, and he took the opportunity to do the same. She gave him a slightly apprehensive look as she swallowed. "Have you heard from Hope or Augusta? You mentioned that they were going to execute a warrant at Michael's home and office."

He sighed. "I don't want to ruin your appetite."

She pressed her perfect lips together. "What did they find?"

"They found more traces of the explosive used to kill Jess. It was on the floor of his basement and a storage locker rented by his trucking company. They also found financial records from an offshore account that traced the Hornbrook blackmail payments to him."

"So he really was behind that too. Why am I not surprised?" She studied Hez's face. "Is there anything else?"

"There is." He fiddled with his flatware. "They found a hidden safe that contained files on me, your dad, and you—surveillance pictures, papers that seem to have come from our trash, and other stuff."

She shivered. "He had people watching us the whole time."

"He did—including when I was taking a shower one night at the new house."

Her eyes widened. "That's how they knew about your birthmark!" She reached across the table and took his hand. "I'm doubly sorry I doubted you."

"I would have doubted me too." He put his other hand on hers. "There's more. The file on Ella's death was in that safe."

She gripped his hand. "So he did kill her."

"That's what Hope thinks."

"But why did he want the file on her death? There was nothing in there even hinting that she was murdered, was there?"

"There may have been clues that the police overlooked because everyone thought it was an accident, but—" He hesitated. "Sociopaths sometimes keep mementos or trophies from their crimes."

She turned pale. "I feel sick."

"I'm sorry. I shouldn't have said anything. I ruined our date."

She swallowed. "It's my fault for asking."

His phone buzzed.

She pinned on a smile. "You should check that. Maybe it's good news."

He checked his phone—and his pulse spiked. "It's Bruno! Someone is breaking into the room where he left that fake burner phone."

"The police station is only a couple blocks away!" She pulled back her hand and ran. Hez raced after her, shooting an apologetic glance at their startled server on the way out the door.

CHAPTER 42

SAVANNAH'S BREATH LABORED IN HER CHEST, AND SHE wished she wasn't wearing heels, but she'd wanted to look nice for date night with Hez. He was several strides ahead of her, and it was impossible to keep up. The salty breeze from Bon Secour Bay tugged strands of hair from her updo and blew them across her face. She swiped them away impatiently.

Michael and Jimbo were in custody, so who could be breaking in? It made no sense when the evidence to convict them was ironclad without the phone. Her mind whirled with possibilities, but she found nothing logical to explain them.

The streetlights cast enough of a glow to keep Hez in sight until he reached the corner of the police building and dashed toward the back. Since running was impossible anyway, she slowed her pace before she broke an ankle in these stupid shoes. The police might already be on-scene too.

The door to the front of the police building opened, and a masked man dressed in black darted through. His shoulder plowed into her before she could step out of the way, and she instinctively clutched him to try to stop their trajectory to the ground. They crashed down together, and the pavement scraped her left elbow and leg. His heavy weight was on top of her, but she rolled and managed to get on top of him.

He struggled to toss her off, but she held on. "Hez!" she screamed, holding on with all her might. She couldn't let him get away.

The man succeeded in rolling her over so his heavy weight pinned her down. She wrapped her arms around his neck and her legs around his. She smelled pipe tobacco on his clothing, the same cherry scent her father used. And the man's breath smelled of lemon drops. "Hez, help me!"

Seconds later Hez arrived and got the man in a headlock. "Let go, I've got him."

Savannah released her grip as Hez hauled the guy off her. She got up and reached out to yank off the black ski mask—but she couldn't do it. Familiar brown eyes pleaded with her from the holes in the mask. Her hand shook. Pipe tobacco and lemon drops? It couldn't be.

Hez pulled off the mask and her father's pale face stared back at her. He struggled to escape Hez's grip. "Let go of me. This is a misunderstanding."

A dawning realization widened Hez's blue eyes, and his lips flattened. He gave Dad a shake. "What's the misunderstanding, Pierre? What were you doing in there?"

Dad licked his lips. "I—I thought I saw a burglar, so I was checking it out."

"And you just happened to have a ski mask in your pocket?"

"I, uh . . . It must have been there from a ski trip."

Hez's voice was tight with fury. "And you didn't call 911?"

"I didn't have a phone."

Hez roughly patted Dad down with his free hand. He yanked

out a phone and tossed it on the ground. It was the dirty old burner phone from Bruno's trap.

Dad's lips worked, but no sound came out.

"You had to get that phone, didn't you?" Hez's grip tightened, and Dad struggled for breath. "You were behind Ella's death."

Her dad thrashed in Hez's grip. "No!"

Hez went on, building the damning case against her father. "Her file was the one thing that made no sense for Michael to have in his possession. Why would he want it if he was involved? He would have known everything that went down. He had just as much dirty evidence on you as you had on him, didn't he?"

Something in her father seemed to break. He slumped and twisted his hands together. "No, no, you don't understand. Ella would have been perfectly safe if Deke hadn't screwed up. And I made sure the ransom money wouldn't have come from you—I had a softhearted, rich widow ready to pony up the price. It would have been a few hours, and Ella would have been back home safe and sound. It was Deke's fault, not mine."

He cared so little for his own granddaughter that he would be willing to traumatize them all? Dozens of memories slammed into her brain: Ella running to climb into her grandfather's arms, the way she called him "Pops," her dimpled smile when he stopped over. His apparent love had been nothing but a sham.

Bile burned the back of Savannah's throat, and she rushed to the grass to vomit up the oysters and bread she'd eaten a few minutes ago.

Her father's voice penetrated her fog of horrified revelation.

"Savannah, I never meant for anything to happen to her. It was an accident."

She straightened and turned to stare at him with new understanding. Loathing toward him had stripped away any illusions still clinging from her childhood. Was he even capable of love? What kind of man would do this?

"You were already skimming money from TGU. Why would you risk Ella's life for more? She loved you."

Her father's eyes watered. "I—I got into a spot of trouble with a gambling debt. It wasn't supposed to happen this way."

A rush of movement came from the back of the building, and Augusta burst into view with two uniformed officers. She clapped cuffs on Dad and glanced at Hez with a question in her eyes.

"He confessed to orchestrating the kidnapping attempt that killed our daughter," he said in a bereft tone. His hands fell away as one of the officers led her father, still protesting, away.

The strength ebbed from Savannah's legs, and she sank onto the grass with tears surging to her eyes. Hez settled on the grass beside her and pulled her into his arms. She wept against his chest. "How could he?" she whispered. "How could he?"

Michael leaned against the wall of the exercise yard at the Bay Minette jail, watching a basketball game. The hot June sun and thick humidity slowed the players to a jog and took the spring out of their jumps. Michael wasn't interested in basketball, but he didn't have anything better to do.

A big, heavily tattooed man walked up and nodded to Michael before taking a spot along the wall, bringing the now-familiar scent of unwashed male body with him. Patrick Jefferson was one of several of Michael's employees who had been rounded up during the smuggling raids and were still at Bay Minette awaiting trial or serving short sentences. "Morning, Mr. Michael. How'd the arraignment go? Is your lawyer workin' on a plea deal?"

"Pled not guilty, of course. As for a plea deal . . ." Michael shrugged one shoulder. "My attorney is meeting with the DA today, but it doesn't matter much. I'll be in prison for the rest of my life."

They watched the game in silence for several minutes. Then Patrick nudged Michael and nodded toward the far end of the yard. "That him?"

Michael looked in the direction Patrick indicated. Under the watchful eye of a guard, Pierre Legare wandered along a weedy strip of grass, shuffling like a zombie. His normally perfect silver-streaked brown hair was matted on one side, and his face was unshaven and slack. Michael doubted Pierre had slept much since his arrest two days ago. "Yeah, that's Pierre Legare."

"Heard about him on the news last night. The TV in the recreation area had him on every channel." Patrick made a face like his septic tank had just backed up. "Killed his own granddaughter and pinned it on ol' Deke. Those Legares are a bad bunch."

"Couldn't agree more."

"Trash. Total trash."

"Yep."

Patrick lowered his voice and leaned toward Michael.

"Wanna take out the trash? I'll bet we can get to him, even in protective custody."

Pierre's gaze wandered across the yard and found Michael. Recognition and surprise flickered in his bloodshot eyes for a moment, but his face went blank again after a few seconds and he went back to meandering.

"Not worth it." Michael turned to Patrick. "Man's already dead."

Patrick shrugged meaty shoulders. "If you say so." He turned back to the basketball game, leaving Michael to his thoughts.

Already dead. Pierre had lost everything he cared about—his money, his reputation, his pampered lifestyle. His facade had been ripped away, exposing the decayed soul underneath for all to see. He loved to lord it over everyone he met, and now even the common criminals in the yard looked down on him—and rightly so. Pierre now lived in what Walt Whitman called "hell under the skull-bones," and Michael had no intention of freeing him through physical death.

Michael had suspected Pierre's role in Ella Webster's death from the moment Deke told him about the mystery phone calls in the aftermath of the drowning. Michael knew he hadn't called Deke, of course, and Pierre's ongoing snooping easily could have discovered that Michael used burner phones and voice-altering software. The thought of a man kidnapping his own grandchild for money was stomach-churning but perfectly in character for Pierre Legare.

Michael had scoured the files he had on Pierre for evidence proving his suspicions. He even had Tammy grab the file on Ella's death in hopes that it might contain a puzzle piece or two. He'd come up dry, but Deke's confession had set the

Websters on the trail, just as Michael had hoped it would. His nephew wasn't the sharpest of the Willards, but he had unintentionally set a Legare to catch a Legare. Beautiful. And to make the situation even sweeter, the news stories about Pierre were sprinkled with tidbits Michael knew came from his file.

Michael had won. His victory had come at a steep price, but it was complete. And yet . . .

They said vengeance was a dish best served cold, but Michael felt like he was holding an empty icy plate. Everything he'd done, everything he'd sacrificed, led him to this point. He had come to the end of the mission he set himself—really the end of his life—and he finally gripped the prize in his hands. But somehow he held only ashes.

CHAPTER 43

SAVANNAH SMOOTHED THE CHAMPAGNE LACE DRESS AND its sequins over her hips. The skirt flared and swirled just above her ankles, so it was perfect for the white sand. A recording of the Beach Boys sang "Wouldn't It Be Nice" outside the tent as the guests made their way to the chairs. A fresh sea breeze blew in from the bay just yards away. Hez's parents had come from Oregon, and they sat with his cousins on Hez's side of the guests. Her side held only friends.

If only Jess were with her.

She stared at her image in the full-length mirror Nora had thoughtfully brought for her. Tendrils of auburn hair trailed along the curve of her cheeks and a few more along her neck. Her green eyes were luminous with excitement, and her lips couldn't stop smiling. Makeup had masked most of her bruise, but pictures would always be a reminder of what they'd gone through to get here.

June 20, her wedding day. She'd thought it would never come.

Nora inserted a few flowers in Savannah's elegant updo. "Hez will lose his mind when he sees you." She stepped back and studied Savannah's face. "You doing okay? It's only been two days since, well, everything happened."

Savannah nodded. "I shouldn't have been surprised by my father's depravity. It was on display often enough throughout my life, but I didn't want to see it. At least we know what really happened. This is a new beginning for me and Hez. I hope Ella knows and that she's smiling and laughing in heaven at how happy we are. She has no pain, no trauma. All that is past for her, and I'm focusing on that, especially today."

Nora's glasses misted, and she took them off to clean them. "You're a wise woman."

"You look beautiful in that dress. I caught a glimpse of Graham ogling you."

Nora's cheeks went pink. "Things are going well."

Savannah twirled, relishing the way the dress moved with her. "That's an understatement." The murmur of guests chatting in the chairs stilled as the music changed to the Beatles' "Here Comes the Sun." She gave Nora a little push. "I think that's your cue."

Nora nodded and grabbed the bridal bouquet of clematis and anemones, then thrust it in Savannah's hands. "I've got the ring for Hez. I'll see you at the altar, girlfriend." She picked up her matching nosegay and headed out of the tent.

Savannah's pulse throbbed in her neck, and she pulled in a lungful of salty air to calm herself. These were all people she loved, and while she missed her sister, it would be the perfect day because it would end with a wedding ring on her finger and Simon as their son.

The music thumped out the beginning dramatic notes to the "Bridal Chorus," and she stepped through the tent opening. A white paper runner sprinkled with clematis petals beckoned her to the beautifully decorated arch where Pastor Forrest waited with two other figures beside him. Hez and Simon—the ones she loved so much.

They wore khakis and matching tropical shirts in a blue that matched the waves rolling onto the white sand. The three of them would form a new family today, and she blinked back happy tears at the thought. They would experience this miracle together in the next few minutes.

She focused on Hez's face radiating joy, pride, and commitment. His blue eyes never left her as she walked toward the arch with the sea as a backdrop. They'd had their challenges, but he'd been steadfast at working his way back to this moment. And so had she.

She reached the arch, and Hez took her hand in a confident grip. "You're beautiful," he whispered.

She stepped into place beside him, and they repeated their vows, the same traditional ones they'd said once before, but she didn't fear a breakup. They'd grown and learned from their mistakes. They knew how to handle conflict and trials, and they each meant the "so help me God" promise.

He slipped her wedding ring on her finger, and the familiar weight of it felt like coming home. His eyes glimmered with moisture when she slipped his on and it settled in its spot.

"Hez, you may kiss your bride," Pastor Forrest said with a smile.

A broad smile lifted Hez's lips, but his eyes held serious intent, and he took her in his arms. "I'm never letting you go again," he said for her ears only.

His lips came down on hers, and she tasted that promise in his ardent kiss. She wrapped her arms around his neck and swore her own devotion the same way. The guests clapped and a few hooted and whistled. Her cheeks were hot when she pulled back.

He cupped her cheek in his hand. *To be continued,* he mouthed.

Their pastor held up his hand. "There's one more detail to be tended to before you can congratulate Mr. and Mrs. Hezekiah Webster. The picture isn't quite complete." He stepped to take a paper from his wife's hand as she approached. "Simon, this involves you." He glanced at the guests. "Miz Willard, would you mind coming up?"

Helen frowned like she might refuse for a moment, but she rose from her front-row seat and came to join them. She edged close to Simon and didn't appear much taller than the ten-year-old. She pressed her lips together, and her questioning gaze darted to Savannah, then away again.

The pastor raised the paper in his hand. "The court has granted Hez and Savannah's request to adopt you, Simon. Your name from this day forward is Simon Willard Webster."

Simon gasped and turned wide eyes toward Savannah. "Really? I'm your son—and Hez's?"

Savannah embraced him and inhaled the spicy scent of his

shampoo, the same one Hez used. "I've loved you like a son ever since I saw your face in England. And I think your mom would want us to honor your Willard roots as well. You're the best of both of us." She released him and gestured to Helen. "Your great-grandmother is a wonderful role model for you. Love your family like she does."

"I—I don't know what to say." Helen wiped tears from her eyes. "I need to tell you something, Savannah. I wasn't sure you were genuine, but I thought maybe you were as good as you seemed. I was trying to help from the sidelines. I had the envelope about Martine left on your porch. And the one with Deke's phone bill."

"I wondered who left those. Thank you."

"I love my son, but I didn't hold with his methods. I knew the feud needed to end and that maybe you were the one to end it. I'm glad I was right. Bless you, Savannah." She gripped Hez's hand. "You too, Hez. I'm proud to share my great-grandson with you, and I wish you both a long and happy marriage." She released Hez and embraced Savannah in a cloud of gardenia perfume.

Savannah gave her a fierce hug and choked back tears before returning to Hez's side. His hand enveloped hers, and they turned toward the standing guests. A chorus of cheers erupted from the group when the pastor introduced them.

He tucked her against his side. "Right where we belong—together."

The sun came out from behind a cloud, and its bright glow was a reminder of the promise of their future.

Hez took her hand and nodded to the DJ. "I want to dance with my bride." The Righteous Brothers began to sing

"Unchained Melody," and tears came to her eyes. "We danced to this on our first Valentine's Day together."

"I said I had a surprise for you, and this is part of it." He pulled her into his arms. "Now and forever, babe, now and forever. And we're going to Tahiti. Nora has your things all packed."

EPILOGUE

IF ONLY WILLIAM WERE ALIVE TO SEE WILLARD HALL. HELEN had heard years ago that the half-finished ruin on campus would be called Legare Hall, but that wasn't what was on the engraved invitation she received for the grand opening. And sure enough, the proud Willard name gleamed on the facade outside.

Helen had dressed up for the occasion in her best blue dress, the one she'd worn for the last anniversary dinner before her husband died ten years ago. It had hung in the closet ever since, and she'd even caught a whiff of his Lagerfeld cologne when she slipped it over her head.

The new air-conditioning kept the humid August afternoon at bay, but Helen had still found herself nodding off in her chair during the grand opening speeches. She couldn't hear well, and most of them weren't worth listening to anyway. A lot of blathering on and back-patting from people who had nothing to do with this. Only one person had the right to crow about it, and Helen hadn't talked to her yet.

Her sensible pumps clattered on the mahogany floors as she wandered Willard Hall. She stopped in the office and stared at the portrait of Joseph Willard, patriarch of the family, with the same nose that many of his descendants had inherited, including Helen herself. She hadn't even had to change her name when she and William married, joining two of Joseph's distant lines.

The ornate desk below the portrait had come from her bungalow and had been beautifully restored. An open photo album lay on its surface, and she flipped with pride through the pictures of the excavation of the Willard Treasure. The place did proper homage to her family and their contribution to the university.

The scent of coffee and appetizers drew her back to the massive rotunda, where she snagged a crawfish egg roll on a minuscule plate along with a glass of wine. She spotted the woman she'd been watching for. Savannah Webster walked her way with her hand on her husband's arm. Her auburn hair was a little shorter since Helen saw her at the wedding last year. Hez's expression of pride was no doubt due to that baby bump under Savannah's tan sheath dress.

Savannah stopped in front of Helen. "Miz Willard, I'm so glad you could come." She swept her hand around the massive rotunda. "What do you think?"

"I love it all. This hall, the Winona Willard Neonatology Center you're building, everything. I never thought I'd say this to a Legare, but my thanks for what you've done here. Justice has finally come for the Willards, something I thought was a pipe dream."

Savannah's green eyes softened. "There's no need to thank me—it was the right thing to do, and I'm honored I got to be part of it."

"The right thing isn't always the easy thing, girlie, as I've seen in my family. You could have used that money for other needs here and no one would have known."

"I would have known."

The right thing to do wasn't easy for Helen either, and she took a sip of courage from her wineglass. "Some of my family hurt you both, and I'm sorry for that. I hear the two of you are visiting Deke at the prison in Jefferson." She'd winced when she'd heard he was assigned to a maximum-security prison, but the boy had made his own bed.

Savannah's smile faltered, and she glanced at Hez, who took her hand. "Deke asked us for forgiveness once, and we weren't ready to talk about it with him. Until now."

"Whoo-ee, that's a lot of forgiving. Can you even do it?"

"It will be a journey. Your family has a lot of forgiving to do too."

Helen put her plate and wineglass down on a nearby window ledge. "I'd be proud to have you as a travel companion on that journey."

She held out her arms, and Savannah enveloped her in a hug that nearly swallowed her whole. Helen didn't mind having a strong woman like Savannah lead the way into unknown territory.

A NOTE FROM THE AUTHORS

DEAR READERS,

Thanks for coming with us on the final stage of Hez and Savannah's journey! We enjoyed every minute, and we hope you did too. We do our best to make every detail in our books as authentic as possible. That involves a lot of research, of course, but we love it. Much of the research is boring—but sometimes we come across nuggets that are worth sharing. Here are a couple from this book:

Dead man's switches: As the name implies, these are designed to be triggered by someone's death or incapacitation. There are real computer programs similar to the one Bruno created, but dead man's switches aren't limited to the virtual world. They're common in heavy equipment, for example, where they automatically turn off potentially dangerous machines if the operator dies or is incapacitated. Dead man's switches are also a key element of nuclear strategy, where they're sometimes called "fail deadlies" (as opposed to "fail safes"). One famous dead man's switch is the "letters of last resort" written by every incoming British prime minister. These are sealed handwritten orders to the commanders of Britain's nuclear missile submarines with instructions to open them only if Britain's leaders are all killed.

Private islands: There are hundreds of privately owned islands scattered throughout the Caribbean, ranging from uninhabited reefs to large islands with exclusive luxury villages. Some real estate agencies specialize in selling or renting these places, and some of them are surprisingly cheap—though not quite cheap enough for authors whose names aren't Rowling or King.

We hope you've had as much fun reading the Tupelo Grove saga as we had writing it! Shoot us an email and let us know what you think.

Blessings,

COLLEEN COBLE

https://colleencoble.com
colleen@colleencoble.com

RICK ACKER

https://rickacker.com
contactrickacker@gmail.com

DISCUSSION QUESTIONS

1. At the end of chapter 33, Michael says, "Justice is coming." Hez says the same thing a few pages later. Did either of them get the justice they wanted?
2. Did Pierre receive justice? Why or why not?
3. "I sat with my anger long enough until she told me her real name was grief." This quote, often attributed to C. S. Lewis, expresses a deep truth. Simon's outbursts and misbehavior had their roots in grief over the death of his mother. To what extent was Michael's rage driven by grief over the loss of Marie and Jess?
4. As reflected in the book, Alabama, like many states, makes it very difficult to terminate a parent's rights, even when that would be in the best interests of the child. Do you agree with that rule?
5. How has Savannah changed over the course of the Tupelo Grove series? How about Hez?
6. Forgiveness has been a major theme throughout the series. How has forgiveness—or the lack of it—shaped the following characters:
    a. Hez
    b. Savannah

   c. Michael
   d. Helen

7. Pierre has done terrible things and never asked for forgiveness, but he is still Savannah's father. What should she do?
8. As you may have guessed, one of us (Colleen) loves home renovations. Rick, on the other hand, just wants to hire a contractor and get it over with as fast as possible. How about you? Do you enjoy or dread home improvement projects?
9. We went back and forth over where to send Hez and Savannah on their honeymoon. We considered an African safari, a European river cruise, a beach in Hawaii, an apartment in Paris, a houseboat in Washington, and a bunch of other options before settling on Tahiti. Where would you have sent them? Do you have a favorite spot for a romantic getaway?

ACKNOWLEDGMENTS

Our huge thanks go to our HarperCollins Christian Publishing family for trusting us to do this new thing of writing together! They've worked hard to make it successful—and succeeded. We are so very grateful, especially to publisher Amanda Bostic, who has always been able to steer us through the murky waters of publishing. Thank you so much!

A special thanks to our freelance editor Julee Schwarzburg, who has been a tremendous help throughout this series. She caught our vision early on with the first book and has guided us with a deft hand. Thank you, Julee!

Thank you to agents Karen Solem, Julie Gwinn, and Ami McConnell Abston for your help in figuring out the new direction as well. We both appreciate you so much. Karen left for heaven in January 2025, and Colleen will be forever grateful for her guidance and friendship these past twenty-five years!

A heartfelt thanks to Anette Acker, Rick's sweet wife! She read every word and offered great suggestions and was a much-needed sounding board for direction and brainstorming.

We have such great friends in the author community who have been wonderful supports through this new journey.

Denise Hunter and Lynette Eason in particular have been steady influences and encouragers through it all.

A heartfelt thanks to our beta readers as well. These readers are longtime fans who unanimously loved the book and thought it felt very cohesive. Thank you, Nikki Bee, Deb Blower, Cat Brown, Nancy Cantrell, Chandler Carlson, Jodi Edwards, Kathy Engel, Marcie Farano, Dawn Heist, Gay Lynn Hobbs, Per Kjeldaas, Janith Marker, Beverly Moore, Bubba Pettit, Gail Pettit, Vincenza Rabenn, Joni Truex, Ruth Ann White, and Leah Willis!

Honestly, it has felt like God himself dreamed up this partnership and handed the idea to us, and we're so thankful for his guidance and provision for this new venture!

From the Publisher

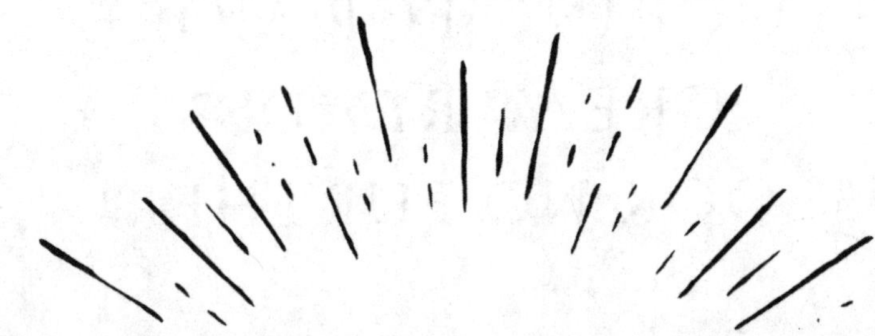

GREAT BOOKS

ARE EVEN BETTER WHEN THEY'RE SHARED!

Help other readers find this one:

- Post a review at your favorite online bookseller
- Post a picture on a social media account and share why you enjoyed it
- Send a note to a friend who would also love it—or better yet, give them a copy

Thanks for reading!

LOOKING FOR MORE GREAT READS? LOOK NO FURTHER!

Visit us online to learn more:
tnzfiction.com

Or scan the below code and sign up to receive email updates on new releases, giveaways, book deals, and more:

@tnzfiction

DON'T MISS THIS GRIPPING STAND-ALONE NOVEL FROM COLLEEN COBLE AND RICK ACKER

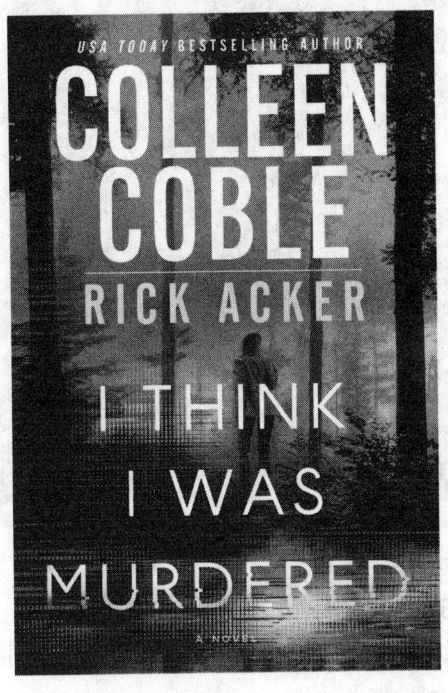

Available in print, e-book, and audio

ABOUT THE AUTHORS

EAH Creative

COLLEEN COBLE IS THE *USA TODAY* BESTSELLING AUTHOR of more than seventy-five books and is best known for her coastal romantic suspense novels.

Connect with her online at colleencoble.com.

Instagram: @colleencoble

Facebook: colleencoblebooks

X: @colleencoble

RICK ACKER WRITES DURING BREAKS FROM HIS "REAL JOB" as a supervising deputy attorney general in the California Department of Justice. He is the author of eight acclaimed suspense novels, including the #1 Kindle bestseller *When the Devil Whistles*. He is also a contributing author on two legal treatises published by the American Bar Association.

You can visit him on the web at rickacker.com.
Instagram: @rick_acker
X: @authorrickacker